SOUL
CATCHER

SOUL CATCHER

A NOVEL BY

COLIN KERSEY

ST. MARTIN'S PRESS
NEW YORK

Design by: Sara Stemen

Library of Congress Cataloging-in-Publication Data

Kersey, Colin.
Soul catcher / Colin Kersey.
p.   cm.
ISBN 0-312-13606-4
1. Winds—Washington (State)—Seattle—Fiction.   2. Seattle
(Wash.)—Fiction.   I. Title.
PS3561.E6617S68   1995
813'.54—dc20   95-32436
CIP

10 9 8 7 6 5 4 3 2

For my wife, Joyce, and daughter, Jesse

Acknowledgments

A proper acknowledgment of everyone who was responsible in some way for helping me write this first novel would resemble the telephone book of a small community, including both white and yellow pages. In the interest of brevity (not to mention our precious natural resources) I therefore wish to thank the following individuals for their crucial contributions:

mentors and friends, Elizabeth George and Jo-Ann Mapson;

Camp Pine Writers, Jo-Ann, Alexis Taylor,
Marilyn Shultz, and Clark Hepworth;

my sister, Diane Thompson;

pastor and friend, Bob Ewing;

my brilliant editor, Keith Kahla;

and my extraordinary agent, Victoria Sanders.

The white man will never be alone.
Let him be just and deal kindly with my people,
for the dead are not altogether powerless.

—CHIEF SEATTLE

They have sown the wind,
and they shall reap the whirlwind.

—HOSEA 8:7

SOUL
CATCHER

Prologue

Black Wolf waited until the bones glowed red before reaching into the fire and pulling one out. It was hot and he jerked his hand away. The air in the sweat house was dense with smoke and he wiped a lean brown arm across his eyes to clear them. When the blackened caribou bone had cooled enough, he picked it up, turning it carefully in his hands so as not to break it before he had studied its cracks and deciphered their meaning by the light of the fire.

At the first faint rumble, he lifted his head, turning it in the direction of the sound in order to listen with his better ear. Hoofbeats approached. Thousands of them. More than he had heard since he was a young boy on his first hunt with his father. The ground began to shake. Dust and twigs fell from the roof, exposing narrow shafts of sunlight within the sweat house's tenebrous interior. Black Wolf closed his eyes and inhaled deeply as the sound grew louder. . . .

And suddenly he was a caribou running side by side with the rest of the herd. The vapor from his labored breath joined with the other animals' as they raced into the frigid interior of the white mountain. Their hooves echoed like thunder against the stone walls of a long, dark tunnel. Ahead, he saw a light that grew steadily until the herd poured from the tunnel into a vast cavern whose walls glistened ghostly white. Icicle-shaped deposits, large as trees, hung from the vaulted ceiling. In the center of the milling herd, bearing a huge rack of antlers, stood a tall, white creature on two legs that was half man and half caribou. Atikwapeo. Eyes like red coals turned upon Black Wolf.

The herd parted for Black Wolf as he approached the powerful spirit. Atikwapeo drew a circle in the dirt, using a long, carved bone. At the bottom of the circle, he quickly sketched a land of mountains surrounded by water. Then, he drew a tall man-figure with a wolf's head and tail. Next, the bone scraped the shape of a much smaller man. Beside this, he made several slash marks to indicate its age—thirteen. There was something odd about the second figure and Black Wolf had to lean close to see that the boy had no ears. When he had finished, Atikwapeo dragged the sharp point of the bone across the two figures, making a deep gouge in the earth. As the caribou stamped and grunted nervously, bright red blood began to fill the gash and spread across the circle.

SEATTLE, FRIDAY, 4:43 P.M. It looked like a dead animal sprawled across the bus seat. The Greyhound driver hesitated, unsure what to make of it. Ever since finding a lunch bag stuffed with ten and twenty dollar bills, Jerome had made it a regular practice to examine the bus after all the passengers had left. He had found sunglasses, a radio, a pair of crotchless panties and even two tickets to a Supersonics basketball game. But never anything as big as this rattylooking heap of leather and fur. Gingerly, he prodded the pile of ancient animal skins with the toe of one of his non-regulation Nikes.

"Time to dee-part. Move it or lose it. Hear what I'm sayin'?"

Jerome drew back a step as the curled, gray shape began to unfold slowly with a whisper of leather against leather. The seat groaned and the faint odor of long-ago campfires and pine needle forests invaded the rear of the bus. He thought about calling security, but those guys took forever to show up and were scared of their own shadows.

The figure sat up stiffly and blinked under a tangled mass of long, silver hair. Dark skin covered the skull closely like a well-worn saddle, creased by age and a frown of temporary confusion. The lips and chin were tattooed in an intricate pattern of tiny crosshatched black lines. Sunken cheeks accentuated the high cheekbones and hooked nose.

"Look at this! What we got here?" Jerome asked. He shot a quick glance back along his exit route before studying the man's attire. Strips of what looked like fur from a large, black dog were attached to the chest and shoulders of the hide body wrap. His feet were covered in the same hide-like material, now shiny with wear, the nap having disappeared long ago.

"Where—am—I?" The voice was halting.

"We arrived in Seattle ten minutes ago. Nobody else left on board but you. You going to Portland?"

"No," the old Indian answered. "This is my final stop."

"Well, it's mine, too," Jerome said. "So, I'd be much obliged if you'd get off my bus so's I can go home."

The Indian stared at him for a moment before putting his sinewy hands on his knees. He struggled to rise. Jerome saw that he was having difficulty.

2

"Hey," he asked, extending a hand. "You okay?"

For answer, one of the gnarled hands grabbed his wrist with surprising strength and the Indian pulled himself up. He stood, teetering briefly, before letting Jerome go. Although the Indian was hunched by age and ailments, Jerome was forced to look up to study his face and, as the old man shuffled past him, his body wrap fell open to reveal several long fangs, yellowed with time, that clacked together among bits of feather and beads strung on a leather thong.

Perhaps it was the evident age of the artifact that interested Jerome, or perhaps it was the way the teeth and bones seemed to hold the light. "That's some mean-looking necklace you've got there," Jerome said. "Wanna sell it?"

The Indian pulled the wrap tightly shut and looked at him with dark, distant eyes.

"You no sell heart," the Indian thumped him on the chest, "Black Wolf no sell necklace."

"Swap you for my watch?" Jerome called after the old man as he exited the bus in silence.

Black Wolf, shaman of the Caribou People, stared up at the many tall buildings that shot up like a monstrous forest of trees competing for sunlight. Seagulls swooped by jutting towers. Steam curled upward from their steel and glass pinnacles. Here and there, the skeletons of construction cranes stood among the buildings, poised delicately, like enormous blue herons.

How different the city was since the time he had come here as a young man with pelts of Arctic fox, lynx, and marten. It had been during the time of the great battle across the sea. Trolley cars, filled with laughing soldiers, sailors, and their girlfriends, clung to overhead wires as they descended the steep hills, carrying the young men to the waterfront where they boarded the gray ships. Then, he had found the city that sprawled among the mountains and waters to be merely ugly. Now, the many buildings blocked the views of the Cascade Mountains to the east, the Olympic Mountains and Puget Sound to the west, and Tahoma, the one called Rainier by the whites, to the south. This disrespect of holy spirits was insolent, he thought. More, it was evil. He spat on the concrete sidewalk.

The city throbbed with the sound of engines. The noise hurt his ears, the acrid smell of gasoline and diesel fumes stung his nose, and, for the first time since he had begun the preparations for his long journey, doubt crept into his mind.

Black Wolf had studied the pattern of cracks in the fire-blackened caribou shoulder blades carefully, yet the bones had not shown him how ghastly the city had become, nor was the meaning of the vision entirely clear to him. Was it not Atikwapeo who directed the herd when to move to the Barren Grounds for spring and when to come back to the forest in the late fall? And had not Atikwapeo told him to go south to the white man's land? Or had he—Black Wolf—become so old that he had lost his medicine? Perhaps he had misread the portents. For a moment, the knot in his belly felt as if it had been seized by a claw as he remembered the drawing of the boy and himself and the blood—the bright red blood welling up from the ground. Black Wolf clenched his fists. It was too late for looking back now. Much too late.

He became aware of people stepping around him. Some looked at him out of curiosity. Others kept their eyes down, pretending that he was not there. Black Wolf adjusted the medicine bundle that hung by a thong over one shoulder and began to move his aching body toward the setting sun. Soon, he would need to ask for help from one of the whites, but for now, he was very tired and he chose to ignore them as they waited like cattle on street corners or crossed inside the painted lines. He was wary, however, as he walked among the cars that crowded the streets like the herds of caribou he had known as a boy.

In summer, his people had herded the caribou with spears into the lakes and rivers. In winter, they had driven the animals into pens made from young fir trees. Black Wolf had spurned the use of rifles, preferring the killing be done with bow and arrows, as his ancestors had done. Once the caribou had covered the Barren Grounds like a mantle, but it had been many years since their return. Since the whites had come with their oil drilling rigs, the herds had begun to disappear, their numbers shrinking each year until, finally, there were none. Even the white man's scientists could not explain it. Now, Black Wolf did not think the totem animal of his people would ever come back.

Before another season came and went, he knew that he, too, would die. But because his body had once been so strong, it fought the final battle with a ferocity that would not let him slip easily into the spirit world. He would have preferred to remain among the silent lakes and forests. But he was the last—the only one of his tribe who had not already died or surrendered to the white man's ways by moving to their cities. Since the death of his wife, Talks With Moon, the previous spring, no one remained to ease his loneliness or care for his needs, and he had finally given in to leaving the land he loved. His bones could no longer withstand the sub-zero cold, nor could he still hunt effectively or fish beneath the ice for his food. When the snows and the winds came, even the rivers ceased to flow. The approaching winter would have found and humiliated him by starving him to death. All his life, he had eagerly anticipated nature's rhythmic cycle. Now he looked forward only to this moment and the next. He was a man of no seasons.

After receiving the vision of Atikwapeo, he had put torch to the lodge and sweat house. Then, pausing only to bid farewell to the spirits he had known from boyhood, he had turned his back on the land of his people and journeyed south that he might meet his final enemy, as he had met all the others in his long life, without fear.

He came at last to a street corner that provided a view to the west. The sun was setting behind the Olympic Mountains, standing pale and rugged above the dark line of distant land. Below, the ferry-boats and cargo ships crisscrossed Elliott Bay. The sea was the color of a mountain lake in winter; the water glistened like frozen snow.

Black Wolf faced the sun, letting its glow revive the embers of the tiny fire that still glimmered in his chest. He had saved the money that his daughter sent him over the years, refusing to spend it because she had moved away and married a white. Once, many years before, she had come to visit him, bringing her half-breed children, but he had refused to see her. He stood inside the lodge door, listening to her sobbing entreaties with eyes pressed shut against the pain in his chest until, finally, she left. For a long time, the money had stopped. And then one day, it had started coming again, a few dollars every month.

Now, with her last tattered envelope tucked in his buckskin shirt, he had come to find his daughter so that he might spend his final months with family. The daughter of a Caribou shaman could not refuse him a warm fire and hot food to take the chill from his bones. It was "the way." Women listened to men, bore the young, dressed and cooked the meat and even dragged the sledges, heavy with carcasses and supplies. For a moment, he wondered if living with the whites for so long had made his daughter forget her upbringing. Then he remembered the money and was assured that it had not.

5

Black Wolf continued toward the waterfront, still far below, where he hoped to find lodging for the night. In the morning, he would approach the innkeeper or some official to help find his daughter's residence.

Arriving at the Pike Place Market, he was shocked again by the many changes. Where farmers and fishermen had once sold their fresh goods from the backs of their trucks in an open field, now a stream of cars and people wound through the maze of buildings. The stalls of produce and fish peddlers had closed for the day, but he could still smell the earth-rich aroma of vegetables, the sweetness of apples and salty tang of seafood.

The thought of food made his stomach groan. It had been early that morning, several hundred miles away, when he had last eaten, and then just a roll and coffee. He began to watch for a diner like those that he had seen on his long bus ride.

A hand grabbed one of his arms from behind. Turning, he looked into the bleary eyes and pox-ravaged face of one from the lost tribes. The grinning, toothless face moved in closer to his own. The stench of liquor and urine from the outcast Indian was nearly over-powering.

"Come," the face invited. He gestured drunkenly toward a small, ragtag band whose half-dozen members sat or slouched in an alley doorway, sharing a bottle wrapped in a paper sack. "Join powwow. We make big medicine." He threw back his head and pantomimed drinking.

"Get away," Black Wolf commanded and resumed walking. Again, the man grabbed his arm.

"Wait. Where do you go, Old One? You are one of us."

The old Indian removed the man's hand. "Black Wolf is Na-Dene, from the 'first people.' You are worse than slave." His hands chopped and slid through the air, using the sign language he had learned as a boy. "You dead." The other Indian's bleary eyes blinked and seemed to clear for a brief moment. The toothless mouth hung slack. Then, Black Wolf turned his back and con-tinued on, shutting out the insults that followed him.

On the corner of another large, fortress-like building, Black Wolf spotted two small, interlocking arches of brass, set into the used-brick exterior. The smell of food and the warm lights attracted him inside.

He had become so hungry that, at first, he was unaware of the other people around him. Now, he observed them paying for food and receiving it on trays at a large counter. Black Wolf proceeded to the counter. While he waited his turn, he overheard the profane comments of a young man, followed by female laughter. He turned to face them.

The first of the two young women was tiny and thin; the baggy blue denim pants and sweatshirt only emphasized her emaciated figure. Her lifeless hair hung straight to her shoulders. The other female, taller and heavier, wore her hair in a spiked row down the middle of her shaved head, not unlike the tribal headdress worn by warriors of old. Her lips and nails were painted purple. A tiny gold hoop from which hung a safety pin pierced one nostril. She wore a garment that barely contained her large breasts.

"Long way from the reservation, hey, chief?" the young man asked in a voice like the blade of a rusty knife. His head had been shaved very close to his skull. He wore a sleeveless black shirt and black leather pants. Like the others, he wore military-style boots. While one side of his lips smiled, the other side was turned down, making the overall effect one of a savage snarl. Above a metal-studded, leather arm band, he also wore a blue swastika tattooed inexpertly on one shoulder, Black Wolf noted. But the crossed arms of the emblem were in reverse direction to the Indian symbol for the four winds.

"May I help you, sir?" a voice called from the counter. He turned back to the uniformed young woman who had called out to him. In answer to her question, he pointed to one of the many illuminated photos of food that hung over the back wall. After he had pointed a few more times at the items in the photos or on the trays next to his, she pushed the colored squares on a machine and announced the price.

Using money was a skill he had needed only a few times in his entire life. Trade was conducted in goods. Now, he brought out a handful of bills and change, and handed them to the clerk. "Sorry, sir," the woman said. "I'm afraid we'll have to charge you more for Canadian money."

Black Wolf recalled receiving Canadian money for his U.S. dollars when he bought his bus ticket. He reached inside the buckskin shirt and brought out the thick envelope from which he drew out a few of the U.S. dollars and handed them to the clerk.

"This here's a rich Canuck Indian, for sure," the voice rasped behind him. "A Native American of means. Must be all that money he saved on dry cleaning." The women laughed again.

Black Wolf found their disparaging comments difficult to ignore as the attendant counted out his change. He placed the envelope with the remaining money carefully back inside his shirt. His hunger made his hands shake as he picked up the tray of paper cartons and turned to find his way to the seating area.

"Mmmm. Don't that look tasty?" The man smelled Black Wolf's food and chose a french fry from his tray. "Bet they don't cook like this on the reservation, hey, chief?" he asked, grinning hugely while chewing the potato.

"*MissaniLtcwin,*" Black Wolf said. Roughly translated, it meant, "its breath stinks like a buzzard."

"Miss-a-what?" The man stopped chewing, his eyes widening in surprise. "What the hell did you say?"

The heavier of the two girls began to laugh, her body shaking.

"Don't you dare laugh at me, bitch! Don't you so much as smile!"

All motion and noise in the restaurant came to a halt.

"Calm down, Ajax." The small one interceded for her friend. "She don't mean anything."

Black Wolf walked to the farthest corner of the restaurant and sat by himself. He opened each of the cartons and wrappers and smelled their contents. The small fish patty tasted unlike any fish he had ever known, but he was so tired and famished that he troubled only to pick off half the breading with an arthritic forefinger. He remembered how the rivers had once teemed with salmon, how he had speared the heavy fish, smoking the flesh to preserve it for winter.

He was halfway through his meal, alone in his memories, when a french fry, soaked in ketchup, struck the wall, leaving a long, blood-red streak as it slid down and fell onto his table. Another struck his face. Laughter burst loudly from a nearby table. Black Wolf rose, the joints of his knees and hips complaining enough to make him wince. The young man turned to face him, the half-smile, half-snarl twisting his mouth.

"What's the matter, chief?" He sipped his drink noisily from a straw and belched. "Ain't you gonna stick around for dessert?" The dining room was quiet except for the laughter of the man and the larger of the two women, who covered her mouth cautiously. The small one only smiled, her eyes glinting like a weasel's.

When Black Wolf was younger, he would have dragged the cur outside and taught him a lesson in respect that he would be unlikely to forget. Now, he walked past the table without a word.

Several people in the restaurant watched as he made his way to leave. A slender, red-haired boy stepped into his path as he neared the door. The boy's hand found Black Wolf's for a brief moment and the boy's green eyes looked deeply into his own. Black Wolf stared back in surprise as he felt the surge—not a drain as he might have expected, but a transference of energy from the boy to himself. Only once before had he experienced such powerful medicine in one so young—and so fatally gifted. The death of Black Wolf's uncle, a much-feared shaman, had required drastic measures. It was known by the elders of the tribe that entire villages had been wiped out by sickness and starvation for failing to ensure that a dead shaman's spirit was at peace in the spirit world. Until then, the life of everyone in the tribe was at risk. It was of small consequence, therefore, if one must give his or her life for the many. As his own powers grew, Black Wolf had eventually assumed the role of his uncle within the tribe. In sixty years, however, he had never managed to overcome his guilt. Except for the fact that his sister was one year older and still a virgin, it might well have been his body consumed on his uncle's funeral pyre.

His shaman's power told him about the boy's ears and he put out his hands to touch them. Before he could do so, however, a young woman with yellow hair cut like a boy's stepped between them.

"No!" she said, pulling her son out of reach. "Keep your hands off my son!" Then, perhaps recognizing Black Wolf's wounded pride, her flashing blue eyes seemed to soften. "I . . . I'm sorry."

Struggling to maintain control, Black Wolf exited the building. This was the boy in the vision—he was certain of it—but meeting him so soon had caught him off guard. And the young woman was like a she-bear who believes her cub in danger. Had she, too, seen the future, or was she merely acting on a mother's natural instincts? In either case, Black Wolf reasoned, she was right to worry. He shook his head. This part of the vision troubled him. Even if he somehow found the boy again, how could he approach him with the mother around? He must seek another sign from among the sacred items in his medicine bundle. But first, his mind and body needed rest.

He had walked three blocks before his anger and confusion had diffused enough that he remembered his plan. A stairway descended between the buildings toward the waterfront. Below, in the deepening twilight, he could see the lights of the ferryboats that cruised between Seattle and the nearby islands. Ignoring the protests of his knees, he started down the stairway.

Someone had spray-painted the same unintelligible letters again and again on the stairway walls. This was probably meant to discourage outsiders from entering tribal territory, he guessed. Of such warnings he was not heedless, but he had long since left behind the familiarity and safety of his own country. Since the vision in the sweat house ten days before, his future had been determined. From now on, for however long it might be until he drew his final breath, he must live in the land of his enemy.

Halfway down, the light bulb was shattered within its protective grille, but this did not slow him. His eyes were used to seeing in far less illumination. He heard something behind him and stopped to listen, cocking his head so that his good ear was turned toward the sound. Only the scurrying of rats, he decided.

When he finally reached the waterfront, he faced yet another surprise. The flophouses and bars were gone. In their place stood warehouses, a few shops, and a large aquarium. All looked to be closed for the night. He stood in a large, deserted parking lot. Overhead, an elevated roadway roared with the passing of automobiles. The vibration caused small pebbles to fall to the ground below.

He was too tired and his knees too sore to go back up the stairs the way he had come. He would have to find a place down here to stay. He was considering whether he could walk as far as the ferry terminal—perhaps he could spend the night there—when he heard the laughter behind him. Even before he saw them, he knew it was the three.

"Hiya, chief," the voice rasped.

So this was how it would be.

The adrenaline began to flow through his blood. He felt stronger, more powerful than he had in years. He reached for his skinning knife, then remembered that he had not thought it necessary to bring. A pity. Above the noise of the traffic, he could hear the three breathing. Farther away, vehicles exited a ferry with a metallic clang.

"Why did you run out on us, chief?" the man asked.

"We were hoping you'd join us for a party," the large female joined in.

"Yeah. A war party," the man said, adding a few poor-imitation war whoops. They laughed, mocking him.

"Usually, I'd just ask you for your money and be gone." The

man placed his hands together, locked his fingers and stretched so that each of his knuckles popped. "But you made me look bad, chief. Now, you gotta pay the price."

For a few heartbeats, the half-smile, half-snarl twisted the man's face. Then he struck quickly, using his boot-clad feet. Black Wolf took the blow, the heavy skins helping to diffuse the pain. Another kick, harder than the first, caused one knee to buckle and he nearly went down. Recovering his balance, he backed up slowly, his eyes following the young man's every movement. Like the grizzly, he waited patiently for the right moment.

"That was close, wasn't it, chief?" the young man jeered, breathing heavily. "Better say your prayers. Next time's gonna be it. I'm a homicidal engine of destruction. A meat-eating, heat-seeking missile that's locked on your red ass."

He came now with his fists, the two women cheering him on. Black Wolf reached out with one hand, caught an arm, twisted powerfully with his other hand and heard the man's shoulder pop as the bone was wrenched from its socket. The snarling one yelped in pain.

Angered by his coup, the big female came now. She tried to kick him in the groin, but he caught her leg and threw her onto her back. She landed heavily, her face turning red as the wind departed from her lungs.

Black Wolf grunted in satisfaction. He had just begun to savor the thought of victory when he felt the small one land on his back. A blade bit into his neck and he groaned as much from surprise as the pain. He hadn't considered her to be as dangerous as the others. Before he could throw her off, she struck again, this time getting his face.

Black Wolf managed to remain standing, defiant as he faced his enemies. His fingers held the flap of skin that had once been his cheek in place while, with the base of his hand, he pressed against his neck to staunch the hot, sticky stream of blood. The small female helped the man to stand. The other sat up and coughed.

Already, he could feel his arms and legs losing their strength and he knew that he was quickly reaching the end. He turned away, moving toward the ferry terminal again. Even though he was dying, he needed to get away from these carrion-eaters. He had gone only a dozen faltering steps before all vitality left him and he stumbled to the ground.

He thought of many things as he lay there, cheek pressed against the asphalt: of long-ago battles, his first caribou hunt, of snowshoe-ing by the light of a full moon. How the earth had laughed when his son was born. And how the heavens had wept when he died. Then he remembered again the sweat house vision, the drawing of the man with the wolf's head, the boy with no ears, and the blood. Now he understood. The boy would serve him well in the spirit world. Before Black Wolf's spirit could know peace, however, one more thing was necessary. For that, he must hold on to life yet a while longer, no matter how great the injury to his pride.

By the time he felt the kicks, he no longer felt pain. Only his anger remained as he listened to the man's furious epithets inter-mixed with grunts of pain.

"C'mon, Ajax, let's go!" one of the women pleaded.

"First, get the money," he said, his voice quivering with the pain of his injured shoulder.

The small one fumbled with his robe. She gasped and drew back.

"What is it?" her friend asked.

She held the thick envelope before her. "There's blood all over it."

"How gross," the heavy one said.

"What about this?" The small one pointed to the medicine bun-dle.

"Forget it," the man ordered. "Take the money and gimme the knife."

"What for?" the other female asked.

"Just give it here and shut up!" A moment later, the young man was straddling his back. "Grab his hair. I'm taking me a scalp."

With his eyes squeezed tightly shut that his enemies might not see into his heart and the pain that was hidden there, Black Wolf felt the knife sawing through his hair. Silently, he endured this last in-dignity until, at last, he felt the release of his hair and heard the man's cry of victory.

Though he feared that he had very little time left, the old one waited until the three had left. It took all of his remaining strength just to roll over to face the sky one more time. His hand found the medicine bundle. From within its ancient recesses, he withdrew a handful of ocher-colored powder. With his other hand, he clasped the necklace.

The North Star glittered coldly in the night as he began the nearly soundless chant. Williwaw must come. His death must be avenged.

I

Storm Warnings

SAN JUAN ISLAND, SATURDAY, 10:00 A.M. "Byron! Where are you, boy?"

Helen Anderson shut the door and stepped out into the crisp morning air. She frowned as she strode through the most recent layer of scarlet and gold leaves that had fallen during the night. She had waited a full thirty minutes—twice what she would have allowed a human—and still no Byron. His absence caused an unwanted gloominess to settle behind her brow.

It wasn't like Lord Byron, her Airedale terrier, to not be back in time for their constitutional. In fact, Byron was about the only thing she could depend on. They hadn't missed a walk together since Helen had brought him home as a pup.

She wore a goose down vest, unbuttoned, over her turtleneck sweater and tweed wool pants to ward off the chill. Today being a game day, she wore her gray hair tucked up into her lucky, purple stocking cap with "Huskies" imprinted on it in gold letters.

Keeping one eye out for her companion, she left behind her leaf-littered driveway to walk along the narrow blacktop road. She couldn't imagine what had delayed him unless he'd had an accident. The odds of that were slim, however, especially in the off-season. One of the pleasures of living on the island was its remoteness. She could walk down the road seven days a week, rain or shine, and, often as not, never see a passing car or truck. And the few coyotes on the island were too small and intelligent to tackle anything as large as Byron.

Helen decided to push the worry from her mind. It was far too splendid a day for worrisome thoughts. With its vibrant colors and clean-smelling air, fall was her favorite time of year and days like today made the long, damp Washington winters almost bearable. She had retired from teaching high school English in Seattle to live alone and write. Forty years of teaching Shakespeare to teenagers had given her an appreciation for quiet. Twice a year, more if she got antsy from the rain that sometimes stayed too long like a bad cold, she took the ferry to Anacortes and then drove to Seattle for a week of shopping, attending plays and visiting those few students who had stayed in touch. The nearby village of Friday Harbor provided for her immediate needs: a market for groceries and a hardware store for repairs. It also provided a pub for her vice—dart throwing. Her steely demeanor under pressure had earned her the nickname "Heartbreaker." So fond was she of this moniker that she now used it when signing onto the electronic bulletin board that linked her computer with hundreds all over North America.

Not having a dog running ahead of her did have its advantages, Helen discovered. While Byron was good company, he also frightened away the birds and animals. She had gone only a short distance, less than half a mile from her home, before she came upon a doe who watched her for a frozen moment from fifty yards up the road before disappearing silently into the secrecy of the dark forest. The Douglas fir, madrona, and alder trees formed such a dense canopy that even on a sunny fall day, the forest remained veiled with mist. Helen stared after the doe, hoping to catch another glimpse of the stately animal, but she was gone, swallowed up by the thickly wooded land.

The road often took her near the water. Through the trees, she caught occasional glimpses of Low Island and, beyond it, Vancouver Island. Arriving at one such opening, she walked out onto the rocky outcropping that provided a panoramic view of Haro Strait. A great blue heron lifted off, wings beating gracefully as it rose up over the tranquil salt water.

Standing on the fir-needle-carpeted knoll that overlooked the rocky beach below and eavesdropping on the gulls calling to each other over the gentle breaking of the waves, she found it difficult to reconcile the site's gruesome history with its stunning vista. According to local lore, the earliest white settlers had unknowingly brought smallpox with them to the islands. In a futile effort to combat the fever, hundreds of native Indians had thrown themselves into the icy waters only to die of pneumonia shortly thereafter. Forever more, the picturesque inlet would be known as Smallpox Bay.

A melancholy sigh far behind her in the trees told her that the breeze was picking up. It was time to get moving again. Where was that dog?

"Byron?" Helen whistled. "Where are you, boy?"

A pair of black shadows swept by overhead, their obscene cawing resembling the demented laughter of lunatics. Helen shivered as if a cloud had passed between her and the sun. The air seemed to have dropped several degrees in temperature, yet the sky remained an unbroken field of blue. She shoved her hands into the pockets of her vest to keep them warm.

The wind's sigh built into a low-pitched whine as she walked back across the small bluff. Sodden leaves began to take flight; several became plastered to her clothing. Across the road, the trees began to creak and groan and, for a moment, she imagined the forest waking, as if it were a giant thing come to life.

She was both relieved and startled when Byron burst from the underbrush, running at full throttle toward her. His teeth and gums were exposed in a frightening grin. No doubt, he had seen trouble and it was not far behind.

"What's the matter, By?" Helen hugged him to her. "You look like you've seen a ghost."

The terrier licked her hand once before struggling to free himself from her arms. He turned to face the road, ears flat against his skull. From deep within his throat came a rattling sound.

"Leave it be, Byron, whatever it is. Let's make tracks for home."

Helen began walking again, but found the going difficult. She was forced to lean far forward as the wind increased its pitch. A blizzard of leaves and twigs stung her cheeks as the wind buffeted her. From deep in the forest came the snap and crash of large limbs and trees going down. Byron charged forward, his growl replaced by fierce barking that was all but drowned out by the wind's scream.

"Come back!" Helen cried, but the words were torn from her mouth.

The dog struggled to make it to the opposite side of the road. For a brief moment, he crouched, legs braced, facing the direction from which the wind or whatever it was approached. Then his body was picked up and hurled into a tree in front of her.

"Byron!"

Horrified, Helen struggled to reach him. She had managed only a few labored steps before she was blasted off her feet and over the edge of the bluff.

DECEPTION PASS, SATURDAY, 10:47 A.M. Some twenty-five nautical miles south, Ann Bessani stood just inside the cabin hatchway and sipped coffee from a large plastic mug. From her cozy vantage point, she could observe her husband, daughter, and father-in-law in the open cockpit of their twenty-four-foot sailboat. The wind behind them, they were flying wing and wing, with mainsail out to one side of the boat and genoa out full on the other. Sailing downwind as they were, there was no sensation of a breeze, but judging by the hiss of the water rushing past the hull and rudder, Ann knew they were moving at a steady if unremarkable clip.

At the last minute, she had decided to join the others. She couldn't refuse her daughter's entreaties. And, she had to admit, it was a glorious day for sailing: sparkling blue skies and just enough breeze to make sailing fun without being too scary.

She glanced over at her daughter. Clothed in a bright orange life jacket over her snow skiing outfit, Megan was curled up with Paddington Bear, pointing out clouds, seagulls and anything else that moved to a charmed grandfather. With his silver hair, unshaven face and Dutch seaman's cap, Angelo Bessani looked the epitome of an old salt. For all of that, his boating experience was limited to fishing for salmon once a year at Westport on one of the large, ocean-going charter boats.

Ben's seafaring knowledge was only marginally greater. With a college sailing class behind him, he had proved a quick study. His grasp of the proper way to handle the tiller and trim the sails had impressed Ann. What he lacked in skill, he generally made up for in caution. While they had owned the boat nearly four years, only rarely had they ventured out of Lake Washington and into the vastness of Puget Sound with its 600-fathom depths and forty-seven-degree water. Protected by land masses from the deep swells of the Pacific Ocean, the Sound was still a far cry from the relative security of Lake Washington, surrounded as it was by restaurants, marinas and beautiful homes with large green lawns, many with their own docks. Out here, no one would be apt to see them if anything should happen. And it was too far to swim, given the coldness of the water. She stared down at the sinuous green expanse that billowed around their boat, and shivered. She could never look at the ocean without feeling tiny and helpless.

"Hey, you feeling okay?" Ben called out from the tiller. "You don't look so great." Her husband was dressed in a heavy wool sweater, faded blue jeans, and deck shoes.

"Nothing that a hot bath, fire, and a good book wouldn't cure," she answered.

"Book?" Ben exclaimed. "Why read about life when you can live it, right Megan?" He winked at their daughter who smiled in return, flattered as she always was by her father's inclusion of her in this

16

"Let's get mom" conspiracy. "Can I get a refill?" He held his mug out to Ann. It was the one with the illustration of a schooner on it that she had bought him for Father's Day. With a narrow top and wide, heavy, rubber-coated bottom, it provided perfect stability on heaving boat decks. "And how about a smile to go with the coffee?"

Ann forced a smile before turning to leave. Then, out of nowhere, a puff of frosty air hit them from the northwest. The sails suddenly ballooned and lines snapped taught. A draft sneaked inside her windbreaker and Ann felt a cup full of something oily and unspeakably cold spill inside her stomach; its numbing contents quickly spread throughout each area of her body.

"Hey!" Angelo called. "Now we're moving!"

Megan giggled and curled up even tighter with Paddington.

Ann searched the horizon for the cause of her dread, but could find none. Satisfied that there were no other boats or obstacles in their path, she retreated below.

Setting her own cup down, she spooned instant coffee into her husband's mug. She had just picked up the stainless steel teapot from the tiny, two-burner gas stove when the boat lurched violently forward. Her first thought was that they had hit a submerged log. Steaming hot water from the teakettle splashed onto her knee. "Damn!" The sound of an explosion punctuated her cry. When she poked her head up through the hatch, Ann saw that the genoa had torn loose from the cleat and was snapping angrily about in the suddenly increased wind. The boat immediately began to turn and heel dangerously over onto its side as it came around into the wind. Water flooded in over the port-side rail and into the boat. Ann read the fear in Ben's face and felt her own heart hammering away. The veins in his hands and neck clearly visible, Angelo strained to uncleat the jammed mainsail sheet. Megan huddled in the corner of the cockpit, frozen in terror.

"Stay put. I'm coming, Megan!" Ann yelled over the gunfire-like flapping of the genoa. The backstay was stretched so taut that it sang. "It's okay, Ben! Let it head up!" Lacking her husband's practical experience, she had read everything there was to know about sailing, especially what to do in an emergency.

But Ben ignored her. "Coming about!" he yelled, pushing the tiller over to one side with all his strength. It was the first and last sailing mistake that Ann ever saw her husband make.

The boat now veered the other way. The boom swept back across the cockpit with the force of a falling tree.

"Ange!" she shrieked, too late.

There was a noise like a metal baseball bat striking a ball as the boom struck her father-in-law in the back of the head. Angelo toppled overboard, one hand thrown out as if to catch the cap that tumbled out of sight.

"Dad!" Ben cried out in anguish.

Ann barely had time to consider the sight of her father-in-law floating face down when water began pouring in over the starboard rail and the boat heeled over in the opposite direction. What happened next was like those few, confused half-seconds during an automobile accident before the spinning car comes to rest. Ann was sure the wind had shifted to the northwest, but suddenly it seemed to come from the east. And then, they were going over. The boat lay down with a shudder like a tired, old horse, letting the entire ocean rush into the cockpit and down into the galley. The curtains she had so proudly made and installed above the stove ignited briefly from the still-burning gas flame and were just as quickly quenched as the boat continued to roll and fill with water. She heard a loud tearing noise, as if the boat were being rent in half. The noise ended abruptly, but the boat remained upside down.

The shock of the cold water enveloping her body sent her muscles into spasms. Terrified that she was trapped in a sinking boat and desperate to find her daughter, Ann kicked toward the boat's stern, using her hands to fend off the Styrofoam cups, paper towels, and rigging that clutched at her. Filtered, green light showed her the way to the surface.

"Mommy!" she heard Megan scream the instant she reached air. Pausing only to gasp for breath, she swam toward her daughter, bobbing in the orange life vest.

"You okay?" Ann asked, in between gasps. "Where's Daddy?"

Megan shook her head. Tears sprang from her eyes and rolled down her pale cheeks.

Ann searched the water frantically for any sign of Ben. Behind her, the algae-covered bottom of their boat bobbed nakedly in the water. Remembering from her reading that boats generally float, even when capsized, and that you should always stay with the boat, she coaxed her daughter toward it. There was also the problem of hypothermia. She had read somewhere that a person could become comatose in as little as twenty minutes. Yet, unless a Coast Guard helicopter out for a Sunday cruise just happened by, any rescue was likely to be an hour or more away. Ann wrestled with increasing panic as she considered what to do.

"Everything's gonna be okay. Help Mommy swim to the boat."

Her daughter's eyes, wide with terror, darted from side to side like a pair of frantic searchlights. "Where's Daddy? And Grandpa!"

Ann recalled Angelo being knocked over the side of the boat. She clenched her daughter's shoulders firmly, as much to control her own fear as Megan's. "Don't worry, honey. I'll find them. They're probably on the other side of the boat."

The hull was slimy-wet and provided nothing to hold on to. High up on its center, the torn fiberglass mounting that had once housed the keel pointed jaggedly toward the blue sky. Now, Ann understood the tearing noise that she had heard earlier and why the boat had remained upside down. Without the heavy, lead keel, there wasn't enough ballast to right the boat.

A thin line of blood ran down her arm and into the water. Ann noticed that the skin on the back of her hand was torn. Ominously, she couldn't feel the wound—couldn't feel her hand at all. She wanted to believe that none of this was real. If she could just close her eyes for a moment, perhaps she could go back to sleep. A cold wave slapped her in the face, bringing her back to reality.

"See that thing?" Ann asked, spitting out briny water and pointing at the broken keel housing. "I'm going to push you up so you can grab it, okay?"

Megan's teeth were already chattering so hard she was having a hard time talking. "Who's . . . who's going to save us?"

"Everything's going to be fine," Ann lied. "But you have to be a big girl and hold onto that thing for all you're worth. I can't find Daddy and Grandpa if you won't help me." Ann forced her daughter to look into her own eyes. "Understand?"

"Okay," Megan whispered.

Kicking hard, Ann grabbed her daughter by the waist and lifted her as far out of the water as she could. "Grab hold, Meg," she coached between sputters as she swallowed salt water.

"I can't," Megan cried.

"You have to. Stretch. Please, honey," Ann pleaded, feeling her strength ebb.

"Got it," Megan shouted at last, her rubber boots scrabbling up the side of the slick hull. She hugged the stump of the keel, one leg draped over either side of the boat.

"Good girl. Now, hang on. Don't let go no matter what. Not until someone comes to get you. Hear me?"

"Where are you going?" Megan cried. "Don't leave me!"

"Mommy's going under the boat, Megan. You hang on. Scream if you see Daddy, okay?"

Ann considered taking off her waterlogged ski jacket and pants. Underneath, she wore long underwear. No time now, she decided, as she plunged her face into the ice-cold water. Other than a ghostly white sheet that trailed off into the invisible depths, she could see nothing. She struggled to swim underwater with numbed limbs in waterlogged clothes.

Ben was nowhere near the tiller that swung from side to side in the current. Her lungs begging for air, Ann forced herself to continue to look around. The boat made curious, echoing sounds as it rocked gently in the waves; water sloshed in the compartments and air bubbles rose in streams from the galley.

She peeked into the hatchway to see if by some chance Ben had swum into the galley to find her and had become trapped. Plastic knives and forks, paper plates, a Dr. Pepper bottle and seat cushions floated or drifted in a jumbled confusion. But no Ben.

She began to sink beneath the boat. Her legs had become lead weights which dragged her down. Everything numb and warm now. It would be so easy to just close her eyes.

A muffled scream coming from far, far away. Her daughter, Megan. So far.

Another scream. Must go to Megan.

MYSTERY BAY, WHIDBEY ISLAND, SATURDAY, 11:02 A.M. Tom finished the last of his tuna sandwich and tossed the empty Baggie down into the bottom of the aluminum boat. Torn leader packages, a candy wrapper, and two empty soda cans rolled about in the small pool of water that had gathered there.

He studied the tip of the stout fiberglass fishing pole standing in the nearby rod holder, ever alert to the telltale bobbing that was evidence of a fish nibbling at the cut herring bait hanging some forty feet beneath them, but the pole remained motionless as it had all morning. He glanced at his friend's fishing pole. It, too, stood motionless in its rod holder on the opposite side of the boat.

Before the sun had risen, they had ridden their bicycles down to the Poulsbo Marina on the west side of Whidbey Island. After renting the fourteen-foot boat with the money they had earned as deck-hands during summer vacation, they had motored to the quiet cove where they'd caught salmon, cod, and rockfish in the past. Not today, however. Today, they hadn't had a single nibble. Not even a mud shark.

"Where are the fish?" Tom asked, his eye following the heavy monofilament line down into the placid salt water.

"Must have taken the day off," Osky replied.

They sat and watched their poles in silence. They had been best friends since third grade when old, senile Mrs. May had seated them together on the first day of class. Together they had learned to swear, smoke, and drink and if their grades weren't anything their mothers could brag about, well, there were plenty of kids who did worse stuff.

Reaching inside his down vest, Tom found the crumpled pack of cigarettes. "Got a match?" he asked.

"Yeah." Osky stood up, turned around and dropped his pants. "My butt and your face!" The boat pitched to one side as he hooted.

"Idiot! Sit down before you drown us both."

Still laughing, his friend urinated over the side of the boat before zipping his pants and sitting back down.

"Toss me a light, turkey."

"Catch," Osky said.

Tom grabbed the matchbook just before it sailed past him and into the water. As he lit his cigarette, something in the distance over his friend's shoulder caught his eye. At first, he studied the patch of black water passing the boat with a lack of concern. The weather at this end of the island could be really fluky: quiet one minute and ugly the next—kind of like his dad. He squinted his eyes as the rippling surface appeared to change course, moving toward them with greater speed.

"What the hell is that?" he asked.

"What?"

"That dark stuff. There." He pointed. "On the water coming toward us."

The other boy glanced briefly over his shoulder. "Just the wind. Gimme back the matches." Osky struck a match, cupping his hands to shield the flame. Before he could light his cigarette, a frigid gust blew the match out.

"Damn it!" He kicked the tackle box.

Tom tried again to get his friend's attention. "Look, Osky, white-caps."

"In this cove? No way."

Then the gust hit them. The boat drifted a few feet, riding the crest of a small wave.

"Whoa! Surf's up!" Osky giggled nervously.

Tom had a good grip on either side of the boat and saw that his friend had done the same. Things were definitely getting weird. The air tasted sharp like the snow on a skiing trip. The boat began to turn in a slow circle. "What's going on?"

"Somebody must have pulled the plug!" Osky said over the growing turbulence.

Tom thought his friend's joking was poorly timed. The boat had completed a circle and was beginning to spin faster. It began to rise and stand on one end. Fishing line from the two poles still in the rod holders wound around them with a high-pitched racheting noise, drawing them closer together as the boat spun, faster and faster.

"Whirlpool!" Tom yelled. Their hands fought in vain to stop the line from binding them together. As the line wound around Tom's face, it cut into his skin and he screamed. His ear felt as if it had been torn from his head. He could taste warm blood mixed with with salty tears running into his mouth as they continued to re-volve.

Osky tried to rise. "Make it stop!" he wailed in a nearly unrecognizable voice.

"Don't stand. . . ." Tom warned. And then they were falling from the spinning boat.

22

2

Counting Coup

SEATTLE, SATURDAY, 11:15 A.M. Evan Baker covered his eyes with his hands and peeked between his fingers in mock horror as his mother attempted to parallel park the ancient station wagon. She elbowed him playfully and continued heaving on the steering wheel of the car that had once belonged to his grandfather. After three tries, they were at last parked within spitting distance of the curb. Adjusting the rearview mirror, Denise blew a lock of fine blonde hair from her face and swore.

A silver earring in the shape of a cross swung from her small ear as her mouth moved. Evan managed only to pick up the words "fool" and "last time" before she turned finally to face him.

What? he signed. He tugged at his hair in imitation of her primping.

"Sorry," Denise said, speaking the word carefully while simultaneously signing her apology by making circles with her hand over her heart. "There I go talking to myself again. I can't believe I just paid thirty dollars for this haircut and it already needs trimming. I've got less hair than you and your haircuts are just five bucks.

"Want to come up to the office with me? I need to finish editing a newsletter and going through my mail. I'll just be a half-hour or so."

He shook his head.

"Are you sure? Bob has a new computer game."

He pinched his uplifted nose, his sign for "yuck," and turned to look out the car window. From many hours of practice, he had earned a reputation as a devastating game player—his initials were recorded on half the arcade games in the city—and computers were how he communicated with his friends. But playing a computer game was poor entertainment compared to exploring.

Knowing his affinity for adventure and also that his handicap combined with his "special talent" made him a lightning rod for attracting both good and evil, his mother tapped him on the shoulder until he looked at her. "Promise you won't leave the car, Evan. I don't want to have to come looking for you. And there are too many weird people downtown." She signed the word "weird" by making a C in front of her face with her right hand, bringing it down in a quick twist and crossing her eyes.

He smiled at her attempt to humor him, but looked away without answering. Once more, he felt her tapping.

"Hey. Love you." Her hands added emphasis to her spoken words as she crossed her closed fists over the heart with exaggerated force such that the word "love" became more like "*Looovve.*"

You, too, he signed back rapidly before turning back to the window to watch the parade of people passing by. He knew the moment his mother had exited the car by the vibration of the door closing. He waited until she had climbed the stairs and disappeared inside the renovated brick office building before getting out of the car. From experience, he had learned that there was no point in worrying her needlessly by telling her his plans in advance. A mom's job was to see that a kid never did anything. A kid's job, on the other hand, was to see that a mom's job was never easy.

Hands shoved in the pockets of his nylon ski jacket, he roamed the brick-cobbled streets, peering into windows of the shops, galleries, antique stores, and restaurants that crowded the historic district known as Pioneer Square. Without the advantages and distractions of sound, he eagerly sought out the old, the new, and the unusual from the merely mundane. He sometimes felt like a diner seated next to the dessert tray at a large banquet and he devoured every crumb. It was a rich and eclectic feast: homeless people with their shopping carts filled with odds and ends, skinny women in leotards driving their Mercedes, soaring seagulls and strutting pigeons, neon sculpture and whale teeth carved into sailing ships, and everywhere the odors of coffee beans and ripening garbage mingling with the salt air.

His favorite store was the curio shop. He spent several minutes browsing among the shrunken heads, blowguns and shark jaws of every size, including some that made you think twice about going near the ocean. Lying in a dusty glass case smudged by countless hand prints, Henry, the mummified, 1,000-year-old Pueblo Indian, seemed to cry out for release, his gaping mouth frozen in a permanent scream. Evan turned to leave and gasped, startled by the sight of an object he'd never seen before in the shop's crowded interior. The pelt of a wolf hung from the wall behind him. Its red glass eyes seemed to glow with an evil gleam. He reached out to touch one of its large black paws, thought better of the idea, and pulled his hand back. Carefully, he edged past the animal, avoiding the jaws with their vicious-looking fangs, and bolted for the exit.

Once he was back outside the store, he felt embarrassed and a bit silly about his reaction. Thank goodness no one was with him. A waiter, clearing coffee cups from a recently vacated patio table, looked up and nodded as he walked by. Evan waved. Soon, the sidewalk portion of the café would close for the season. Today, however, it was busy. Any day now, the city would shed its smiling autumn-gold face and put on its wet, somber, winter one. Keenly aware of its transitory quality, many residents were out enjoying one final sip of their city's candescent beauty. Sea and sky were a dazzling blue; the sky pitched so painfully high that the tiny white whorls of vapor that crossed its highest reaches were impossible to see without hurting one's neck. The sun's amber glow illuminated the peeling magenta paint of a tavern doorway where a bum with crinkled brown face and silver whiskers lay sleeping. His frayed and baggy coat had fallen open, revealing his unzipped trousers. A young black man wearing a school letterman's jacket elbowed his friend and laughed. A large, well-dressed woman with heavy black eyebrows glanced back over her shoulder at the man, a scowl on her face, before hurrying on. Evan waited until they were gone before approaching the sleeping man. Carefully, so as not to disturb him, he lifted the soiled corner of the man's coat and covered him.

The pigeon-man stood in his usual late-morning spot by the iron and glass pergola in the center of the open square, his feet spread shoulder distance apart, arms held straight out from his sides. The pigeons roosted everywhere on his body that there was room to light, covering his arms and shoulders like a cloak of feathers. One even sat upon his tattered cap while dozens of others pecked and strutted about, feasting upon the bread crumbs that he had scattered for them. A few people watched, amused expressions on their faces. Most hurried by, intent on their destinations.

An older couple, probably tourists, huddled over a bus schedule. Seeing him watching them, the man gestured for Evan to look at their map. He studied the man's lips carefully, but, although he could lip read with the best, he was unable to concentrate on his words. Then Evan saw the tiny red X's, like an invading army, spreading behind the man's eyes, attacking the brain. Silent, deadly, they seemed to be multiplying even as he watched. Bile scorched his throat and he fought not to gag. Oh, God, not again.

The man grew more and more agitated at his inability to help them, throwing up his hands and becoming red-faced as Evan stood, unable to speak or even sign, rubbing his hands together as if he could wash away his vision. The woman tried once more to explain their need. Finally, the man grabbed his wife's arm and pulled her away. Evan looked after them, terror, sadness, and relief washing over him.

His preoccupation with the retreating couple caused him to miss seeing the bicyclist passing behind him. He turned and stepped directly into the cyclist's path. Both were knocked to the ground. The cyclist sat up angrily and pointed an accusing finger as his mouth worked angrily. Evan stared at the man's shiny black shorts, tight-fitting shirt, and racing helmet. After inspecting himself for injury, the cyclist stood up, tiptoed awkwardly in his wedge-shaped shoes over to where his bicycle lay on the pavement, one wheel still spinning. Before peddling away, he raised a hand in parting salute, a solitary finger thrust upwards.

Evan became painfully aware that his hands and one knee were stinging from where they had struck the pavement. Examining his knee, he discovered that he had torn a hole in his new jeans. He banged his fist on the ground. His mother would have a cow. Dejectedly, he put his head down and wrapped his arms around his knees. Why did he have to be different? It was bad enough being deaf without the other thing—the "knowing." His mother called it a gift. Hah! Nightmare was more like it. There were millions of things he wanted to know and didn't, like what questions would be included on tomorrow's history test, and plenty of other things he regretted knowing—things that kept him awake at night—like the man just now. What good was a gift like that? Even if he could talk, he couldn't just go up to someone and tell them they had cancer. "Excuse me, sir? Had a brain scan lately?"

He was considering returning to the car to wait for his mother when he felt a warm tongue on his neck. A medium-sized white dog with part of an ear missing and wearing a red kerchief around its neck licked his face as he looked up. Evan hugged the animal. The dog's name was Fortuno and he belonged to Nick, the blind beggar sitting on the sidewalk a few blocks away. After petting the dog for a few minutes, he stood up and limped after it.

Evan tugged on the ear of the white-haired old man. The man grinned and extended his hands until he found Evan and held him close. He smelled of old wool, leather, and sweat. A hand-lettered sign stated that he was legally blind. The seeing eye dog licked the man's hand as it had earlier licked Evan's face and received a treat from the man's pocket.

The beggar patted the ground next to him, indicating that the boy should sit. While Evan sat down, the man dug within his layers of coats to produce a small, metal cylinder. He watched as the old man blew into the device whereupon the dog, which had been sitting quietly near them, leaped up and began licking the beggar's face, much to his amusement. In addition to his surprise, Evan felt a strange tingling sensation in his head. Holding his hands over his ears, he stared in fascination as the beggar blew the whistle again. Fortuno continued to lick the beggar's face.

He tugged on Nick's arm until he finally got his attention. The white eyes and sunburned face turned toward him, the wrinkled hands with their short, sausage-like fingers holding up the miraculous whistle for him to see. Hands shaking, Evan took the small whistle and blew into it. Again, he felt the tingling sensation deep in his head. Now, the dog was knocking him over, licking his face as he blew again and again.

A wide smile that displayed his badly rotted teeth spread across the beggar's face, his sightless eyes glistening as he ran a hand through Evan's hair. He had never before heard the boy laugh or, for that matter, make a sound.

The wind's speed and fury increased as it neared the enemy camp. A concentrated force of immense energy, it shot high over the tree-covered, emerald hills toward the city nestled among the brilliant blue waters. The one called Black Wolf had summoned it to punish those responsible for his death and to find the boy with no ears. Now it fought the urge to annihilate anything and everything that stood in its path. Revenge was near at hand, but a good warrior first counted many coup before the battle.

At the north end of the city, a number of brightly colored kites fluttered high above the rusting black metal towers, once part of a gas-cracking plant, that jutted up from the small park located on the shore of Lake Union. The sudden gust snapped the restraining strings on paper birds and plastic dragons and sent them spiraling crazily toward the lake's surface as children and adults stood watching, mouths agape.

The rainbow-hued sails of a beginning windsurfing class likewise made an irresistible target. The wind swooped low now, the water rushing upward to greet it. Yelps of surprise and pain rang out as sailboards spun out of control; crisscrossing and ricocheting like pins toppled by a bowling ball. In seconds, not a single upright sail remained. Scattered moans rose

*from the heads that bobbed among the floating boards, but the wind was
gone as quickly as it had arrived.*

Seattle Times reporter-at-large, William "Billy" Mossman, and his
wife, Julie, were enjoying muffins and coffee at one of the tables
outside the Starbucks coffee shop. Their view included Westlake
Plaza, Fourth Avenue and Pine Street, all of which were crowded
with Saturday shoppers, many of them drawn to the Nordstrom
store across the street.

"Look, Billy," Julie nodded toward the Plaza where one of Seattle's few remaining mounted police officers had paused for a moment to let several young admirers crowd around and pat his horse.

"A dying breed." Billy sipped his decaffeinated café au lait and
frowned.

"You don't think they'll keep a few on, just for public relations?"

"I doubt it," he replied. "The Mountain Bike Force has proven
so successful, both in terms of making arrests and performing trick
riding for kids, I think they'll put these guys out to pasture—no
pun intended—as soon as the election is over."

"A shame," Julie said. "Somehow, patting a bicycle on the fender
just doesn't pack the same emotional wallop for me."

"That's progress," Billy said. "Ain't it grand?"

As the horse and rider departed from their view, Billy's attention
turned toward the opposite side of the street where tiny workmen
labored high above them, installing windows in Seattle's newest and
largest skyscraper, the ninety-eight-story Olympic Life Insurance
Tower.

"It'll be all faced off in two more weeks," he said, a touch of defeat in his voice.

"You did your part, Billy," Julie patted his arm. "No one can
accuse you of not raising a red flag over the mayor's latest shenani-
gans. Like Lucy my hairdresser says, 'Feed the pigs what they'll
eat.' "

Billy smiled to hide his frustration. Once, years before, his columns had been syndicated, appearing in *Time* magazine, *Newsweek*,
and the front pages of all the major dailies. Now, he was relegated to
the *Seattle Times*' metro section, covering grand openings and other
P.R. events like the completion of a new office tower—in short,
crapola. But he was damned if he'd let his wounded pride spoil his
day off, especially his time with Julie. They had been married for six
years now. Both had grown children by previous marriages. Since

28

moving to a houseboat on Lake Union, having brunch downtown and people-watching had become one of their favorite things to do on weekends.

A young woman struggled less than successfully to keep her dress from blowing up around her hips as she crossed the street. Billy looked out at the construction workers who worked at street level on the new building, many of whom had stopped what they were doing to stare. "I bet those guys spend half their time gawking."

"I'd love to see one of them crossing that intersection in a dress," Julie said. "Since that monster has gone up, the wind has picked up noticeably on the street."

"C'mon, Julie," he said.

"C'mon yourself," she replied. "On a chilly day, with the wind blowing and the rain coming down, you'd swear there was a tornado on Fourth Avenue."

"You mean a hurricane," he corrected.

"Whatever."

As if on cue, a sudden gust of wind hit with such force that it overturned their table and sent some of the others rolling into the street. Plates, trays, and coffee cups went flying and a number of people were knocked down. Screams erupted around them.

"What's going on?" Julie yelled.

Before he had time to consider an answer, there was a sound like a bomb detonating as a panel of granite from the Olympic Tower hit the street, shattering windows and felling pedestrians with shards of stone.

"Stay down," Billy yelled, his combat training taking over. Another panel landed on an automobile, crushing the top. The horn blared. Crouched behind their table, he glanced at his wife and saw that she was terrified but unhurt.

"You okay?"

"I think so." Her lip quivered.

"Get inside." He nodded toward the Westlake Center, less than fifty feet away. They ran, crouching, for the doors.

"You should be safe here, but stay away from the glass. I gotta go."

"Be careful, Billy."

He touched her cheek, then ran back outside, his head tucked as far down as it would go into his shoulder blades. A fine dust hung in the air over the bodies that sprawled on the sidewalks and street, and the screams of the injured competed with the car horn to drown out any rational thoughts. Several construction workers had run to the car that had been struck and were trying to free its occupants. Others stood in shocked silence.

Billy looked up to see two workmen, three-quarters of the way up the building, striving desperately to hold onto one of the large windows that had evidently just been put into place. In silent horror, he watched as the sheet of black glass flung first one and then the other tiny figure to their deaths. Unrestrained, the window dropped toward the street. Then it appeared to catch a gust of wind and as he watched, unbelieving, it began soaring down Fourth Avenue.

A reporter's sixth sense for news compelled him to follow. Hurrying after the flying window, he stepped over a body that lay where it had fallen on top of a storm drain. A long, slender leg was thrown outward at a ninety-degree angle, ending in a bloody foot. Billy recognized the young woman who, just a few minutes earlier, had struggled to keep her dress under control while crossing the street.

Above, the dark bird began to descend again. Billy ran faster, straining to see where it would finally come to rest. Although he had covered less than a few hundred feet, already his breath came in loud wheezes and his legs were stiffening. At the end of the block, the police horse stood patiently but its rider was nowhere to be seen. The window was dropping swiftly now, a hawk stooping toward its prey. Billy had just picked out the mounted police officer with his wide-brimmed hat from among the confusion when he realized that the window was headed directly for him.

He tried to shout but lacked the air. "Huhhh!" he tried again. The officer glanced up at Billy from where he was kneeling. Still running, Billy pointed up at the sky. The officer looked up in time to only stare in fascination as the window descended toward his body. With a shattering crescendo, the glass disintegrated into a million tiny dark stars that rained like shot upon the surrounding pavement. The horse reared up on two legs, letting out a terrified squeal, and launched itself down Fourth Avenue in the direction of Pioneer Square, the sound of its clattering hooves echoing in the sudden silence.

Evan glanced at his watch and saw that there was still a little time before he would need to return to the car in order to avoid worrying his mother. Too excited by his recent discovery with the whistle to wait patiently in the car, he decided to continue his explorations a few minutes more.

In Occidental Park, sitting beneath the brilliant, rust-colored canopy formed by the leaves of London Plane trees, were a small number of Native Americans, the ragged remains of Seattle's once numerous tribes. According to his history teacher, long ago they had ruled the surrounding land and waters. Now, these few descendants drank themselves into a desperate amnesia. The side of one of the brick buildings that bordered the park had been painted like a billboard whose message read, "Seattle: America's Most Livable City." Evan wondered if the city's many homeless and Indian people would agree.

Remembering the elderly Indian at McDonald's, Evan ventured nearer to get a better look at one who appeared to be sleeping on a park bench. Something about yesterday's encounter with the Indian had both intrigued and frightened him. Touching him had been like touching the posts of his train set's transformer.

The reclining Indian suddenly woke and began to scramble away with surprising agility. Evan looked up and saw a horse galloping directly at him. Effortlessly, it leapt the park bench the Indian had just vacated. In a matter of seconds, it would run him over, but his feet felt as if his shoes were nailed to the ground. He could only stand, staring stupidly, as the horse bore down upon him, sweat-soaked sides heaving, nostrils flaring, huge eyes rolling in its head and strings of foamy saliva swinging from its jaws. The air grew dense with the stink of fear and sweat. At the last instant, he was thrown hard to the ground.

A tall, blue scarecrow with long, black hair pulled back in flying braids suddenly appeared between Evan and the horse, arms raised. Startled, the horse slid to a stumbling halt and reared. Being careful to stay just beyond striking distance of the pawing hooves, the tall figure kept his arms raised. As the horse's hooves descended, the man closed in quick as a snake, one hand grasping the reins that dangled from the frothy, metal bit. As the horse reared again, the man hung on. When it descended, he leaped onto its back and pulled the reins back tightly.

The horse bucked again and again, all four feet leaving the ground. Then it hopped, straight-legged, from side to side. But the man would not let go. Finally, after several seconds, the horse shuddered violently and stood still, head bowed, lathered sides heaving.

Then Evan's mother was there, pulling him to his feet, crushing his body to hers. He could only grin.

*

"Oh, Evan," Denise said, forgetting at first to sign. "You scared the spit out of me." Tears ran down her cheeks. "Why did you leave the car? I thought we had an agreement. . . ." Before she could finish, two long blue legs appeared beside them. Denise looked up into dark, unsmiling eyes. Jet black hair was pulled back into braids from a smooth, brown forehead. One hand gripped Evan's shoulder.

"Why didn't you run, boy? Are you a statue? You could have been killed."

Denise brushed his hand off and stood, her face flushed. "Leave my son alone. He's just a boy. Besides, he can't hear you. He's deaf."

The Indian stared at Evan in surprise. Denise noticed that he was dressed in a three-piece suit, now torn at the shoulders.

Meanwhile, Evan was signing like he was possessed, his hands flying through the air, faster than she could follow.

Denise stopped his hands. "Whoa, Evan. Not so fast. I can't understand you."

He signed again, more slowly. *What's his name? Where did he learn to do that? Can he teach me? Ask him to dinner. Please, Mom.*

Denise sighed and faced the Indian whose profile was turned to her now as he looked north. She became aware for the first time of what sounded like an army of sirens converging some distance away.

"What is it?"

"I don't know," he answered. While they stood listening, a fire truck rumbled past them; the shriek of its siren punctuated by insistent blasts of a horn. "Whatever it is sounds like major league trouble."

"Maybe aliens have invaded Nordstrom."

He turned, for the first time seemed to really see her. "I'm sorry for yelling at your son. My name's Paul Judge. Is he okay?"

Denise glanced at Evan who was tugging on her arm with one hand and signing with the other. "Oh, I think he's more than all right, thanks to you. My name is Denise Baker and this is Evan."

Paul signed something to her son.

Evan signed back.

"I didn't recognize whatever you signed," Denise said. "Was that American Sign?"

A hint of a smile flickered across his face like sunlight on grass. "No, Plains Indian. It means. 'We meet again one day soon.' " He nodded at the horse who remained standing nearby and started to back away. "Before he causes any more trouble, I had better call the police and tell them about their escapee."

"Wait," she called after him. "Your suit. At least let me pay for a new one. You saved my son's life."

He paused. "My grandmother used to say. 'All rain eventually returns to the one great spring.' "

Denise watched him for a moment as he lead the horse away. Now there's a novel way to meet a man. Forget supermarket produce sections, like all the women's magazines recommended. Just stand your kid in front of a runaway horse. Too bad her conversational skills were so rusty. Not that she had time for men or companionship in her life anyway.

"*Well, Evan,*" she signed her son, "*now that you're alive and safe, I'm going to have to make you wish you weren't.*"

The whirling blades of the small police helicopter swatted the blue column of air, the noise reverberating off canyon walls of concrete, steel and glass. A child's high-pitched wail blended with that of approaching sirens as Billy stood on rubbery legs in the middle of Fourth Avenue and surveyed the carnage.

A dozen bodies lined the sidewalk, feet pointing neatly toward the street. Emergency teams worked side by side with bystanders to aid the injured. Sitting on a nearby curb, Billy's wife tried to comfort the driver of the car that had taken a direct hit from one of the granite panels. Her white blouse now stained crimson, the woman stared in silent shock as firemen used the Jaws of Life to tear at the crumpled metal that had once been a Toyota in an effort to free the bodies of the children trapped within.

After he had recovered sufficiently from the sight of spattered blood and flesh from the mangled officer, Billy had phoned the city desk with his eye witness account of the tragedy and advised that all available reporters and photographers who hadn't already been assigned the story be dispatched to the scene immediately. Now, he analyzed the heat in his cheeks and the tremors that shook his stomach and realized that he hadn't felt this way since the fall of Saigon.

Here was life and death, separated by an instant. And here he was, too: confident in the knowledge that being in the blood-red dust of catastrophe and reporting the fierce hum of action was what he, Billy Mossman, did better than anyone. Early in his career, he had listened and watched and, later, written words that made people put down their newspapers and stare unseeing at the dining room wall. Words that seared into brains. Words that gripped chests tightly so that sometimes a tear might roll down a weathered cheek. Words that made people feel outrage.

Staring up at the Olympic Life Insurance Tower with its gaping black holes from the missing panels, Billy considered his wife's earlier remarks. Could the combined effect of an ninety-eight-story office building and a freak gust of wind have caused this destruction? Or had a developer's rampant egotism and the political machinations of the mayor finally overstepped their bounds?

3

Light Beams

SAN JUAN ISLAND, SATURDAY, NOON. Helen woke to tongues of fire lapping at her ankle. Her lip was cut—she could taste the blood—and the rest of her body throbbed. Even her hair hurt. She moaned and opened one eye to find herself staring eyeball to eyeball with a crab.

"Piss off!" she shouted, more startled than afraid.

The small crab scuttled sideways out of reach. The sight of driftwood lying like bleached bones in a tangled jumble above the tide line and the odor of seaweed dying on the rocky beach brought back the memory of her fall: a tremendous wind coming through the woods like an invisible creature, tearing limbs off trees. Her dog, Lord Byron, had been savagely hurled against a tree and her own body tossed from the bluff like a bag of leaves.

"Byron!" she called. She tried to whistle through her smashed lips and failed. "Here, boy," she called again, but there was no answer. The idea of her longtime companion lying injured and unable to respond impelled her to try and get up. She couldn't bear the thought of his dying because she couldn't get him to the vet in time. Helen also needed to assure herself that what she remembered had actually happened. Even though she lay face down on the beach, cold hard rocks pressing into her cheek, a part of her still refused to believe it. Perhaps others had suffered. She needed to know.

First, she had to move. Gingerly, she twisted the upper half of her body so that she could see the fire that was burning her right foot and ankle. Instead of flames, she discovered that her foot was being lapped by icy salt water. Her relief was fleeting as she realized that the tide was coming in. A few minutes more and the water would be up to her face.

Groaning, she pulled herself forward a few inches on her elbows. She could see the bank from which she had fallen some twenty feet overhead. The climb would have to be done on her stomach, a few inches at a time.

"Son of a bitch." She spat blood onto the rocks.

To top it off, Byron might die before she reached the top. A spell of dizziness forced her to close her eyes as she weighed this thought.

"Byron," she called out one last time. "Hang on, boy." If he was going to die, then at least she'd try to see that he wasn't alone when the time came.

Another wave arrived, this one riding up to her knee, and she knew there was no other choice but to get going.

"C'mon, you old fart. This is no time for a vacation." Gritting her teeth against the pain, she began pulling herself forward, pushing with her good foot.

Hours later, she found her dog lying near the tree he had struck. "Byron," she called, but his eyes only stared past her. "Come back here!" she pleaded. "You can't leave me now." Then she wrapped her arms around his stiffening body and wept.

Helen was on a cruise ship, waltzing with the captain, when she woke again. Over the gentle breaking of the surf below, she could hear something approaching from far away. She lay panting on the edge of black asphalt. The pain from her swollen ankle, splintered fingernails, ruined elbows and knees came in waves that made the illusory boat rock gently. Occasionally, the chills came, too—so violent that her jaws ached from her teeth chattering. It was night, either that or she was going blind. She was no longer certain.

Passing in and out of consciousness as through an ocean mist, Helen struggled to listen. The road was beginning to grow brighter. The sound of an engine increased steadily. The tires whined like those of a truck, she decided, as reality returned for another brief visit. Perhaps it was Stan, coming to pick her up for the Saturday night dart tournament at Harrigan's.

"Good old Stan," she whispered. "I'll bake him a cake, if he doesn't run me over." She waved her arm.

There was the sound of old brakes squealing—bad brakes, Helen thought as she closed her eyes and waited for the impact. Instead, she heard tires skidding to a stop followed by the thump of a door. Then came footsteps and a shadow crossing in front of the blinding lights.

"Oh, Lordie," Stan said softly. "That you, Heartbreaker?"

DECEPTION PASS, SATURDAY, 8:12 P.M. "So, how are you planning to spend all this money you've earned?" Ted Hanson asked his son. He spoke over the sound of the massive diesel engines that hummed beneath the rear deck of the sixty-five-foot fishing trawler. Smoke curled from a pipe clenched between his teeth as he stared out over the large steering wheel into the darkness of Puget Sound.

"Don't know yet, Dad," Brian answered, shrugging his larger shoulders. "I'm looking forward to a little partying soon as we get the boat tidied up."

Ted shook his head sadly. "I don't see why you and Debra don't take a week or two and go to Hawaii. You've earned it. Heck, I'll even pay for it."

Brian stared silently out the large windshield. His coarse dark hair, long overdue for a trim, hung low over his square face yet couldn't hide the frown line in his forehead.

Even before leaving on the fishing trip to Alaska, Ted had been disturbed by the trouble he sensed between his son and daughter-in-law. Not the confrontational type, he had waited until now, less than two hours cruising speed from home port in Ballard, to bring it up, even though he had agonized privately for months.

The tobacco smoke hung silently above them, a blue cloud in the small, well-lit cabin. Outside, stars bloomed, distant flowers in a field of night.

After thirty years on the water, Ted's subconscious recorded something wrong before his eyes had time to identify the problem. His hand came back on the throttles.

"Hit the lights, Brian. There's something out there." Instantly, the sea lit up for fifty yards in front of them.

"Where, Dad?"

"One o'clock." Ted struggled to keep the thing in sight as it disappeared regularly among the slow black rollers. A ghostly white shape came into view as they drew near.

"A whale?" Brian asked.

"Naw. A boat. Damn!" The sight of a boat floating upside down miles from anywhere meant only bad news, not to mention a delay. After six months in Alaska, Ted wasn't exactly thrilled to have their homecoming interrupted by some idiot who had dumped his boat.

"Keep a sharp eye out for survivors," he warned. He cut the engines back almost to idling to approach the boat slowly. "Rag boat, looks like."

"Are we going to tow it in?"

"Can't. Looks like it's bottom up," Ted answered. "The Coast Guard's gonna have to pick it up. I'll radio its position."

They were within forty feet of the hull when Ted suddenly stopped the engines. "God almighty! I was staring at a patch of seaweed on the hull when it rolled over and looked at me! Arturo," Ted spoke into the intercom. "Get your ass up here. We got a rescue."

Brian ran aft toward the hoist. The deckhand appeared seconds later, wearing only blue jeans and wiping sleep from his eyes.

"Get a spotlight on that boat and keep it there, Arturo."

The sound of an outboard engine starting up came from the stern.

"Careful," Ted said through the microphone as the small, inflatable boat came into view. He stood at the cabin doorway, straining to pick out objects in the dark water. Using the starboard stairway railing to swing himself down to the deck, he watched anxiously as the light illuminated a body clinging to the broken keel. Brian put the Zodiac's engine in neutral and now Ted could hear a child crying over the waves that slapped heavily against the trawler.

"Where's Mommy?" the small form wailed as Brian struggled to get her into the Zodiac.

"Don't worry, honey," Ted called. "We've got you now. Everything's gonna be all right."

The whine of the outboard began again and then died suddenly. The white hull gleamed eerily in the spot lights. Around it, sky and sea were one, a living, black thing. Ted tried to make out his son and the raft but they were now out of the beam of light.

"Brian? What the hell's he up to, Arturo?" he shouted in frustration. "Can you see 'em?"

"There's a body tied to the rudder." Brian called back.

At the other boat's stern, he saw his son untie a kelp-draped rope and haul a lifeless form into the boat.

"Bring the boat around to port, Brian," Ted yelled. "We'll pick 'em up there."

Moments later, Brian had maneuvered the inflatable along side of the trawler. Arturo dropped down into the Zodiac and handed up the girl and her mother while Brian fended off the larger boat. The woman was comatose, her blue lips contrasting sharply with her pale white skin. The girl couldn't take her eyes off her mother and was shivering so hard that her crying came in jerky snuffles. Ted figured she'd be in shock soon if she wasn't already.

"Get cocoa for the girl, wrap her in a blanket and put her in my cabin," Ted ordered Arturo. He tested for a pulse, then put his ear to the woman's mouth.

Brian had climbed out of the dingy and made it fast to a stern cleat. Now he hovered over his father and the woman. "How is she?"

"Looks like she's been in the water a long time. Too long, probably."

Brian smacked a fist into his thigh. "We can't just give up on her, Dad. What's her little girl gonna think?"

"Then help me get her into the shower. We might be able to save her yet."

Picking up the lifeless woman, they carried her below to the small bathroom that doubled as a shower stall.

"Now get back up there and drive this tub as fast as she'll go to Edmonds," Ted said. "Radio for an ambulance to meet us at the docks."

Ted kicked off his deck shoes and stripped off his jacket before turning the water on as hot as he could stand it. Then, sitting on the floor, still wearing his jeans and shirt, he cradled the woman against his chest, holding her head up out of the spray of water as the room quickly filled with steam.

"Stay with me, honey. You can make it," he coaxed as both engines roared to life, flooding the small cubicle with vibrating sound.

"She gonna live?" Arturo appeared in the doorway and began peeling off the woman's sodden vest, sweater and pants.

"God only knows."

Ann Bessani heard a sound like thunder as an enormous white-winged horse galloped toward her, hooves pawing the air. A feeling of absolute love and contentment filled her as the huge creature swept her up, cradling her under one wing.

"Look, skipper." Arturo pointed to the woman's head resting against Ted's shoulder. Tears ran down her cheeks in the rising steam.

4

Final Preparations

SEATTLE, SUNDAY, 7:53 A.M. The phone rang again. Billy opened one eye, momentarily enjoying the sweet smell of slept-in bed clothes while his wife fumbled with the phone. "Hello," she asked at last. "Who is this? Just a moment."

She rolled over to face him, one hand cupping the receiver. "It's Mayor Grenitzer," she whispered. "He doesn't sound like he just called to say hello."

Billy was instantly awake.

"Good morning, Mayor." He sat up and squinted at the alarm clock's enormous red numerals, one of his few acknowledgments of middle age.

"Good morning, my ass. What is this crap about yesterday's tragedy having something to do with the Olympic Life Tower?" The mayor's voice sounded distant; probably using a speakerphone, Billy guessed. That meant he was at his office and, this early on a Sunday, that meant trouble.

"Well, Mayor," he started to explain, his tongue still thick with sleep, yet the memory of the neat row of bodies coming back into all-too-clear focus.

"I thought you were a decent reporter." The angry voice cut him off. "Responsible. Until this nonsense! C'mon, Mossman. Venturi effect? Geophysics? You must be crazy. I'm surprised the *Times* would print this crap."

"I called your office." Billy felt his stomach began to knot. He wondered who else might be listening to their conversation over the speakerphone. "They said you were unavailable for comment."

"So you just write what you damn well please, is that it? The election is barely three weeks away and you write a bunch of cockamamie stuff that makes it sound like I betrayed the public trust. What utter bullshit!"

Billy listened to the sputtering voice with growing detachment. After all, it had been Grenitzer and his cronies on the council who had jammed through the approval over the objections of most of the community. Still, he'd never heard the mayor quite this hot. Normally, the little bastard was fairly even-tempered. Then again, until today, Billy had written only what Douglas Truitt, city editor, expected of him. By presenting a mostly whitewashed portrait of the city, his columns rarely offended anyone. After the accident yesterday, however, the bear was out of his cage and there was no going back. Billy was committed to finding the truth and if his story about the Tower had touched a nerve, well, so be it.

"I didn't just 'write what I wanted,' Mayor. I checked it out. Dr. David Thomas is one of the world's foremost authorities on geophysical forces and their effects on bridges, buildings, and other structures. He showed me a letter to the city planning commission warning that this kind of thing could happen if a ninety-eight-story building were erected in that location. The proximity of Queen Anne Hill, the freeway canyon. . . ."

"Crap, crap, crap, Mossman! Your story stinks worse than a four-holer in July. First of all, Thomas is an academic eccentric and full-time weirdo. None of his theories are accepted by the people who actually build things. Second, my staff tells me he's politically ambitious—wants to run for office down the road. Add it up. The guy's hot for a little free press. Along comes this freak gust of wind and the opportunist blames it on a fucking building, for Chrissake. Now I understand that proverb, 'It's an ill wind that blows nobody good.' My opponent must be laughing his ass off right this minute. My God, what a gift!"

His wife, Billy noticed, had given up on sleeping in and was getting up.

" 'Here's my chance at a Pulitzer,' is that what you were thinking, you asshole? If they give awards for stupidity, I'm nominating you, Mossman!"

"Mayor . . ." Billy tried to get a word in.

"So, now you probably want to start testing the aerodynamics of buildings before they're built, huh? You overweight numbskull! Buildings don't fly, for Chrissakes. They just sit there on their asses—like you."

Despite his indignation, Billy could feel a laugh building somewhere near his toes. The foulness of Grenitzer's language this early on a Sunday morning was absurd. "Excuse me, how do you spell 'Chrissakes?' Is that with or without a 'T'?"

"Listen here, Mossman. You write any more horseshit about this and I'm going to turn your ass into the world's largest wind tunnel.

Boeing will be able to fly 747s through there!''

Unable to restrain himself any longer, Billy began to chuckle.

"Enjoy yourself while you can. We'll see who has the last laugh." The line went dead.

Billy was still grinning when he reached the living room. The drapes were open, displaying Lake Union immediately outside. Ducks swam around the small sailboat moored to their dock. The smell of percolating coffee filled the floating houseboat. Still wearing her robe, Julie eyed him warily from the kitchen.

"What's so funny? He was so obnoxiously loud, I could hear every word and what I heard didn't sound especially humorous."

"You missed the good part." Billy put his arms around her waist and pulled her close. The softness of her body next to his felt very good. He could feel himself becoming aroused.

Julie freed herself and turned to face him. Her dark eyes reflected her worried tone of voice. "He's got powerful friends. If he wants, he can make life difficult for us."

"Let him try," Billy said, remembering the mayor's threat.

"You really think the Tower caused those deaths?"

"Hey, my dear, don't you remember? You were the one who suggested it in the first place."

"Yeah." Julie nodded slowly. "But it feels like there was something more to it than just that."

"Feels like?" Billy was not amused. "I can't write stuff like that. People would laugh. I might as well go to work for the tabloids. Besides, like I told Grenitzer, there's a scientific theory predicting what happened."

Julie looked at him over her coffee cup. "Maybe the world isn't the nice, neat scientific equation everyone wants it to be."

"Now you tell me." Billy headed for the bathroom. His erection was gone and taking a pee was suddenly the most important thing in the world.

"I can't believe the bastard would write such crap." Grenitzer scowled across the stacks of binders and computer printouts that covered his aircraft-carrier-size desk at the two men seated opposite him. "What on earth possessed him? Up till now, I actually enjoyed his column. You don't suppose Wilson slipped him a few bucks to assassinate me in print?"

His aide, Bud Phillips, stared into his coffee cup, as if looking for wisdom there. "I admit the timing is highly suspicious, but I don't think so. Mossman had a pretty decent reputation back some ten years back. Then a story on political payoffs blew up on him."

"What'd he do, make the story up?" Grenitzer asked.

"Nah, it was probably true. Trouble was, he made the fatal mistake of attributing a number of damaging quotes to one fictitious person instead of several real ones. Then the Senate subpoenaed him and he was forced to admit it. Caused quite a scandal. He lost his job, his wife, the whole ball of wax."

Earl Massey chuckled. The developer of the Olympic Life Tower was a large man in his early sixties. Behind the men and all along one side of the thirtieth-floor office, large windows gave a panoramic view of Puget Sound, now cloaked in early morning fog.

"I'm going to call Peters, the publisher, and try to get the jerk canned," Grenitzer said.

"Now, just a minute, Jack." The developer's voice was reasoned and cool which made Grenitzer despise the man all the more. "Let's talk this over. I know Peters very well. We both belong to the Seattle Athletic Club. He'll wonder why you're making such a big fuss out of a half-baked story. Better just let it lie."

Massey was dressed like he had just stepped off his yacht. He wore a red and blue crewneck sweater, white chinos, and Topsiders. Despite the silver in his full head of hair, he could have passed for ten to fifteen years younger than his real age. It was one thing to dress younger, Grenitzer thought, but how did the bastard carry it off at home? His latest wife couldn't be thirty years old yet. And that was another reason why he resented Massey.

"Look, I've got a job, not to mention a reputation, to protect. We're only three weeks from the election and the polls have Wilson ahead by ten percent."

Phillips nodded in confirmation that his numbers were still accurate. His aide was dressed today in his usual style: expensive sport coat, V-neck sweater, slacks, and loafers. Maybe he had a polo match later. Still, nobody in this town was more politically astute. Bud had been the architect of the public relations campaign that had resulted in Seattle being named "America's Most Livable City" for each of the previous five years.

Massey slurped his coffee before speaking. "I don't think Wilson's got a chance, Jack, no matter what the polls say. The whites are scared of him, the Hispanics will vote for their own guy and the Orientals despise blacks even more than they do whites."

Grenitzer frowned at such a gross oversimplification. "That's a load of crap. Bud's got an informant planted on Wilson's election team and she says Wilson's considering coming out against busing one week before the election. If he does, he'll get the black vote, most of the white vote, the Vietnamese, Chinese, and Japanese vote, and the Latino vote, too. The whole enchilada."

"So, Jack," Massey edged closer to the desk, shooting a quick, conspiratorial glance at Phillips, "why don't you head him off by doing the same thing first?"

"Because I can't, dammit!" Grenitzer leaped to his feet and began pacing behind his desk.

"We can't touch the busing issue," Phillips explained. "If we say we're *for* busing, Wilson will accuse us of being racist. But, if we say we're *against* busing, Wilson will also accuse us of being racist. It's the old catch-22."

"Clever old coot, isn't he?" Massey lifted his large frame from the Queen Anne chair and walked across the room toward the coffee pot.

"I fail to see the humor," Grenitzer said. "It's your Tower of Babel that's created this mess."

Massey turned around slowly, one finger pointed menacingly. "Listen, you little two-bit hustler. You might do well to remember who's been supplying your campaign coffers with plenty of cash over the years. Not to mention the vacation to Israel. You've ridden a far piece on my back. Now, it's time we stuck together. Am I clear?"

"I've ridden on nobody's back, you son-of-a-bitch."

"Gentlemen, gentlemen." Phillips stood, holding both arms up, palms raised, as if to keep the two men apart. "This is getting us nowhere."

Grenitzer walked to one of the many plaques that decorated the wall behind his desk. This one was the Enterprise Award, presented to him by the National Association of Chambers of Commerce, in recognition of his support for small business. Shit. There were so many interest groups today, it was impossible to please anyone, let alone everyone. Hardly a day went by when he didn't have to fight his way through a line of pickets just to get to work. Striking school teachers, gays for equal housing, Greenpeace . . . If Wilson got elected, good riddance. The city could go to hell as far as he was concerned.

"Jack?" Phillips called out. "We still don't have a plan of action."

"Go ahead, Bud. Let's hear what you have to say." Both he and Massey seated themselves again.

"What about confronting this thing head on?" Phillips asked. "Say we hold a press conference."

"Now you're talking." Massey nodded his enthusiastic agreement. "I can get Walter Eggenburk, the retired dean of the UW's School of Architecture to discredit Thomas," Massey interrupted. "We can get structural engineers, physicists, whatever it takes to roast this guy publicly. Make him look like a real grandstander."

"I think it's the only way," Phillips said, nodding. "Can you really get the dean?"

"Don't worry about that. I can get anybody."

"What do you think, Jack?" Bud asked. Both men turned toward him.

"When? We need to stop the train before it gets rolling."

"Let's do it tomorrow morning, right at the Tower," Bud said.

"Is that wise? Our city inspection crews will be crawling all over every inch of that building to check it out. Their report won't be complete for at least a week."

"Of course it's wise," Massey said. "If you're standing there along with the dean and our own engineers, why, there won't be anyone present or who sees it on the news who won't think that the Tower's fine—that there was just some kind of little bitty twister yesterday."

"Are you really sure about this?" Grenitzer asked. "What if there's another accident? Can you imagine the crap that would hit the fan? All someone like this Mossman needs is a hint of a story and he'll turn it into front page news. Next thing you know, camera crews from CNN and *60 Minutes* will be parked outside in the loading zone. There'd be lynch mobs scouring every inch of this city for both our asses."

"Jack, don't make me spell it out for you. It's got to be at the Tower and soon." Massey smacked one large palm onto the table top, causing his cup to jump and coffee to slosh into the saucer. "I've got to get that thing leased up immediately or the debt service will eat me alive."

"But what if you got a bad shipment of bolts from Taiwan? Or if one of your guys is on the take?"

"The Tower's fine, dammit!"

Massey's face had become red. Grenitzer wondered if he was

45

about to have a stroke. Go ahead, asshole, die. But not in my office.

"What do you think, Bud?"

Bud shrugged. "Sooner we get the air cleared, the better able we'll be to face off with Wilson. You know he'll try to use this."

Grenitzer nodded. "Okay, Earl. You take care of the dean and the engineers. Bud will take care of the rest. Right, Bud?"

Huge, gray and silent, the enemy camp lay sleeping in the thin, morning light. Along the tree-lined, residential streets, barely a handful of people were out. These were runners whose shirts and shorts hung loosely on their bodies and whose calf muscles were like woven strands of good hemp rope.

Only the mournful call of a foghorn intruded upon the stillness of the waterfront. The gulls had fled. Below the Alaskan Way Viaduct, high up among the concrete supports, the pigeons hid with small, blinking red eyes as below them, Styrofoam cups, cigarette butts, and paper containers that once held fish and chips were caught in a whirling dance.

Here was where Black Wolf had fallen. This was the place of desecration where his blood yet stained the ground.

> *Hear me, Old One,*
> *hear my song of death.*
> *From the sacred white mountain far, far away,*
> *where not even the eagles dare to fly,*
> *I have come to make war*
> *on this people who have wronged you.*
> *Rest easy on your spirit journey, Old One.*
> *I will avenge your death.*
> *Aiyee, few of the enemy yet know of me,*
> *but soon, all shall know my wrath.*
> *Let them beware.*
> *This is my song of death!*

The keening sound of the wind became an enraged howl.

A paper sack containing an empty pint bottle was snatched up and hurled against a brick wall. The crash woke a wino named Chuck from a dream of bacon and eggs and hot coffee. Peeking out from his cardboard cocoon beneath a stairway, he was amazed to see the whirling cloud of debris and to hear the wind's screaming. An automobile, abandoned the previous night, rocked with the wind's buffeting. The car began sliding sideways, leaving a trail of black tire marks. Then, as the wino rubbed his eyes, the front end lifted and the auto was thrown end over end with an ear-rending crash onto the railroad tracks like a discarded child's toy. Shattered glass windows and chrome trim littered the pavement. Chuck withdrew quietly back into his shelter. He crossed himself, though he was not Catholic.

"Are these the last days, Lord?" he asked the roof of his RCA home. "Am I thy last prophet? Death and destruction have I seen. Yeah, speak to me from the burning bush, Lord, and I shall lead thy people." He began to hum "Jesus Loves Me." It was the only hymn he could remember.

With a final shriek, the wind bolted up onto the double-decked expressway. The driver of a Volkswagen van that had been headed south was surprised to find himself staring up at the sky for a brief moment as his van became airborne. He jammed his foot on the brake and turned the steering wheel first one way and then the other in an effort to control his vehicle's new-found ability before the van landed on its roof and screeched to a halt.

Following the highway north, the wind entered the Battery Street tunnel. Hurtling from the tunnel with a roar, it blasted the newspaper racks that stood in front of the Tiki Hut restaurant, releasing papers into a funnel cloud that whirled above the city.

Two miles up the highway at the zoo, a pack of timber wolves began to howl. A bald eagle, recuperating from a gunshot wound, thrashed about his small pen, flapping his useless wings. The howling of the wolves was soon joined by that of the coyotes and Australian dingoes. The monkeys scampered about their concrete island, chattering excitedly. Peacocks cried and macaws and elephants trumpeted their alarm. In the big cat zone, the lions, tigers, pumas, cheetahs, and snow leopards growled their displeasure while pacing their compounds. The solitary jackal laughed hysterically and hurled himself against his cage while the birds in the thirty-six-foot-high aviary took to the air with a rush of beating wings.

Then, in the space of a heartbeat, all was silent.

Above the wakening city, the mountains called. The wind longed to return to their pure white silence, but there was much to be done. First, he would scout the enemy before returning to the high place. Yesterday's raid was but a taste of things to come.

SEATTLE, SUNDAY, 10:40 A.M. Evan intercepted the pass and, using short, controlled kicks, dribbled the ball swiftly between the other team's halfbacks. With no sound to interfere, his concentration was focused like sunlight through a magnifying glass, heightening all other sensory information. The playing field was a three-dimensional grid upon which he was aware of the movement of opposing players as well as teammates as his feet skimmed the wet grass, dribbling the ball toward the distant goal.

He was also aware of his mother standing with the other spectators lining the soccer field but was easily able to edit out this information. Not so easy to ignore was the other thing that hovered just beyond the horizon of his conscious thoughts. Although the anticipation made his stomach turn flip-flops, he forced himself to store his foreglimpse until later.

From the right, he sensed the ground vibrating with the approach of a defender. He veered left, stopped abruptly, and then darted right. The other boy sailed past him, lost his footing and sprawled on the ground.

Approaching the penalty box, Evan waited for the defense to commit their attack to him. At the last possible instant, he passed off to the winger on his right. The collision with their fullback flipped him over, landed him on his back and knocked the wind out of him.

He lay staring up into the sky and the sweaty, red faces of his opponents who stood around him, hands on hips, discussing him as if he were a frog dissected on a table. Though he watched their lips, he couldn't understand a word they were saying as he struggled with the task of trying to get his lungs jump-started. He wondered if he was dying.

His mother, no doubt, was having a fit. Evan's team was not only smaller than other teams and undermanned, but deaf. Yet, for all that, they had a winning record against non-handicapped teams. Their coach, once a star player on the British World Cup team and now a recovering alcoholic, attributed their success to an uncanny ability to sense one another's moves. Whatever it was, it worked. Evan's team was leading their division and would move up into the next division if they managed to finish the season in first place. But, even more important, they had proven themselves capable of winning in the hearing world.

After what seemed like hours, he was able to sit up. Evan closed his eyes and waited for the black nausea to evaporate. While he rested, the vision came, blood-chilling and unwanted. Suddenly, his nausea was gone.

He was running from the wolf he had seen in the curio store. Wherever he ran, down street after street, even into buildings, it followed, relentless, unstoppable. As if watching a video tape on fast forward, Evan saw himself run into an alley. Too late, he realized that he was cornered with no way to escape. The wolf knocked him to the ground and pinned him beneath its massive paws. He heard it howl, then felt a stabbing pain as its jaws closed on his throat. The illusion was so real that he grabbed his neck in terror. Then he saw something that gave him hope. At the entrance of the alley, an Indian sat bareback on a great black stallion, wearing only a loin cloth and war paint.

Evan opened his eyes and scanned the surrounding fields and parking lots. He half expected to see Paul Judge, his rescuer from the previous day sitting astride his horse, ready for battle. But there were only the players and their families.

Hey, Ev, one of his teammates signed. *Miss your nap?*

He grinned through his pain as the coach and one of his teammates helped him stand. Because his team had only enough players to make up a side, he stayed in the game. His lip felt like it had swollen to the size of a pillow and his hip throbbed painfully, but he could still run. Evan waved to his mother and was glad when she waved back.

An hour and a half of soccer, pizza, and Pepsi later, they were home.

"Take off your shoes and throw those clothes in the hamper before you sit on any furniture," Denise signed.

Evan raced upstairs ahead of her, taking the steps two at a time. Denise followed, shaking her head as she marveled at his energy. Even more unheard of, he had actually done what she'd asked without being asked twice. That was the weird thing about raising a kid: just when you got used to them being one way, they changed to being another.

She noted the light layer of dust that had settled on the walnut console table at the head of the stairs. Some other time, she sighed.

The tiny green light on the phone message recorder blinked in the half-light of her small, upstairs bedroom. Denise sat down on the Victorian-era oak bed and pushed the play button.

"This is Grenitzer. Where the hell are you? Have you read the *Times?* We need to call a press conference for tomorrow morning at the Olympic Life Tower. Call Bud the moment you get in."

"Terrific," Denise sighed, falling backward onto the bed. She had been looking forward to reading the Sunday paper and mowing the lawn before the grass got too high and the rain resumed. Now, she covered her eyes with her hands as she contemplated the work that would need to be accomplished even before Monday began: phone calls to editors, locating the tables, chairs and PA system, writing a news release and a fact sheet and then seeing that they were distributed to the wire services. She'd be lucky to get a couple of hours' sleep. And all for a client who had never once thanked her or even acknowledged her efforts in the six years she had worked on his behalf.

She lay motionless for several minutes and considered quitting for perhaps the hundredth time. When at last she looked up, Evan was standing in the doorway watching her, his face partially hidden in the shadows. She stretched her sweat-suit-clad legs out in front of her and stared at the toes of her sneakers. Finally, she turned to him and hoped that he couldn't see the moistness in her eyes in the dim light.

"How would you like to run off to Mexico, live on the beach?"

Evan nodded enthusiastically, coming over to sit beside her on the bed. He smelled of soap and shampoo. She stroked his damp hair and took solace in the warmth of the thin body that nestled against hers.

"You could fish for our food and I would write children's books that sell for millions—"

The sound of an automobile entering the driveway and approaching the house interrupted her. Denise stared at the open window where the lace curtains she had made when they first moved into the house still hung, simple, white and uncomplicated. A car door squeaked open and then thudded shut. The nearly imperceptible vibration was enough to propel Evan streaking out of the bedroom and down the stairs.

The doorbell rang. Denise approached the door cautiously, descending the stairs one at a time. After the mayor's phone message, she was not eager to face any more surprises. Halfway down, she saw with dismay that the door stood wide open. Denise began preparing her most aggressive defense to purge the intruder—salesman, Jehovah's Witness, or subscription-selling fundraiser—as quickly as possible from her rapidly evaporating day of rest. She was nearly to the bottom stair before she could see past Evan to whoever stood in the doorway. Her surprise was such that she nearly stumbled. Her ex-husband, Ron, wearing a Seahawk jacket, looked up from Evan and smiled as she approached. He looked like he might have gained a couple inches around the middle since she had last seen him. His curly red hair looked a bit thinner on top, too.

"Hello."

"Hi," Denise replied, letting it sound like the question it was.

"I thought Evan might like to take in a Seahawks game with me this afternoon." He reached in his pocket and produced tickets.

Having prepared her defenses for something else entirely, Denise was momentarily without words. She looked to Evan, as if he might offer her some clues as to how she should proceed, but he was shifting his weight from foot to foot and avoiding her gaze. If she didn't know better, she might have thought he looked disappointed, but how could that be? He did not often get a chance to attend professional games, much less see his father.

"So, tell me. Were you out for a Sunday drive, just happened to be passing our house and remembered you had these tickets in your wallet?"

"I tried to call a couple of times." Ron smiled sheepishly.

"Bullshit."

"Now, Denise, is that proper language to be using in front of a twelve-year-old?"

"Thirteen. But then, how would you know?" Denise read the hurt in Evan's eyes and realized that she had once again lost her senses. Ron did that to her. "Okay, look, I'm sorry. It's not turning out to be one of my better days."

Ron tousled Evan's hair with one hand, as if that would make all those missed birthdays okay. Evan winced and pulled out of reach. "How'd he get the lump on his head?"

"Soccer."

"He plays soccer?"

"Yeah. Excellently, I might add."

"Hey, hey! Way to go, Ev!" He put out a hand to be high-fived. Evan smiled sheepishly and slapped Ron's hand.

"Let's try starting over," Ron suggested. "Can Evan go to the Seahawks game with me?" He glanced at the expensive-looking gold watch on his wrist. "We should be back by six, easy."

Try as she might—and God knows her mother wanted her to try—she couldn't forget that this was the man who had split soon after Evan was born. The pregnancy had been an accident, coming early in their senior year of college. Ron had wanted her to abort the fetus. Only after he realized her determination to keep the baby did he offer to marry her. Later, unaware that Evan was deaf, Ron and his family had been quick to assume that he was retarded—undoubtedly some wayward gene from Denise's family, her mother-in-law had implied. Already under strain, their marriage had come unglued.

Now, she wanted to slug Ron, knee him in the groin and pluck out his pale blue eyes. Instead, Denise bent down and looked into Evan's innocent eyes, signing carefully.

"Want to go with Ron to the game? It's okay with me. I'm going to be busy with work."

Evan smiled, put his arms around her neck and hugged her painfully. "Okay, Ma."

He didn't speak often, usually only in the bathroom and never in public places, but when he did, her heart sometimes felt too large for her chest.

"Dammit, Evan," she whispered, holding him at arm's length. "You really know how to get me."

Denise stood up finally and smiled at Ron. "You guys win."

The three of them walked outside in silence. A willowy, young woman with long, light brown hair stepped out of the black sports car. She wore a black leather jacket and pants and a belt that glittered with silver conchas. The turquoise ring on her right hand was nearly the size of a small animal.

"New set of wheels?" Denise asked Ron. "Nice finish. Anything under the hood?"

"Denise," Ron said, ignoring her questions, "this is Monica."

"Hi." Her smile was lovely, her teeth were perfect and she couldn't have been older than twenty-four. Denise glanced next door to see if the neighbors were watching. A drapery swung back into place. That ruled out homicide—too many witnesses.

"Where's Evan going to sit?" Denise gestured toward the car. Evan was admiring the rear spoiler and wide tires.

"There's a jump seat," Monica said. "Of course, he can sit in my lap, if he wants."

"I want him to have his own seatbelt."

"Relax." Ron put a hand on her shoulder. "There are belts in the back." She drew back from his touch.

"Please don't feed him too much junk."

A moment later, the engine roared and the car backed down the narrow driveway. Denise returned Evan's wave and stared after the car, her arms crossed over her chest as if to hide the ache inside.

"Okay, Ma," The words had burned into her brain, permanently branded there. What a kid. With the toe of one of her sneakers, she kicked at the grass that would soon be too long to mow. "Guess we'll have to raise a herd of dairy cows." She glanced again at the neighbors' window as she strode toward her house and noted the same drapery swinging closed. Now, there's a dull life, she thought.

5

Signs

SEATTLE, SUNDAY, 6:30 P.M. Nicolo Tambakis counted the change in his cup by size and weight. There were also a few bills. These, he knew from experience, were probably ones. Sundays were the worst. Even on days the Seahawks played, the amount of money hardly justified the time. He came anyway to sit in his regular place on the sidewalk by the little park and to measure the days by the taste of the air and by the sounds and smells of the people passing. Every day was a blessing from God to be caught and held firmly like a strong, fat trout and then released.

He would show the money to the priest at the mission as he did every day. Other than the deaf boy, Father Janowsky was one of the few people that he trusted. The Father would take only the ten percent for a tithe plus a little for his room and meals. The rest was deposited to his bank account.

"Come, Fortuno. It's time for you to go to work."

A warm tongue licked the hand that he held out. Nicolo found the collar without difficulty and attached the harness. Without this bit of leather around his throat and chest, the dog was just like any other. But with the harness on, Fortuno became all business. Once he had managed to stand, the dog led the way, slowly, to allow for his probing with the cane and his halting steps. Sitting all day on the hard concrete sidewalks, his legs had become heavy and numb. I must have slept a good while, too, he thought. His keen hearing told him that the crowd from the football game had already departed; the streets were now deserted as they were every Sunday evening.

Rhythmically, he tapped with the cane, seeking the telltale curbs and parking meters that served him as signposts. The dog stopped and waited patiently at stop lights while Nicolo enjoyed the fading warmth of sunlight on his face. Soon it would be winter. He shuddered with the memory.

For much of his life, he had lived on the streets, sheltered by a stairwell or an overpass. The money had run out not long after he was blinded while working at the shipyard. His wife and daughter had left him soon after that. Once he had accepted his fate, the handicap had become manageable. Now, however, there were too many bad people. Once, it would have been unthinkable to attack a blind man, but no more. He had been beaten and robbed not once but many times. The weather hurt him now, too.

He had avoided the mission initially because the other men were always loud and stupid and sometimes cruel. The priest had persisted over the years, however, inviting him to stay whenever the weather was especially bad. Finally, one frostbitten Christmas when his toes had lost all feeling and he was afraid he would lose them, he had stayed for good. Now, he had his own room where he and the dog slept. You are a lucky man, Nico, he thought.

He was still smiling as he heard the dry leaves skittering down the sidewalk. A powerful breeze blew icy tendrils in under his coats. Above his head, a sign began to swing on rusting chains. The dog growled protectively.

"What is it, Fortuno?" He bent to stroke the dog and found that the hair on his neck was standing on end. "What makes you so angry, my friend?" He listened with all his considerable skill. The wind was stronger now and louder. He wrapped the scarf tightly around his neck. The dog began to whine in a high-pitched manner that Nicolo had never before heard. Something approached rapidly with a hollow thumping. Aware of his helplessness, he stood and faced the sound. His eyes watered and his face stung with the impact of dust and grit. A shiver ran down his spine that made his entire body feel cold as death and a foul taste rose in his throat as the menacing noise closed on him. A plastic garbage can, he realized, as it tumbled past. A bass drum beat loudly in his chest.

"Silly old goat," he admonished himself. "And you," he called to the dog as he returned to his tapping and probing. "What's the matter? You never see a garbage can hopping down the street before?" Nicolo laughed heartily.

His laughter was cut off abruptly as a blast of air made him stumble. Like a falling skater, he threw out his arms in search of a handhold. His hand found a lamppost and he held on with one arm, his cane clattering to the sidewalk. The other hand still clung to the harness.

The wind screamed like an angry beast. Nicolo had to let the dog go to grasp the lamppost with both hands. Desperately his fingers searched for purchase on the smooth metal pole even as he felt his feet leaving the ground. His hands, once powerful from loading ships, felt as if tendons were snapping and tearing away from the muscle and bone. And then he was flying.

At first, Nicolo covered his sightless eyes with his arms. At any moment, he expected to crash, face first, into a building. Instead, he was hurled upward. His senses told him that he was rising very high, very fast.

He was swept away by a powerful river of air that smelled of snowy peaks and evergreen trees. The wind was all around him. Every small movement of an arm or leg changed the flow of air currents, but seemed to have no effect on his speed or direction. The wind's howl was deafening, yet Nicolo was no longer afraid. He crossed himself. If God had chosen this moment to come for him, well, who was he to argue?

He remembered a family picnic on the Island of Samos, being a boy running in a sea of windblown grass on a hill that overlooked the white-toothed Aegean and there being a great *zephyros*, how he had put out his arms and tried to fly. "I'm a bird," he had yelled to his sisters and their cousins. Their parents had called them back and they had climbed in the cars and driven back to town, but not before the white tablecloth had taken flight, his mother, father and aunts and uncles all chasing after it while the children shouted with glee. He smiled at the memory and tried to flap his arms but the wind was too strong. Had one of the diners in the revolving restaurant high atop the Space Needle chanced to look in his direction, they would have seen what looked like a much older and humbler Superman, sans cape, hurtling through the darkening evening sky.

Now the glacial air smelled of barnacles crusted on rotting, salt-water-washed pilings. I wonder what will happen to the dog, he thought. And then he plunged beneath the frigid waters of Puget Sound.

SAN JUAN ISLAND, MONDAY, 6:45 A.M. Helen sat up in bed. The effort caused her to wince and she squeezed her eyes tight as the pain stabbed, an ice pick in the center of the brain. She waited until it had passed before opening her eyes again.

The pain was a clear reminder of her current physical state. Dr. Gardner had warned her that a mild concussion was nothing to fool with and had prescribed plenty of bed rest. Easy for him to say, Helen thought. Her thirst to identify the villain responsible for her beloved pet's death would not be denied. The wind or whatever it was that had thrown Lord Byron savagely against a tree and blown her from the rocky bluff onto the beach below must have hurt others or caused damage elsewhere, but finding this out had proved difficult. Neither the doctor nor the nurse who had admitted her had known anything about reports of severe winds or a storm on Saturday night. Waking briefly from a drugged stupor on Sunday, Helen asked the nurse who offered her a bed pan whether she had heard about any news reports of wind damage.

"A wind?" the nurse asked. "I think they had something happen in Seattle. I'm not sure. Are you done? Now rest. You need to be quiet." And Helen had fallen back into her oblivion.

She stared at the television that hung from just below the far ceiling. She looked around her for a remote control to turn it on, but couldn't spot one. From the other side of the curtain that draped between their beds came the smooth, even breathing of her unseen hospital roommate.

She eased her feet to the floor and stood, testing her weight on her bandaged right ankle. Not too bad, she thought. She took a step, using the bed for support.

"Holy Mother of God!" Her ankle felt like someone had smacked it with a hockey stick. She sat back down on the bed and rubbed the swollen joint, stiff from the bandages. "Perhaps we're being a bit hasty."

The breathing continued on the other side of the curtain, the only sound in the otherwise silent hospital room. The pale green walls and medicinal smell brought back painful memories. "Hospitals are where people go to die," her father had confided to her. "When my time comes, don't let some guy wearing a white smock and driving an expensive automobile convince you that I'd be happier in a place that smells like a morgue. Just take me home, sit me in the rocker by the window where I can feel the sun and leave me be." His last request still haunted her.

She had been visiting New York to take in the theater when the call had come from her aunt. "Charley's had a bad spell," his sister had explained. Helen had taken a taxi to Newark and caught the very next plane to Seattle. All too vividly, she remembered running up the steps of the Veterans' Hospital, riding the elevator that stopped at every floor, hurrying past the gurneys laden with wasted, old men. The smell of urine and medicine gagged her. When she had finally seen her father's pale, unconscious face and his shrunken body lying beneath the sheets in the crowded room, she had panicked. "What did you do to him?" she screamed. And then, before the startled orderlies could react, she had raced down the emergency stairway, burst through the doors and collapsed on the entrance steps, the sweat soaking her dress and forming a small pool beneath her on the marble as she wept.

Now, Helen regarded the white closet door set in the opposite wall and counted the large, dark brown and white tiles that formed the checkerboard floor between the bed and the door. Ten steps, she guessed. Whether her clothes were still in the closet or whether there were any hope of getting out of the hospital once she was dressed, she considered only briefly before putting both feet on the floor once again.

Shutting her eyes, she tried again to walk, this time leading with the other foot. A liquid warmness filled her foot and ankle but the pain was less severe.

Her roommate didn't wake until Helen had finished dressing and was halfway to the door. The drapery hadn't been closed all the way and Helen saw the young woman's curly dark head lift, the eyes attempting to focus. "Just checking out, honey," Helen whispered. "You get some rest now." The head dropped back onto the pillow, the woman rolled over and soon Helen heard her peaceful breathing resume.

She opened the door to the hallway and peered out. The stillness at this hour was eerie; the place appeared to be deserted. She closed the door behind her and shuffled down the hall. She was almost past the nurses' station when a young woman stood up to challenge her.

"Just where do you think you're going?" she asked, a *People* magazine clutched in one hand.

"I'm on my way to visit my sister." Helen smiled innocently. Never tell the truth if a lie will do, she thought and hoped that her soiled clothing, bandaged foot and missing shoe weren't too obvious. "She asked if I could come early today."

"I'm sorry," the young woman replied, "but we don't permit visitors until eight."

"Oh, what time's it now?"

"It's not even seven yet," the nurse replied, glancing at the colorful plastic watch on her arm. "You'll have to wait in the lobby."

"Thanks, miss," Helen said. She was careful to keep the counter between her and the nurse as she hobbled painfully down the corridor.

The lobby contained a bench-like sofa and a couple of matching chairs, too ugly to invite theft, but no newspapers. Helen opened the door and spotted a combination pharmacy and general store down the street that looked as if it might be open. "Barely out of field goal range," she said. She dialed Stan from the pay phone in the lobby, using her credit card number.

"I'm ready to go home," she announced when he picked up the phone.

"Hey, Heartbreaker," the groggy voice answered. "That's good news. How about if I'm there around ten or so?"

"Sure. I'll be sitting on the curb across the street."

"Does that mean you'd prefer my arrival be sooner?" Stan asked warily.

"I wouldn't want to inconvenience you."

"What about twenty minutes, then?"

"Take your time," she answered and hung up the phone.

Halfway across the street on her way to the small store, the pain returned to her ankle with a vengeance. She tried to hop and fell instead to the pavement. The few cars that were on the road passed her slowly. One driver nearly stopped, leaning his head out the window.

"A little early to be hitting the sauce, hey lady?" he asked.

Helen crawled on hands and knees to the curb where she rolled up the cuffs of her dirty tweed pants and inspected her bandaged ankle. She unbound it tenderly. Bloated and purple, it leaked blood from her pores. Aghast, she covered it loosely again in the bandages.

She was sitting on the curb, shivering in the early morning mist, when Stan arrived in his pickup truck. Seeing her friend cheered her. She tried to rise and failed. Stan jumped from the cab and came around to help her.

"My God, Helen. You sure you know what you're doin'?" he asked as he struggled to lift her into the cab.

"Thank you for coming, Stan." She put a hand on his arm while he rested. "I had to get out of there. Bloody deathtrap."

Stan looked over at the small wooden-frame hospital across the street and shook his head. "You are about the most hard-headed broad I have ever known." He started to shut the door but she stopped him.

"I've got two more favors to ask."

"I knew this wouldn't be easy," he sighed.

"First, I need you to get some newspapers: yesterday's and today's."

"Which ones?"

"All of them."

"And?"

"I'd like you to drive back to where you picked me up the other night."

Helen watched him return from the store a few minutes later. Under one arm, he had a weighty-looking bundle of newspapers which he handed her through the window. In his other hand, he held an aluminum cane with four prongs forming a square pattern. He placed the cane in the back of the truck.

"What's that thing?" she asked as he climbed into the driver's seat.

"Something to help you get around for a few days. And please be careful with it, Helen," he said as the truck's motor came to life. "I've got to return it in good condition or lose my ten dollar deposit."

Within moments, they were out of town on the narrow, two-lane, blacktop road, winding past small farms and the startlingly large mansions put up by the Californians. Some of these monuments to conspicuous consumption were designed to resemble castles with massive stone walls and turrets. One even sported a drawbridge and moat. Helen searched the countryside for wind damage while she simultaneously scanned the newspapers for items related to a freak storm.

"I don't believe it!" she said. "It's right on the front page of the *Times*: 'Twelve People Killed by Tower's Rain of Death.' " The ice pick returned, probing behind her eyes. Helen gasped, dropping the paper and covering her eyes with her hands.

"This is dangerous, Helen. You should be back in that hospital bed with your eyes closed. Not getting all worked up reading the newspapers."

"Bullshit." Helen straightened up and stared out the front window, wiping a tear from her eye. She piled the newspapers beside her on the seat. "We're almost there," she said.

Approaching the bluff, she felt her heartbeat quicken with the appearance of several downed trees and branches. "Stop," she commanded.

Stan slowed the truck obediently to a halt. Helen opened the door.

"For God's sake," he protested.

"I've got to get a closer look," she answered and continued to exit the truck.

"Wait." Backing up a short distance, he ground the gears into first and they lurched into the forest, bouncing hard over fallen tree limbs and rocks.

"See?" Helen pointed to the damage. Trees lay across one another, roots exposed to the sunlight. Several larger trees still stood, but displayed gaping wounds where branches had been torn off. It looked like a giant had come through—a pissed-off-giant.

"What did I tell you? Incredible, isn't it?"

"Pretty strange, indeed. Surprised I didn't feel it blow or have the power go out over at my place."

"But look at the damage, Stan. It only hit this little area. There's nothing over there."

"Must have been a funnel spout. Just touched down here and kept going. Lucky you didn't end up in Kansas."

Helen considered this while she rubbed her bandaged ankle. The engine coughed and continued to idle hoarsely while, outside the cab, a family of chickadees called to one another.

"Can we go now?" Stan asked.

She nodded once before turning to face him. "Yes. Thank you, Stan. Please take me home now."

The house seemed dreary, as if saddened by Byron's loss. She stared at the half-empty dog dishes for a long minute before entering the kitchen. She tossed several aspirin in her mouth and chased them down with a swallow of Jim Beam mixed with cold water from the tap.

"Fire's lit in the stove." Stan rejoined her. "Anything else I can do? Be happy to stay a while."

Helen put her arms around him and hugged his wiry frame to her. "You saved my life," she whispered.

"Thank God I saw you, Heartbreaker. You were about done in for sure."

She let him go. There was work to be done.

She waited until he had driven away before hobbling over to the hall closet. Helen found her father's wooden walking stick and admired its well-worn finish and the inscription on its silver crown,

"C.A., with love, H.A." She tossed the aluminum contraption into the closet and shut the door. It was time to fire up the computer and make a few phone calls. But first, she would pay a visit to her small garden and the fresh grave which Stan had dug there.

6

Second Sight

SEATTLE, MONDAY, 10:50 A.M. Billy was a step and a half away from being in the *Seattle Times'* one and only, slow-as-a-bad-joke elevator when he remembered his overcoat. Already running late, the temptation to just get on the elevator and go was almost, but not quite, overpowering. Memories of the morning's chill and the average length of the mayor's speeches made him turn back. He nearly ran over the intern on his way to his office.

"I was just coming to see if you'd left yet," Gretta said, hurrying after Billy on her high heels. "There's a phone call for you."

"Tell 'em I've left. I'm already late for the mayor's press conference at the Tower."

"It's a woman," Gretta persisted. "She's calling long distance. Something about the wind on Saturday."

Billy stood in his office, poised to leave, his coat over one arm. "Probably just another senile old bag whose cat ran away." He sighed and glanced out the window. Down at the street level, people were bundled up against the chill and scurried to get wherever they were going. Judging from the battalion of large, gray, cumulus clouds moving in to take up their positions, rain would be falling soon, if it wasn't already.

"Sorry, Billy," Gretta said. She ran her fingers nervously through her thick, shoulder-length brown hair. "Do you want me to take it?"

"No, Gretta. You did right. Don't let my whining inhibit you. You never know which call might be for real." Billy grabbed the receiver and stabbed a finger at the blinking light. "Mossman." He waved Gretta off.

"The Olympic Life Tower wasn't responsible for those people's deaths."

"Who are you and why not?" Billy asked. At least his caller knew how to get to the point.

"I'm Helen Anderson. I live on San Juan Island and on Saturday morning, a wind like nothing I've ever experienced came out of nowhere and blew me right off the embankment and onto the beach."

"Listen, lady. I'm late for a . . ."

"Mr. Mossman, I think the same wind that hit here early Saturday morning hit downtown Seattle a little later."

"That's well over a hundred miles from here," Billy said. "Are you sure you didn't have one too many shots of brandy in your morning coffee, Helen?"

"After I got out of the hospital, I had my friend drive me to the place where it happened. There are trees and limbs down all over the place."

"So tell me, how come nobody else knows about this?" Billy glanced at his watch. It was eleven. The press conference would be starting any minute now.

"There may be others who do know, Mr. Mossman. There's a story in the Whidbey Island paper about a sailboat capsizing on Saturday that might be related."

"Might be. Come on, lady. Got any facts? We could sure use a few. About all I'm hearing from you so far is that you got a sore tush and some free firewood. If this was a wind storm, we would have serious damage all over the western part of the state. Now, forgive me for being rude, but I'm late."

"I know it sounds fantastic, Mr. Mossman, but, just like in your column yesterday, this wind seems to have struck only small concentrated areas. Almost like targets . . ."

Billy set the receiver down carefully in its cradle. Like many of the calls he received, the woman's story was too weird by a half. He'd already checked out the Whidbey Island story and a couple of other weather-related items from around the greater Puget Sound region, and the result was as clear to him as clear could be. The only logical explanation for the deaths on Saturday was the design and location of the Olympic Tower in combination with a sudden, strong gust of wind.

He was finally in the elevator when he heard his name called for the second time. It was the intern again. Billy swore silently as he pushed the door open button and held it. The other passengers stared at him.

"What now?" he asked.

"They found the bodies of those two missing boys," Gretta said.

Billy stood an instant longer, finger still depressing the door open button as he sorted through his cluttered memory for relevant information. With a shake of his head, he stepped off the elevator. He walked silently up to where Gretta stood and placed an arm around her shoulders. This was not as easy as he would have liked. She was at least five foot ten and, in her heels, stood taller than he by a good two inches. "The kids from Poulsbo?" he asked. "Who found them and where?"

"Half the fishing fleet's been out looking for them. The coast guard just announced that their bodies finally surfaced. I guess it takes a few days in the cold water before the bodies blow up with gas and float to the top."

"Accident or foul play involved?"

Gretta shrugged her shoulders. "It does sound pretty strange. They say the bodies were tied together in fishing line."

Billy studied the young woman, a college senior whose spelling was atrocious, but whose long legs would no doubt help her scale the male-dominated corporate ladder in record time. On the other hand, his own spelling had caused many a professor to question the validity of his career choice. Spelling or no spelling, it was time to find out what the kid was made of.

"Rule number one," he began, " 'pretty strange' doesn't cut it in reporting. We need facts. Now, this kind of stuff's ordinarily not my beat, but find out when the autopsy's going to be and the name of the coast guard captain. One more thing: get me copies of the *Whidbey Island Gazette* for the past few days. And, Gretta?"

"Yes, Billy?"

"I'm very late for the mayor's press conference. So will you just take messages for me? Please?"

Billy walked slowly back to the elevator, pushed the button and stared silently at the light over the door.

Denise cradled the Styrofoam cup between her frozen hands and took frequent sips of the hot liquid to combat the chill. The large U.S. and Washington State flags that stood behind the speakers' table made popping noises in the sharp, blustery wind and the sky had turned a menacing black that threatened rain at any moment.

Her raincoat, five years old now and missing its zip-out liner, was no match for the damp air that whipped around her legs. Zip-out liners were a lot like men: they were never there when you needed them. The lack of sleep combined with the weather made her feel physically vulnerable, as if she were getting a cold. But there was something else, too, Denise thought over the sound of her chattering teeth as she studied the assemblage for the cause of her unease.

Something indefinable that made the muscles at the base of her skull knot painfully. Perhaps, she rationalized, it was the horrifying awareness that several unfortunate people, including three children, had met violent deaths in this very location just two days earlier. Knowing that lightning never strikes twice in the same place was just a myth wasn't helping her relax. Whatever the source of her tension was, she didn't want to be here.

The Tower's major corner, facing Fourth Avenue and Pine Street, had been notched with a two-story high entrance of polished brass that sheltered revolving glass doors. The entry was raised from street level by a flight of broad steps. This made it a perfect location for holding press conferences. From her vantage point behind and to the left of the speakers' table, Denise could survey the entire gathering.

The mayor was sitting at the opposite end of the speakers' table from her own table with its flame-heated coffee urn, bags of Styrofoam cups and stacks of press kits. Short and bald with heavy eyebrows, Grenitzer reminded her of a troll. On the mayor's right stood Walter Eggenburk, former Dean of the School of Architecture at the University of Washington, who was taking questions from the gathering of news media representatives. Lean and elegantly middle-aged, he had nevertheless managed to climb incredibly high on her shit list by virtue of the patronizing manner he had displayed when Denise introduced herself earlier that morning.

"In the future, Miss Whatever-your-name-is, I'd appreciate it if you'd review any articles with me that mention my name before they're released to the media."

"I'm sorry, sir, but I had very little time."

"Never time to do it right the first time, but there's always time to go back and repair the damage later." He patted her arm. "Did they teach you that in school?"

Denise stared after Eggenburk, fuming, as he walked away. "They taught us to think, to organize, to write and who to call, but they sure as hell never taught us about dealing with assholes like you in forty-eight-degree weather when you've been up half the night."

Bud Phillips, the mayor's aide, overheard her and pulled her aside. "Are you out of your mind? Get a grip, Denise."

"I'll get a grip all right. He can kiss his alleged manhood good-bye if he gives me any more lectures," she answered.

On the mayor's left, nearest Denise, sat Massey, the building developer, who nodded agreement with Eggenburk's words. No hat covered the older man's steel gray hair.

Camera crews from all the local television stations, including both independents and network affiliates, crowded the stairway. Their equipment vans filled the loading area immediately in front of the sidewalk. On Fourth Avenue, traffic moved at a snail's pace as drivers craned their necks for a better look.

In addition to the TV news teams, Denise recognized the call signs of several radio stations on the microphones that crowded the portable lectern. Among the newspaper reporters, she spotted Hayes of the *Times* and Satherwaite of the *Post-Intelligencer.*

"Thank you, Dean Eggenburk," she heard Mayor Grenitzer say. "So, ladies and gentlemen, if there are no more questions, I recommend we adjourn the press conference before we get wet." Please, no more, Denise thought.

"Just one, Mr. Mayor," a voice called out from the cluster of reporters below. The crowd parted around a middle-aged man of husky build wearing a rumpled overcoat. His sandy hair and ruddy face reminded Denise of a scoutmaster.

"Go get 'em, Billy," a voice in the crowd called out.

"Well, well, if it isn't Mossman. Have you got any more new scientific theories for us today?" Denise could see Bud giving Grenitzer the knife-across-the-throat gesture. With the election so near, she could understand Bud's concern should the mayor overreact to Mossman's charges. Dignified, politically correct responses were sometimes missing from Grenitzer's repertoire, especially when he became emotional.

"Sixteen months ago," Mossman began, "the City Council debated whether to grant a permit for a ninety-eight-story tower after the planning commission called it—and I quote—'a hideous example of corporate ego running amok and an opportunity for disaster.' Yet, in a matter of twenty-four hours, the permit was approved."

"So?" the mayor interjected. "Haven't you ever heard of compromise? One side gives a little, the other side gives a little . . ." Denise saw Bud shaking his head from side to side and mouthing the word "No."

"A little?" Mossman retorted. "You call the construction of a ninety-eight-story tower over the objections of the city populace and the planning commission a 'little compromise?'" The crowd chuckled.

"C'mon, Mossman. This is a building the city can be proud of." Grenitzer waved his arms expansively to include the entire crowd. "San Francisco has nothing like this. L.A. has nothing like this. A city needs its pride. Need I remind you, we were named 'America's Most Livable City' for the fifth year in a row? And, if I'm re-elected," his voice rose, "I promise we'll be 'America's Best City For Business,' too."

Scattered applause broke out. A few of the reporters could be heard talking and joking among themselves. Eggenburk leaned back in his chair and nodded at Massey who clapped his gloved hands enthusiastically. If it hadn't been so damned cold, Denise would have liked to march down and stand beside the beleaguered Mossman to offer her own rebuttal to the mayor's politically-motivated repartee. Doing so, however, would mean moving to another city, if not another state. Bud would make sure she never worked in this town again.

An eager breeze chose that moment to lift the bags of cups and the stack of glossy press kits that had been supplied by the developer and send them tumbling toward the building entrance. Denise rose and ran to recover them before the papers spilled out and littered the streets. As she bent to retrieve several of the kits, she was greeted by thunderous applause. Startled, she wondered for an instant whether the mayor had actually said something intelligent or whether her underwear was showing. Then she looked up and realized that the sound was the beating of wings as a thousand seagulls and pigeons burst into flight from several nearby buildings. Their numbers swelled rapidly, further darkening the sky. Even as she marveled at their instinctive ability to fly in formation, she saw their formations rapidly deteriorate into utter chaos.

I wonder what spooked them, she thought as she stood up, her hands full of plastic bags and press kits. She wished again that she were somewhere else and that she could rub the back of her neck where it remained cramped. Denise blew the bangs out of her eyes and was about to walk back to her table when a powerful gust rocked her backwards. In her sneakers, she might have remained standing. In heels, however, she landed painfully on her rear. Her hands, stinging from trying to break her fall, still clutched the now torn plastic bags and disordered press kits. The flags clattered to the ground and an ear-splitting moan erupted from the PA system speakers.

"Dammit!" Denise looked up as if to ask "What's next?" and saw a huge shape falling toward the crowded steps. "Look out!" she screamed.

Billy looked up and saw his death falling from the sky. Then, instinct took over. He took two steps and leaped into the crowd of reporters and cameramen surrounding him, knocking as many down with him as he could.

The granite panel landed so close, he felt the air rush by, followed by the deafening impact. Instantly, he felt stabbing pains in his legs and back. Just like shrapnel, he thought. And then he passed out.

A woman screamed. Denise scanned the devastation, unable to move, her ears still ringing from the concussive force of five hundred pounds of granite smashing onto the steps below her. The large, flat stone panel had fallen into the midst of the news people who had been standing on the building's steps, scattering them like broken toys. A television crew was filming the area near the largest parts of the stone where at least a dozen bodies were down. Scattered moans rose from the scene of confusion.

The mayor, Denise noted with grudging admiration, had remained at the lectern and taken charge. "We need ambulances," he spoke into the microphone. "Somebody call 911. Anybody who's not hurt, pitch in or stay out of the way. As soon as we get this area cleared, I want the streets closed around this building." The dean, meanwhile, had managed to crawl under the table. Massey stared up at the Tower, one hand held to his head as if dazed.

"Denise!" She tried to identify the voice calling her from the moans that hung in the air. "Denise, answer me. Are you okay?" Bud crouched down beside her. "My God, you're bleeding." He brushed her cheek with his handkerchief. It came away red. Denise realized that her cheek felt as if she had been stung by a bee.

"I'm okay, I think. What happened?"

"Another panel fell from the Tower." His eyes darted upward. "That's gonna be all she wrote for this thing—at least until they figure out what's going on. Are you sure you're okay?"

"Yeah, I . . ." she started to say, then looked down. Her skirt and coat were up around her thighs, her pantyhose had a run the size of the Mississippi River, one of her new black pumps was missing a heel and her butt hurt like she'd been blitzed by a linebacker. "What am I saying? For that matter, what am I even doing here?" Bud's face showed surprise. "I don't even like this job!" Her teeth

69

were chattering again and she could feel tears coming like the dark rain clouds. Her hands curled into fists as she fought to regain control.

"You're okay." Bud's face softened into a brief smile. "I'd be pretty worried if this was your idea of a good time. Here." He put his arm around her and helped her up. "Let's get under the doorway where it's safer."

Denise let herself be led for just two steps before halting. "Wait a minute. Those people . . ." She nodded toward where the stone had landed.

"Forget 'em," Bud said and tried to pull her along.

"They need help."

"You really are out of your mind. Can't you see that the sky is falling? One more chunk of granite and we're history."

Denise looked up in time to take a raindrop in the eye. The Tower rose like a massive tombstone, dwarfing the people below. "C'mon, Bud. Be a hero for once."

"Sorry, Denise. That's not what I get paid for. Besides, I've got a family to think about and so do you. Heroes are the most selfish people in the world."

"What about the families of these people? Are they less important than yours or mine?"

He bowed and smiled cynically. "Be my guest. I'll live to fight another day."

The rain began to fall in earnest. Denise hobbled back down the steps to where the injured lay, avoiding the shards of stone that littered the stairway and leaving Bud to huddle with several others under the building's brass entry. Her thin coat was already soaked through and clung to her body. So this is what being a Popsicle feels like, she thought.

As the wailing of fire engines and aid cars approached, she recognized the black braids of a figure kneeling over a middle-aged reporter who lay propped against the stairs with his eyes closed. Rain and blood were forming a puddle beneath one of the man's legs.

"Paul?"

Paul Judge looked up; for just an instant, his eyes reflected surprise.

"Help me with this guy. His leg needs bandaging before he loses any more blood." He pulled a small silver knife from his pants pocket and opened the blade.

The reporter's eyes fluttered open and he regarded Paul and the knife. "Just don't stab me with that thing. I don't need any more pain."

Denise pouched his trousers above the thigh and glanced at Paul as he poked the knife through, slitting the soaked fabric down to the cuff. A furrow in the flesh just above the knee pumped bright red blood. The man groaned at the sight of the wound and closed his eyes, his head falling back onto the step.

"Don't worry," Denise reassured him. "Just a scratch."

"Give me your tie, and a handkerchief, if you've got it," she said to Paul. "Where did you come from, anyway?" She watched as he stripped the tie from his white shirt collar beneath his heavy overcoat and handed it to her. "Are you some kind of superhero, always arriving in the nick of time?"

"I was just up the street at the Convention Center and heard the commotion." Paul lifted the man's leg while Denise wrapped the tie tightly around the wound, using the handkerchief as a compress. "But, weird as it sounds, I expected something strange to happen."

"You knew this would happen?" She waved an arm at the destruction. In the sunless gloom, red and blue lights flashed eerily from emergency vehicles that jammed the streets as the rain continued to fall heavily. Clothing of victims and rescuers were stained with dark splotches, whether from blood or rain, Denise couldn't tell. Urgent voices called out among the huddled and prostrate bodies and sirens rent the leaden air. The police had taped off the area around the Tower. Across the street, the crowd huddled in small islands under store awnings.

Paul nodded, avoiding her eyes. "Woke up with this strange feeling. What about you? What are you doing here?" He looked at her. A drop of rain hung for an instant at the end of his nose. "Yesterday a runaway horse, and today this little picnic. I wouldn't want to be your insurance agent."

"This is my job. I helped set this up."

"You planned this?" Paul grabbed the injured man by the arms and pulled him up into a sitting position. He pushed up one of the man's eyelids with a thumb; only the white showed. "Got to get him some blood fast." He lifted the unconscious body onto one shoulder and walked, hunched over with the weight, toward the flashing lights.

Denise looked around for any more unattended victims but, thanks to fast action by both the emergency personnel and good Samaritans, most had already been loaded into aid cars. The few who remained were surrounded by paramedics in their bright yellow rain slickers.

Paul returned and removed his coat, wrapping it around her shoulders. "You'll catch pneumonia if you don't dress warmer."

Denise didn't mind the frown of concern that crossed his smooth, brown face. Before she could say thanks, a voice boomed over the P.A. system. "They have sown the wind, and they shall reap the whirlwind."

Startled, Denise jumped. "Jesus!"

"I don't think so, but you're in the right ballpark," Paul said as the voice continued.

"Behold, I will break the bow of E'lam, the chief of their might. And upon E'lam will I bring the four winds from the four quarters of heaven, and will scatter them toward all those winds; and there shall be no nation whither the outcasts of E'lam shall not come. For—"

The P.A. system died abruptly. Probably Bud or someone else had pulled the plug. Denise searched the throng for the source of the voice. She finally spotted him. Two policemen had hold of either arm—his hands were cuffed behind him. She caught snatches of his loud protests as the police propelled him forcibly down the steps directly toward where she and Paul stood.

"Hinder not the word of the Lord," the agitated man said. "I'm Chuck, prophet of the Most High."

He actually did resemble a painting of Jesus, Denise thought, albeit a Jesus who hadn't bathed in quite a while. His long, brown hair was plastered to his thin, bearded face. He began shouting at the top of his lungs as he was thrown into the back of a squad car. "And I will bring evil upon them, even my fierce anger, saith the Lord; and I will send the sword after them. . . ." Then the door slammed shut, drowning out his voice.

". . . till I have consumed them," Paul completed the verse.

"Wow, I'm impressed. Are you a minister?" Denise asked.

"Just a former mission school student."

Another voice, this one using a megaphone, interrupted them. "Please clear the area. Anyone not injured or a member of the city emergency crews, please clear the area. I repeat . . ."

"Sounds like good advice." Paul turned up the collar of his suit which was quickly becoming saturated by the rain. "What about lunch?"

"If you'll let me buy. I still owe you a suit."

"Forget it. How did you get here?"

"My car's parked in the loading zone. Damn! I almost forgot. I had to sign my life away for the tables and P.A. system. I can't just leave without them."

"I don't think they'll let us stay here any longer," Paul said. "There must be a hundred firemen just standing around. Let me see if I can coax one into helping us."

They were hauling the tables to the back of the station wagon when the fireman who was carrying the percolator called back to them. "Looks like you won't be going anywhere in this thing for a while."

"Now what?" Denise hurried to the front of the car.

He didn't have to answer. The windshield was one massive jigsaw puzzle.

"Must have taken a hit from a good-sized chunk of rock," Paul said.

"What am I going to do?" Denise sagged against the front fender. The rain had eased temporarily but, judging from the sky, it was likely to resume, prestissimo, soon.

"Put everything in the car and leave it. This area's going to stay roped off for quite some time. After lunch, I'll drive you home, then come back for your car."

Denise studied Paul's strong, angular face. It was a handsome face, even fascinating, but most of all, it was an Indian face and its strangeness both attracted and made her wary. For the first time, she noticed a tiny, white scar that ran diagonally across one side of his chin. Although she still wore his heavy coat over her own drenched version, she shivered.

"That's chivalrous, but don't you have important things to do?"

"Not so important that they can't wait for an hour or two. Let's lock up your car. We can take the Underground Metro back to where my car's parked."

A minute later, they were walking across the street toward the Westlake Center and the entrance of the underground bus tunnel that linked Pioneer Square and downtown. With her missing heel, Denise was forced to limp. "Wait a sec." She leaned on his arm. She smacked the other shoe against the curb, breaking off the heel. "Thanks. Now, I can at least walk without looking like Dr. Frankenstein's assistant, Igor."

Paul smiled. "I seriously doubt anyone would make that comparison."

"What did you mean back there?" she asked, stepping awkwardly in her heel-less shoes. "You said you woke up with a feeling that something was going to happen?"

"My grandmother called it second sight. She said we were all born with the ability to see into the future, know important things that were going to take place ahead of time—even our own death, but that whites and even most Indians had lost it."

"This 'second sight,' could it tell you when people were sick and what was wrong with them?" Denise asked cautiously.

"If you were a shaman."

"A shaman?"

"Medicine man. Someone with special healing powers. Why do you ask?" Paul studied her.

"No reason," she said, but her response sounded insincere, even to her. "Do you have these special powers?"

"I don't think so. Certainly not enough to use it effectively." He stopped walking and stared down at the sidewalk as if remembering.

"What is it?" she asked.

He looked at her without smiling. "You'll think I'm crazy."

She took his arm. "No I won't. Please, tell me."

"I had a vision on Saturday, just before that riderless horse showed up. I was in my office, trying to locate a file, when I got so jumpy, I couldn't concentrate. So I made myself relax, closed my eyes, took deep breaths. And I saw your son."

"You saw Evan?" Denise couldn't believe her ears.

He frowned. "A boy anyway."

"Whew!" She forced a laugh and they started walking again. "You had me going there for a second."

"Whoever he was, he was being followed by someone or something I couldn't quite see, but that felt dangerous. So, I went downstairs for a walk. Less than ten minutes later, I saw the runaway horse."

"Thank heaven for that. If it hadn't been for your premonition, Evan could have been killed. I can't thank you enough. He's all I've got. I don't know what I would do if he were ever seriously hurt or . . ."

A long black car pulled in beside the curb just ahead of them and a window disappeared down into the rear door.

"Looks like your horse lost a shoe. Need a ride, lady?"

Denise recognized Bud. "Oh, yes. I'd do anything to be warm again."

The rear door opened. Bud moved over and Denise saw that Grenitzer and Eggenburk were sitting inside. "Do you mind if my friend, Paul Judge, rides with us?" she asked.

Bud glanced at the mayor. "We're kind of in a hurry, Denise."

Grenitzer nodded. "You, me and the spin doctor here are going to need every trick in the book to fix this one."

Paul held the door for her. "Go ahead. I'll take the bus."

"No, that's . . ."

"It's all right," Paul said. With Bud taking her hand and Paul insisting, Denise let herself be shepherded into the car. The relief of being out of the damp cold and into the warm, plush comfort of the car was tempered, however, by the discomfort of leaving Paul behind and riding with the three men.

"Your coat—" Denise started to say as the door closed. And then the car was moving, pulling out from the curb and into the traffic lane. Denise peered through the rain-streaked rear window at Paul, standing by the curb.

"I must say, you have some interesting friends, Denise," Bud said.

Paul stood watching until the sleek, black limousine had disappeared. His suit had long since lost any water resistance so that it clung to his body and offered no protection against the rain or chill. Though the Metro tunnel entrance where he could escape the weather and catch a bus back to the warmth of his office was only twenty yards away, he lingered yet a while, his mind combing through events, actions, words, and even dreams as he struggled to make sense out of the last forty-eight hours.

He liked this woman, how she had risked personal injury to come to the aid of the man at the Tower. But he was wary as a trout in a clear mountain stream. Today was not the first time he'd been left standing in the rain by a white woman. As a naive college freshman, he would have given anything just to be in the company of the young, beautiful, white woman he had made eye contact with in the campus commons. And for a few, brief weeks, he had succeeded— only to be used, paraded in front of her senior class friends and then abandoned on the front steps of her sorority like a sack of garbage. It had felt the same way when the mayor's limousine had driven away. Unlike the first time, it no longer surprised him. On the other hand, he was forced to admit, it still cut.

Confusing as his attraction for Denise was, his concern for her son was much greater and more immediate. It *had* been Evan in his vision—he was almost certain of it—and the thing that had been following him had not just been dangerous, but lethally so. The memory of his earlier vision had vanished until its exact repetition this morning, a detail he'd been too self-conscious to communicate clearly to Denise. To be fair, he wouldn't have believed himself either.

He wished he had learned more from Evan. Why would someone be stalking the boy? And why couldn't he see who it was? While he asked himself these troubling questions, he heard the wind rising. The chilled air felt like a knife against his damp skin and he began hurrying toward the tunnel entrance. He reached the glass doors of the Westlake Station just as a sudden strong gust struck. He made it through one of the doors an instant before the other slammed on a large woman who was exiting, pinning her leg against the jamb. The woman screamed as the aluminum bit into her flesh. Blood from the gash flowed down her leg and onto the floor. The noise of the wind as it rushed through the narrow opening was deafening. Paul wedged his shoulder between the door and the jamb and shoved with all the strength that he had. "Pull her out! Now!" he yelled over the tumult. Bystanders dragged the collapsed woman from the doorway. The moment she was clear, Paul dove for the floor. The door slammed with such force that the shattered safety glass blasted them like grapeshot from a cannon.

And, just like that, the wind was gone. Paul rolled over in a puddle of rainwater and glass, amazed to find himself only nicked and still in one piece. A half-dozen bodies still lay curled on the floor, arms and hands protecting their faces. He didn't need second sight to tell him there was more going on here than stormy weather, but right this moment, he didn't have time to think about it. He crawled to the injured woman who lay nearby, whimpering in a pool of blood.

"Somebody call an ambulance," he ordered. Then he borrowed a scarf and, for the second time that day, began bandaging a leg.

7

Long Shots

SAN JUAN ISLAND, MONDAY, 12:45 P.M. Helen tried phoning Ann Bessani's hospital room again. It was a long shot, but then so was being born. As she hoped, a different nurse answered this time. The one who had answered before was probably at lunch. Helen decided to try a new tack.

"May I speak to Ann, please?"

"Are you a member of the family?" the nurse asked.

"Yes. Her husband's family, from out of state."

Helen heard mumbling in the background. Finally, a voice answered.

"Hello?" The woman sounded tiny and distant.

"I'm very sorry about your tragedy, Mrs. Bessani. I'm not really a member of your husband's family. I had to lie. I know you're hurting, so I'll get right to the point. Can you describe the wind that overturned your boat?"

Silence stretched for several nerve-wracking seconds. "Mrs. Bessani? Ann?" Her ears strained to pick up a response. "Please don't hang up. You and I may share something in common, something others need to know about."

"I . . . I'm not sure what you mean," the woman finally answered.

"The wind—was it sudden or continuous?" Helen rushed on.

"Very sudden," the tiny voice finally answered. She cleared her throat. "Pardon me. I've got these tubes in my nose and my throat's extremely dry."

"That's okay, Ann." It was time for another long shot. "What else do you remember? I can't tell you how important this information could be."

"What did you say your name was? I'm not sure what's happened to my memory. Since the accident, I have a hard time remembering names, or even what day it is. People tell me something and, a minute later, I have to ask them what they said. I hope you didn't lose someone, too?"

"Just my dog." Helen stared at the two dog dishes still sitting on the linoleum kitchen floor. If there was a God, perhaps the only way one could truly know His love was by owning a pet. She had to swallow before she could speak again. "My name is Helen Anderson. I'm a retired school teacher from Seattle now living on San Juan Island. On Saturday, I was out for my usual morning walk when a sudden gust of wind threw my dog against a tree and knocked me head over heels. It did a lot of damage to the forest, but only in a very small area. What time did the wind hit your boat?"

Once again, Helen was forced to wait for a reply. "Sometime between ten-thirty and eleven, I think."

"That's what I guessed. It hit me just before that."

"And you think the same wind hit our sailboat?"

"Yes, I do. Tell me, Ann, did you hear about the wind damage in Seattle?"

"I'm afraid I'm rather out of touch. Were there people hurt?"

"Yes, several. Some construction material blew off a tall building and fell on the people below." There was another pause. "Look, I know it sounds crazy."

"Actually, this is the first thing in two days that's made any sense," Ann said. "The coast guard officer thought I was crazy, too. It was just like you said. One minute we were sailing peacefully along and the next, we were topsy-turvy. But I remember now—I think I must have been in shock then—there wasn't any wind afterwards. So strange. It hit us first on one side—we took some water in the cockpit and Ben, my husband, overreacted. Dad got knocked overboard by the boom. Then the wind veered and came around the other side. That's what capsized us."

Helen heard her own heart beating in the receiver. "Wait a minute! It changed directions—you're sure?"

"Yes. And then it was gone. I keep hoping it was just a nightmare."

"This wind," Helen said, "I know it sounds silly, but did it seem . . . *mean* to you?"

"Funny you should say that word. That's what my daughter, Megan, called it. Of course, anything that would hurt her dad . . ." Ann's voice broke off.

"There now. Don't fret, Ann. Your daughter—Megan, is it? She's going to need your strength. I'd like to come see you sometime soon, when you're feeling better, if that would be okay."

"Do you have any idea what could have caused this, Helen?"

"Not yet, but I'm going to do everything I can to find out."

"They're letting me out of here tomorrow. Maybe I could help. Call me, please."

After hanging up, Helen hobbled over to her computer. French doors gave a view onto the lush, green forest where rain was falling, but Helen barely noticed. The pain in her head was so intense, she was forced to close her eyes for a minute. When it eased, she hit the spacebar to turn off the screen saver and see if there were any replies to her urgent bulletin board request. Drumming her fingers on the desktop while she waited, Helen realized that she hated two things more than anything else in the world: waiting and being an invalid.

8

Trick or Treat

SEATTLE, MONDAY, 3:00 P.M. The plastic insides of the bus were still shiny and new-looking, yet, to Evan's observant eyes, the first signs of wear and eventual shabbiness were already obvious. The imitation leather seat cushion next to his was split and one of the overhead lights was broken. It cast a flickering, yellow glow on the surrounding empty seats. Someone had spray painted over the advertisements for rectal itch cream and feminine pads. Neither the gray skies and frequent rain nor the tawdry bus interior had so far managed to dampen his spirits this day, however.

With no soccer practice on Mondays, he usually rode the school bus home. Given the unique nature of a school with twelve grades of deaf students, it was a long ride, with stops all over town, but he didn't mind. Riding high up in the bus, protected from wind and rain, there was always something new and interesting to see. And there was little to go home to. He had no brothers or sisters to play with and the other kids in the neighborhood called him "dummy" when they thought he wasn't watching. His decision not to let his handicap prevent him from doing what "normal" kids did had ironically resulted in making him stand out all the more. Once they learned of his deafness, he became a target for teasing and abuse by the neighborhood bullies. Though he was constantly on the alert in order to avoid them, he sometimes went home with a bloody lip or a black eye from fighting on the neighborhood playground. But, if he hadn't won many rounds, he also hadn't given in.

What with soccer followed by the Seahawks game and not getting to see much of his mother the day before, he had been inspired to skip the school bus and take the metro bus downtown to surprise her. She would lecture him for doing so without warning her in advance, but he was gambling that she would be pleased to have him drop in on her. Perhaps she would even offer to stop somewhere for dinner. And, since she didn't get off work until 5:30, he would have plenty of time to visit the main downtown library first. Its three stories of marble columns, tile floors, and thousands of books were only a few blocks from her office.

Today being Halloween, the bus had a festive feel. The bus driver wore a clown suit, makeup, and a big red nose. A jack-o'-lantern pail half-full of candy corn sat beside his seat. On his way to the back of the bus, Evan passed a little kid dressed as a pumpkin waddling up the aisle for more of the treats. An older girl stole the show with her bleached blond hair cut short, safety pin-pierced nose and spider tattoo peeking above the neck of her black leather jacket. She wore her bus face—a look that denied the existence of anyone else. Rather than a costume, he guessed that this was her normal attire. Some people liked to dress like it was Halloween all year round.

The bus was one of the articulated kind. It was twice as long as an ordinary bus and hinged in the middle with a rubber bellows like an accordion for turning corners. From his seat in the very back, Evan could barely see the bus driver over the heads of the distant passengers riding in the front half.

As the bus proceeded on its start-stop-start-again journey down Broadway Avenue, farting black smoke with each jerky start and stinking of diesel fuel, Evan used the strategic location of the large rear seat to observe his fellow passengers and the people on the street. Like the elephant lady. She was so fat that she had nearly become stuck in the bus doors and, when she finally sat down in his half of the bus after laboring up the aisle, she took up an entire seat.

Outside, an Asian grocer wearing an apron leaned against the doorway of his butcher shop and smoked as a Latino family passed, pushing a grocery cart loaded with children and bags of food. The woman held her coat over her head to protect the food and the children from the rain. Her thin white blouse was plastered to her brown skin so that he could see her bra. Across the street, a small group of mostly black people clustered under the awning of a mortuary. While he watched, four men carried a small bronze coffin out from a large door. A row of cars with their headlights on waited patiently while the men loaded the coffin into the rear of a hearse.

The sight of the funeral procession and the tiny coffin spooked him. A chill traveled through him as he remembered the wolf with the red glass eyes in the curio store the day before. For a fleeting moment, he had the eerie feeling that something large was following right behind the bus, watching him. When he looked, however, there was nothing to see but a plastic grocery bag that fluttered up

81

high in the bus's wake. The feeling had been so strong, however, that he had forgotten to breathe. Now he sucked in air deeply as he continued to stare out the rear window for signs of anything unusual.

The seat and floorboards vibrated as the bus slowed to make another stop. The doors slid open and two girls Evan's age entered the bus, chewing gum and talking as they collapsed their umbrellas and unbuttoned wool coats. One was dark-haired and red-cheeked and wore glasses with large, round frames. The other was fair-skinned and wore her blond hair in a pony tail. Both wore school uniforms, consisting of plaid skirts and white blouses, under their coats.

As they approached the rear of the bus, the dark-haired girl said something and giggled while looking at him. He didn't know for sure whether she had spoken to him or her friend, so he pretended not to notice them. He was both delighted and terrified when they sat on the seat directly in front of him.

His attention now focused on the tops of their heads, he began to feel light-headed from the smell of shampoo. The blond girl's pony tail was tied back with a blue bow with tiny white hearts. As she talked to her friend, she rested a hand, slim and delicate, on the seat back just in front of him. The fingernails were badly chewed. Even so, he thought her hand to be the most beautiful he had ever seen.

The dark-haired girl stole a glance over the seat back. Then another. Evan squirmed uncomfortably and wondered whether they were talking about him. What a cosmic gyp not to know, he thought. With his handicap, they might as well be aliens. He began to hope that they would just go away so that he wouldn't have to explain about his deafness.

Once again, the dark-haired girl's face appeared, but this time it stayed. "My friend thinks you're . . ." She was giggling, making lip-reading difficult. He couldn't catch the last, crucial word. Her friend pulled her down and they wrestled for a few moments while Evan's hopes alternately rose and fell. At last, the dark-haired girl's face reappeared. She took a moment to replace her glasses before speaking.

"What grade are you in?"

He held up eight fingers.

"Do you go to . . . ?" He couldn't understand the name and shook his head "no." His ears were burning now. This was the point of no return. He reached inside his backpack and took out his notebook, but what to write? For a moment, he considered just coming out with the plain truth—*Excuse me, but I'm a freak*. Instead, he sighed, then wrote, *My name is Evan. I go to Bradley Academy for the Deaf. Could you please talk slower, so I can read your lips?*

He passed the note forward. The two heads disappeared. Evan waited. And waited. The seat just inches away from his own seemed too still and he began to think that they had somehow managed to sneak away. When he could stand it no longer, he peeked over the back of the seat and saw the girls' heads huddled together. He turned to watch the people on the street through the rain-streaked window. It was suddenly hard to concentrate.

The dark-haired girl's face reappeared followed, at last, by the blond, pony-tailed one. He saw that her eyes were blue as she handed him a note. She flashed him a smile that displayed a full set of braces. He held the note in hands that trembled. Written in handwriting that looked like tiny flowers were their names, Janelle and Rachel.

How old are you? he wrote beneath their message. *What school do you go to?*

Both hands reached for the note, starting giggles again. After a long minute, Janelle handed back his paper with another folded note attached. There was the name of their school, St. Bartholomew's, their grade level—the same as his—and even their birthdays. There was also a question that caused his face to grow warm: *Can't you talk?*

He struggled with how to tell them about his slowly developing ability to speak. He was afraid that the more questions he answered, the less normal he sounded. Finally, he wrote: *Talking is very hard when you can't hear yourself. I'm learning, but I need lots of practice. Sometimes I make funny mistakes—like saying "Vatman" instead of "Batman."* He handed the note to Janelle and was thrilled when their hands touched for an instant. He held his breath while he waited to see what their reaction would be. Fortunately, he did not have to wait long. The girls' heads bobbed up again and several more notes were passed quickly back and forth. To Evan, each was a gift, far more precious than the latest Nintendo game.

I play the violin, Janelle's last note read when she had passed it back. *I want to be a musician when I grow up. Do you like classical music?*

Evan fretted over this last question before answering. At his school, they had computers that visually displayed musical notes and voices. But the only music he had ever "heard" was when their previous next-door neighbor, a college student, played his stereo with Surround Sound and the floor of their house vibrated. The first time, he thought it had been an earthquake.

I would give anything to hear you play, he wrote.

Janelle seemed unfazed by his shortcoming. *I like art, too. I sometimes visit the museum and galleries to look at paintings and photographs. On Saturdays, I play soccer at Greenlake Park. Would you like to come to one of my games?*

Soccer! As the bus began to slow again, he realized that they might get off at any time. Before they did, he needed to get an address or phone number. While he waited for their reply to his last note, he hurriedly scribbled another one and dropped it over the seat back. A short while later, Janelle's smiling face came up again from the other side of the seat. He had just started to unfold her note when he sensed heavy footsteps approaching. Evan looked up and felt his heart quicken like it did when the roller coaster approached the top of a drop.

The shorter, beefy kid with dark hair, sat down sideways in the seat in front of the girls and winked. The thin one, who wore a grotesque Halloween mask complete with an eyeball hanging from one socket, maggot-infested flesh wounds and heavy stitches around the neck, sat in the seat opposite. They appeared to be seventeen or eighteen, stuck somewhere between being ugly boys and immature, even uglier men.

The heavy boy propped an arm on the seat back. He wore a western-style, rawhide jacket missing much of its fringe. On his hand, he wore a black glove with no fingers and a large cheap-looking silver ring in the shape of a skull. He smiled at the girls who were sitting rigidly at attention. Then he said something that Evan couldn't lip read. When they made no response, he reached up and removed his two front teeth, then stuck his tongue through the gap. Turning his head sideways, he continued to dart his tongue out, making comical faces at the other boy.

Janelle and Rachel grabbed their book bags and stood. Rachel pulled the stop cord. Janelle hurriedly mouthed the word "'Bye," to Evan and turned to leave. The mask-wearing kid was dressed much better than his friend; his denim jacket had "Hard Rock Cafe—London" sewn on the back. The "Monster" extended his leg across the aisle, blocking the way to the exit, and gestured toward the seat beside him. When Janelle shook her head, he held his disfigured head in his hands and faked looking disappointed.

The bus stopped and Evan saw a passenger in the forward half get off and an elderly man and woman get on. Still trapped, the girls were unable to escape before the bus pulled out into traffic again. The other boy, "Rawhide," tugged on Rachel's sleeve as she stood behind Janelle, and made kissing motions with his lips. Rachel jerked her arm away and hid her face in disgust. The boy's hand crept to her plaid skirt. He started to raise it, as if to peek under it. Rachel slapped him. Rawhide held one hand to his jaw and pretended to wipe his eyes with the other. This started both boys laughing.

Janelle reached for the stop cord in the row behind Monster, but he reached over the seat back and grabbed her arm. With her other arm she swung her umbrella at him, but he caught it and ripped it from her hand. Evan saw her scream as the kid in the mask climbed over the seat back. Rachel was now crying and Janelle looked like she was close to panic. Evan jerked the stop cord several times. Almost immediately, the bus began to slow down again. Monster ripped off the mask, threw it on a seat and pointed at Evan. Whatever he said, Evan felt all four faces turn toward him.

Leave them alone, he signed, unsure what else to do.

"What's the matter," Monster asked, "cat got your tongue?" He had a narrow face with greasy-looking blond hair that partially hid his eyes. He smirked at Rawhide. While he was turned away, Janelle grabbed her things and tried to leave, but Monster grabbed her ponytail and pulled her back. Rachel must have cried out; Rawhide covered her mouth with one hand and held up a finger in front of his own in a "shhh" gesture. Evan looked for help. The bus was stopped and the driver appeared to be coming to their aid, but was trapped behind the elephant lady. She blocked the entire aisle as she moved her mountainous form toward the forward exit with the speed of a glacier.

Evan had no plan, just a certainty that the time was at hand to do something. Monster was turned so that he couldn't see him which, given the circumstances, suited Evan just fine. He swung his book bag at the other boy's head with everything he had. It contained only his notebook and a history book, but Monster reacted as if he had been struck by a fastball. He went down in the aisle, twisting in pain. Evan grabbed Janelle's arm and pulled her toward the exit. Rachel had already broken free from the other boy and was ahead of them. They managed to run only a short way, however, before they ran into the backside of the elephant lady. Evan tried pushing to speed her up and only managed to sink his hands into her soft, Jell-O-like flesh. He pounded his fists on her back and tugged on an arm the size of a tree, all to no avail. He turned to Janelle just in time to see her face contort in warning. He jerked his head to the side just before the blow landed. Monster's fist missed his cheek and smashed his shoulder instead. Evan bounced off the elephant lady and onto the floor. He lay gasping in pain, studying the grooves in the rubberized floor. His shoulder felt as if a tank had used it for target practice. Before he could move again, Monster had grabbed him by the collar and pulled him up off the floor. Evan kicked sideways and managed to get him in the one place that was guaranteed to be effective. Monster backed into a seat, holding himself with both hands, his cheeks puffed out like a blowfish. Good one, Ev, he told himself. If he wasn't going to kill you before, he is now for sure. He searched again for the bus driver, still trapped behind the elephant lady.

Evan turned back in time to see Rawhide charging up the aisle. Knowing that he didn't stand a chance of surviving anyway, he launched himself headfirst. His header caught the other boy in the solar plexus, sending both of them sprawling onto the floor. While Rawhide sat up and tried to breathe, Evan swung and kicked furiously. He was clutching a seat leg with two hands, still lashing out with his feet, when he felt a hand tugging angrily at his shoulder. Evan jerked his head around, expecting to see Monster. Instead, the angry bus driver was holding the other boy by the back of the neck with one hand and motioning for him to get up with the other. Ashamed, Evan climbed out from under the seat and stood. The two boys were arguing with the driver and pointing at him. Janelle and Rachel came to his defense. The red-faced driver ordered the other boys off the bus. Before leaving, Monster pointed at him again and yelled something that Evan couldn't lip-read, but understood with perfect clarity. He was startled by the hatred he read in the older boy's ice-blue eyes.

After the boys were gone, the bus driver turned to Evan, jabbed a finger in his chest and pointed outside again. Evan felt his cheeks burning. Under the gaze of the other passengers, he walked to the back of the bus to get his book bag. While the driver watched, he searched his seat and the floor beneath for Janelle's note, but it was gone. Rachel was crying. Although Janelle continued arguing on his behalf, the driver remained unmoved. Janelle reached out a hand to touch his arm as he passed.

86

When he had climbed down off the bus, he was surprised to find himself downtown, still four or five blocks from where he had intended to get off. Rain continued to fall and life was proceeding normally, except that people looked at him strangely. He studied his reflection in a store window and saw that his forehead was cut. Evan took out his handkerchief, spat on it and wiped the blood away. It stung, but his pride hurt far worse.

Other than the pain in his shoulder that made it impossible to raise his arm, his hurts were fairly minor. The feeling that had led him to take the bus in the first place was gone, however. In its place was the bitter ache of loss. He bowed his head and began walking, oblivious to all but the steady rain that fell upon him and the concrete beneath his feet.

He had proceeded only a short way when he felt someone tapping his sore shoulder. An ancient bag lady stood before him, chewing like a cow. She wore a brimless cap and several tattered coats that stunk from being wet. She stopped her chewing for a moment to ask him a question that he couldn't understand as much from the lack of her teeth as from his deafness. He touched his lips and ears and gestured with palms up to make her aware of his deafness. She began to dig among the plastic garbage bags that filled her shopping cart. Evan felt uncomfortable as the search continued through bag after bag. He was afraid that she was going to offer him some food and was embarrassed, since she obviously lived by scavenging. At last, her hand withdrew a small object and held it out for him. It was a tiny, glass horse, missing one foreleg. He accepted the fragile gift, wiped his eyes with the back of a sleeve and smiled at her. She smiled back and then turned away. Evan watched as the humpbacked figure walked slowly away, pushing the cart.

He studied the horse for a moment and loved it, broken leg and all. The library was still a good idea, he decided. It had a men's room where he could wash up before he had to face his mother. It wouldn't do any good to have her see him scuffed up. As much as he wanted her sympathy, he was smart enough to know that she would restrict him if she found out about the kind of trouble he'd gotten into. The worst part was, he had lost Janelle's note. Now, he doubted that he'd ever see her again. He'd never had a girlfriend. Until today, he'd never even really had a conversation with a girl he didn't know and who wasn't deaf.

He began walking again toward the library. He put the tiny horse in his jacket pocket and was surprised to find a folded piece of paper there. He brought out the note and unfolded it carefully to keep the rain from ruining it. At the end of a lengthy paragraph of flower-like words was an address and a phone number. She must have slipped it into his pocket as he was leaving the bus. He put the note back into his pocket and smiled up at the seagulls that soared among the tall buildings.

9

Questions and Answers

Everett, MONDAY, 3:30 p.m. The preliminary results of the autopsies on the two boys were released barely twenty-four hours after their bodies had been discovered. Whidbey Island was still mostly rural and unpopulated, a refuge from gangs, graffiti, and traffic, and a place where the butcher was still someone you knew by first name. The death of two local boys, especially under such baffling circumstances, was big news.

It was Gretta's first time covering a press conference and she had arrived a half hour early. When Billy Mossman had become incapacitated in the accident at the Tower, she had decided to attend it herself. At the very least, she could demonstrate that she'd covered for him. Secretly, however, she'd felt a warm spot grow on both of her cheeks when she learned that he was hurt. Her fantasy was that she'd get a chance to cover the story herself, be noticed and leap frog past the other interns into a full-time job. The odds of this scenario actually happening were highly unlikely, but waiting politely in the wings for a chance that might never come didn't suit her at all. She sipped her Diet Coke and watched the television camera crews setting up equipment and checking sound levels. If she'd learned anything in her twenty-one years, it was that you made your own opportunities in this world.

In consideration of the media, the conference was held at a meeting room in a Hilton Hotel in Everett. Seated at the podium were representatives of the Island County Coroner's Office, Sheriff's Department and the U.S. Coast Guard. A group of ten or twelve reporters arrived, many of them at the last moment or shortly after the conference started. The three people wearing suits could only be television reporters while the newspaper folk were obvious by their laptop computers. Gretta recognized a familiar face from the *Times*. Nevertheless, she scribbled furiously on her yellow legal pad, filling page after page, as she took down nearly every word that was said. No one could accuse her of just putting in an appearance.

The facts were both confusing and few in number. The boys had drowned, their bodies wrapped in twenty-pound monofilament fishing line. They were found about where they could be expected to drift, given the strong currents on the southwest side of Whidbey Island. So far, there was no sign of the boat. Nor was there any sign of drugs or beer in the boys' blood samples. No one had seen them from the time they left the boat launch at around 8:30 Saturday morning. The boys were neither particularly popular nor unpopular at school. No known enemies. They knew their way around boats and had been fishing many times on their own. The families were devastated.

Immediately following the presentation, a number of hands shot up from the audience. As the afternoon wore on and deadlines approached, however, the questions dwindled. Gretta raised her hand when she realized that no one else was going to ask the question that was fermenting inside her.

"Yes, Miss?"

Every face in the room turned to watch her. "I was wondering . . ." Her voice sounded much too high and thin and she cleared her throat. "Has anyone considered that there might be a connection between the boys' drowning and the Olympic Tower accident?"

"The what?" County Sheriff St. Pierre frowned.

After an embarrassing couple of seconds during which there was a good deal of whispering between St. Pierre and the coroner and Gretta began to wish that she could crawl under her chair, Captain Woodbury of the U.S. Coast Guard spoke. "Heavy wind conditions could certainly capsize an aluminum fishing boat, or cause a few panels to come off the face of a building, for that matter. As most of you probably know, we also had a sailboat capsize with loss of life that same day. But such severe events are generally accompanied by moisture and cause much more widespread damage. And even if a gust of wind was responsible," he shook his head sadly, "how these boys came to be wrapped up in fishing line, trussed up like my wife's stuffed pork roast, I have no idea."

"At this point," the Sheriff interjected, "we're not ruling out homicide. Not until we find that boat, anyway."

"Thank you." Gretta wrote down St. Pierre's words.

There were two follow-up questions, one regarding the victims of the sailboat accident; Gretta wrote down their names. And then, as if by common agreement, every one packed up to leave.

Driving back to Seattle, she went over and over the mysterious circumstances of the boys' deaths. Captain Woodbury had labeled the tragedy an unsolved mystery. Every time she recalled his words, her mind would flash back to the first Tower accident, and, later, the woman who had called from San Juan Island. Something told her there was a stronger connection than just a gust of wind running between the incidents. Like her mother often said, "When something smells funny, you can bet that it is." But how to go about finding the connection, if it even existed? What would Billy do? she asked herself. And then she knew.

10

Close Encounters

SEATTLE, MONDAY, 4:45 P.M. Evan picked up his book from the checkout counter and noted the time displayed on the library clock. There was just time to get to his mother's office before it closed. He stuffed *The Deerslayer* into his backpack and slipped outside.

It was raining harder now, the drops slicing through the air like bullets, striking the pavement so hard that they ricocheted up onto his legs. The streets had filled with cars, their headlights peering through the fading light, and the sidewalks surged with the umbrellas of the many people who had just gotten off work and were hurrying home. Evan joined the flow, walking briskly toward Pioneer Square.

Without an umbrella or even a hat, he was quickly drenched. He turned up the collar of his ski jacket and was rewarded by an ice cold rivulet of water that coursed down his neck and halfway down his back. He buried his hands in his pockets in an effort to control his shivering and, once again, was warmed by the touch of Janelle's note and the glass horse. With renewed spirits, he watched for a bus that would take him where he needed to go. On the next block, he found a crowd of people lined up three deep. When the bus arrived a few minutes later, a ship of light in a sea of gloom, he saw that it was packed with people standing in the aisle. So much for that idea, he thought. Fortunately, it was only a half-mile walk to his mother's office.

Much of the city's downtown perched on a hill. Several of the larger buildings straddled block-long portions of the steep grade. Elevators and escalators allowed passage from one street level to another with a minimum of exertion. Seeking temporary relief from the weather, Evan cut through Columbia Center. Until the arrival of the Olympic Tower, the black skyscraper had been Seattle's tallest.

On each floor, the area surrounding the escalators was clustered with fast food restaurants and a variety of shops: dry cleaners, candy and coffee shops, a one-hour photo developer. As he rode the escalators that would eventually take him from Fifth Avenue down to Fourth, Evan spotted two familiarly-dressed figures exiting a magazine and gift shop. Shit! He ducked his head. When he looked again, the boys had disappeared. Maybe they hadn't seen him. Then he glanced behind and above him. Monster shoved a woman aside to get onto the escalator. Rawhide followed right behind. They'd seen him, all right! Evan began running down the escalators, his book bag slapping against his back, weaving among the other riders. At the revolving doorway to Fourth Avenue, he chanced another look back and saw the two young men from the bus barely a hundred feet back and closing fast.

Like a halfback evading tacklers, he sprinted down the crowded sidewalk, then dashed across Fourth Avenue, dodging automobiles. Behind him, he could see the bobbing heads of his pursuers. He bounced off a fat man in a trench coat and landed on his rear. The man wanted to lecture him, but he jumped up and kept on going. The one-way traffic coming up Cherry Street slowed for a light and Evan darted through the cars. He crossed Third Avenue against the light, then took a last look back before deciding which way to go. No boys. He ducked into a narrow alley that ran between the tall buildings. During the day, the alley was often filled with delivery trucks. Now, it was deserted and stunk of urine. He had to run around puddles of rain water vast as ponds and nearly as deep, but at least there were no people to slow him down. He grimaced when he thought about what the Monster and Rawhide would do to him if they caught him here. On the other hand, he didn't think they could catch him. He was the second fastest on his soccer team and these guys didn't look like they were in training for anything other than being mean and stupid. He forced himself to stop for a moment in the pouring rain and scan the alley behind him. The boys were nowhere to be seen. Probably didn't like getting wet, he thought.

He hoped his mother wouldn't get too bent out of shape about his clothes. He had managed to wipe most of the dirt off his jeans and jacket in the library men's room. They were so soaked now, it hardly mattered. And, if she noticed his arm injury, he could say it was from the soccer game on Saturday. But how was he going to explain the cut on his forehead? He was testing some excuses out mentally when he saw a white dog wearing a red kerchief drag a harness past the end of the alley. Although he had only glimpsed it for a moment, he was almost certain it was Fortuno, the blind beggar's dog. When he reached the end of the alley, the dog had disappeared. He ran downhill in the direction in which it was headed, but at the street corner, he fared no better. Had to be another dog, he thought. Why would Fortuno be dragging his harness? The beggar always took it off when he wasn't using him to see.

Moving down the street, Evan looked in doorways and watched for gaps between the cars in order to observe the other side of the street. Just as he was ready to give up, he glimpsed the dog a block away. There he was, waiting for the light to change. He started across the street and almost ran into the side of a patrol car. For a moment, he feared that he would get a ticket for jaywalking, but the officer only stared him back onto the sidewalk before driving on.

Tail between its legs, the dog continued down the next block, nose to the ground as if searching for something. Evan's impatience grew to gigantic proportions. Then he remembered the whistle that the beggar had given him. From his teacher, he'd learned that it was an ultrasonic whistle. Only dogs and other animals could supposedly hear its high-frequency sounds. He pulled the whistle from his pants pocket and blew as hard as he could. The dog stopped, head up and ears pointed, sniffing the air. Frantically Evan waved his arms but, with all the people and traffic, the dog didn't see him. Although he blew the whistle again and again, the dog disappeared around the corner.

Williwaw studied the crowded streets below intently. There it was again. Among the cacophony of roaring engines, squealing brakes and occasional sirens was a new sound, much higher than the rest. Curiosity whetted, the spirit wind twisted down among the towers, swifter than an arrow, seeking the source of the sound. Those pedestrians over whose heads it flew saw only a violent rustle in the trees, a stoplight that swung erratically, or a directional sign that rattled on its post. A few felt a sudden frigid blast like the tailwind of a departing jet and they shivered and drew their coats still tighter about their throats.

Evan thought he had lost Fortuno for good. Then he glanced down another alley and saw that the dog had halted midway to sniff around a Dumpster. Evan started after him, then paused, as he recalled the horrifying vision from the day before during the soccer match. Water lay in oily black pools on the scarred blacktop, rutted by decades of delivery trucks so that the ancient bricks beneath were exposed. Scraps of spoiled food, cardboard, cigarette butts, glass and stuff too crushed and crumpled to identify had formed a stinking sludge that seemed to grow from every nook and cranny. He tried clapping his hands to get the dog's attention. Then he remembered the whistle. Again, he blew into the small metal cylinder. At last, the dog looked back and saw him. Its tail wagged happily in recognition. Fortuno! When a last look around turned up nothing suspicious, Evan ran to meet the dog and threw his arms around it, hugging its shivering body to his own. The dog's feet danced on the wet blacktop. He nearly knocked Evan down in his excitement.

For several seconds, they were oblivious to the rain and the cold. Then, Evan sensed something wrong and looked up. A solitary figure approached. It took a couple of seconds in the dim light to be sure. He wiped the rain from his eyes to confirm that the figure wore a fringed rawhide jacket. Where was his friend? Evan's head swiveled around. Less than twenty yards away, Monster approached from the opposite direction. Fortuno trembled as if he, too, recognized their danger. I'm dead, Evan thought.

He leapt up and ran straight at the larger of the two, thinking he might be slower. At the last second, he tried a move that sometimes worked in soccer, feinting left, then trying to squirt by on the right. He was nearly past the other boy when he tripped over a foot thrown out by Rawhide and went down hard. Unlike the soft grass of the soccer pitch, the street punished him, smashing knees and elbows and stealing skin from his hands. Momentarily stunned, he lay face-down in shallow water and grime that smelled worse than garbage. The stench brought back the long-forgotten memory of a tree under which he had found several dead birds. Forevermore, he would associate the smell with death. A hand, painfully strong, clamped his neck and jerked him to his knees.

Evan stared in terror at Rawhide's sneering mouth. "Gotcha."

The Monster arrived barely a second later. He said nothing, only nodding like one of those stupid Kewpie dolls that some people put in the back windows of their cars. He wore the mask over the back of his head. It was hard to say which side was scarier: the disfigured latex face or the real one with its ice-blue eyes. Fortuno tried to lick Evan's hand. Monster grabbed the dog's harness and looped it around a door handle several feet away. Then he turned his attention to Evan, squeezing his cheeks between the fingers of one hand.

"You're mine now, boy, all mine. This is gonna be fun. Fun for *us*," he nodded toward Rawhide. "Not so fun for you, I'm afraid.

Too bad you can't talk. I'd like to hear you beg for forgiveness. Not that it would really matter. Can you scream, boy?" He squeezed tighter. "We're gonna find out. A real scientific experiment. What do you think, Chuck? Can the dummy scream? Ten bucks says I can get him to scream."

Evan tried to swing at him and missed. Then a knee caught him in the face. Pain sparked in his brain and he felt the crunch of cartilage. His nose swelled as if inflated and pumped blood into his mouth.

"How you like that?" Monster taunted him. "Try this on for size." A foot landed in his stomach.

Evan retched, doubling over so that his face would have touched the ground if Rawhide hadn't still been holding him by the neck. Blood flew from his nose, spattering the tops of Monster's cowboy boots and making him all the more angry. Once again, he lifted Evan's head, forcing him to look at him.

"Now look what you done. I'm gonna have to teach you some manners." He reached inside his jacket and pulled out a long, slender knife and whipped it open. "Hold his arms." Rawhide let go of Evan's neck and forced his arms up behind his back until tears sprang from his eyes.

"Pay attention now. Class is about to start." Monster brought the knife up to Evan's face, first waving it before his eyes, then pressing the cold, wet steel to his throat. Evan felt the blade begin to bite into his skin and he flinched. Then the blade slipped down between his shoulder blade and the book bag strap. One strap gave way, then the other and the bag slipped from his back. Rawhide yanked the nylon parka down around his elbows so that it pinned his arms to his side.

As Evan sucked in his breath and wriggled desperately to escape from Rawhide's grasp, Fortuno reappeared, his broken harness now hanging from his shoulders, and sank his teeth into Monster's hand. He tumbled to the ground, the knife skittering away. When his attempts to jerk his hand away failed, Monster swung his other fist at the dog, but the dog wouldn't let go. Evan tried to stand, but Rawhide kneed him in the back. Pain and rage contorting his face, Monster continued to smash his fist into the dog. Then something caused Fortuno to suddenly stop his attack and lift his head. Evan stole a look in the direction the dog was looking; his only hope was that Paul or someone was there. But, except for a garbage Dumpster, the alley remained empty. His hand now free, Monster rolled to his feet and kicked. His boot caught the dog just below the ear. Stunned, Fortuno dropped to the ground, his breathing evident by the rapid rising and falling of his side. Tears sprang to Evan's eyes. Monster stood up, holding his injured hand with the other, and kicked the dog again. Then, he bent down and retrieved the knife. This time when he looked at Evan, there was something more than just meanness in his eyes.

Arms still pinned, Evan struggled unsuccessfully to slip Rawhide's grip on his neck as the other boy approached. *Go ahead and kill me, you stupid jerk!* Evan wanted to say. But he couldn't talk and, even if his hands had been free, the boys wouldn't have understood him. Then a frigid breeze swept the greasy, blond hair past the monster's eyes and a smell of Christmas trees filled the air. Evan felt the ground moving, as if a heavy truck had entered the alley. The others felt it, too. Now, they all turned to where the Dumpster stood. Slowly but methodically, it moved toward them on its stubby steel wheels.

"Who's there?" Evan saw Monster call out.

"Somebody's playing games," he said a moment later. "Go check it out."

While Rawhide went to investigate, Monster pointed the knife at Evan's face. "Don't be thinking no ideas about escaping. I hardly started with you yet."

As soon as the stocky boy reached the Dumpster, it stopped moving. Rawhide walked around it cautiously. When he reappeared on the other side, he grinned and shrugged his shoulders. Monster signaled for him to rejoin them. He had taken only a few steps before the Dumpster started following.

Monster was ready to chew steel. "Check underneath!" He pointed.

The gloom from the rain and the lateness of the day made it difficult to see under the Dumpster. Clearly unhappy, Rawhide was forced to get down on his knees in the wet alley. He had no sooner lowered his head when the Dumpster seemed to lurch sideways, one wheel coming down on his hand. The wind was much stronger now. Unable to run due to the knife pointed at his face, Evan witnessed Rawhide's agony as he howled and thrashed about. As the Dumpster continued to roll farther up his arm, he alternated between trying to fend it off with his free arm and waving desperately for the other boy's help, but Monster only watched, mouth open in dumb fascination. Within a few brief seconds, the Dumpster was pressed against Rawhide's anguished face, then it folded his head back like a rag doll. A couple of seconds later, the Dumpster had passed completely over his body, and was continuing toward Evan and the other boy and moving faster.

Monster wiped his mouth with the back of his good hand and started to back away. "Guess it's your turn next, kid," he said. "I'm outta here." Eyes still on the Dumpster, he turned and began jogging down the alley in the opposite direction. He had taken a dozen or so steps when a blast of wind struck. A fire escape parted from the upper floors of the brick building and swung down like a black metal scythe. Monster must have heard it because he looked up barely an instant before an iron stair step slammed into his throat, separated his head from his body and sent it rolling back down the center of the alley, a soccer ball with pale, blinking eyes, greasy blond hair and a Halloween mask.

Like a crazed nightcrawler, Evan twisted and squirmed out of the prison of his coat. He jumped to his feet, grabbed the heavy dog and ran as fast as he could past the motionless Dumpster and Rawhide's body, his heart knocking in his chest as if it wanted out.

Only when they had reached the end of the alley and the relative safety of the crowded sidewalk did he stop to catch his breath and make sure they weren't being followed. Then he threw up.

"Hi, Roxanne, this is Denise Baker. I'm sorry to bother you, but is Evan there? I've already tried the school and about everywhere else I can think of. Did Bobby see him get on the school bus by any chance?"

Denise was sitting in the dining room, really nothing more than a wide passage between the kitchen and living room. While she waited for Roxanne to track Bobby down, Denise held the phone receiver between her neck and shoulder and peeled the tinfoil wrapper from another candy kiss. Twenty minutes earlier, the bag of Halloween candy had been full. Now it was half-empty. With each call, her anxiety level had cranked up another notch. How many calories does a heart attack burn off? she wondered. After studying the nutritional information panel, she set the bag back down on the small pine table, silently toting up the caloric damage. With a sigh, she decided it would take a calculator and gave up.

"He didn't see Evan at all? Thanks for checking anyway, Roxanne. I know, he'll probably walk in the door as soon as I hang up. By the way, you wouldn't happen to have a spare set of leg irons?"

Denise glared at the television flickering in the living room, a silent but insistent housemate, and saw once again the videotaped sequences from the accident at the Tower playing on the evening news. She stood up, ran her fingers through her hair and felt her frustration bubbling and foaming upwards like an exploding can of soda. "Where could the little creep be?" This becoming independent business was out of control. First, there was the horse that nearly ran him over when he wandered away from the car in Pioneer Square. Now this. Enough was enough! She would put her foot down big time. She was considering grounding him for an entire month—possibly two—when she heard footsteps on the porch followed by the doorbell ringing. Denise walked quickly to the door, heart pounding, as conflicting thoughts raced through her mind. Had she locked Evan out? Or was it a police officer come to tell her that he'd been kidnapped?

She opened the unlocked door to find a girl, younger than Evan, dressed as Princess Jasmine, and a woman who was probably her mother standing on the porch.

"Trick or treat."

"Oh." Denise sighed with a mixture of disappointment and relief. "I nearly forgot. Be right back."

Denise retrieved the bag of remaining candy and sent the princess and her mother happily on their way with a couple of the chocolates. Even before their footsteps had departed her porch, her eyes were scanning the neighborhood for any sign of Evan. The setting sun was veiled by squadrons of heavy black clouds that marched across the sky, providing nightfall with an early jump. Flickering light lit the smile of a jack-o'-lantern on the porch of a house across the street. Evan had slung a rope tied like a hangman's noose from the top of their own porch, a decorative touch whose ominous overtones she now regretted. At the end of the street, she could see the lights of a solid line of cars making slow progress down Forty-fifth Avenue. The heavy, moisture-laden air made her shiver and she retreated back inside the house to consider her options. She could put on her coat and walk the neighborhood, but it would take too long to check out all his possible hangouts on foot. Of all the nights not to have a car.

Paul Judge had called about the damage to her Mercury even before she'd reached home. The message on her answering machine had been short and to the point. "Your car's in the shop. They'll call you later with an estimate. The guy told me he thought he could turn it around in a day." And that, she was certain, was the last she would ever hear from him. Then she remembered that she still had his coat. Giving it back presented an awkward opportunity that might be difficult—not to mention embarrassing. She didn't have his address and he hadn't left his number on the answering machine.

She still felt badly about how she'd left him standing on the street corner in a downpour as she'd driven away in the mayor's limo. She'd spent the better part of the afternoon in the mayor's office listening to Grenitzer and Bud argue about whose idea it had been to hold the press conference at the Tower.

The television news continued to replay the Tower footage. Denise pushed the off button and watched the bad news fade into a fuzzy white pinpoint before winking out entirely. If only she could do the same to her brain. Who could she call for help? As much as she hated to admit it, there was only one person she could turn to. She picked up the phone, punched in the number and listened to the rings over the protests of her conscience. A woman's voice answered.

"Hello?"

Denise pictured the willowy young woman who had climbed out of Ron's Porsche on Sunday. What was her name—Monique? Monica?

"Hi. This is Denise Baker. Is Ron there?"

"Oh, hi, Denise. He's not home yet."

"Is he working late?"

"Ron?" She laughed. "You must be kidding. He's usually home by now except on Monday nights, he goes to a sports bar downtown to watch football."

"Do you know the name of the bar?" Denise thought she detected the woman's hesitation. "Listen, I'm sorry to trouble you but I may need Ron's help. Evan's not home yet and I don't have a car."

"What happened to your car?"

"It got conked by a rock in the accident at the Tower today."

"You had an accident?"

"Look, I don't have time to explain. I'm worried about my son. Will you just tell me the name of the bar so I can call Ron?"

"Geez, Denise." Monica sounded wounded. "I don't know the name."

"I'm sorry. Forgive me for taking my troubles out on you. If he calls in, will you please ask him to call me? It's an emergency."

"Sure. I can call and leave a message on his car phone."

"That would be a big help. Thank you."

Denise hung up the phone. Now what? Without the television on, the house was too quiet. Thus far, she had barely managed to control her steadily-increasing alarm. She was beginning to feel like the boy with his finger in the dike as the secret terrors that normally lurked just offstage in her imagination jostled for attention. Like men who picked up young boys and hurt them in unspeakable ways, or car accidents that left kids comatose. She fought to push her irrational fears back into the dark recesses of her mind.

Her mother would probably call every hospital in King County. What about the police? Did a missing boy rate a call to 911, or did the situation have to be life threatening? And would they tell her to wait and file a missing person report after twenty-four hours? Denise reached again for the phone; it was time to find out.

After waiting for nearly five minutes, she finally got a tired-sounding operator.

"Please state the nature of your emergency."

"My son is missing."

"How old is your son?" The woman's voice was suddenly all business.

"Thirteen."

"And how long as he been missing?"

"He's normally home from school by four, at the latest."

"Ma'am, it's not even six o'clock and it's Halloween."

"So? He's over two hours late!"

"Has this happened before?"

"Never," she lied.

"Have you tried his friends?"

"Yes. None of them has seen him."

"Hang on, please, and I'll transfer you to someone in Missing Persons."

"Thank you." Denise felt better. At least she was doing something.

"Officer Dowling. How may I help you?" It was a voice that had known more than its healthy share of cigarettes and coffee.

Denise was repeating the information that she had told the operator when a beep signaled that she had another call waiting. "Excuse me, Officer. Could you please hold? This might be my son calling."

"Hello?"

"Congratulations! You may have won a brand new Pontiac

101

Grand Prix. . . ." the automated voice stated enthusiastically.

Denise pushed the hang-up button twice in disgust. "Officer? Are you still there? I'm sorry."

"Was that your son?"

"No. Just a computer telling me I've won a new car."

"You, too, huh? I must have won sixteen of those damn things in the last two months."

Denise barely had time to appreciate his sonorous laugh when the phone beeped again. "Oh, oh. Another call coming in."

"Go ahead."

"Denise?"

"Yes?"

"This is your mother."

"Hi, Mom. Can I call you back? I'm on the other line."

"Of course. Is everything okay?"

"Yes, fine." How did her mother always know when she was in trouble? "I'll call you back later tonight or tomorrow." A part of her regretted not being able to tell her mother about Evan's disappearance. But, living three hundred miles away in Spokane as they did, what good would it do?

"Sorry again. My mother this time."

"That's all right, Ms. Baker. I think I've got all the facts. Let me ask one more question: Does your son sometimes tell you he's going to do one thing and then end up doing another?"

"Yes, but—"

"I've checked the computer and, so far, there are no reports of a boy turning up. Odds are he's just having fun somewhere, forgot to look at the clock and will turn up soon. I'll be honest with you; we don't have any surplus manpower to check this out right now. The wind and rain have caused a lot of traffic accidents and the mayor's had us block off the streets downtown around the Olympic Life Tower, adding to the congestion. What with the traffic and its being Halloween, a lot of people are probably going to be a little late getting home tonight.

"Now, please do us both a favor and don't panic. I'll stay on the computer, just in case something turns up. And if you haven't heard from your son by eight o'clock, give me another call—I'll give you my extension—and we'll start a door-to-door search if we have to."

"But wait, you don't understand. He's deaf. He could be lost or hurt and unable to call me."

"Is your son also retarded?"

"No," Denise answered and resented his question.

"I understand your anxiety, ma'am, but your son's being deaf doesn't really change the situation as far as we're concerned."

Denise felt the first tear sear her cheek as she hung up a moment later. She laid her head on the table and pressed her palms and fingers into its corner surfaces, but there was no give. The truth, she had to admit, was just as unyielding. First, she had failed in her marriage. That was bad enough, but hardly unique. Then, hard as she had tried, she had failed to provide the security and comfort level that she and her son required. She was excluded from lunches with the guys at work, treated like someone with half a brain. She had even suffered the indignity of being passed over for promotion, because, according to her boss, the "guys" didn't feel she was a team player. But what did it matter? Now, she had to face something about herself that was worse—much worse. As a mother, she was turning out to be a total, unqualified bust.

She raised her head so that her chin rested on the table. A telephone book lay just a few inches away. After searching the columns of names for several seconds, during which time she had to wipe her eyes on her sleeve twice in order to read the tiny print, she finally found what she was looking for. There was no address given but the phone prefix was the same as her office.

She listened to the phone ringing and forgot to breathe. An answering machine clicked on after four rings. "Dammit! Is everybody at a sports bar?" She forced herself to wait until the beep to leave a message anyway.

"This is Denise Baker," she blurted into the phone. "I'm sorry about leaving you stranded earlier today. I still have your coat and now I really need to talk to you. My son—"

"Denise? Hang on while I shut the machine off. Still there?" Paul sounded out of breath.

"Yes." She sniffed.

"I just got in. What's up?"

"I know you probably think I'm a bitch for running out on you today—I can't believe that happened—but, unfortunately, I need to ask another favor. I've tried everyone else—"

"What's the matter?"

"Evan. He never made it home from school and I'm worried he's stranded someplace. He can't call me." She tried to prevent the quiver in her lip from working its way into her voice. "Could you . . . would you be willing to check my office to see if, somehow, he might have gone there? I'm afraid to leave the house in case he shows up here. I called the police. They aren't willing to help for a couple of hours at least. I know it's asking a lot," she rushed on. "Especially after all you've done. You don't even know us."

"Just out of curiosity, why are you calling me?"

"Because . . ." There was that damn quiver. "Because I don't know what else to do and because, for some reason, I trust you. And," she swallowed, "because I could really use a friend."

"Where's your office?"

She told him.

"Stay by the phone. I'll call you within thirty minutes."

II

Pursuit

SEATTLE, MONDAY, 6:16 P.M. Paul Judge padded up the stairs, silent as a thief but for the creaking of old, wooden floor joists. He was dressed in black from head to foot—black leather jacket over a sweatshirt, black jeans, and black athletic shoes—and his unbraided black hair hung straight to his shoulder blades. He passed the door to Denise's firm and, seeing no one, proceeded to the other levels of the building. Each floor was lit by a single ceiling fixture. All the offices were closed and dark. He tried the well-worn brass knob of a restroom door and determined that it was locked.

Back at Denise's office, he checked the door to assure himself that it was also locked, then squatted and studied the floor. He touched a hand to a small pool of water and smelled his fingertips.

A moment later, he was downstairs, drinking deeply of the air that had been purified earlier by the heavy rain. A ten-year-old Mercedes sedan gleamed with Teutonic pride at the curb. A single eagle feather hung from the rearview mirror. The streets that often teemed with people during the day were now deserted and, even for a Monday night, seemed singularly quiet. But if the streets were dead, the night was alive with an energy all its own that awakened his senses and stirred his blood. Why this was, he could not have said.

As he considered where a boy who couldn't speak might go on a cold and windy night, Paul observed two men and a woman, dressed in conservative business suits, appear suddenly from around the nearest street corner. Lost in conversation and walking into one another as if slightly inebriated, they had almost passed by before they noticed him. There was a sudden intake of breath from the woman.

"It's Cochise," the shorter of the men whispered loudly.

"How." The other man raised a hand in salute. The men snickered.

"Shhh," the woman scolded.

105

"Have you seen a young boy by himself, maybe twelve or thirteen years old?" Paul asked.

"Your son?" the woman asked.

"No. He's got light skin, freckles, red hair."

"Whatsamatter?" the shorter man asked. "He steal your horse?" The men's loud guffaws rent the quiet night.

"Guys!" The woman elbowed the shorter man in the side.

Paul ignored their drunken insults. Living in Seattle, you either got used to it or you moved on. The only Native Americans most people saw were the disenfranchised and downtrodden. The others, like himself, were too busy working, networking, and overcoming obstacles that most whites didn't have to think twice about. The end result was that people who wouldn't think about slurring a black, Latino, or Asian, slurred Indians without even realizing it. Paul figured these guys weren't necessarily mean, just not very bright.

"Thanks, anyway." As Paul walked to the car, the three continued on, stealing looks over their shoulders.

"Think that's his car?" a man asked.

"Yeah, and it's a lot nicer than yours," the woman said.

Paul cruised the streets slowly in the Mercedes, windows rolled down, the heater purring softly over the rattle of the diesel engine. "Crazy," he said to himself as he waited at a stop light. The kid was probably home by now, eating dinner and solving math problems. And even if he did find him, who was to say whether he wouldn't run away? They had seen each other only once and for less than five minutes. And, Paul recalled, he hadn't exactly been Mr. Congeniality.

He passed The Elliott Bay Book Company and noted that it was closed. Nothing seemed to be open except for a seedy-looking tavern, a holdover from the days when Pioneer Square had been a rough and tumble area of bars and flophouses. Now, in addition to the art galleries and specialty shops, the historic quarter housed the tony offices of numerous ad agencies and P.R. firms, C.P.A.s and attorneys. His own office and apartment were located just a few blocks away on the southern fringe of the International District. Hardly a ten-minute walk, but a world away in terms of cachet.

On his second tour of the area, he saw a man urinating in front of a large bus route map at the entrance of the underground bus station. The car coasted to the curb and he got out to study the map. Having ridden the route many times, he needed only a quick glance to confirm what he already knew. The tunnel intersected with the Westlake Center and the monorail before ending at the Convention Center. A blast of warm air, smelling of diesel fumes, escaped from the tunnel opening. Paul started down the steps into the tiled cavern.

A few minutes later, a bus rumbled up and the doors whooshed open. Paul climbed up onto the stairway.

"Have you seen a deaf kid, twelve or thirteen years old?" he asked the driver.

"No."

Paul started to exit.

"I seen a kid with a dog. Don't know as he was deaf. He never said nothin'."

"A dog?" Paul thought back to the pool of water in front of Denise's office.

"Yeah. Told 'em he couldn't ride with the dog. Felt sorry for the little bugger. No jacket. Drenched to the bone. Wouldn't leave without the dog though."

"How long ago was that?"

"This is my second or third loop since then, so maybe twenty minutes, give or take."

"I got a hunch this might be the kid I'm looking for. You see which way he went?"

"Yeah. Into the Center. Listen, buddy, I gotta go or they're gonna think I died down here."

"The Center?" Paul had to shout over the revving of the engine. "I thought you said you wouldn't let him ride because of the dog?"

The driver shrugged. "Felt sorry for the little bastard."

"Thanks."

Back at the entrance, Paul looked for the nearest phone booth. Denise answered before he heard it ring.

"Any word?" he asked.

"No. Oh, my God. I was hoping you had found him by now."

He could hear the fear in her answer, even stronger than before. "I checked your office—nothing. I may have a lead, though. What was he wearing?"

"His blue parka, jeans, a flannel shirt, and athletic shoes—white ones."

"One more thing. Do you know anything about a dog?"

"No." Denise sounded confused.

"I'll call you again, in thirty minutes or less." He hung up the phone and frowned. It didn't fit. No jacket and a dog. But as the moon, ghostly as a spirit, appeared from within the clouds, somehow he knew he was on the right path. Like his grandmother used to say, "The eyes can find the trail, but sometimes only the heart can find the truth."

The breeze stirred fitfully, bending a small, ornamental cherry tree in its protective iron girdle and causing the remaining leaves to rattle. Nearby, a "Re-Elect Grenitzer for Mayor" cardboard sign fluttered from a light post. Paul zipped his jacket and walked briskly back to the car. A small group of young toughs was circling the Mercedes like a pack of dogs. He strode through them, ignoring their bluster, saying nothing that would provoke them. It was getting so there were gang bangers, drug dealers, and vicious punks everywhere you looked, people that would just as soon blow you away as look at you.

As he drove the mile north to the Westlake Center, he tried to think like a boy trying to get home. The Center was brightly lit and open late—a place to grab something to eat or just hang out. It also connected with just about every bus line either entering or leaving the city. Yeah, he considered, it was a good place to check out.

After the incident in the alley, when his legs would let him stand, Evan had run back to his mother's office. It had been closed, however, by the time he arrived. Tired, discouraged, and so cold he couldn't keep his teeth together, he had led the dog back to the beggar's usual place on the sidewalk. This time, however, it was just like any other vacant sidewalk space; the blind man was nowhere to be seen.

Now the dog sat patiently and waited while Evan considered what to do. Although it had stopped raining, his wet shirt and jeans clung to his body as if he'd been swimming in them. With every step he took, his feet squished in his shoes. His chill went deeper than soggy clothes, however. For now, he tried to block the vision of Monster's head rolling down the alley and of Rawhide's mangled body. He had lost his book bag containing his library book and homework, and, to make matters worse, his jacket. Janelle's note and the horse were still in one of the pockets. As heartbreaking as that was, there was no way he was going back for them. He had the dog and they were alive. That was all that mattered now.

The ride on the underground bus had helped to restore his dampened spirits if not his attire, but now he watched, crestfallen, as the other bus with the lighted reader sign that said "Wallingford" rolled away from the curb and disappeared down the street. With it went all hope of catching a bus home. You could ride around on downtown buses all day for free—and he had done so in the past— but to get home, he needed bus fare. Even if he had the money, this driver, unlike the previous one, wouldn't bend the rules and allow the dog to board. So here they were, a mile closer to home, but still stuck downtown. It might be only twenty or thirty minutes by car, but it would be a journey of at least two or three hours on foot. If he could just get someone to call his mother, she would come get them. But so far, he had had no luck.

He entered the Westlake Center, leading the dog on a length of twine he salvaged from a litter barrel, and tried signing the people hurrying to or from the buses. Most people pretended he didn't exist. He probably looked no different than the dozens of street kids they saw every day, panhandling for drugs and food. Due to the storm and it being a Monday night—not to mention Halloween—the crowd of people returning home from work or shopping had quickly thinned out until only a few remained. Still, Evan refused to give up. There had to be someone who would help. He rode the escalator up to the third level to try there. Most of the dozen or so fast food restaurants and shops were closed except for a sandwich shop. He borrowed an order pad to write a note, but the two Latino workers didn't understand his written English. Then he spotted an older woman eating a sandwich and reading a magazine in the souvenir shop. She looked up as he approached and frowned.

"No dogs allowed in the store," she said with her mouth full and turned back to her reading.

Evan caught enough of what she said to understand but waited patiently, refusing to leave. After several moments, she looked up again, clearly annoyed. He put the dog down and signed that he was deaf. Then, knowing she probably would not understand, he pointed to paper and made writing motions.

"What's the matter?" She rolled her eyes. "Can't a person eat dinner in peace?"

For a moment, Evan thought she was going to kick him out. Then she reached beneath the cash register, found a scrap of paper in the waste basket and put it in front of him. He took one of the pens that were for sale, one that had an umbrella that opened and closed attached to the eraser, and wrote his name and phone number, trying not to smear the ink with his wet hands and shirt. Then he handed it to the woman who regarded it suspiciously.

"This better not be a trick," she said, "or I'll call the cops."

She had just started to push the buttons on the phone when an older boy and girl, dressed in Seattle "grunge," came into the store. The boy headed immediately for a rack of clothing.

"Hey, Shelley. Check out these shirts," he said. He held up a sweatshirt with an illustration of a lovesick duck and the words "I'm quackers over you" imprinted on it. "Like this one?" The girl glanced up from examining the glass paperweights containing miniatures of various Seattle scenes. One slipped from her grasp. She tried to catch it with her Doc Marten-clad foot and succeeded only in kicking it onto the tile floor where it broke, spilling a glittering, oily substance. Fortuno sniffed at the spreading pool.

"Way to go, Shell," the boy said. "Now you've done it."

"Stupid kids!" the clerk said in disgust. "Would you mind leaving things alone unless you're planning to buy?"

Forgetting that he couldn't hear her, she said to Evan, "Look, no one answers and I've got to watch the store, so take your dog outside, okay?"

Evan picked up Fortuno again. Through the store window behind the woman's back, he saw that the monorail had arrived. The doors slid open and a handful of passengers got off the brightly lit cars. No one was waiting to get on and the ticket taker looked bored. He waited until the girl behind the counter had turned away, then pushed open the door and ran, darting under the railing and into the car.

The ticket taker, a college sophomore, looked up just in time to see boy and dog disappear into the rear car. "Hey, you!" she called out. "C'mon back here! You'll get me in trouble." She picked up the phone to call security, punched the first digit and then, after looking around and seeing no one, reconsidered and put the receiver back in its cradle. "Who cares?" she mumbled to no one and went back to reading *Norton's Anthology of English Literature.*

Evan huddled on the floor with the dog to avoid being seen. The monorail wouldn't take them home, but at least it was headed in the right direction. Looking back on it now, he realized that he probably should have stayed outside his mother's office. At least there, he had a roof over his head. And while it might have taken a while, eventually his mother would have found him, although she would have been plenty angry from having to drive back downtown. After what had happened earlier to the two boys, however, he wasn't about to stay alone in an empty building. Even the nearly empty monorail was better than that.

A few minutes later, he felt the footsteps of someone else getting on, followed by the door closing. Then, with a lurch, they were gliding away from the station. He climbed up on the seat and patted the cloth surface for the dog to join him. A couple seated several rows back appeared not to notice him. Through the glass bubble windows, he watched the Westin Hotel slide by. The drapes were open in one room, the television on and the lights warm and inviting. He sighed and scratched behind the dog's ears. They were still a long way from Wallingford and home.

Williwaw looked out over the city from the high place and gloated. Below, the streets were still cordoned off with flashing lights from his earlier raid. The enemy appeared to be angry and confused, swarming in all directions at once like an anthill that has been disturbed. This was a good sign. Several had died this day and passed on to the spirit world. Many more would follow in the days to come.

He noted with keen interest the bullet-shaped monorail as it headed north through the heart of the city, winding its way on a single wide track supported by concrete pylons. He watched the monorail because the enemy's ingenuity never ceased to amaze him, and because the boy with no ears was on it.

Paul spotted the flashing lights of the barricades on Fourth Avenue and swung the Mercedes west to avoid them. Navigating the alternating one-way streets took only a little extra time as the streets were nearly empty. He approached the Westlake Center, a three-story, triangular-shaped building from the north and parked nearby underneath the monorail.

As he walked the short distance to the Center, he heard the monorail cars rumble by overhead and he stopped for a moment, watching a newspaper tumble down the street like a drunken gymnast as the buses came and went, and felt the sense of doom come again like an alarm, starting in his stomach and spreading quickly throughout his body. It was the same feeling he had experienced last Saturday and again this morning. Only once before Saturday in his thirty-four years had he felt this way.

He moved swiftly but cautiously, his eyes searching every dark corner, his ears attuned for the faintest cry, sensing danger at every step. The boy was gone—he was sure of it. But where? There was no trace of him outside by the buses. None of the handful of people who remained remembered seeing him.

After a quick tour of the exterior of the building, he continued the search inside. Again, no one remembered seeing a deaf boy, or a boy and a dog. He checked out a record shop decorated with Halloween ghouls and heavy-metal-inspired graffiti, then took the escalator to the food level. At the sandwich shop, he explained who he was looking for by using a combination of English, Spanish, and gestures.

"Sí, sí. Allí," the attendant answered. He pointed to the souvenir shop.

"Gracias," Paul said.

The only store still open, the souvenir shop stood out like a lighted beacon. "Excuse me," Paul said to the heavy-set, older woman who sat behind the counter. "Have you seen a deaf boy and perhaps a dog this evening?"

The clerk looked up at him over her spectacles. Under her scrutiny, he felt his blood rise as if he had been slapped on the face, but the flames of his anger were doused by the habitual control he had learned from a lifetime of such incidents.

"Do I look like the Answer Lady?"

He wanted to say, "You look like an overweight bigot." Instead he spoke in a polite but firm voice, "Where did he go?"

"I don't have the faintest."

He stared at her, tried to think like the boy. "Did he try to communicate, maybe write a note?"

She hesitated, then fished a crumpled piece of paper, still damp, out of the wastepaper basket.

Paul recognized the number and his adrenaline spurted. "So, did you talk to his mother? Did she come to get him?"

"I tried calling but there wasn't anyone home."

He stared at her in surprise. "Do you mind if I use your phone for a moment?"

"Yes, I most certainly do mind." Her face reddened. "First, I'm the Answer Lady, now I'm a frickin' telephone operator. You can use the pay phones like everybody else."

"I will," Paul said as he backed out of the store. He was angry now, angry enough to say something he'd regret later.

Outside the store, he clenched the railing overlooking the lower floor and forced himself to think coolly. He could see no pay phones on the second floor and guessed that they would be either on the first floor or in the underground bus station. He had just stepped on the escalator that would take him down when a motion caught his eye. He ran back up the escalator and out the exit door to where the electric-powered monorail cars had just arrived and now sat silently.

The young Asian ticket taker wore a Seattle University sweat-shirt. Her eyes took on a look of confusion at his rapid approach.

"Did you see a boy and a dog?"

She began nodding her head even before he finished the question. "They sneaked on," she blurted. "It's my fault."

Paul smiled briefly in appreciation of her honesty. "Good for you. Do you mind if I search the cars?"

"Is he in trouble?" she called out as he stuck his head inside each of the cars.

"No. He's deaf and doesn't have a way home. If you see him again, please call this number." He handed her Evan's note from the waste basket.

He wanted to get to the car and make tracks for the Seattle Center while the trail was still hot. Instead, he forced himself to call Denise again.

"Paul? Have you got him?"

"I'm at the Westlake Center. Just missed him. But don't worry, I know where he is now."

"Where?"

"The Seattle Center."

"But why?" Her voice was nearly hysterical. "What's there?"

"I don't know. I think he's just trying to get home anyway he can. A girl saw him sneak on the monorail with a dog just a little while ago."

"A dog? The monorail I can believe. He loves anything that moves. But where would he get a dog? Are you sure it's him?"

"I'm sure. In fact, he tried to call you. Were you unable to answer your phone anytime in the last several minutes?"

"Are you kidding? It's never been more than four inches from my hand!"

"I thought so. He gave a store clerk your number to call, but she either didn't try or got a wrong number."

For a few seconds, there was only silence on the other end of the line. "Denise? Are you there?"

"I'm sorry. For a second there, I nearly lost it. It's a good thing I wasn't with you. I might have killed her."

"I've got to go," he said. "Stay by the phone. If he manages to get in touch with you tell him to meet me at the base of the Space Needle."

"Paul?"

"Yes, Denise."

"Thank you."

He hung up the phone and exhaled slowly. The bad feeling was there again, only now it was worse. He began to run toward his car.

SEATTLE CENTER, MONDAY, 6:44 P.M. The monorail car glided to a halt. Using the twine leash, Evan led Fortuno out of the car and down the platform stairway, walking a few steps behind a couple bundled in rain coats. Except for them, the Seattle Center appeared to be deserted on this cold and damp Halloween night. Just ahead, the steel skeleton of the Space Needle jutted brightly against the night sky like a huge camera mounted on its tripod. The woman turned and gave Evan a concerned look, then said something to her companion. She was about the same age as his mom, perhaps a little older, but dark-haired and not much taller than himself.

He wondered what his mother was doing. By now, she was probably not only worried, but plenty angry, too. He'd be lucky if he got to leave the house for anything other than school for the next six months. But, as cold, wet and hungry as he was now, and after what he'd been through today, even being grounded was okay. As soon as they reached the Space Needle, he would figure out a way to have someone, maybe this woman, call his mom so she could come get them. The Needle's restaurant was sure to be open, even on a Monday night.

More than anything, he wanted to be home. He missed his room, his computer with all its games and, most of all, the modem. With a modem, he could "talk" just like regular people. More than once, his mother had awakened to the clicking of the keyboard keys and found him behind the closed door to his room, carrying on multiple conversations on one of the dozens of electronic bulletin boards he frequented. She got concerned if he stayed up past midnight on a school night and she had a fit over the telephone bill every month. But, for the most part, she understood his need to communicate. He hoped she wouldn't be mad enough to take that privilege away.

114

Other than her thing about eating broccoli, she was a pretty cool mom. She might even go easy on him when he explained about finding the blind man's dog. He couldn't tell her about the other stuff though—the guys on the bus or the thing in the alley. Telling her things like that would only make it worse. You had to protect moms from scary stuff like that or they got bug-eyed and had a heart attack.

He turned up the collar of his shirt and held the collar closed with one hand as the breeze freshened. A Halloween tradition, the Space Needle Restaurant and observation deck were decorated like a flying saucer with lights that pulsed as they revolved slowly overhead, completing a full turn every sixty minutes. Still trailing the couple, Evan guided the dog toward the base of the Needle and the entrance to the elevator. The hostess opened the door for the couple, but held up a hand to prevent Evan from entering. When he saw that she wouldn't let him pass, he dropped the twine dog lead and tried signing her. A look of confusion crossed her face. Fortunately, the dark-haired woman noticed his difficulty and came back to help. Fortuno lapped at the water that lay in mirror-like puddles on the asphalt as Evan watched the two women argue and looked for something to write with. The nice woman returned and knelt, making it easy to watch her mouth.

"I'll pay for you to enter," he saw her say, "but the attendant won't let you take the dog. I tried, but I can't get her to change her mind. She says there are health code regulations."

I don't mind waiting outside, he signed. *I just need someone to call my mother and tell her where I am.*

She shook her head and held up her palms to indicate that she didn't understand. Evan made writing motions with his hands. She called her male companion over to join them.

Evan felt the wind tugging at his shirt and pants. Goose bumps crowded his arms and legs. A fresh wind often brought more rain, but this felt crisper, colder.

"Write on this," the woman said, handing him a checkbook and pen.

She nodded after reading his message. "I'll call her myself. But don't you want to wait inside where it's warm?"

Out of the corner of his eye, Evan was watching Fortuno growl at something. He shook his head. He couldn't leave the dog.

"Then wait here," she advised. "I'll come back down as soon as I talk to your mom."

115

The couple disappeared into the elevator and he ran back and wrapped his arms around Fortuno. The ferocity of the growl vibrating throughout the dog's shivering body startled him. Had he not seen what happened to Monster and Rawhide earlier, he might have ignored it. Now he stroked the dog to calm it and turned to follow anxiously the glass elevator with his eyes as it climbed slowly up the Space Needle. Inside the lighted glass bubble, he could just make out the couple standing next to the elevator operator. Everything would be okay soon, he told himself. The woman would call his mother and she would come to pick them up.

A strong gust caused him to lose his balance and he sat down in a shallow puddle. Fortuno's excited behavior grew still more frantic. It was all Evan could do to keep the dog from bolting from his arms. The low temperature of the breeze made tears run down his cheeks. He wiped his eyes with the back of one arm and scanned the surrounding area. He could see no reason for the dog's alarm, just a row of trees that bobbed in the wind, but the air suddenly smelled of snow and he knew it was here.

Whatever the thing was that had killed the two boys, it had found him. He tasted vomit as he relived the horror from the alley. When he closed his eyes, his spatial sense went crazy, telling him something unusually large and powerful was approaching. He ducked as it swooped by overhead. Fear jetted through his arms and legs, making them spasm out of control, and he might have screamed. Then he was picked up and carried along on a foaming mountain of frigid air. For one thrilling instant, he rode its invisible curl like a body surfer. His head was the sea and he swam with the moon and the stars. They made a "humming" sound inside his head. Then he rolled along the wet pavement, cast up on the beach like a gasping fish. When he looked up, bruised and terrified yet exhilarated, too, he saw that every light—the Space Needle, street lamps, the monorail cars—had gone black. His nose and cheeks burned as if they'd been frostbitten and his eyes, ears, mouth, and nostrils were filled with grit. The wind-thing was gone. That wasn't all that was missing. Fortuno! Ignoring his fear and shaking off his minor hurts, he ran deeper into the Center seeking the dog. After all he'd been through finding the dog, he wasn't about to lose him now. His eyes were nearly blind from the flying dust and grit. To top it off, all the street lamps were out, making it virtually impossible to see. He stumbled into a fallen tree and had to fumble his way back out and around its twisted branches.

Past the Food Circus building, he was amazed to see the International Fountain still working, shooting sprays of colored water high in the air from dozens of jets to a rhythmic beat he couldn't hear. As he continued to watch, however, he saw that something was very wrong with the huge, bowl-shaped fountain. Instead of graceful, geometric patterns, the spray was suddenly blown far to one side, and then slapped to the other, like a small child playing with a lawn sprinkler. Against this amazing, multicolored backdrop, he spotted Fortuno leaping high in the air, snapping his jaws as if trying to bite the spray.

Once again, Evan thought of the whistle. He dug it from a pants pocket and blew it as hard as he could. Incredibly, everything stopped. The dog quit leaping and stared at him. The fountain returned to its usual, boring routines. In the sudden calm, he ran to Fortuno and grabbed the leash. The dog hardly seemed to recognize him, however, and fought to free himself, showing his teeth and snapping at the twine. Evan dropped to his knees, pulled the dog to him and tried to calm it.

He managed to quiet the dog after holding it close and stroking it for several minutes. There was no sign of the wind-thing. He stood, signaled for the dog to follow and took a few steps back toward the Space Needle.

Then the fountain started to dance again, washing them with waves of colored spray.

Paul drove up Fourth Avenue, the Mercedes thundering past the few other cars on the street. At Vine Street, he was forced to wait impatiently for a light to change. His nerves were already stretched paper thin and he grew more anxious as the heavy car began rocking in the wind and the signal light swung at a forty-five-degree angle to the road. A tramp staggered a few steps, sat down hard and crawled to shelter in a nearby doorway. A sound like an approaching steamroller caused Paul to turn just in time to see the world rolling down Vine, its white polar caps, blue seas, and green land masses barely distinguishable as it spun directly toward him.

He threw the car into reverse and spun the tires as the globe hurtled by, narrowly missing him. It crossed Fourth Avenue, bounded off a parked car and continued on, heading east. After his initial surprise, he realized that the enormous rolling sphere was the lighted symbol from the top of the *Post-Intelligencer* building. In the second it took to consider this, stoplight after stoplight winked out, along with every streetlight and building on the long avenue. In the midst of a sudden, howling windstorm, Paul shifted back into drive and jammed the pedal to the floor again.

Driving with his high beams on and slowing only marginally at intersections, Paul continued north toward the Center. As he turned onto Clay Street, he saw that the KOMO Radio and Television Building had been abbreviated to the MO Building. He maneuvered around its microwave transmitting dish, lying in a crumpled heap. On Broad Street, he dodged several branches that lay across the road and drove through a river of leaves that fluttered like enormous moths in the headlights.

He turned the car onto Fifth Avenue where there seemed to be no wind at all and found a place to park in an unlit, nearly deserted lot. The small, parking lot booth lay on its side and the attendant sat on the ground, leaning against it.

"Did you see a young boy and a dog?" Paul asked the young black man.

"Didn't see a thing." He rubbed his head.

"Need help?"

"Just the license number of whatever hit me."

Paul left him and ran toward the Space Needle which, for the first time in his memory, was dark. The evening air was now eerily still. After causing considerable destruction, the wind had vanished as quickly as it had arrived, leaving the normally impeccably maintained grounds littered with broken tree limbs, downed signs and large patches of roofing tar paper.

The Space Needle appeared to be deserted. Then he spotted the elevator stuck more than half-way up. He pushed open the entrance doors, stuck his head in and called out. A nervous woman's voice answered. A moment later, she appeared, a ghostly face in the lightless interior.

"There are people stuck up there," she pointed. "What do I do?"

"Just stay calm," Paul said. "Help will arrive soon." Would it, he wondered? There was no telling how widespread or extensive the damage was or where the wind might be headed now. This wind seemed capable of changing direction at will. But there was no time to ponder this now.

"Did you happen to see a boy and a dog?"

She nodded, surprised. "They were just here!"

"See which way they went?"

"Sorry."

118

He found a row of unlit pay phones at the Food Circus building and punched 911 to report the power outage. The first phone was dead. While he tried the second, a wave of trash and leaves floated in and around his legs like a chattering ocean wave that hid his shoes. The wave of detritus retreated thirty yards, then came again, continuing to build in size and strength as the phone went unanswered. The wind whistled in the trees. An intense burst slammed him against the phone stall. He pulled the hair out of his eyes in time to see a giant, black bat closing on him, wings flapping, deadly silver talons glinting in the moonlight. He dropped the phone and spun just as the bat smashed into the metal shelter.

He stared at the umbrella with bent spines and whose rapier-sharp point had pierced the metal side of the stall exactly where he had been standing. Another man might have crossed himself and reflected that life was too full of such strange mishaps. Because he was Indian and could more easily accept things he neither saw nor understood, Paul said instead, "Why have you come and why do you try to kill me?"

In the wind's murmured sigh, he almost thought he heard it answer. Then it retreated as if to gather itself, curl its rage beneath mighty wings, and launch itself once more. And in the momentary lull, he heard barking coming from somewhere near.

Evan huddled with Fortuno under the cold, soaking spray of the International Fountain, anxious to run away from this thing he could somehow smell and feel but not see, yet knowing instinctively that there was nowhere they could run fast enough to escape. Whatever it was, he knew full well from his experience in the alley that it could be deadly. Yet, as it had just demonstrated with the water, it could also perform the most wonderful tricks. So he kept his head down, arms wrapped around the dog, until, finally, the wind disappeared again and the fountain returned to normal. Only then did he look up.

None of the fallen leaves that littered the concrete plaza around the fountain stirred, yet Fortuno continued to bark, his body struggling for freedom, as if he still sensed the wind nearby. Evan let the dog pull him along on the length of twine, afraid of what he might discover, but also thrilled, as if he had stumbled across a grizzly bear in a city park.

Fortuno towed him away from the illuminated fountain toward the dark shadows and hulking, black shape of the Opera House. A column of trees provided a visual and sound barrier between Memorial Stadium and the rest of the Center. As they proceeded down the tree-lined walkway, the dog grew more and more agitated until, finally, it stopped. Evan knelt to pet the dog and read the terror in its frenzied barking and quivering limbs, in the eyes that no longer saw him. Love surged through him. With a pang of regret, he tied the cowering dog to the nearest tree. And then he walked softly onward by himself, goose bumps crowding the skin of his arms.

A few moments later, he saw it. At the very end of the row of motionless trees, one tree leaned and bobbed like a dancer listening to headphones. There was no turning back now. He had to know what it was that had killed the boys and followed him. As he approached cautiously, the tree became dead still except for the tiniest movement in its uppermost branches. Evan's throat grew dry.

It came gently at first, pushing, pulling, lifting him ever so slightly in his shoes. He resisted the urge to spread his arms, afraid he might actually fly. Instead, he kept his arms at his side, palms forward, to show that he meant no harm, aware that, if it wanted, it might kill him as easily as it had Monster and Rawhide. He stood, staring up into the tree while the wind alternately teased and bullied him. Stripped of their leaves, three long, slender, sucker-like branches swayed like snakes. One nearly touched his face, then jerked away. He felt the touch of another runner on the small of his back. All three branches were now pulling him toward the tree. Evan extended a hand slowly to touch the trunk, now just inches away, and forgot to breathe. Gingerly, he ran his fingers over its chipped and peeling bark. Then came a rushing, flooding, thundering avalanche of black pain as anger mushroomed in his head. It took him a stunned moment to realize that it wasn't his anger. Then he had to wrap his arms around its trunk and lock his hands together as the wind began whirling around him, faster and faster, sucking the air from his lungs.

Towering black clouds hid the moon and dappled the sky like a herd of Indian ponies as Paul ran toward the sound of a dog barking. At the end of the Food Circus building, he came upon the Flag Plaza where the poles that flew the flags of all fifty states during the daytime now lay snapped and strewn about like a gigantic game of pickup sticks. Beyond them, a dazzling oasis in the blacked-out Center, brilliant jets of colored water spouted and burst in time to the strains of a Bach fugue. Above the music of the International

Fountain's carillon bells, he heard the dog as it continued to bark, more hoarsely than before. He pressed on, running now, the bad feeling awakening the memory of his mother's horrible screams. He came upon the dog tied to a tree, straining against its twine leash. Paul left it leaping on two legs, the spittle flying from its jaws, and continued to run in the direction of the powerful sound of a waterfall.

At the end of a long row of cherry trees stripped of their leaves, he found the boy clinging desperately to the trunk of a tree. Around him whirled a miniature cyclone from whose center came a nearly deafening noise like rushing water. The air smelled like the frigid glacier water that clouded the rivers in spring, so cold that it took his breath away. Evan's shirt appeared to have been ripped off and his ribs shown plainly in his pale body. Even his shoes were missing. Paul started to come nearer when the boy's head lifted. Eyes huge and pleading, Evan shook his head in warning.

Paul circled the tree warily, the umbrella still fresh in his mind. He beckoned the boy with his hands. "Can you let go?" he mouthed the words.

Evan shook his head again.

Paul stretched out a hand in the midst of the howling melee. The wind screamed. Twigs, rock, and grit that were caught up in the cyclone slammed into his body, cut his face, stung his eyes and drove him back. He crouched down and reached again for the boy. The wind pounded him so that he had to crawl forward on his hands and knees while his lungs fought for air. It felt as though he were in a wind tunnel, unable to see clearly or breathe. A rock gashed his forehead and momentarily dazed him. He was almost there; another couple of inches and he would grab the boy and roll away. Just as he was about to touch the boy, the wind shrieked and he was sucked outwards, flying backwards at tremendous speed. An instant later, his back slammed against a wall. Paul slumped to the ground, stunned and helpless, the air knocked from his lungs. Searing pain enveloped his shoulder and the back of his head, numbing his fingers and toes. Before he had time to recover his breath, the wind swept him up again. He grabbed for a light post and had it ripped from his hand. He was flailing, sailing over the grass and concrete toward the glass entrance of the Opera House. As he passed, he glimpsed the boy, free now, take something from his pants pocket. Then, he wrapped his arms in front of his face, closed his eyes and prepared to die.

121

A moment before he would have plunged head-first through the twenty-foot high, plate glass windows, the wind suddenly died. Paul tumbled to a halt on the concrete entryway. For what seemed like a very long time, he lay spread-eagled, immobile, facing the sky, trying to get his breath back. Only with enormous willpower did he manage to turn his head and see the boy running barefoot toward him. Then he rested his cheek against the damp concrete and focused on breathing.

You okay? Evan asked, pointing at Paul and finger-spelling "O" and "K."

Paul nodded once, the effort causing pain to shoot through the back of his head. At last, he managed to sit up. He rubbed the back of his neck and pointed to the thing in Evan's hand. The boy held out the small metal cylinder and pretended to blow it before handing it to Paul. Paul examined the whistle before giving it back. Now was not the time to ask questions. Even if he and the boy managed to communicate, the wind might come back at any moment. They had to get moving. But first, he could see Evan's thin body shivering uncontrollably. He tried to peel his leather jacket off one shoulder and felt the sharp jab of pain return.

Evan tried to help, tugging gently on first one sleeve and then the other until the jacket came off. Paul offered it to the boy. Shyly, he wrapped himself in its warmth. He held his fists against his chest and thrust his open palms toward Paul as he struggled to rise. Paul grimaced, thinking that the boy was describing the wind playing with him like a tennis ball. Then he heard the chopper approaching.

Evan must have seen his concern reflected in his face. *What?* He shrugged his shoulders and cocked his head to one side.

Paul made circles in the air with one finger and pointed. Evan looked up as a blindingly bright light coming from a helicopter swooped in over the top of the Coliseum, its blades cutting the air like a giant lawn mower. Then Paul was up and, despite a bad limp, pushing the boy toward the chopper.

Evan pointed in the direction of the dog. Paul nodded and Evan ran to free it as Paul continued to hobble toward the shaft of light that circled among the wind-strewn flag poles.

Paul waved one arm to attract the attention of the helicopter as it hovered above the International Fountain. To his left, he saw the boy untie the dog and both come running to join him. Before they reached him, however, the dog stopped and cowered as if he'd been swatted across the nose. "Evan!" Paul yelled. His attention returned to the copter just as something seemed to snatch it by the tail and give it a shake. Paul limped as fast as he could back to where Evan stood, frozen in disbelief as the tiny dark shapes bounced around inside the glass cockpit. Then the copter flipped and headed down, spinning crazily. Paul knocked the boy to the ground and fell on him as the copter crash-landed in the fountain. A giant, yellow flower of flame blossomed in the center of several blue geysers as steaming-hot pieces of glass and metal rained upon them. And then the flower died.

12

Homecoming

SEATTLE, MONDAY, 7:45 P.M. The smell of wet dog mingled with the residual odors of burning plastic and aircraft fuel, saturating the car's passenger compartment and serving as a noxious reminder of their recent ordeal. Windows open, heater blasting warm air, the Mercedes droned past the few other cars headed north on Aurora Avenue toward the city's neighboring residential areas and away from downtown. Evan sat in the passenger seat, cradling the dog on his lap. Paul drove fast but warily, with an eye out for sudden gusts of wind or strange objects blowing across the road.

He felt guilty about not calling Denise. It was now well past the time he said he'd telephone her with an update. He could imagine her anxious state of mind, but none of the phones at the Center had worked, and they were now less than ten minutes away. Taking the time to locate a working phone seemed a waste of time.

After the copter crash, the wind had disappeared, leaving only a burned-out, black skeleton lying in the fountain like a huge, dead insect. One glance told Paul there weren't any survivors. Nor was there any reason for hanging around. Having experienced firsthand the wind's destructive power, he hadn't been about to take unnecessary risks in getting the boy home. They had both been through enough already. With him limping from a bruised hip, and the boy and dog following, they had crept back to the car in the shadows, avoiding the police and other emergency personnel beginning to arrive at the Center. There was nothing to be gained by staying and talking, Paul reasoned. Even if he could have explained what had happened, no one would have believed him. And besides, he didn't have any answers that made sense, at least for now.

He stole a glance to where the boy sat, shoulders hunched forward, staring at nothing, petting the dog over and over as if it were his only friend. He wondered what Denise's reaction would be when she saw her son. The kid had been through a lot. Before the helicopter crash, he had seemed much more animated. The explosion seemed to snuff out the boy's energy along with the lives of the men inside the copter. Paul hoped that it was just Evan's weariness and lack of vocal ability that was causing him to retreat within himself. Physically, the boy seemed to have come through his ordeal pretty well, just a lot of superficial scratches and some bruises. But who knew what wounds might lie undetected, just beneath the surface—especially if his own boyhood experiences were any guide? Paul's hands tightened on the steering wheel as they hurtled across the long George Washington Bridge, spanning the Lake Washington Ship Canal.

A few turns after exiting the highway, they were pulling into a driveway, two narrow ribbons of concrete separating two of the modest World-War-I-era bungalows so prevalent in Wallingford. Paul put a hand on the boy's shoulder and shook him. When he didn't move, Paul reached across the boy's lap and opened the door. Evan glanced up at him briefly, then climbed out and walked around the car, the dog close on his heels. Denise burst through the front door and came running down the porch steps. She knelt in the ankle-length grass, hugging the boy to her. Determined not to be left out, the dog stood on his hind legs and licked the faces of both son and mom. Paul turned off the engine and sat for a while, too sore to move. He tried to imagine what it must be like to be a single mother trying to raise a deaf kid and waiting by the phone to learn if he was safe. People used to say that women were "the weaker sex." Now there was a fine myth.

When Denise finally let go of her son, tears glistened on her cheeks in the glow from a streetlight. "Where have you been?" she asked, signing and speaking simultaneously. "And where are your clothes? Your shoes and shirt are missing and your hair looks as if it's been permed in a blender!" She wiped a small cut on his cheek with one hand. "And what in God's name are all these scratches?" She stared at the numerous tiny tracks of dried blood that stood out on his pale skin. "Are you okay?"

Evan turned to the dog, pretending not to "hear" her. Denise tugged until he looked at her. "What's the matter, Evan?"

She shot a worried look at Paul who was still sitting in the car with the window rolled down. "He's like a zombie. What happened?"

"Give him a little time. He's probably exhausted," Paul said, his weary voice adding credibility to his words.

But Denise was anxious to know what had happened. "Dammit, Evan, what's going on?" she said, forgetting to sign and shaking her son in frustration. "Those shoes were brand new. And where's your backpack?"

Evan glanced away, the bare toes of one foot stubbing the grass.

Denise sighed. "Who's your buddy?" she nodded toward the dog.

He finger-spelled the name.

"Fortune—Fortuno?" Denise asked, petting the anxious dog and searching for a license tag. "That's an interesting name. Do you know who he belongs to?"

Paul climbed out of the car and was unexpectedly moved when the boy came running back to take his arm.

Denise followed her son. "Oh, my God. What happened to your face! Will somebody please tell me what happened? You both look like you've been through a war."

Paul and Evan exchanged a look that said neither was anxious to be first with an explanation.

"Did you get in an accident? You didn't phone. I was afraid something terrible had happened—and, from the look of you both, I was right!"

Before Paul could answer Denise, they both heard the phone ring.

"Is that yours?"

"Probably Officer Dowling," she said. "I've been calling him every ten minutes for the last two hours. Come in and get cleaned up. I'll make dinner," she shouted to Paul as she ran up the stairs to answer the phone.

Evan climbed up the porch, still wearing Paul's leather jacket, the dog following. Paul closed the door to the Mercedes and studied the night sky while listening to the hum of traffic emanating from the nearby Interstate 5 freeway.

"Who are you?" he asked softly. "What brother of the wind comes to the white man's city and why?"

Something was out there, causing mayhem and killing people. While this disturbed and even frightened him, the wind's mystery did not trouble him to the same degree that it would have affected the typical white, raised on the rigid disciplines of logic and science. A deeply spiritual woman, his grandmother had taught him to believe that life was one big and, for the most part, beautiful enigma. Pretending to comprehend it was arrogant, not to mention foolhardy. Failure to live in harmony with nature was to break the sacred hoop and invite calamity, such as the death and destruction

126

brought now by the wind. Given the disrespectful abuse of land, sea, and air by generations of whites, it was hardly surprising to an Indian that retribution was finally come.

Denise, on the other hand, would need a rational explanation. So would quite a few other people after tonight, including the police. He and the boy had probably as good a description of the wind as anyone—if you could describe something that was invisible. But Paul didn't want to be the one to explain this. Let some other poor fool try, he thought as he limped up the porch steps. Living in a white world was difficult enough without taking on the thankless task of trying to convince an entire race of people that what they knew as "truth" was, in fact, just a hypothesis. Funny how the same people that could accept the miracle birth and resurrection of Jesus could not for a minute understand the Indian concept of a spirit-animated world.

At the door, the whispering sound of the breeze rustling leaves in a plum tree made him turn one last time before going inside. A covey of leaves rattled down the sidewalk and, for an anxious moment, he feared that the wind might have heard his thoughts and come to finish the job it had started earlier. He waited several seconds, his breathing slowly returning to normal. It was nothing, he decided.

He washed his hands in the bathroom sink, then dabbed with a wet rag at the dried blood from the laceration on his forehead where the rock had hit him. He would have a nasty scab for a while, but didn't think it needed stitches. Too many facial scars were probably not good for one's career, especially an attorney. "Settling out of court" might give someone the wrong idea. There was very little he could do for his other aches and pains. His left hip was swollen and tender from striking the pavement in front of the Opera House and his shoulder felt stiff and raw—too stiff to lift his sweatshirt to get a look at the damage. He found a bottle of Extra Strength Tylenol in the medicine cabinet and downed four.

After completing his self-inspection and cleanup, Paul wandered through the tiny dining room to the kitchen, noticing the books of poetry that lined the top of an antique sideboard. Denise looked up from opening a large jar of marinara sauce as he entered the kitchen where the air was already dense with steam from a large kettle of boiling water. When he had seen her earlier that day, she had worn a dark business suit. Now, she wore blue jeans and a long-sleeved, white peasant blouse. Her casual dress and lack of makeup made her look softer and more vulnerable. Tired as he was, he decided that he was very glad to see her again.

"Hope you like spaghetti," she said. "Besides being one of the few things I know how to cook, it's about the only edible thing left in the house. I have this habit of eating when I'm upset."

The boy and dog bolted into the room. Evan smelled of soap from a hasty shower. He wore striped pajamas in a size too large. Denise caught him by the sleeve and bent to look him in the eyes.

"Evan, I told you the dog can stay, but only if you keep him on the back porch. Put some baloney in a bowl and water in another."

"Any chance there's a cold beer with my name on it?" Paul asked, as the boy dug through the refrigerator.

"Sorry. There might be a bottle of wine hiding above the fridge."

"Sounds fine." Paul found the bottle and began rummaging through drawers for a corkscrew.

"Second drawer, center. But first, let me see that cut," Denise took his arm and made him turn so she could inspect his face. She smoothed a few loose strands of hair away from his eyes with her fingertips. "Not too bad. You could let your hair hang down over your forehead for a few days and no one would ever notice. Now, lift your shirt."

"What for? I'm okay."

"No, you're not. I saw you wince earlier and again just now." She lifted the neck of his sweatshirt and stood on tiptoes to have a look. "There's blood on your shoulder. Here," Denise pulled a pair of scissors from the drawer where she'd told him to look for the cork-screw. "Let's try this."

"Wait," he started to protest, but she was already starting to cut through the waistband.

He heard her intake of breath as she pulled the two halves of his sweatshirt away from where it stuck to his back. "Wow! That must have hurt." He leaned against the counter, adjusting most of his weight onto his good right leg, as she sponged his shoulder and back gently with a wet towel.

"Please tell me what happened to you and Evan. Were you at-tacked?"

"Not in the way you probably think. Let the boy tell it. I think it will help him if he gets it out. Otherwise, it will eat away at him. Later, I can fill in any gaps." He went back to pulling the cork.

"So that *what* doesn't eat at him? I tried again upstairs to get him to talk while coaxing him into the shower. Nothing. Just this off-in-the-ozone-look. He has these tiny little scratches and bruises every-where that he wouldn't tell me about either. Now, I see that you're in even worse shape. Won't you at least tell me why Evan was wearing your coat, and why there's no trace of his jacket, shirt, or shoes?"

As he released it from the bottle, the cork made a loud pop. "It's a weird story."

"How weird?" she said.

"Very. And I only know part of it."

"Hang on a sec. I'll get some bandages." She returned a minute later with a tube of ointment, gauze, and tape.

He was silent while she snipped tape and bandaged his shoulder. Then she opened the door to a small laundry room. She reappeared holding a flannel work shirt. "Here. My dad's. Try it on. Speaking of weird, that phone call wasn't the police. It was a woman who said she was supposed to call me to come get Evan. She claimed she'd been stuck on the elevator at the Space Needle for over thirty minutes."

While Denise was assisting Paul with the shirt, the sleeves of which were at least two inches too short, Evan reappeared from feeding the dog and saw them. He made the sign Paul had seen earlier, thrusting clenched fists outward from his chest.

"He says you were very brave," Denise said. "Why, Evan?" Denise signed back, her impatience obvious not only by her voice but by the way her hands jabbed in the air. "Tell me now what happened."

The boy looked down, but Denise caught his chin in her hand, forcing him to look at her. "Listen to me," she said. "I'm your mother. That makes me head chef, valet, chauffeur, and witch doctor, not to mention sole provider. For the last four hours, I've been going nuts wondering where you were and what had happened to you."

Evan twisted his face out of her hand.

"Evan Baker!" Denise's hands signed forcefully. "Either you tell me now what happened or, so help me, you can forget dinner."

Still he refused to sign.

"Go to your room then! And stay there until you're ready to treat me with a little respect." The boy turned and left, climbing the stairs slowly to his room. Denise looked at Paul. Tears again streaked her cheeks and her pale skin was flushed. "What am I doing wrong?"

"Guess I better go first." Paul handed her a glass of wine. "Mind if we sit down?"

Denise turned the burner under the kettle of now overcooked noodles to low and Paul followed her to the tiny dining room table. He figured starting with the hard facts was the best way. "A police helicopter went down right in front of us."

"A helicopter? Was anybody hurt?"

"Two men. Both dead."

"Good Lord. Evan's probably in shock." Denise stood.

"Wait." Paul put a hand on her arm. "There's more." He could hear footsteps, a chair scraping the floor, as the boy moved around upstairs. Good. That meant he wasn't lying on his bed, overcome with grief. "You asked if we were attacked? Well, you guessed right. Only it wasn't people that attacked the boy and me. It . . ." He paused and sipped the wine. "This isn't going to be easy."

"Try me," Denise said.

"It was the wind."

"The wind?" She shook her head in confusion. "What do you mean?"

Paul shrugged. "I warned you it wasn't going to be easy."

"You were attacked by the wind?"

"That's what got the chopper, too."

Denise stared at the ceiling.

"Well," he said after a while, the frown that creased her forehead and her silence making him uneasy, "aren't you going to laugh, or at least tell me I'm crazy?"

"Oh, sorry, Paul. I was thinking about something strange that happened at the Tower. Just before the panel fell, there was a big gust of wind," Denise said. "It was strong enough that it knocked down the flags and blew me onto my rear end. But even before that, there were all these birds and a smell like—I don't know. . . ."

"Like spruce trees?" Paul asked.

Denise nodded. "That's it! I couldn't have said what kind of trees, but yeah. And, one more thing: it was cold."

"Freezing?"

"Exactly." Denise rubbed her arms beneath the sleeves of her blouse. "So you felt it, too?"

"Not then, but tonight." He nodded.

"What could do that?"

"I'm not sure."

Denise started to stand again. "I think it's time I go upstairs and apologize to my son."

"Before you do," Paul said, "I'd like to make a suggestion. I know it's got to be tough seeing your son behave like this, especially after what I just told you, but maybe I should talk—visit—with him first."

Denise stared at the ceiling, as if trying to see through the floor above and into her son's room.

"Just for a few minutes," he added. "It might help him sort it out. Let the horror of tonight fade a bit."

"You'll bring him back down with you?" she asked.

"I'll do my best."

She nodded. "You saved his life again. Even after I deserted you today."

He stood, looked down into her face as he considered her words. "Some things are just destined to be."

He climbed the stairs slowly, favoring his sore hip. When he reached the landing, there was a sliver of light coming from the door to one of the rooms. He knocked. Evan's face appeared a moment later. When he saw who it was, he opened the door. Paul entered the small room and looked around. Evan sat down in front of a computer and resumed typing away on the keyboard. The screen appeared full of small blocks of text, probably messages. A baseball bat leaned against a corner. One wall bore a large map of the U.S. Against another was a bookcase, its top shelf lined with soccer trophies. Paul picked one up. Evan sneaked a look over one shoulder as he studied it. The lower shelves contained several software packages and a number of books, including a large, pictorial volume on horses. Paul leafed through it. When he had found the page he wanted, he showed the boy, pointing first at the horse, then himself.

Evan pointed to the computer screen, typed, *What's his name?* Then leaned to one side, inviting Paul to use the computer to answer.

Still standing, Paul typed his reply, *Yakima.*

Can I see him sometime? Evan typed.

You can ride him.

The boy's head jerked around. His hands flew through a dozen signs. Paul understood only the "you" and "me" part. He nodded yes, then typed on the computer again. *That was hard on your mom tonight, not knowing where you were.*

Evan's head hung so low, Paul couldn't see his expression. *Don't you think you should tell her about it? Help her understand how you're feeling?* He waited.

At last, Evan typed, *Maybe. Some of it.*

What part don't you want to tell her?

The two boys that the wind killed. When Evan looked at him, Paul thought his eyes seemed much older, sadder, even hopeless.

When? Paul entered on the keyboard. *Where did this happen?*

This afternoon. Downtown. After I found the dog, two boys caught me in an alley. They were going to hurt me. Then the wind came. It ran over the fat one with a garbage bin. Then it cut off the other one's head.

Paul stared at him. Evan shuddered and tears began to well in his eyes. Paul knelt and pulled the boy to him. Evan buried his face against Paul's chest and gave in to his tears. Sobs racked his shoulders. Paul held the boy tightly for several minutes until at last he felt him relax. Evan sat up and wiped his eyes and nose with one arm of his pajamas.

"Better?" Paul asked.

Evan nodded.

"Let's keep this between you and me for now, okay?"

Evan finger-spelled, "OK."

"Tell me about the whistle. Can I see it?"

Evan jumped up and hurried to his dresser. The whistle was hidden away in his sock drawer. He presented it to Paul, then typed, *I think it's a dog whistle. The blind man gave it to me.*

Paul studied it for the second time, noting the manufacturer's name stamped in the metal.

Do you want it?

No. That's all right, Paul typed and handed it back. *I think you should keep it. I don't know about you, but I'm starving. Shall we go see your mom now?*

Evan stood. Paul put his hand on the boy's shoulder and, together, they went back downstairs. Denise still sat at the tiny dining table, her back turned to them. The dog lay at her feet. At the sound of their footsteps, she turned in her chair to face the boy in his ill-fitting pajamas. Evan hung his head, focusing his attention on the dog. When at last he was ready, he signed his mother and, for the first time, Paul heard him speak. "Sorry."

"Unstable air," Billy snorted. "That's putting it mildly." The red-headed, pseudo-scientist, television weather forecaster with the spectacular chest was insisting that the pocket of highly unstable air that had plagued Seattle over the past three days, most recently at the Seattle Center, was now history. Billy was frustrated being in a hospital with his butt in the air like a beached whale instead of out covering the city's news, like the dead helicopter police. But, most of all, he was pissed at himself for blowing the Tower story.

"I don't get it. Something's wrong with this picture."

"Ease up, Billy," Julie said.

"If God had given that woman brains half the size of her breasts, she'd be another Einstein. Hell, she could even be God! Unstable air. That's like blaming murder on unstable people. How unspecific can you get?"

"Hey, hey, Mr. William S. Mossman." His wife waved her arms overhead as if trying to stop a runaway train which was a fairly decent analogy. "Slow down a bit. You know how I feel about silicone-endowed bimbos. I'm usually the first to throw stones. But aren't you overreacting just a wee bit?"

"Go home, Julie," he growled and glanced at his watch. "Visitors' hours are over, the painkiller is wearing off and I've got some pretty ugly truths staring me in the face." Billy stabbed the remote control and the television screen went blank with a crackle of electricity.

"Seems to me, you're lucky to be alive."

"Call it dumb luck with a capital D. Sorry, kid. I hate to be the one to tell you, but you married an idiot."

"So what's new?" Julie smiled. "Just remember, you said it, not me." She dodged the pillow that he threw at her head, then got up from her chair and sat on the edge of his hospital bed. "I've never seen you this self-critical." She stroked his head. "Why?"

"I was wrong."

"Of course you were. After all, you're a male." She laughed. "Which time are you referring to?"

"The Tower story."

"Why should you know better than anyone else what the real cause of these strange occurrences is? Outside of God, who really knows anything?"

"I know. Me," Billy answered bitterly, thumping his chest with one hand. "Those deaths I wrote about weren't the mayor's fault; they weren't even the developer's fault, much as it galls me to say it. Those guys were just victims, just like the two cops on that helicopter or the carload of trick-or-treaters that ended up in Lake Washington."

"Let me get this straight," Julie said. "You're the only person responsible for finding out the truth."

"That's my job."

Julie started to protest when Gretta appeared in the doorway and waved. If she had heard them arguing, she didn't let on.

"Sorry to drop by so late. Okay if I come in, Mr. Mossman? Boots in security told me about the accident."

"Hello, Gretta. Grab a chair. Julie, this is Gretta Taylor. She intends to graduate from Washington State University School of Journalism in December. Unfortunately, she had the bad luck to be assigned to me for her internship."

"This man is as good a journalist as there is, Gretta," Julie said, watching the young woman sit down. "Just don't believe half of what he says. You two can talk shop. I'm going home." She bent over Billy to kiss him on the top of the head. "You told me you had an intern," she whispered, "but you didn't say she was six feet tall and pretty."

Billy grinned sheepishly and waved his wife good-bye.

"I'll be in tomorrow, whenever they open. Get some rest," she said before exiting the room.

"How are you?" Billy asked Gretta abruptly. "Take the afternoon off?"

"Fine. Hardly. Are you always so warm and friendly?"

"Always."

"Remember the two boys that drowned off Whidbey? I attended the briefing this afternoon."

Billy's eyebrows lifted. "I'm impressed. Find out anything?"

"Coast Guard officer said there was no sign of foul play."

"What about the coroner?" Billy asked.

She shrugged. "They drowned."

"That's all?"

"That's all."

"No drugs?"

"Nothing."

"So who the hell tied 'em up? They have any enemies?"

"Not that anybody knows of. Captain Woodbury called it an unsolved mystery."

"Unsolved mystery, huh?" Billy scowled. "Sounds a lot like 'unstable air.'"

134

"What?"

"You know what the problem is, Gretta?"

She shook her head, a look of earnest confusion spreading across her face, but he couldn't stop now. The biggest story he'd handled in ten years and he'd botched it.

"Reality is a hell of a lot stranger than fiction. An entirely different dimension. Tell me: could anybody make this shit up? Here's a bunch of reporters covering a tragic accident caused by a freak wind that strikes a brand-new office tower when yet another freak wind strikes the same office tower—all within forty-eight hours."

"Pretty freaky," Gretta agreed. "How are you anyway?" She tried to change the subject. "I was worried about whether you'd even be conscious. They said you were badly injured."

"Nah, it's nothing. Just a little granite in the ass. What's happening at the *Times*?"

"You heard about the police helicopter crash? Everyone's still at the plant. The place is a zoo."

"Yeah, I heard—about fifty-three times, so far." He gestured toward the boob tube mounted on the wall. "What's the scoop?"

"The SPD spokesman says based on their initial evaluation, the cause was either a severe malfunction, wind shear, pilot error or some combination."

"That's really pinning it down. Those idiots."

"They've had me proofing all the stuff as fast as it's written, so I probably know as much as anyone at the *Times*. The information so far says they were hovering over the International Fountain, when suddenly, for no apparent reason, the helicopter fell to the ground."

"Know who the chief investigator is yet?"

"Yeah, a guy named Rizzo-something."

"Rizzoletti. I know him. A good guy. Can you get me his telephone number and where I can reach him tomorrow?"

"I guess so. Sure. Soon as I get back."

The lights blinked twice and a woman's voice announced over the intercom that visitors' hours were now over.

"Fucking way to die," Billy said.

Gretta nodded and remained silent.

"Keep me posted, Gretta. Anything and everything. You're my arms and legs now."

The young woman rose to leave. Well, arms maybe. Those definitely weren't his legs.

"Say," Billy had another thought, "remember that old broad that called this morning, just as I was going out the door? What was her name?"

"Sorry, Billy. I don't think she said."

"That's okay. Listen, I want to talk to her. Can you get somebody in accounting to print out a list of my incoming calls? Shouldn't be too difficult to find her. Said she was calling from one of the islands—San Juan, I think."

"Sure. I didn't know they kept track of calls like that."

"What's the matter? You been talking to your sweetheart in Spokane every night? Don't worry about it, kid. They keep track of everything. Nothing better to do."

"When are you coming in?"

"I'm getting out tomorrow, but I'm gonna have to work at home for a couple days until my butt heals enough so I can sit down. No big deal. I'll just modem my stuff in. By the way, you're getting baptized in the newspaper business. Tired?"

"Not at all. Are you kidding? This is great!"

"Careful, kid. Once you get ink in your veins, you're hooked. It's pretty powerful stuff."

"I can handle it."

"Yeah?" Billy studied her. Lack of confidence was clearly not her problem. "Call me as soon as you got anything."

"Don't worry." She stood up. "I won't let you down."

Evan skipped over the stuff on the bus and picked up the story with the appearance of the blind man's dog, the words tumbling out in aerodynamic bursts. Mother and son's hands flew fast as nighthawks. Denise also spoke to clarify her signing as well as to help Paul follow their conversation.

"Wait a minute. What blind man?" Denise asked. "How do you know him?" Paul ate in silence and listened intently to Denise repeat what the boy signed.

The old man that always sits on the sidewalk by your office.

"He's old and blind?" Denise's eyes widened. "You mean that pathetic creature sleeping on our back porch is somebody's seeing eye dog? Evan Baker! How's the poor man going to get around? He may be lost, wandering around downtown. . . . Oh, my God." She held her face in her hands. "Didn't you try to find him?"

That's why I was late getting to your office, Evan lied. *We looked ev-*

erywhere we could think of. He took another mouthful of spaghetti and glanced at Paul.

"Ask him if he means the white-haired beggar that sits in front of the banjo place on Second Avenue."

Denise didn't have to sign. Evan began nodding enthusiastically even before Paul had finished his description.

"You know him?" Denise asked Paul.

"I don't know his name, but he should be easy to find. He's been a fixture in that same spot for years."

"Don't seeing eye dogs usually have a collar or something?"

Paul nodded. "The ones I've seen usually wear a harness, at least when they're working. I seem to remember that the old man's dog also wore a red kerchief around his neck."

Denise and Paul both looked at the boy who was chewing a piece of bread and studiously ignoring them. Denise tapped the top of his head to get his attention.

"Did the dog have a harness and a red bandanna?" she asked.

Evan nodded.

"And did you take them off?"

No. There was a short pause. *I mean, yes.* Evan squirmed uncomfortably, remembering the alley. Fortuno had somehow managed to break his harness in order to bite the boy he called Monster. The red bandanna must have come off at the same time. But he couldn't tell his mother that.

"That's just great," Denise said, frowning. "Now what do we do, call the police again to locate a missing blind man? Officer Dowling will have me committed."

"There's a police sub-station located in Pioneer Square," Paul said. "Call and ask if someone reported a missing seeing eye dog. Tell 'em we think it belongs to the old man that sits in front of the banjo place on First Avenue every day. They'll know who you mean. Probably even know where to find him."

Denise called the police while Evan finished his third helping of spaghetti. Paul gathered the empty plates. Denise hung up the phone just as he was preparing to wash them.

"Please sit down, Paul," she said. "You've done enough for one day." Her words reminded them both of the scene at the Tower. For just a moment, both were silent as they remembered the earlier incident.

"What'd the police say?" he asked.

"You were right," Denise said. "There's only one person there tonight—a woman. She didn't know his name, but she knew him. No one has called or reported a missing dog, however."

"Did she know where he lives?"

"Just that he lives somewhere near, probably a shelter."

"I'll check to see if he shows up in his usual spot tomorrow," Paul said.

"What if he doesn't? What if he's hurt? Could Evan get in trouble?"

"Don't worry. If he doesn't show up, I can ask around, see if anyone knows where he is."

Can we keep Fortuno? Evan asked.

Denise reached out a hand and touched her son's arm briefly before signing. "I'm sorry, Evan, but we can't keep someone else's animal, especially a seeing eye dog. We'll have to give him back."

Evan didn't think that the blind man would be claiming his dog. Whenever he tried to remember the old man, all he could see was a blank space where his face should be.

"Tell me the rest of the story," his mother signed. "What happened after you got to my office?"

And so he told her and Paul about sitting in front of her door, of running back to the stores and finding them empty, of getting a bus ride downtown and then taking the monorail. When he told about the mean lady in the souvenir shop and the crowds of people that wouldn't stop to read his note, his mother looked away, biting her lip. Then he told them about taking the monorail to the Seattle Center, meeting the young woman at the Space Needle, and chasing the dog.

Evan paused in his story, not sure how to continue.

"Go on," Denise signed, then squeezed his arm in encouragement.

I saw this thing, playing in the fountain, making the water do weird stuff.

"What thing? What exactly did you see?" Denise frowned. Paul remained silent.

I don't know. I couldn't really see it—just what it was doing to the water. Then it left.

"What did you and the dog do then? Is that when Paul found you?"

He shook his head. *We followed it.*

"Followed it? I thought you couldn't see it."

138

I couldn't. But the dog knew where it was. It made him crazy. He barked and growled a lot. I had to tie him to a tree. Then I walked closer, real slow.

"So, did you find whatever it was?"

He nodded. *It was in the tree, the last one. It made the branches shake. I was just watching. Then it grabbed me.* Evan realized he had forgotten to breathe and sucked in a loud breath. The room seemed too tight, the air too thin. His mother was sitting straight in her chair. Paul stared at his wine.

Denise signed for Evan to continue.

The blood rushed to his cheeks as he described the wind's anger, how it had shrieked inside his head.

"You heard something making angry talk inside your head?" Denise's eyebrows shot up. "Evan, this is no time for stories!"

He looked to Paul for support.

"Why was the wind angry?" Paul asked. He glanced up at Denise to sign for him, but Evan shook his head that it wasn't necessary.

The boy's hands trembled as he signed. *Bad people hurt it. Now it will hurt them back.*

"What bad people?" his mother asked. "And why did it hurt you and Paul? You aren't bad people."

All bad. We're its enemy. A tear grew heavy, spilled from one of his eyes and cascaded down his cheek.

Denise got down on her knees and hugged him to her. "Thank God you're safe," she said, looking into his eyes and squeezing his shoulders tightly in her hands. "That sounds really scary. But you're home now and I'm going to take care of you. I want you to forget it ever happened. It's gone. Whatever it was. Forever."

Paul watched as Denise led Evan back upstairs to bed. He ran a hand down his tender hip and was not at all convinced that the wind was gone. But he hoped that her words would help the boy.

13

The Visitant

SEATTLE, MONDAY, 9:33 P.M. Paul yawned and closed his eyes, willing his bruised and tired muscles to relax, like flat stones sinking in a quiet pool. He could hear Denise moving around upstairs. It was a family-sort of sound—a sound that he had heard all too infrequently in his thirty-five years.

He needed to get home and get some rest. Tomorrow was a work-day and, after today's events, he would be even more behind in his caseload than normal, a status he could ill afford. Leaving the white woman and her son now, however, was more difficult than he would have ever imagined just a few hours earlier. He found himself being drawn inexorably closer to the boy. Both were loners. In Evan's deafness and his own skin color, they also shared a kinship in handicaps they had to overcome. Or maybe it was simply the kid's incredible bravery that attracted him. Whatever it was, this development, while surprising, didn't especially disturb him. Having missed out on the benefits of having a father himself, he found that their growing bond rather pleased him. Denise, on the other hand, was another matter entirely. He smiled, remembering her ordering him around earlier while inspecting and bandaging his injuries. He would not soon forget the touch of her hands. And by filling his wineglass before excusing herself to put Evan to bed, she had seemed to indicate that she wanted him to stay. He fought his urge to want this woman, and even more alarming, to trust her.

He left the unfinished glass of wine on the table and stood. He was almost to the door when he heard Denise's soft footsteps coming back down the stairway. He turned to say good-bye, instead found his eyes lingering over the way her breasts pressed against the soft cotton blouse, the lean length of her legs and the narrowness of her pale ankles.

"Please don't go yet," she said. "We have a lot to talk about." She put an arm, slim and white, through his and led him to the sofa in the living room. "Evan said you were very brave tonight. That you risked your life to save his." She folded her legs beneath her on the small couch.

Paul also sat down, ignoring the stiffening in his hip, and shrugged. "I'd say he was probably responsible for saving mine, too, although I'm not sure how."

Denise leaned forward. "Okay, you're going to have to help me out here. How is it possible that a thirteen-year-old could save your life? Please understand, I'm the mom that has to show him how to hang up his clothes and occasionally how to untie his shoes."

"I was on my way to becoming a big hit at the Opera House when he blew this whistle and the wind just stopped."

"A big hit, as in kapow?"

He nodded.

"A whistle? I don't understand."

"Looked like a dog whistle." Paul shook his head as he considered all the disconcerting questions this day had brought. "To satisfy my own curiosity. I'm going to check into the whistle, and some other things. I don't know that I'll learn much if anything. You know, all this happened just a couple of hours ago, yet it already sounds ridiculous—even to me. Frankly, I'm surprised you haven't phoned the men in white coats long before this."

"You must be kidding. One look at the bruise on your shoulder and the marks on my son was enough to convince me that the two of you underwent a major ordeal. And, after the horse nearly ran Evan down on Saturday, nothing really surprises me anymore. Besides," her eyes held his, "you don't seem like the type."

"What type is that?"

"To make up a story like that." The muscles in her jaw tightened. "I learned several things today—none of them very flattering. I thought I had friends—people I could count on for help. Yet you're the only one who came when I called and I know nothing about you. I don't even know if you have a family. Your wife is probably at home, putting the kids to bed and wondering where you are even as we speak."

"No." He smiled at her unlikely description. "No wife, no family."

"Girlfriend then."

"No girlfriend either."

"Boyfriend?" She raised her eyebrows.

"No. No boyfriends."

"I didn't think so, but you never know. So, tell me: how did a man with a name like Paul Judge become an attorney—or is it just another made-up name, like Oceanview Estates?"

"It's my real name. Also, a very boring story."

"I'm a good listener."

"In the old days," he began, "it was customary for an Indian to have a name that was the result of a vision quest, or described a particularly telling incident in his or her life. Signs of wealth or acts of bravery were very popular. In the case of my grandmother, she became the judge of our tribe after the death of my grandfather. Whenever one member of our tribe had a dispute with another, they would come to her to settle it. When it was time for me to enter school, she had them write in her last name, Judge."

"Do people tease you about your name?"

"All the time, but they also remember it."

"What kind of cases do you handle?"

"None that you've heard about. I'm a public defender. Mostly I handle indigents."

"How noble."

"Not really. I was trained in criminal law. In fact, I thought I was going to be a prosecuting attorney. A big star." He shrugged. "This was the best I could do."

"Because of your skin color?"

He paused, her boldness surprising him. "Perhaps the need is greater where I ended up."

"Yeah, right. I wish I felt as generous about others' motivations as you."

"Do I detect a trace of bitterness?"

"Sorry. Must be the wine. My daddy always said my mouth would get me in trouble." She took a sip from her glass and quickly changed the subject. "You mentioned your grandmother. What about your parents? Are they still alive?"

"I have no idea."

"Goodness! Open mouth, insert foot."

"It's okay. It happened a long time ago. We lived in a little one-room shack in Butte. They fought a lot. My father was a miner. Never came home until he was drunk. One night, after I had gone to bed—I was maybe five or six years old—he started hitting her. I tried to make him stop, but I was too small." He studied his hands. "He dragged her outside, screaming. After a while, the screams stopped. I never saw either of them again. The next morning, my grandmother drove up in an old pickup truck and hauled me off to the res.''

"Is your grandmother still alive?"

"She died during my sophomore year of college."

"Any brothers or sisters?"

He shook his head. "What about you?"

She sighed. "Mom and Dad still live in the same house in Spokane where I grew up. Dad had a heart bypass operation two years ago. Now, he's scared to be away from his doctor or his medication for very long, so they don't get around much anymore. I had an older brother once. He died when I was just a kid—about Evan's age. Cystic fibrosis; never even graduated from high school. I'd give anything to have him back. I can't tell you how many times I've wished I had a brother to talk to. And yet—this sounds terrible—I can't remember what he looked like. Isn't that awful?

"When I met Ron, my ex-husband, it was like I'd finally found the brother I'd missed. Unfortunately, we got married. Biggest mistake of my life. Turned out we were just pals—not soul mates. I was too young and stupid to know the difference."

Paul looked into her eyes and felt rising conflict, wanting to protect her, yet fearful, too.

"How long have you been divorced?"

"Since Evan was a year old."

"Must have been difficult."

She laughed ruefully. "Worse than difficult. Evidently, I had contracted the rubella virus while I was carrying Evan. At any rate, he was born deaf, but we didn't know at first. When he was about six months, we started to get scared that something might be wrong. Ron's parents thought he was retarded. They blamed me. Even before we had Evan tested, Ron suggested we consider institutionalizing him. Now, when I look back, I can see he was just worried about finishing school. But, at the time, I lost it. Told him to get lost. Threw his stuff out on the lawn. Even had the locks changed. It's been just the two of us ever since. I had to get a job, finish school and see that Evan got the special care that he needed."

"You've done a good job. He's a neat kid. Can anything be done about his hearing?"

"We're doing as much as we can. He's in a private school for the deaf where they learn to sign, read lips and even speak. His advisor says he's getting good enough that he can transfer to a public high school, if he chooses. But he's shy—like I was. Doesn't like to practice talking in front of people. I don't know. It's his decision.

"As for treatment," she said, "they say there's no hope for congenital deafness, but I read the medical journals and talk to the specialists. It kills me to think that he may never be able to hear music, or laughter."

She pulled her knees up and hugged them to her chest.

"Let's talk about today. What do you think it was—the thing that attacked you and Evan? He said it spoke to him in his head."

"I don't know." Paul shook his head, remembering.

"It scares me when he says he hears things in his head," Denise said. "I've never told this to anyone else, but he thinks he knows what's going to happen to some people. Talk about creepy. I don't know whether it's total baloney or not. I mean, what can I do? Walk up to a perfect stranger and warn them to stay away from railroad crossings for the next few days? Once, he made me call my mother to make sure she was all right. Turned out she was just on her way out the door to go shopping. So, we had a nice chat and hung up. Five minutes later, she tripped over a rake in the garage and broke her hip. Maybe we should put together an act—'Madame Lazonga and Her Wonderboy Tell Your Future While You Wait.' Cash in advance only, please."

Paul laughed softly. "I wondered why you were so interested in learning about shamans and second sight earlier today. Sounds like Evan could have some pretty strong medicine."

"What's that mean?"

"It's another way of saying he may have spiritual or psychic gifts."

"You believe in that stuff?"

"Grandma had what the people in the tribe used to call 'big medicine.' After I started high school, I remember walking with her one day in the tall prairie grass and she said 'Listen.' I couldn't hear a thing. Grandmother said, 'No, boy, listen with your heart, not just your ears.' I tried, but I still couldn't hear anything at first. Then, after a while, maybe the hum of bees searching among the clover or the whisper of the wind. 'Listen to the ancestors,' Grandmother said. 'Our ancestors are here. Everywhere are ancestors. Today they are happy.'"

"Did you ever hear them—the ancestors?"

"Not until after she died. I won a scholarship to Gonzaga University, but the competition and pressure were incredible. To top it off, I wasn't exactly popular. One night, during my sophomore

144

year, somebody jimmied the lock on the Coke machine in the dormitory and stole the money. I got blamed."

"Why you?"

"Some pretty strong circumstantial evidence. I was the only one staying there at the time. I had no money, no family. Couldn't go home for Thanksgiving vacation like the others. Mostly, I was just Indian. Anyway, the upperclassmen decided to hold a trial. There was no proof, of course, just a lot of accusations. Even though I was officially cleared, I became an outcast. One day, I decided to skip classes and hitchhike back to the same meadow where Grandmother had tried to teach me to listen. I wasn't sure I could make it through school and was feeling sorry for myself. All afternoon, I tried listening with my heart, like Grandmother had said. Nothing. I sat there, getting more and more hungry and cold. And then, just before the sun went down, the clouds drifted away and a warm breeze sprang up. It felt like eighty degrees, yet this was early December. I believe that it was Grandmother's spirit that I felt on the prairie that day."

"So what are you saying? That what happened at the Tower was caused by a spirit?" The skeptical look on Denise's face said everything. "Look, I know it's Halloween, but you can't expect me to believe that a spirit stole my son's clothes and backpack?"

"It's one possibility," he said.

"You can't be serious!"

Paul shrugged. "You asked what I thought. I told you the truth."

"Look, I don't mean to be rude. These are probably just the beliefs you were raised with, but—" An eerie sound interrupted her. "What on earth is that?"

"The dog."

Paul's hip had stiffened and he had to struggle to get up from the couch. Denise grabbed his arm.

"Are you okay?" she asked.

He only nodded as he walked to the front window. He pulled the drapery aside and stared out into the night, the muscles in his jaw tightening as the sound increased in pitch.

"We've got to make him stop before the neighbors call the police," Denise said.

"It's here," Paul said.

"What?"

"The wind."

*

Evan was snorkeling in water so clear that beams of sunlight radiated through it like light streaming through the stained glass windows of a church. The waves rocked him gently as he searched for shells among the swaying sea anemone and the brilliant yellow, blue, and green fish that darted just out of reach. He took a deep breath and dove, kicking with his flippers until he reached the sandy bottom. As he drifted back to the top, he examined a small shell fragment that he had retrieved before letting it sink back into the depths.

He cleared his snorkel with a blast of air and looked for his mother on the beach. She waved a tanned arm from her beach chair. He returned her wave before resuming his search.

The shallower depths were picked over and he decided to venture into deeper water. Finding a narrow channel crowded with schools of fish, he swam through it to the other side of the reef. The swift current was much stronger, reducing visibility from over a hundred feet to less than twenty. The water was colder, too. He had just decided to turn back when he glimpsed something hidden in a deep depression among the coral. He had to wait until the currents parted the seaweed again to get another look. Whatever it was, it had a pinkish glow. He dove down to have a closer look. He had to swim hard just to get near. Aware of the moray eels that lurked with razor sharp teeth among the coral formations, he reached a hand gingerly to touch the object. He expected the surface to be hard, instead it was soft and fleshy, as if alive. How weird. He stared in fascination, hardly aware that he was holding his breath under water, when two eyes suddenly blinked open. Startled, Evan accidentally sucked in some water. He coughed into his snorkel and fanned his arms to get away, but a hand suddenly shot out from the coral and seized his arm. Evan kicked, twisting furiously, but the hand would not let go. His lungs were bursting now. He fought desperately to free himself as the hand pulled him down where the icy-blue-eyed, grinning face of Monster was waiting, surrounded by a halo of waving, blond hair. "No!" Evan tried to shout, his silent cry tumbling from his mouth in great torrents of bubbles that rose toward the surface and burst. The severed head only laughed as the hand pulled him to it. The jagged coral tore into the skin of his arms and shoulders and the water began to cloud with his blood.

Evan woke, gasping for breath, his heart crashing like waves in his chest. His body was drenched in sweat. The blankets had been kicked off and the bed was so damp that he was afraid he had wet it. He had to fight the impulse to run next door to his mother's room and tell her about the nightmare and the real event that had inspired it. If he said anything, however, he knew that he'd have to spend the rest of his life within ten feet of her. Mothers didn't want to know the truth about what their sons did. They thought they did, but they couldn't handle it.

While his heartbeat and breathing slowly returned to normal, his attention was drawn to the *National Geographic* map of the world that hung on his wall. Shadows from the window played across the map's surface. He watched the leafy tendrils as they swept across Texas and Oklahoma, attacking the southeastern states and Mexico. His mind knew that the shadows were just the result of a night breeze stirring the branches of the birch tree in the backyard. There was something creepy, however, about the way the vine-like shadows twisted and curled. Almost like an octopus looking for lunch, he thought.

Reluctantly, his gaze swung to the window where the tree limbs danced against the glass. Even from the bed in the dim moonlight, he could see the glass quivering in the frame as the branches crawled against the outside of the panes, exploring the seams where glass and wood met, as if looking for a way into his room. He pulled the covers tighter around his neck, and as he watched, wide-eyed, the branches continued their exploration. Then he remembered that the window latch was loose. He sat up so fast that the mobile suspended above his bed swayed, the cardboard warplanes dancing round his head. He hadn't mentioned the latch to his mom. After all, nobody could reach his second-floor window. Now, he eased himself down from the bed and tiptoed to the window. With alarm, he saw that the latch had worked its way to within a hair's breadth of being open. He grabbed it with both hands and twisted it shut. The wind reacted angrily, shaking the window glass so violently that he thought it would break or fall apart. He backed up, never taking his eyes from the window. Dust from tiny air currents swirled around the room, causing the mobile to spin and papers to take flight. Any second now, the wind would be in his room. From the top of his dresser, he grabbed the whistle and blew for all he was worth. And, just like that, the wind was gone.

He stood staring out the window and shivering in his pajamas for several seconds, waiting for his heartbeat to return to normal and watching anxiously for any sign of the wind's return. When he detected his mother's footsteps on the stairs, he scooped up the bedding on the floor and climbed back into bed. A moment later, the door opened and light from the hallway spilled across the room. He pretended to be sleeping as she bent over him, kissing the top of his ear and pulling the comforter up over his shoulder.

The mobile still turned slowly. Denise assumed that opening the door had disturbed it. She stood over her son and listened to his breathing. It sounded much too fast. He must be dreaming. She considered waking him, wanting to hold him to her chest, yet didn't. "Love you," she whispered in the still room. Then she glanced over at the carved angel, bought at a swap meet and missing the tip of one wing, that stood on top of his dresser among the baseball cards, Swiss Army knife and other incriminating evidence of a boy's life. "Watch over him. Please." On her way out the door, she was forced to step over several sheets of paper that littered the floor.

She found Paul in the backyard, standing beneath the silver birch, staring up at Evan's window. The clouds had momentarily parted and a three-quarter moon was reflected in the glass. She shut the door carefully to keep the dog, now quiet, from getting out. Paul turned as she walked toward him in the long grass, glistening with dew. Unlike her blond hair and pale skin, his black hair and dark skin seemed like a natural part of the night and the outdoors.

"Evan okay?" he asked.

"Sleeping. What about out here?" They spoke in hushed voices to avoid rousing the neighbors.

"It's gone."

Denise hugged her arms and shivered. "How can you tell? And what makes you think it was the wind?"

"That dog is like having radar."

"But, even if it was the wind, why here?"

"I don't know how it tracked us here," he said, "but as to 'why,' it's got to be either the dog or your son."

Denise's mouth moved, but no words came forth. "C'mon." She tried to smile—it had to be a joke. She stared at Paul's unsmiling face and felt her emotions spinning out of control like a speeding car on a slippery corner. "No!" she said at last, too loud. "It can't be!" she whispered. "The wind isn't an intelligent being that tracks people down!"

"You said yourself there was something weird going on at the Tower," he said. "This has got nothing to do with the weather. If

Evan really has psychic gifts, that could explain why the wind is following him."

"Look, I admit, a lot of weird stuff is happening,"—Denise
waved her hands, refusing to believe—"but the wind isn't a creature! It's not possible!" she said. "You're out of your mind."

Paul let out a long sigh and began limping toward the back door.
Denise grabbed his arm after he had gone a few steps.

He winced.

"I didn't mean to yell or hurt you," she whispered. "I'm scared,
Paul."

"I know." He put his hand out and she took it.

"I can't believe what's happening." She looked up into his strong
face. "Or how dependent on you I've suddenly become."

"Looks like I may need to depend on you to get up these stairs."
Paul tried climbing the steps of the back porch and was forced to
lean on Denise for support.

"How bad is your leg? Can you drive?"

"It's my hip. I bruised it."

They reached the top of the porch.

"Sure you wouldn't like a hot bath and some aspirin?"

He rubbed his jaw. "What would the neighbors say if I stayed
overnight on your couch?"

"Are you kidding? *Good Morning America* will probably make it
their lead story tomorrow."

"Yeah. You're probably right."

"Hey." She waited until he looked at her. "Even if they did, it
wouldn't matter. I'll make up your bed."

He stood for a long moment, silent, as if listening to the night
sounds.

"Good," he said finally. "I'll leave before sunrise."

14

Deadlines

SEATTLE, MONDAY, 11:34 P.M. It was only natural,
Gretta told herself, that she would be the one to take the phone call
from the one who called himself "Chuck." She gulped down Diet
Coke to wash down a mouthful of devil's food cake, a leftover from
the staff Halloween party. Nearly everyone else in the newsroom
had gone home. Most of those few who remained were working on
the power blackout and helicopter crash at the Center for tomorrow's early edition. An assistant editor was updating the day's
earlier big story about the mayor's press conference at the Tower.
Anyone who had a wind-related story was trying to call Billy Mossman, unaware that the reporter was hospitalized with superficial
flesh wounds. Gretta was taking his calls. And a strange batch of
calls they were, from a hysterical mother's report of costumed kids
tumbling down the street, their bags of treats scattered over several
blocks, to the huge plywood initials missing from the roof of the
Lake Washington Yacht Club.

When the "Chuck" call came, she was sitting at Billy's desk,
proofing a story about the mayoral race.

"Taylor," she answered, having heard Billy reply "Mossman" so
many times.

"Who?"

"Taylor, Gretta," she said with a little less confidence.

"I don't believe I know you, do I?" The deep male voice spoke
with a southern accent. "I was calling for that feller, Mossman."

"Mr. Mossman is in the hospital. I'm a colleague of his. What
can I do for you, Mr. . . . . ?"

"A colleague?" The voice sounded both suspicious and slightly
inebriated. "Are you a real reporter then? What kind of stories do
you write?"

"All kinds," Gretta said.

"Well, Miss Reporter, you know about this wind that's been
kicking butt lately in our fair city?"

"Yes?" She reached for her pen and discovered it was out of ink.

Of all the stupid times to quit. Frantically, she began opening and shutting desk drawers, searching among rubber bands, paper clips and last year's *Sports Illustrated* swimsuit edition for something to write with. "Wait just a sec." Where did Billy keep his pencils? Finally, in the bottom drawer, she found a three-by-five card with a pencil taped to it. "Looking for this?" the note read. In smaller handwriting, it continued, "Next time, stay out of my desk." It was signed B. Mossman. With the phone clenched between ear and shoulder, Gretta ripped the pencil from the card. "Okay. Go ahead."

"I seen it."

"Pardon me?"

"I was blind and now I see."

"Was this an operation that allowed you to see?"

"No. Christ, what a featherhead! I have seen the wind that kills. For they have sown the wind, and they shall reap the whirlwind."

"You saw a whirlwind?" Gretta wrote "whirlwind" on a telephone message pad and noted an alarming desire to imitate the man's drawl.

"It hath no stalk: the bud shall yield no meal: if so be it yield, the strangers shall swallow it up."

"What on earth are you talking about?" Gretta said a little too loudly, causing an editor to glance up from her terminal and frown. She was beyond being tired and this man's infuriating mannerisms were getting under her skin.

"The wind is come and it ain't taking no prisoners, no ma'am. Ask not for whom the bell tolls, it tolls for thee!"

"I'm sorry, but you're not making any sense."

"Those who oppose him he must gently instruct, that they will come to their senses and escape from the trap of the devil, who has taken them captive to do his will."

"So long." Gretta hung up the phone and shook her head. The guy was definitely a quart low. What a day she'd had. Her first press conference and now this character. Every minute in this job was going to make good storytelling when she talked to her friends back in Pullman. She decided to call her boyfriend, Peter, even though it was nearly midnight. She was reaching for the phone when it rang again.

"Taylor," she said.

"So you think you can handle a big story, lady? I got me the biggest story of the century and I'm willing to give it to you for free."

Gretta sighed. "I've got deadlines to meet," she lied. "What did you say your name was?"

"Chuck. Now, listen here, Miss Deadlines. I've seen the thing that's causing all the trouble—killing people and making a mess of buildings and such—and I can show you where it hangs out."

"Killing people—what thing?"

"I ain't saying no more till you get here."

"When?"

"When? Why right now, by God. 'Less you don't mind if it kills a few more people while you're meeting your deadlines."

Gretta looked at her watch absently, as if she didn't already know how late it was. She resented being treated as if she was a paid staff reporter. On the other hand, wasn't that exactly what she wanted?

"Okay, where?"

"Meet me in front of Pier 65 in half an hour."

Gretta hung up the phone and leaned back in Billy's chair. More than likely, going to meet this guy would turn out to be a total waste of time. Probably just some drunk. Billy got calls like this every day and ignored them. Gretta had just about decided to skip showing up when she remembered the call earlier that morning. What about that lady up on San Juan Island? Billy had hung up on her when she called, but now he wanted her phone number. She picked up the framed eight-by-ten black and white photo sitting on the corner of the desk. Billy was wearing a khaki vest, pants, and floppy brimmed hat and standing among a small group of men. Many of the men were half naked, posing with their weapons and wearing silly grins, cigarettes dangling from their lips. The photo had been signed by several of the soldiers.

Okay, so what was the worst that could happen if she went to meet this guy—maybe waste an hour? The upside, however, was a story that could get her noticed, maybe even pave the way for a full-time job as a reporter. She remembered something her first journalism professor had said: "Great stories don't happen behind a desk." There was no need to be totally irresponsible, however. She dug through her purse until she found the tiny can of pepper spray and transferred it to her suit pocket. If this guy had any ideas that weren't strictly business, she'd let him have it.

On the way out of the building, she ran into Andy mopping the floor. The janitor was short and painfully bowlegged, but the muscles bulged along his arms and shoulders so that the faded fabric of his work shirt ballooned at the buttons like sails.

"Hey, there. Going to call it a day?" the old man asked.

"Nah. Got work to do."

"Yeah?" Andy stopped mopping and looked her over. "You working on that Center stuff?"

"Could be something connected with that. I'm checking out a lead for Billy."

"Take care. I never seen it so crazy out there when I was coming to work. Stuff blowin' all over the place."

"Thanks. I will."

She drove the few blocks down to Alaskan Way and then over to Pier 65, practicing what questions to ask. Based on some of the calls she'd taken earlier, she half expected to see buildings destroyed. But Gretta saw no signs at all of wind damage. After parking the car under one of the few street lights, she looked around cautiously. This part of town wasn't lit very well and the lack of traffic and people felt a bit spooky. She got out of the car and walked toward the murky parking lot area under the viaduct. The air was damp and smelled of rotting fish. She stepped carefully over the trolley tracks, listening hard for any note of danger. Other than her heels crunching on the gravel bed, the only sound was the occasional *whoosh* of a car on the viaduct overhead.

She remembered reading somewhere that criminals could spot potential victims by the way they walked, so she strode purposefully, shoulders back, chest out. She carried the pepper spray in her right hand.

"That you, Miss Deadlines?"

The voice came so near as to startle her. She whirled to see an older man, dressed in ragged clothes and a watch cap, leaning against one of the viaduct's concrete supports. "You walk like you messed your underpants, lady." The figure shook for a moment before erupting into a fit of coughing.

Gretta remained silent and kept her fists clenched at her side.

"I reckon I'd be scared, too, if I was as green as you, kid. You sure you're a reporter?"

"Ah'm sure." There was that stupid drawl creeping into her voice. "You must be Chuck. Now, what exactly did you see?" she asked, speaking carefully.

"C'mere." Chuck led Gretta to a dark area of parking lot directly underneath the viaduct, mumbling to himself as he went. She caught only "Suffer the children, and forbid them not."

A moment later he stopped and pointed.

"See that?"

Gretta peered closely at the ground, but could see nothing unusual. "What am I looking for, exactly?"

"Bloodstains."

"From what?" She squatted and ran her left hand along the asphalt where it seemed darker.

"An Indian, least I think that's what he was."

"So what happened? You think the wind killed him?"

"Why me, Lord?" Chuck rolled his bloodshot eyes heavenward, hands stretched out. "Eyes have they but they see not: they have ears, but they hear not."

Gretta felt her ears redden. First, this escaped lunatic had made her feel like a scared girl and now, stupid, too. "Are you gonna tell me what happened or not? I get enough patronizing during regular work hours."

"Some kids killed the Indian," Chuck said. "That's what got the wind riled up, in my opinion."

"Wait a minute—where were you when this happened?"

"I was under there," Chuck pointed to the area under a stairway. "That's my current residence."

"Very nice, I'm sure. Did you tell the police?"

"Faw! Then I'd be the one cooling my heels. They nearly threw me in jail today just for trying to warn people. Besides, telling the cops wouldn't solve anything."

"Why do you say that?"

"I told you already. I saw the cursed wind! It blew shit—pardon my language, Lord—all around here. Then it picked up this junk heap and tossed it like a cornflake."

"When was this?"

"Two, three days ago. I ain't exactly sure." Chuck stroked the stubble on his chin.

"What did it look like?"

"You can't see the wind. No, ma'am."

"But you said—"

"Just this great big, whirling cloud of cigarettes, paper cups and everything that was on the ground, not tied down, all flying around like a twister."

"Maybe it was a twis—a cyclone." Gretta stood up and wiped her hands on a handkerchief.

"Nah." Chuck shook his head and frowned. "I seen twisters before. In my youth, we had 'em. Big, tube-worm-like things. You could see them coming for miles, sucking up whatever got in their path. Scarier than a one-testicle fortune teller."

"What makes you think this wind-thing is causing the other stuff that happened?"

"I think it's pissed off at us for killing that old Indian."

"Us? I thought you said you weren't involved?" Gretta had barely got the words out when a loud drumming made her jump for the second time. "What is that sound?" She had to shout to be heard over the racket.

Chuck was staring up at the pitch-black underside of the viaduct. "Pigeons."

"Pigeons? Is that all? My God! For a minute there, I thought the world was coming to an end." Gretta laughed at her jitters and noted that her teeth were chattering. The air was frigid where her skin was exposed. She pulled the collar up on her suit coat. "Look, Chuck," she yelled. "Why don't I take your name down and a place where I can reach you later? I'm starting to freeze my tail off."

Chuck said something that was drowned out by the noise.

"What did you say?" Gretta shouted.

"I said it's too late for writing things!"

Gretta stared at him in surprise, expecting to see a smile. Instead, she saw a quiver in the man's lips and a drool of spittle running down his chin.

"Would you mind not doing that? You're starting to scare me."

"No man knows when his hour will come," Chuck said.

Gretta had only a moment to ponder this before the wind hit her with a deafening roar. It spun her around and knocked her back several steps before she could recover her balance and filled her eyes and throat with sandy grit. Through stinging eyes, she saw Chuck struggling to run away. He reminded Gretta of a man trying to walk in ocean waves. He got only a dozen steps before the wind picked him up and hurled him headfirst into a concrete pylon with a snap like the breaking of a stick. The body slid to the ground, leaving a long, dark smear.

The wind that had buffeted her was suddenly gone. Gretta had been leaning so far forward that she lost her balance and fell to her knees. In the renewed quiet, she heard the excited cooing of a thousand pigeons and felt a sudden attack of incipient diarrhea. She began crawling toward her car. Although the wind had seemingly disappeared, she knew that she must leave or die, although she could neither stand nor walk.

It was slow going. Her hands and knees stung where gravel bit into her flesh. "Damn you," she whimpered. Her nylons were ruined and she resented Billy for not being around when she needed him.

Gretta looked up to see how much farther she had to go to reach her car and had to look twice due to the tears that blurred her vision. She started to wipe her nose with the back of her hand, then stopped. The car was still there, less than two hundred feet away now, but the parking meter was rocking back and forth like a metronome. She remembered what Chuck had said about the wind tossing a car like a cornflake. Her legs trembled like reeds as she tried to stand.

She looked back the way she had come. A dark stairway led up to the Pike Place Market, but she knew she could never manage it in her present condition. Farther down Alaskan Way was the ferry terminal. She had taken several shaky steps in its direction when she heard a popping noise. Gretta stopped and looked over her shoulder.

The parking meter was a silver arrow streaking toward her back in the dim moonlight.

15

Hoofbeats

SAN JUAN ISLAND, TUESDAY, 8:17 A.M. The thirteen-inch Sony television beamed brief, gaudy flashes of color and made disgustingly friendly if less than intelligent early morning conversation from the kitchen counter. The somewhat more subdued voices of KIRO Newsradio chattered in the background from her bedroom clock radio. Helen raised her cup of tea to her lips and felt the return of the ice pick probing behind her right eye. She hurried to set the bone china cup down on its matching saucer, a treasure from one of her antique-hunting trips to Victoria, British Columbia. In her pain, she misjudged the lip of the saucer and struck it a glancing blow with the cup. Tea sloshed onto the pressed, white linen tablecloth that covered the small wooden table and began to spread outward in an ugly brown stain. "Bloody hell!" She threw down the newspaper she had been reading. It fell to the floor where it lay like a child's crude tent. She was eager to learn more about the strange and deadly events in Seattle, but her headaches had turned her favorite activity, reading, into something akin to crossing a minefield.

When the pain had receded enough that she could stand, she picked up the delicate cup and saucer and examined them carefully, caressing the saucer's ragged edge with a finger. It was only a small imperfection, one that wouldn't affect their utility. Still, Helen knew that she would never take pleasure from them again. She limped slowly to the kitchen counter and set them both in the box of items to be donated that she kept under the sink.

It was not starting off to be a pretty day. The pain pills weren't working, her ankle showed no improvement, and Byron's absence made every hour drag. Other than Stan who had called last night to check up on her, no one else had phoned or stopped by. Normally, Helen appreciated the quiet. Now it threatened to overwhelm and capsize her fragile emotional state. She thought of going back to bed. She had spent most of last night tossing and turning, unable to sleep. When the morning paper had arrived just before dawn, she had been standing at the kitchen window, porch light on, waiting.

In the last three days, several people had died of wind-related circumstances: Ann Bessani's husband and father-in-law in the sailboat accident, the people killed by falling granite and glass from the office building, including the mounted police officer, and, last night, two more officers in a helicopter. Although the toll of death and destruction continued to mount, the news media persisted in identifying the cause as abnormal weather conditions. It was all so bizarre that she had begun to question her own memory. As time passed, she was less and less certain that she had actually seen the wind pick Byron up and hurl his body into a tree. No wind she'd ever seen did that. It was probably just her imagination working overtime, but the wind had seemed mean, even vicious.

Stan had suggested that perhaps the gust that killed her dog might have been a freak of nature, like a rogue wave. A former merchant marine, he'd heard stories of a spectacular wave rising up out of nowhere to crush ships and send men to their watery graves. Was there a rogue wind, Helen wondered? And, if so, did it have a name? She'd feel better if she could at least find a label for what had killed Byron.

Helen shivered. The temperature in the house was barely sixty-five degrees, her usual practice for this time of year. She liked to say that she was born with her own, personal, nuclear reactor inside to keep her warm. It had helped her save money on heating during the winters. Now, however, when she needed it most, her metabolism seemed to be failing her. Perhaps she was running low on fuel. The thought of food was unappealing.

She turned off the television and stared out the kitchen window. Rain fell in silent sheets, streaking the window like tears. Tiny silver knives marched up the driveway, varnishing the asphalt with a glossy black sheen. The trees, some of them eighty feet tall, weaved and bobbed with the breeze, their tops drooping under the weight of a slate gray sky.

"Time to punt," her father used to say when nothing seemed to be going right.

Helen opened a nearby cabinet door and saw the whiskey bottle within. She hesitated, remembering the driver calling out when she had stumbled and fallen while leaving the hospital. Might help her to sleep, however. She was saved from further deliberations when the dot matrix printer began clattering in the next room.

158

Reading the tiny letters on her computer monitor had always been difficult and was now virtually impossible, so Helen had programmed the computer to automatically print out any electronic mail as soon as it was received. She tore the paper off when it had finished. It was addressed to "(:-. . ." which was the hacker's symbol for a heartbreaking message and also short for her handle, Heartbreaker. The sender was one Grasshopper from Kodiak Island in Alaska. The message was short.

"IMHO, sounds like you got yourself a Williwaw, though never heard of one so far south. Most people believe it's only an Indian legend, but had a nasty experience with one a few years back.

"On my way to Prudhoe for 3. Call then if you want. P.S. . . . Like your handle."

It was signed ":-x," the symbol for "Kiss," followed by a phone number.

Helen stared at the message, her hand shaking. "Williwaw," she whispered. The word made the hairs stand up on her arms and the back of her neck. She reread the note quickly. What did "3" mean—hours, days, or weeks? Grasshopper's message was frustratingly short of specifics. She quickly dialed the phone. Perhaps there was still time to catch him before he left. She continued to study the message while she waited for the call to go through. "IMHO" was computer slang for "in my humble opinion." Helen suspected that anybody who used the term wasn't in the least humble.

On the fourteenth ring, a man's voice finally answered. "Damn it to hell, Audra! I told you to quit buggin' me."

"This is Helen Anderson. I'm calling for Grasshopper. It's about the bulletin board message you sent. The Williwaw."

"Oh, Christ, what a relief! I thought it was this lady friend of mine, Audra Cummings. She can talk for an eternity without coming up for air. So, you're Heartbreaker? No offense, lady, but you sound just a little bit old to be breaking many hearts."

"You don't exactly sound like a spring chicken, yourself, Grasshopper." She clutched at the chair arm as another stab of the ice pick came and went. "Now, can we please get down to business? I'm laid up physically and you seem to have a schedule to meet, correct?"

"You got balls bigger'n a Kodiak bear, lady. What exactly do you want?"

"Everything you know about this Williwaw you mentioned."

Helen sat down at her desk and pulled out a drawer to rest her foot on. "Tell me how you first heard about it and what happened to you."

"Okay, but I only have a sec. We're due up north in a few hours. All I can tell you is that Williwaw is a real ass-kicker of a wind. Indians believe it's a spirit that guards their holy places. Personally, I always figured it for just some more Eskimo bullshit. Then, one time, I heard about this lake from another bush pilot that wasn't on any map. Cheechakos will pay anything to fish where it ain't been picked over, so I try to check out tips like that. At any rate, I didn't spot it on my first look-see. Must have been my second or third trip when I found a likely candidate way up in the Arctic Circle. We're talking ice, colder than Judas's heart, even in July. Just the middle of the lake was thawed, so I went in on pontoons.

"So, I'm sitting there, nice and peaceful, not a cloud within a hundred miles, got a line dangling in the water for trout, when, next thing, this Williwaw hits. Not a hint of warning. Before you can say 'Muktuk,' the plane's on its nose, going down faster than a sea lion with a killer whale on its ass. If I hadn't been standing on a pontoon, taking a leak, I'da been fish bait, for sure. Didn't even have time to send out a distress signal."

"I'm surprised you survived," Helen said.

"I was real lucky. Eskimo found me, took me back to his barabara and had his wife cuddle up in bed with me, both of us naked as a couple of jaybirds. She wasn't much to look at—must have weighed two hundred forty pounds—but she thawed me out in no time. Later, the fellow hauled me by dog sled over three hundred miles to the nearest civilization. Never saw my plane again. Friends helped me get started again."

"Sounds like you have some mighty good friends, Grasshopper."

"That's what Alaska's all about, lady."

"How big are these Williwaws?"

"Big? You mean like size? No idea. All I know is they're powerful sons-a-bitches. Fellow told me they clocked one over one hundred miles an hour once."

"Who?" Helen grabbed a pencil from the can on the desk. "Who clocked one?"

"The Weather Service, of course."

"The U.S. Weather Service?"

"You got another kind, lady?"

"Wait a minute, you're saying the government knows about these Williwaws?"

"They may not subscribe to the Indian 'spirit' business—you got to experience that firsthand to believe it. And what with all the cruise ships and airplanes filled with tourists now days, they ain't likely to advertise 'em, know what I mean? But they sure do know they got 'em. Now look, lady, today ain't exactly a national holiday and I got a long flight to make."

"Thanks, Grasshopper. You've been a big help."

"Good luck, lady. Hope my mouthing off about your handle didn't hurt your feelings. If you got a Williwaw, you got a tanker-load of trouble, that's for sure."

Helen hung up the phone and rubbed her ankle. A moment later, her hands were flying over the keyboard as she dialed into the computer database. The printer was silent for only a few seconds before it began clacking away.

"Williwaw or willywaw or wulliwa," the print-out said. "1 a: A sudden violent gust of cold land air common along mountainous coasts of high latitudes. b: Any sudden violent wind. 2 a: A violent commotion or agitation such as a storm or tempest. b: Can reach 113 miles per hour after the wind builds up on one side of a mountain and suddenly spills over into what may appear to be a relatively protected area. Considered the bane of Alaska mariners. See also Taku."

"Now we're getting somewhere," Helen said. With a sense of urgency as if she had just discovered the cure for AIDS, Helen frantically searched through the scraps of paper for the phone number of the *Seattle Times*.

"Mr. Mossman, please," she said, when the operator answered.

"I'm sorry, Mr. Mossman won't be in today. Can I give you to someone else at the News Desk, or would you like his voice mail?"

Helen considered quickly: if she hadn't convinced him in their first phone conversation, voice mail was probably not going to work any better. "No, that's all right," she answered at last. She'd been a fan of Mossman since well before she'd retired. It was one of the reasons she still took the afternoon *Times* in addition to the morning *Post-Intelligencer*. But he had a reputation for being a world-class skeptic and getting him to listen to her was going to take some thought.

Helen's gaze swung to the picture window where the forest

seemed to press in against her small house. Pain or no pain, there was only one way to present her information, she decided. She found the ferry schedule under the number for Ann Bessani. It took a magnifying glass to read the tiny print. She saw that there was just time enough to do a little more research on the computer before she would need to leave in order to catch the next ferry.

SEATTLE, TUESDAY, 8:55 A.M. All laughter and talk died the moment Paul entered the Pioneer Square police substation. He left his umbrella standing just inside the door. Dreary morning light from a large window joined with the harsher glare of fluorescent tubes to illuminate what had once been a dress shop before most retail stores moved uptown. A tall, blond officer, wearing a crew cut and a wispy mustache that failed to disguise his youthful face, leaned back in a metal chair behind a desk, hands gripping the chair's arms. Two more officers, a male and a female, dressed in rain gear, studied Paul over the tops of their coffee cups from a wooden bench in the otherwise unoccupied waiting room.

Still favoring his left hip and leaving a trail of raindrops on the vinyl floor, Paul approached the desk which bore a small plastic bowl containing Halloween candy. The younger man watched him silently, as if unsure what to do.

"I'm looking for the blind man that usually sits outside the Blue Banjo."

"Well, he ain't here." The Viking-like officer winked at the others.

"I can see that," Paul said. "I thought you might be able to help me track him down."

"I thought it was Indians who were supposed to be good at tracking."

Paul's face, like his feelings, remained frozen. At last, the Viking stood up and walked to the café door that separated the room from the next. "Hey, Sarge. We got a guy out here can't find somebody."

A few moments later, a large, older man appeared through the swinging door.

"What's up, chief?" he asked. He leaned against the desk, one leg resting on its worn, wood surface, and unpeeled the wrapper from a miniature Hershey bar.

Paul repeated his question.

"Sounds like Nick," the woman volunteered. She looked to be in her late twenties with a pretty face, dark eyes, and hair that she wore in a tight roll. Paul noted that her shoulders were wider than some men's.

"What do you want him for?" the sergeant asked, still chewing the candy.

"Nick run off with your squaw?" the Viking asked, sniggering.

The sergeant rolled his eyes.

"Someone I know, a boy, thinks he may have the man's seeing eye dog."

"How'd the boy get the dog?" the sergeant asked. His bushy gray eyebrows seemed to grow together as a note of suspicion entered his voice.

"He said he found the dog running loose downtown."

"When was this?"

"Yesterday afternoon."

"Poor blind bastard is probably lost, trying to find his way home."

"That's enough, Peterson."

"I haven't seen Nick in a while, have you?" the woman asked the man seated next to her.

"Don't believe I have. But, what with all the weird stuff that's been going on, I haven't really been paying much attention."

"I tried the donut shop on the corner," Paul said. "It's been two days since anyone there saw him."

"Check the computer," the sergeant ordered. "See if we got anything on the old fart."

"Surname?" Peterson asked.

"Tambakis, Tamales—something like that," the sergeant said.

Peterson tapped out instructions on the keyboard and then waited. "Here it is: Nicholas Tambakis, age unknown, Greek citizen, reported missing at 9:30 A.M. on Monday."

"Who filed the report?"

"Father Janowsky."

"Looks like old Nick may have skipped town," Peterson said.

"Not likely. Not without his dog anyway," Paul said. "What about this priest? Do you have a phone or an address where I can reach him?"

"Sorry, chief," the sergeant said. "We're not allowed to give out that information. You might be intending ol' Nick harm. That's quite a scratch on your forehead, by the way."

"May I leave my name, in case you find him?" Paul dug in his wallet for a business card. "He'll want his dog back."

"Sure, chief," the sergeant said, taking his card and nodding his head in the direction of the two officers in rain gear. "We got a lot of staff with time on their hands to check this out." The two officers exchanged looks and stood as Peterson raised his eyebrows and made faces at them.

"Mr. Paul Judge, Attorney-at-Law," the sergeant read aloud from the card. "You know, you look familiar to me. Wasn't that you kept us from throwing away the key on that peeper last spring?" He searched the bowl for another candy.

"Sam wasn't a Peeping Tom, Sergeant." Paul said. "He just made a poor choice about where to take a leak."

The two officers in rain gear chuckled.

"Yeah?" the sergeant glared at them. "You're so damn smart, maybe you oughta change the name on your card to Mr. Judge and Jury."

While Peterson hooted, Paul turned and walked to the door where he retrieved his umbrella. "I don't make the rules, Sergeant."

"Thank bloody Christ for that, at least," he said, his mouth now full of candy.

Paul exited into the pouring rain. He had walked two blocks in the rain on his way back to his office when a black and white cruiser eased up to the curb beside him. The window rolled down and he was surprised to see the woman officer.

"Mr. Judge? Climb in. I'll take you to where Nick lives." After he was sitting in the passenger seat, she said, "Don't mind the guys." Paul nodded as he absorbed the throaty purr of the cruiser's large engine, the leather smell of the officer's holster and the lethal sight of the riot gun in its holder by his left knee. "We've lost three uniforms since Saturday," she continued. "Everybody's a little freaked out."

Paul realized with a start that he had been connected circumstantially with all three deaths, having caught the runaway horse and witnessed the helicopter crash.

"Something wrong, Mr. Judge?" She looked him over while they waited at a stoplight, the windshield wipers punctuating her words. "You look a little shaken."

"I didn't realize that you'd lost so many people," he lied. The light changed and she tromped on the gas pedal so that the cruiser's tires spun momentarily on the wet pavement. "By the way, thanks for the ride. I still don't know your name."

"Rodriguez. Call me Lucy." After a short pause she said, "Pretty crazy, huh? And all because of this weather. First, Ewing gets creamed by a falling window. Then Bristol and Haas go down in the chopper. We can normally go a year or two without losing anybody. Now, suddenly, we're going down like flies."

A pang of guilt, the result of his experiences with the wind and the chopper crash, made Paul wince. But there was no way he was going to be the first one to start talking about a killer wind. He had enough troubles. A white might at least get listened to, but an Indian? He'd be lucky to get a padded cell—without the pad.

"Here we are," Lucy announced as they pulled into the loading zone in front of the Sisters of Mercy Mission. Paul recalled normally seeing several men standing or sitting on the concrete steps with the green peeling paint. Today, due to the rain, the steps were empty. Paul remained seated while Lucy called in on her car radio.

"Okay, I'm cleared," she said a moment later. "Let's go."

Paul took out his umbrella, but Lucy was out of the car and up the stairs before he could get it open. He limped after her as she strode through the loose knots of men sitting on benches or standing about inside the clean but decrepit building. Piles of bedding and personal belongings lined the walls of the large hall. The smell of cigarette smoke, coffee, and sweat was stifling. Paul spotted a familiar face.

"Hello, Bob. You ever collect on that judgment?"

A small, neatly dressed man of about sixty looked up from playing chess. "Are you kiddin'? Not a friggin' dime. All I want is justice. That's all," the small man continued.

Paul took a card out of his wallet and handed it to him. "Call me next week."

"We gonna kick some butt, Mr. Judge?"

"Something like that. Just don't forget to call," Paul said and hurried after Lucy who had stopped to wait.

"Where's Father Janowsky?" Lucy asked a tall, cadaverous man with a scraggly beard.

He pointed to a door in the back. "What's he done now?" he called after her.

"Oh, nothing much. Stealing from the collection plate, trying to pawn the candlesticks, the usual," she said over one large shoulder as she continued to the doorway.

Paul followed her through the door and found himself in a kitchen. A lean, athletic-looking man was washing dishes at a large,

165

stainless steel sink. His sleeves were rolled up. Coarse black hair covered his arms and head except for a large bald spot.

"Morning, Father," Lucy called out over the sound of running water and a radio blaring a traffic report. "How's the human salvage biz today?"

The priest looked up and smiled. He turned off the water, wiped his hands on a thin, gray cloth and switched off the radio.

"Officer Rodriguez. A pleasure, as always," he said, extending his hand. "You have some word on my lost sheep, I hope?"

"Sorry, Father. Still working on it. This is Paul Judge." She nodded in his direction. "He's also looking for your man. Thinks he may have his dog."

"Mr. Judge." The priest shook his hand, a frown creasing his face.

Paul guessed Father Janowsky's age to be about the same as his own, although the priest's wire rim glasses and thinning hair made him look older.

"You have Fortuno?"

"Well, not me, actually. A boy that knows the blind man found the dog yesterday afternoon roaming the streets."

"Roaming the streets? You're sure it's Nico's dog?"

Paul nodded.

"Not a good sign." The priest took a cigarette from a crumpled pack in his shirt pocket and tapped it several times on the back of his hand. "I keep saying I'm going to quit." He searched his pants pockets absentmindedly. "Would either of you happen to have a light?"

"Sorry," Lucy answered. "When did you last see him, Father?"

"Sunday morning." The priest finally found a book of matches in the pocket of his shirt. He lit his cigarette, then carefully held the match under the faucet for a second before tossing it into a pail under the sink. "He was at morning services. After lunch, I asked him if he wanted to listen to the Sonics game on the radio in my room, but he said that the weather was much too fine for taking a day off. He left a few minutes later with the dog. Can you imagine? A blind beggar and he wouldn't take a day off. I've never known such a religious man."

"Is there anyone he might stay with? Did he have any friends?" Lucy glanced at the clipboard she held.

"No one that I know of." Father Janowsky shook his head

slowly. "But, he knew—knows everyone: shop owners, waitresses, the police."

"Did he ever mention a deaf boy?" Paul asked.

"Oh." He looked away for a moment, as if trying to remember. "I seem to remember him mentioning a boy. But I can't remember his name. Perhaps he never told me."

"Evan? Does that name ring a bell?"

"No, not really. Is he the one who found Fortuno?"

"Yes. He's anxious to give the dog back, but also anxious to keep him as long as he can."

"Of course. I understand. He's a good dog," the priest said. "I think the boy should hang on to him—until Nicholas returns, that is." He held the cigarette under the faucet until it was out, then threw it at the pail, but missed. It lay soggy and brown on the concrete floor. "I called all the hospitals in town," he said, still staring at the butt. "Nothing."

"Did you try the morgue?" Lucy asked.

He let out a long sigh. "I suppose that's where we are, isn't it?"

"Was he carrying any I.D.?"

"I doubt it. Credit cards and driving licenses are pretty rare items down here."

"Then be sure to check out any John Does at the county medical examiner's offices. I can't take time off to go with you, Father," Lucy said. "But, perhaps Mr. Judge . . . ?"

Paul glanced at his watch and considered his ominously growing lack of billable time. The missing man really wasn't his problem and he'd done what he'd promised to do. On the other hand, something told him that the wind was involved. And, if that was the case, it was going to be everybody's problem, whether they knew it or not. "I can spare another hour, I guess."

The priest looked up from the cigarette on the floor. "I would appreciate it very much," he said.

"Mr. Judge." Lucy held out her hand. Her grip was that of a weight lifter. "I've got to get back to my rounds, but I hope our paths cross again soon. And Father, let me know what you find out."

"Of course."

"Nice lady," Paul said in the awkward silence after she had departed.

"Yes. Quite." The priest stooped to retrieve the butt and

dropped it in the pail. "Did you bring a car?"

"No, but I live just a few blocks away."

"Never mind. We can take mine. But perhaps you'd like to drive. Driving in the rain has never been my game, if you know what I mean."

"Son of a bitch!" Billy slammed the telephone receiver down in its cradle. "It's nine-thirty and Gretta still hasn't shown up at the *Times.*"

"For God's sake," Julie said, "it's only nine-fifteen and she's just a kid. Besides, we'll be home in a few minutes and you can call her from there. Come on, Billy," she said, her voice clearly conveying her frustration. "The attendants have other patients, too."

"I guess you're right," he sighed as the two male nurses lifted him from the hospital bed into a wheelchair with a large, foam rubber donut on the seat. The pain made him grimace. "But she's no damn reporter."

"What is it you do, Mr. Judge?" the priest asked a few minutes later when they were laboring up First Hill. The car was a ten-year-old Toyota station wagon with 140,000 miles on the odometer. It coughed and hesitated when starting out and reeked with the stale odor of cigarettes.

"I'm an attorney." He was forced to hunch over the steering wheel in order to see through the fogged window where the wipers slapped ineffectually.

"Such an apt name. Criminal, corporate, divorce, torts?"

"Public defender. As a matter of fact, I've represented some of your houseguests."

"No doubt. For being so unencumbered, they have a surprising number of problems. Still, it's a good thing you do."

"Nothing compared to you, Father."

"Me?" The priest looked away momentarily, as if embarrassed. "I do nothing. I open the doors in the morning and I shut them at night. In between, I cook, I clean, and, mostly, I pray. Tell me, do you believe, Mr. Judge?"

The question caught him momentarily by surprise. "Yes," he answered.

"You were raised a Catholic?"

"Is it that obvious?"

168

"Just an inspired guess. Tell me, when was the last time you went to confession?"

"When I was thirteen, maybe fourteen."

"I see. Now, you believe, but you're not one hundred percent sure what you believe. You wonder how God can permit the suffering. Am I right?"

Paul nodded. "Close enough. At mission school, I learned about the white man's God. And at home, I heard about the Great Spirit from my grandmother. I tried to make them one."

"And has the operation been successful?" The priest was looking at him over the rims of his glasses. Paul thought he detected the hint of a smile.

"Not consistently. Grandmother taught me that everything was sacred—not just this particular building or that individual. She also said it was okay to study the Bible, but to go easy on asking God for favors—like a winning Lotto ticket—or making others wrong because they believed differently. It seemed to her that the whites often used Jehovah to suit their own petty needs."

"She sounds like a very wise woman, Mr. Judge. I have this very unorthodox belief. It's that though each man's God is different, yet they are all the same. Great Spirit, Jehovah, Jesus, Buddha—one and the same. It's like the story of the blind men touching the elephant. You know it? The elephant is so large and multifaceted that each person feels something different. By the way, don't quote me. As long as you believe, it will be okay. Some day, the mysteries will be explained to us. Like the thing that is happening now to this city."

Startled, Paul jerked his head around to stare at the priest. "What thing?"

"The thing that is killing some people and making others disappear." The priest pointed ahead.

Paul looked back to the road just in time to avoid rear-ending a bus that had stopped to make a left hand turn. The Toyota swerved to the right and was small enough that they were able to squeeze by. Fortunately, no one was getting out of one of the parked cars that lined the street.

"You know what this 'thing' is?" Paul asked, driving more cautiously now. Father Janowsky did not appear to be ruffled by their near miss.

"No, but I can almost believe that I feel it."

Paul frowned as he drove. The sky appeared even darker ahead, as if they were driving into a storm.

"You said 'killing people.' What did you mean?"

"Just what I said—killing them. And making people disappear, like Nico."

"You have proof?"

"Just the word of street people. Hardly what the media would call a reliable source. On the other hand, their stories have a certain, gritty resonance. Especially when you measure them against someone like Nico's disappearance. A man like Nico would never just disappear. Yet, if the boy hadn't found the dog and you hadn't come forward, the police would have ignored me." Father Janowsky turned to face Paul. "You're going to think that I'm losing it—and maybe I am—but I fear that someone or thing has opened a gate."

"A gate?"

"Between the heavenlies and us. 'For our struggle is not against flesh and blood, but against the rulers, against the authorities, against the powers of this dark world and against the spiritual forces of evil in the heavenly realms.' Ephesians, chapter six." The priest opened the tiny glove compartment, withdrew a handful of parking tickets, and studied them. "Do you like to watch basketball?" he suddenly asked.

"Occasionally."

"Perhaps we could attend a game together sometime."

Paul was troubled by the priest's abrupt change of subject, but wasn't ready to discuss his own fears. In any case, he was forced to delay further questions and concentrate on driving as they arrived at Harborview Hospital. A small sign that read KING COUNTY MEDICAL EXAMINER, followed by an arrow, led them to the back of the medical complex. He found a parking space near an unobtrusive office entrance at one side of the building.

"Here we are," Paul said. He got out and waited with the umbrella. The priest stumbled as he exited the car.

"I hate this."

"Do you have to do this often—identify bodies?"

"Too often and not often enough. You would think it would become routine after awhile," he continued. "The men I have to identify have made their choices, after all. But I've never been very good at facing up to the horror of death. If I had to identify children, I'd be a total washout." He shook his head. "That's why I could never be a parish priest. They see it all."

Most people visiting the hospital would never know this area existed, Paul thought as they entered the door and went down a short flight of steps. Father Janowsky went directly to the counter that separated the small reception area from the busy office behind.

"Somebody here has a green thumb," Paul gestured toward the thriving ficus plant that dominated one corner of the room.

A young woman rose from a desk occupied by a computer. "Can I help you?"

"We're trying to locate one of the residents of the Sisters of Mercy Mission," Father Janowsky said. "He's been missing since Sunday."

"Name?"

"Nicholas Tambakis, but he may not have been carrying identification."

She returned to her desk and punched the name into the computer. A middle-aged Chinese woman wearing a lab coat and consulting with one of the other office workers, looked up from her clipboard and caught Paul's eye before disappearing down a hallway.

"We don't have a Nicholas Tambakis," the young woman explained. "We do, however, have a number of John Does. If you'd like to sign in and wait just a moment, I'll let the people in I.D. section know you're here."

They had waited only a couple of minutes before the Chinese woman returned and approached the counter.

"Excuse me. I do not wish to be rude, but you are an American Indian, correct?"

"Yes?" Paul steeled himself. What was this? Had she never seen one before?

She put out a hand. "I am Dr. Chan, Director of I.D. Section."

"Paul Judge. This is Father Janowsky. We're trying to find out if you have one of the father's missing residents. Unfortunately, he may not have been carrying identification."

"I see. I have a John Doe I would like you to see. He is one of several, but most unusual. If I help you, perhaps you will help me?"

"I'm afraid I don't have much time, Doctor."

"Oh, I promise this will only take five minutes, but it could solve a big mystery. We have no identification, no money, no watch, nothing except some rather odd body markings and a primitive-looking necklace. A real anachronism. Won't you help us, Mr.

Judge? We don't like mysteries in my profession."

Paul shrugged. He could feel himself sliding deeper into a hole whose sides were crumbling in after him. "Okay, but . . ."

"Come, let us start at my office."

She led the two men down a sterile hall past doorways marked "Toxicology Lab," "Crime Lab" and "AFIS." They entered a door marked simply "ID." On one side of the room was a row of a dozen large, stainless steel refrigerators. On the other were several waist-high tables where a trio of gowned and masked attendants looked up from the microscopes and other lab equipment.

"Here," Dr. Chan said, gesturing to a small, carpeted office. "Please be seated." From a file cabinet, she produced a large manila envelope. "I do not usually hang on to personal belongings. Articles of clothing and jewelry are usually photographed and then kept with the body. But this seemed too important."

She spread a clean, white sheet of paper on her desk, then picked up one end of the envelope. Something dark and blood-stained slithered out, startling the priest.

"Good Lord," he whispered and crossed himself.

Paul stared in silence for a moment before examining the four-inch claws, bits of feathers, bones, beads, and sea urchin quills strung on a leather thong. At the bottom was a small leather pouch, black with age, blood or both.

"Seen one of these before?"

"Sure," he said. "In a museum." He touched one of the claws. It was ice cold, as if it had just come out of a freezer instead of a file cabinet.

"I think you are right, Mr. Judge. But this did not come from a mannequin or a glass case. It was found on a body that came in early Saturday."

"Must be a ceremonial piece. Nobody wears stuff like this."

"Nobody?"

"Not that I know of. I'm no expert, you understand. I went to a powwow once as a boy. Most of the tribes from Western Canada and the U.S. were there. You never saw so many beads, bonnets, and ceremonial trappings. But I never saw anything quite like this."

"Please, excuse me once again. You are saying it is fake?"

"No." He spoke slowly, unable to tear his eyes from the neck-lace. "I'm just saying it's like something out of a time machine. The real stuff is long gone. Museums and private collectors bought it all up at the turn of the century for a couple of bucks. Half of it's now in Russia and Europe. Do you think . . . could I possibly try it on?"

Dr. Chan and Father Janowsky both stared at him. Paul couldn't have explained his fascination with the artifact, or why he wanted to try it on. He was relieved when they didn't ask for an explanation.

"Be my guest," Dr. Chan said.

Gingerly, he picked the necklace up and slipped it over his head. *Immediately, the room grew dark. Nausea gripped him as his senses reeled with the sudden shift in time and place. Paul felt as if he had been transported to a long tunnel carved out of rock. Even more bizarre, he seemed to be running on four feet, surrounded by a herd of animals that jostled him. The entire herd was running toward a faint light that lay ahead; the animals' noisy respiration and clattering hooves were deafening. The light grew steadily larger and more ominous. Paul understood that ahead of him was the boy and something else, too. Something final and without hope. Death—both his and the boy's. Then, he heard his name being called as if from a great distance.*

"Mr. Judge?"

He removed the mysterious artifact and laid it again on the paper. Only when the necklace was out of his hands did the vision end. The last thing he saw before it faded entirely was a large black wolf, watching and waiting.

"Are you okay?" Father Janowsky asked.

He nodded, still a bit overcome by the experience produced by the necklace. "Yeah."

The priest wore a concerned frown on his face. "You looked like you left us there for a moment."

"Where do you think such a thing might have come from?" Dr. Chan asked.

"I have no idea. Why not ask an anthropologist or someone who specializes in Indians?"

"I did and they weren't very helpful. One thought the necklace was hundreds of years old. Another thought it might be a movie prop."

"Where was the body found?"

"Near the waterfront."

"May I?" Father Janowsky pointed to the necklace.

"Of course."

He ran his fingers over the necklace with one hand while, with his other, he clenched a strand of rosary beads that he took from his pocket. "So cold. Amazing."

Dr. Chan nodded. "Yes. I noticed it, too. In fact, I placed it in a

173

vacuum bottle and then sampled the temperature in the bottle."

"And?" the priest asked.

"After five minutes, fifty-six degrees Fahrenheit. After ten, forty-one point four."

"Incredible."

Paul remained silent, thinking about finding the boy and the wind, how cold it had been.

"What's in the medicine bag?" he asked.

"A bit of charcoal, some herbaceous earth, and several teeth."

"Teeth?" Father Janowsky asked. "What kind?"

"Another piece of the puzzle." Dr. Chan loosened the leather thong and poured the contents of the small pouch onto the paper. "There are two different kinds of teeth. These"—she pointed to two exceptionally long fangs—"are the incisors of a canine, possibly a very large dog or wolf. These, on the other hand,"—she pointed to a number of tiny white objects—"are from a child, probably twelve or thirteen years old."

Paul glanced at Father Janowsky whose lips were pressed tightly together in a straight line.

"I have used up my five minutes, Mr. Judge. But if you have another five, I would like to show you something even more remarkable."

"Father?" Paul asked. The priest nodded.

Dr. Chan placed the necklace back in the envelope. A few moments later, she led them through two sets of swinging metal doors into a large, chilly room with a powerful antiseptic odor. On one side, built into a wall, were what looked like forty or fifty file cabinet drawers. On the other were three stainless steel tables. Hoses ran to stainless steel sinks nearby. Three large drains were set in the gleaming linoleum floor.

Dr. Chan checked the numbers on one file-cabinet-like drawer against a number on the manila envelope. The drawer slid open silently.

"Remarkable," Father Janowsky said.

Glassy, distant eyes stared from the gray, martyrly visage. Huge sutures of waxed twine went down the sides of his skull to the ears. The body was wrapped in plastic, the arms and legs trussed tightly by rope. A tag hung from one gnarled toe. It was just another dead Indian, Paul tried to tell himself. But something about the man's appearance filled him with sadness, like finding an enormous tree that has blown down.

174

"We have an Indian male of taller than normal stature, approximately six feet two inches and weighing one hundred seventy-eight pounds. I would estimate his age to be between seventy and eighty, although it is difficult to gauge accurately because his lifestyle appears to have been so radically different from what we commonly use as standards." Dr. Chan's voice was professionally cold and impersonal. "The teeth are quite worn, but contain no cavities or dental work. Note the facial tattoos. Other noteworthy markings include numerous scars of indeterminate age."

Dr. Chan pointed with a ballpoint pen to a couple of black outlines. "These discolorations of the face and throat are stab wounds. Death was the result of the throat wound. Forty-eight hours after the autopsy, during the course of our standard re-examination, we also discovered several latent bruises to the extremities, abdomen and torso. This is consistent with the bloody footfalls on his garment.

"We know that our John Doe was in a fight to the death. That he was killed by a single-bladed knife from behind by either a woman or a small boy. That he was kicked repeatedly after he was already down and fatally injured. And, most unusual, that he was scalped,"—again, she used the pen, this time to point to the corpse's silver hair—"although not in the traditional Indian manner where both the scalp and hair are removed. His histamine level was much higher than his serotonin, meaning the victim died within fifteen minutes of his injury.

"From the condition of his lungs, which contain considerable particulate consistent with wood smoke but none whatsoever from pollution, we know he was not from this area, or any place, for that matter, where there is substantial population and the use of petroleum fuels. "Which," she sighed, "includes at least half the planet. So there we are, Mr. Judge. I have told you everything we know. Any guesses as to who our mystery man was, or where he was from?"

"I'd say he was from the north."

She nodded. "Any idea how far? The Okanogan perhaps?"

"No, I'm familiar with the Okanogan, but I've never heard of tattooing. I'd say much farther north."

She frowned. "You think these markings may be Eskimo? This would contradict with his physical height and appearance."

"The designs may be Eskimo, but he is probably not coastal. Somewhere inland. What was he wearing?" Paul asked.

"Some type of tanned animal hide—possibly deer or elk."

"Or caribou. I'd guess he's from the sub-Arctic interior of Canada."

"What about the sea urchin spines?"

"Like the tattoos, something he and his people acquired by interaction—probably trading—with other tribes."

"I'm impressed," Father Janowsky said. "You seem to know a great deal about your fellow Native Americans."

"Not as much as I'd like," Paul said. After his grandmother's words of instruction, "Remember ancestors," he had read everything he could find on Indians at the university library.

"I agree with the Father's most accurate assessment," Dr. Chan said. "What else can you tell me?"

"A big shot."

"A chief? Or medicine man?"

"Both."

"Why do you say that?"

Paul stared again at the face which, even in death, displayed incredible dignity. "I don't know." Then he remembered the necklace and the feeling of being in a long tunnel. "What about his medicine bundle? Where is that?"

Doctor Chan looked confused. "Medicine bundle?"

"A large pouch." Paul described its approximate size with his hands. "It would have contained his pipe and tobacco, perhaps some bones, a rattle, other items he saw in his dreams."

"You have already seen everything."

Paul remembered the tunnel with its growing light and the feeling of inescapable death that lay just ahead. He turned to the priest. "Father Janowsky, remember what you said about a gate being opened?"

The priest nodded. "I remember."

Dr. Chan looked to both men for an explanation. Paul decided this was not the proper time or place to bring up spiritual matters. Father Janowsky evidently felt the same way as he, too, remained silent.

"One more question, Dr. Chan," Paul said. "What do you know about dog whistles?"

"Dog whistles?" Father Janowsky looked momentarily confused. "Ah, yes!" He beamed. "Like the one I gave to Nico?"

"Dog whistles emit high-frequency, ultrasonic waves," Dr. Chan said, "which can be heard by dogs and other animals over long distances. Ultrasonic cries are also how bats can fly and catch their prey. It's the same principle as sonar."

"And don't doctors use ultrasound to check on the health of unborn fetuses?" the priest asked.

"Exactly," Dr. Chan replied. "There is research going on to determine other potential medical benefits of ultrasound, even including rehabilitation of severe hearing loss."

"Wait a minute," Paul interrupted. "Are you saying a deaf person might be able to hear a dog whistle?"

"From what I understand, yes, it's possible," Dr. Chan said.

16

Journeys

SAN JUAN ISLAND, TUESDAY, 10:40 A.M. The town
was mostly deserted, but even on a fall weekday, long after the tourists had returned to the mainland, Friday Harbor remained
crowded with the ragtag fleet of fishing and pleasure craft that rode
at anchor, seaweed-laden mooring lines drooping from their bows.
Sodden nylon yacht club burgees hung sadly from the rigging of a
large wooden ketch that claimed Portland for a home port. Condos,
two-story shops and a few evergreen trees, broken only by the infre-
quent, emerald sweep of lawn and the glass and cedar visage of a
handful of houses, crowded down close to the rocky shoreline.

Helen looked at her watch for the third time in the past two minutes. According to the printed schedule in her purse, the ferry
should already be tied up and off-loading vehicles.

Rain drummed on the hood of her car and occasionally struck
her in the face when it glanced off the partially opened window.
This irritated her to no end, but she was unable to close the window
all the way without fogging up the windshield. Two rows of cars, a
truck, and a pair of hardy bicyclists wearing ponchos waited patiently in the steady downpour. A large, gray, female Western gull,
looking ever so drab compared to the male version, strutted between them, searching for a crumb of donut on the rain-darkened
asphalt, before finally wheeling away with a mournful screech. The
driver to the right of her read his newspaper and sipped coffee, stoi-
cally oblivious, in typical native fashion, to the weather. Ahead of
her, a young mother grew more and more frazzled as her bored children wrestled back and forth over the front seat, causing the car to
rock. A curly-headed boy sucking on a bottle that dangled from his
lips labored to push his stuffed animal through the vented rear window.

Restlessly, Helen glanced back at the pay telephone, standing vacant outside a restaurant less than a block away. It was quite routine
for the ferries to run a few minutes late. Still, she felt her anxiety
level rising by the minute. The trip to Seattle would involve taking a

ferry to Anacortes with a short stop at Lopez Island followed by an hour and a half drive to Seattle. The entire water portion of the trip would take less than two hours through some of the most scenic waterscape in North America. Once she was on the ferry, however, she would be cut off from all communication with the mainland. Helen found the thought troubling.

After a final survey of the still empty inlet, Helen opened the car door and got out. The driver of the car behind hers eyed her suspiciously as she limped past his vehicle, using her father's cane for support. Helen empathized with what he must be thinking: If this gimpy old bag doesn't make it back in time, I could miss the ferry.

The first number she tried was Mossman's. The *Times'* operator informed her that he was still not in. Next, Helen pulled the slip of paper with Ann's number out of her purse. After dialing, she looked behind her and discovered that the ferry was in the process of docking. She recognized the quaint shape of the Hiyu, the smallest of the ferries that served the islands.

An answering machine clicked on and she waited for the beep before speaking rapidly. "Ann, this is Helen Anderson. It's Tuesday morning and I'm on my way to Seattle to talk to whoever will listen. I've been doing some research and might have uncovered what happened to us. There are these winds called 'Williwaws' and they've been clocked at 113 miles per hour. But the really interesting part is that the Eskimos believe them to be spirit winds. I know it sounds a bit woo-woo and all that," she twisted the telephone cord in her hand, "but if it's true, Ann, this Williwaw could cause a lot more hurt and damage before it decides to leave. Anyway, I have to go, the ferry is loading right now. I'll call you when I get in." She started to hang up, then added, "Hope you're better."

Helen hung up the phone. She had done all she could for now. As she bowed her head in the rain and hobbled back to her car, she had no doubt that the irate honking was meant for her.

Even in person, it was not going to be an easy task to get Mossman—or anyone else, for that matter—to accept her story about a wind that could target small areas, that could pick up an animal and hurl it against a tree, or attack a sailboat from two different directions. Like Grasshopper said, who would believe it unless they had personally experienced it? As farfetched as it was, however, Grasshopper's explanation about a spirit wind was the only one that made sense.

"Sorry," she said as she passed the driver who glared at her from the car behind hers. She climbed into her car, started it and drove toward the gaping mouth of the waiting ferry, oblivious to the teddy bear lying in a shallow puddle, a single glass eye staring up at the achromatic sky.

SEATTLE, TUESDAY, 11:00 A.M. The phone rang and Denise reached for it with her left hand, the other never leaving the computer keyboard.

"This is Denise," she said and resumed inputting the rough draft of a story she was working on.

"How's the survivor?"

For a second, she thought it was Paul.

"Wonderful," she replied.

" 'Wonderful?' You didn't tell me you had a new boyfriend, Denise. I'm jealous."

The words drenched her like a pail of cold and dirty dishwater and Denise became immediately wary, retreating deeply into her professional persona. "Bud," she sighed. "What's up?"

"Hmmm, the air suddenly feels a bit frosty this morning. My bedside manner either needs a refresher course, or perhaps I need a new bed?"

"Excuse me, Bud, but did you have a reason for this call? I've got tons of work to get out."

"That's my girl—all business as usual." He sighed. "We need to follow up the Tower conference, Denise. The election's eight days away and Wilson suddenly wants to debate our guy."

"Why suddenly so brave?" she asked. Wilson had turned down cold several opportunities to debate Grenitzer so far, preferring to sit on his lead.

"He might be a bit rattled. Yesterday's Tower accident got excellent play, in spite of everything that went wrong."

"This late in the game, can't we just turn him down?"

"Risky, my dear, very risky. Don't you remember? Back in May, his regalness, in one of his customary lapses of intelligence said, and I quote, 'Any time, any place.' "

"But that was the primaries."

"Same thing. The voters will think he's reneging because he's got something to hide. That Mossman story couldn't have hit at a worse time."

"But the downside of a last minute debate is enormous. I can't believe that you've decided to go ahead?"

"No way. Wilson would turn it into a three-ring circus—the Tower, busing, you name it. Here's the catch, Denise: we can't very well turn it down, but we could be the loser if we go ahead. So, we need a touchdown and a two-point conversion, something that will put Wilson away. Understand the problem?"

"Yeah, okay, let me think." Denise tapped a pencil on her coffee cup and considered options. A framed photograph of Evan in his soccer uniform stood among several fat file folders and the morning newspaper's scattered remains. "I can see why Wilson might be worried," she said. "KOMO TV ran that bit with Grenitzer at the lectern, taking charge after the accident."

"That was priceless. The little schmuck surprises me sometimes, I must admit."

"We'll have results of the latest telephone survey later today," Denise continued. "I think it will show the mayor close to dead even, if not a little ahead. Considering he was ten points down last week, that would be pretty impressive."

"I agree. So all we need is to stage another disaster and we're home free." He forced a laugh. "Sounds easy enough for someone with your talents. Any ideas?"

"What about a follow-up to the copter accident last night at the Seattle Center?"

"Like what—another press conference? I'm not tracking you."

"What about a memorial ceremony dedicated to the two cops that died? And we can include the mounted police officer that died on Saturday, too."

"Hot idea, Denise! I definitely like it. Can't you just see it, cops lined up fifty deep, flags lowered and presented to the victims' wives? Jack can eulogize Seattle's finest, getting in a lick about the crime rate and needing more police. There won't be a dry eye in the city, except those of Wilson and his people. Denise, I could kiss your lovely—never mind. Be ready for lunch in half an hour, I'll pick you up in front of your building. We've got a lot to do in the next few hours. You better start with the Center people. I'll let the cops know what we're doing."

Denise hung up, simultaneously elated and disgusted, and noticed the red message light blinking on her phone. "Sorry I missed you," the recorded voice said. "I couldn't find any trace of Nicholas Tambakis, the blind beggar whose seeing eye dog Evan found. I did meet Father Janowsky, the priest who runs the shelter where he stays, and I may even have found some answers about the wind—

nothing that makes any sense yet. I'm on my way to Issaquah to see some friends and try to sort it all out. I'll call you when I get back. Oh, the priest says it would be fine if Evan kept the dog, at least until Tambakis turns up, if he does."

"Shoot." Denise was more than a little sorry that she hadn't gotten to speak to Paul. Despite the depressing weather and a heavy workload, until Bud's call, she had felt a lightness she hadn't felt in a long time. She was still puzzling over what it all meant.

She had lain awake most of the night, listening and thinking. The story about the wind was unbelievable, yet she didn't think Evan or Paul would lie to her. And even if their stories were hard to accept, the scratches on her son and Paul's bruises were not something that you could fake. Then, there was her own experience at the Tower when it seemed like every bird in the city had simultaneously taken flight a moment before the violent gust of wind hit. Whatever the explanation behind it all was, only one thing mattered: Evan was safe, and all because of Paul.

Twice she had gotten up to check on Evan. Both times, she stood at the top of the stairs, listening for the whisper of Paul's breathing on the couch downstairs. But whether he, like her, couldn't sleep, or was just a very quiet breather, she couldn't hear a thing other than the old clock in the entry.

Early in the morning, she had risen, showered and gone downstairs to make coffee and ask him if he'd like breakfast. Instead of a sleeping man, however, she'd found only a single sheet of paper, folded in half, lying on top of the neatly folded blanket and pillow she had provided him.

We are all children of the same mother. She who brings rivers from the mountain to the sea also brings you to me.

Denise called his number in case he was still there, but there was only his recorded voice and she hung up without leaving a message. "Men," she said.

Grenitzer called twenty minutes later.

"Bud's come up with another stroke of genius: a memorial service for the dead cops. We need to do this right, Denise. No screwups, okay?"

It was all she could do to keep from spitting on the phone. She'd been in the business long enough to expect Bud's taking credit for her idea. That kind of thing happened every day in her business. What she hated most was knowing that he knew she wouldn't say anything. She couldn't afford to jeopardize her job.

Billy leaned against the kitchen counter, staring at the steady rain that dimpled the surface of Lake Union, without really seeing it. Two things kept him from enjoying the view outside their houseboat: his sore butt and the missing intern.

He'd just hung up the phone after talking with Douglas Truitt, the city news editor. No one remembered seeing the young woman since late last night when she'd been holed up in Billy's office. What the hell was going on? It wasn't like Gretta to disappear. Especially when she'd just been offered her first chance to actually do some investigating.

Julie was at work, and he was bored to death being away from the newsroom. He'd always thought that writing in such a quiet, peaceful environment would be nirvana. Instead, it had turned out to be like taking several shots of Novocain to the brain. Even eight cups of leaded coffee hadn't helped. He was feeling more wired, stupid, and frustrated by the minute. He wasn't supposed to drive yet, but Gretta wasn't supposed to disappear, life wasn't fair, bears didn't live in the woods and all that other baloney. She was probably just home with a hangover, or shacked up with some stud.

"I'll kill her," he said to the empty rooms. He got a hat and raincoat from the hall closet and wrote a note to Julie, just in case she got back before he did. At the last minute, he remembered to take his rubber donut. Then he drove to the *Times*.

ANACORTES ISLAND, TUESDAY, 12:00 P.M. At the familiar sight of the Anacortes ferry landing, Helen felt herself begin to relax. Beneath her feet, the Hiyu's steel deck vibrated with the comforting rumble of its massive diesel engines. The rain had slowed to a tolerable drizzle and she leaned against a deck railing sipping the last of the coffee from her thermos. Now that the trip was nearly over, she could enjoy the bite of raw, salty air and the flash of whitecaps against the rolling gray seas of Puget Sound. A small, red cabin cruiser raced by them, skipping over the waves.

The trip hadn't been entirely uneventful. Shortly after leaving Friday Harbor, they had sighted a pod of killer whales keeping pace on their left flank. Many of the automobile passengers had exited their vehicles to watch the tall, black dorsal fins of the orcas appearing, then disappearing, like the rise and fall of swift and deadly undersea carousel horses.

Unlike the superferries with their large, extensive cabin areas which included cafeterias, the Hiyu was so small that many people kept to the comfort of their cars. An exception was the mother and her children that had been in line directly ahead of Helen back at Friday Harbor. Soon after boarding, they had climbed the stairs to the ferry's small lounge. Now the young boy and girl returned to the auto deck, racing between the cars and arguing over a plastic devil mask that the girl wore.

At the sight of the mask, Helen realized that the previous night had been Halloween. Since moving to San Jan Island and leaving the hordes of trick-or-treaters far behind, Halloween had slowly evolved into a private party for her and Byron. She liked to carve a jack-o'-lantern and place it on the mantle of the stone fireplace where its flickering glare reminded her of her childhood. Byron had exhibited a fondness for wearing dark glasses and inhaling miniature Mars bars. At the memory of Byron and his brutal death, her coffee suddenly acquired the taste and odor of liquid asphalt. Careful to judge the direction of the wind, Helen threw the remainder over the side.

As the ferry approached the terminal, those people that had ridden out the journey in the passenger lounge began to make their way to their cars. An engine backfired and the cyclists began unsecuring their bikes from the forward rack. Through the gaping mouth of the ferry, she could see a number of cars lined up, waiting at the ferry terminal. A row of long-necked, black cormorants, reminding her of attendants at a funeral, occupied the flat-topped pilings. Beyond them stretched a low hill, once covered by evergreen trees and now shorn of all but a few holdouts, their numbers replaced by a trailer park and several new housing developments.

Before beginning the lengthy drive to Seattle, Helen decided that she would stop at a fast food place and get something to eat. Once in Seattle, she planned to drive directly to the *Times* where she hoped to meet with Mossman. Then she would place a call to Ann, try to see her if possible. She planned to stay downtown, it didn't matter exactly where. If all went well, she'd be back home late tomorrow or early the next day.

They closed to within a hundred yards of the slip. The engines at either end of the ferry were reversed and the boat began to slow. Helen limped the short distance to her car and was nearly knocked off her feet when the girl in the devil's mask careened around a car and into her path.

"Oops. Sorry, lady," the devil said.

The boy caught up to his sister and made a grab for her mask, but she was too fast for him. "Come on, Gena. It's my turn," he whined at his sister's retreating back. And Gena and the boy continued their game of cat and mouse around the deck.

Helen was putting her father's cane into the car when she heard shouts. At the rear of the boat, someone's red windbreaker had become caught up in the boat's draft and now flew, arms outstretched, over the water behind the boat. There was a collective moan as it finally settled into the foam of their wake.

Again, Helen began to climb into her car. This time, an unexpectedly strong tailwind pushed her hard against the door. Pain splintered from her ankle and she had to bite her tongue to keep from crying out. Her pain was forgotten a moment later. The air tasted of hunting wild strawberries in the mountains with her father. The long-forgotten memory made her look around anxiously for its source. "Oh, my God," she whispered. "Not now!"

The full fury of the wind slammed into them at the worst possible moment. It came from the north just as they were preparing to dock. Helen beheld their coming destruction with awe. They were coming in wrong, pushed off course by the wind. Instead of being lined up to go between the massive, twin pilings that had been positioned to guide the vessel into its slip, they were headed directly toward the one on the left. Two crewmen, who stood ready with heavy hawsers to secure the boat, yelled up to the captain, but their warnings were drowned out by the wind. The cyclists scrambled to drag their bikes back from the front of the boat.

They struck the pilings with a vicious crunch. Bodies and belongings flew forward among the vehicles and a horrid screech of ripping wood, grinding metal and human screams rent the violent air. Helen was flung to the deck. Beneath her, the ferry's engines bellowed in protest. She fought to right herself by using the car bumper for support. High above her, she saw the terror-stricken face of a young man standing on the passenger landing as their stern continued to swing around the piling toward the unprotected side of the pier.

Again, they struck. The ferry's steel deck was the size of half a football field and it smashed into the pier's concrete supports like a giant axe blade, the force of five hundred tons driving it home. The roadway buckled and collapsed. Wooden timbers and chunks of asphalt and concrete toppled off the ferry landing and onto the cars parked on the ferry deck with a thunderous crash. The man she had seen waiting on the landing disappeared into the frothy, propeller-churned waters between ship and pier. A groan of metallic anguish rose from the covered passenger ramp. Then it, too, toppled into the bay with a gigantic splash.

It was over in seconds. A valiant warrior going down on one knee, the Hiyu dipped one rail into the sea. Now the waters came in a rush. Helen lost her grip on the bumper and slid several feet on the wave-washed deck until she came to rest, her legs jammed beneath an automobile. She lay on her back, trapped, as the rapidly deepening waters foamed around her. Somewhere an alarm began ringing, or maybe it was in her head. It was hard to be certain of anything in the tumult of screams and confusion. Unlike the other victims, however, Helen was certain of one thing: this was no accident.

"How did you find me?" she sputtered.

The wind hissed in reply. Then a plastic devil mask swept over her into the turbulent seas.

SEATTLE, TUESDAY, 12:30 P.M. Billy inspected his office. Gretta had definitely been here. He could still smell her perfume. He opened the drawers of his desk and noticed that the pencil had been torn from his note. "Gotcha," he said, and smiled for the first time that day. He picked up his memo pad. Nothing. Then he held the top sheet up to the light. He could just see the trace of a word written there. He took a pencil and rubbed the back of the sheet until he could read it. "Whirlwind," he said aloud. His musing was interrupted by a commotion in the newsroom. He did not have to wait long to find out why.

Douglas Truitt stuck his head in Billy's doorway. "Hey! How's your backside, Billy?"

Small talk from Truitt always made him suspicious. "Fine. What is it?"

"Ferry just went down off Anacortes."

Billy stared at him in surprise. "Fatalities?"

"Sounds like it."

He had to ask. "What caused it?"

"Hell if I know." Truitt shrugged. "That's why I'm here. I need someone who can handle a tight deadline. A pro. Can you help?"

"I'm on my way."

"No, you're not. I want you here, assimilating, coordinating, editing. I've got a couple guys on the way. They'll be your eyes and ears."

186

"Reach out and touch someone? No way. I'm no good at long distance reporting, Doug."

"They can get you interviews by phone."

"That's still not being there."

"I know," Truitt said, "but it will do for today."

"This wouldn't have anything to do with my story Sunday about Grenitzer, would it?"

"Look, I'm giving your ass a break in more ways than one." Truitt's face was growing redder by the second. "Take it or leave it." He walked out and slammed the door.

Lunch with Bud was never a pleasurable experience and today was no exception. They sat in the darkest corner of the hideously over-stuffed bar of the St. George Hotel, a throwback to the era of cigars, two martinis, and prime rib for lunch. At several points during their discussion, Bud had interrupted to wave to yet another of his cronies or one of the city's powerful elite. Denise wondered how they could even recognize each other in the dim light. Had to be something in their DNA, a holdover from their cave-dwelling days. Outlining the memorial ceremony to be held at the Center had nevertheless proved surprisingly simple and halfway through their meal, Bud had ordered a bottle of champagne.

"You know I never drink during the day," Denise said when the waiter had left.

"But today is special, my dear." He smiled.

Denise noticed a small patch of stubble on his chin where he had missed with his razor. The small imperfection only added to her contempt. "How so?"

He threw out his narrow chest and took in a deep breath. "I smell victory in the air." Bud had already knocked down two glasses of chardonnay and was obviously feeling none the worse for it.

"A little early to be celebrating, don't you think?"

He put his hand over hers. "Denise, mark my words: after this Center thing, it's in the bag. Another four years in the captain's seat."

The thought gave her no feeling of celebration whatsoever. "And then?"

"Who the hell knows?" he said as the waiter reappeared with their champagne. "In this business, four years is an eternity. You want job security, forget it. It's survival of the luckiest."

"Is this a new theory of evolution—survival of the lucky?"

"Not a theory—a fact. Call it Phillips' Law of Survival. To you, Denise," Bud said over his raised glass. "For duty under fire."

"To luck," Denise added. She sipped her champagne and thought about Paul. She wondered what had motivated him to leave town suddenly to visit friends. Or was he always so flighty? She didn't think so, but she knew far too little about him to make judgments with any certainty. And besides, why should she be worried about his personality traits anyway?

"Is my company that boring?" Bud put his hand on her knee. "I swear, I think you left town for a minute there."

Denise removed his hand as if she were lifting a dead mouse by the tail and dropped it in his lap. "Just figuring out how I'm going to get it all done."

"Always business. Seems to me you weren't always so irritatingly professional, Denise. What happened to your sense of humor, for Christ's sake?"

She could have said that getting to be thirty-four with a thirteen-year-old son, no savings and no money for a new car or the dentist, and being passed over for raises and promotions because you weren't "one of the guys" was what happened. Instead, she gave him her best imitation smile and remained silent. You could talk to men like Bud until you were blue in the face, and when you were done, you were still left with a sanctimonious, patronizing cretin calling you "honey" and giving you little pats on the rear. It was a fact of life for all women, Denise tried to console herself. So how come she always felt like Tonto, abandoned by the Lone Ranger and surrounded by Custer and the 7th Army?

"Okay, be a party pooper." Bud stood, swayed for just a moment, his words sounding mushy. "We can finish this back at your office."

"After this is all over, we'll find time to relax," he said a few minutes later as they were driving back to her office in his plush city car. The swish of the windshield wipers, the effects of the champagne and her lack of sleep made her want to take a nap. "I've got a place on Hood Canal I'd like to show you. We could take a three-day weekend. Just the two of us."

Denise sat up straighter. They were driving into an underground parking garage near where she worked. "Excuse me, what are you talking about? Should I call your wife and ask what clothes to wear?" She could feel her cheeks redden.

"I figured we'd just skip the clothing," Bud said. "Do a little strategizing in the ol' hot tub."

"You must be drunk, Bud. Even you're smart enough to know that's sexual harassment."

"What's the matter with you, Denise?" Bud sounded flustered as he parked the car on the lowest level.

"Me?"

"All work and no play makes for a pretty dull life. After all, we're not getting any younger."

"Speak for yourself." As disgusted as she was, Denise tried the rational approach. "C'mon, Bud. Let's call it a day. You'll just feel silly when you get back to your office and sober up." She unfastened her seat belt to get out, but Bud grabbed it, used it to hold her in as he pressed against her. "Bud, don't do this!" Denise said as he ran his right hand through the short hair on the back of her head. She struggled to open the door. He tightened his hand on her head, forcing her face toward his. She felt his wet lips on hers for just an instant before she elbowed him sharply.

"God damn!" He grabbed his side.

Denise used the opportunity to get out of the car.

"Hey, can't you take a joke?" Bud continued to rub his rib cage.

"If I want comedy, I'll pay a cover charge!" She slammed the door.

She hurried up the ramp to the street level, then walked back to her office, the rain striking her face. If not for the other pedestrians, she might have let the tears come. Instead, she stamped around the block once before trusting herself to enter her office building. Once there, however, she headed straight for the women's room. Denise blinked through moist eyes at her flushed cheeks in the mirror. "Bastard," she said, the word a hard bullet in her mouth.

A tall black woman looked up from the other end of the bathroom counter top where she was applying a fresh coat of lipstick. "You having one of those days, too?"

Denise nodded, embarrassed, and searched for a paper towel.

"Here, girl. You look like you could use a good cry." The other woman handed her a wad of tissues from her briefcase. "Let me guess. Are you feeling demeaned and humiliated because of, A, one man in particular, B, men in general, or C, all of the above?"

"I can't believe I let them get to me," Denise said.

"Listen, don't waste any tears over a bunch of extinct dinosaurs.

Men are like those Stegosaurs, all horns, muscles, and scales and a brain the size of a walnut. The only reason they're on top is because we let them. I tolerate one to mow the yard, change flat tires, and take the kinks out now and then, but when I need a little intelligence and tenderness, I snuggle up with the dog and a good book."

Denise had to smile. "Thanks. I needed that."

"Hey." The woman touched her shoulder. "I'll probably need you to remind me what I just said someday real soon. Deal?"

"Deal."

ISSAQUAH, TUESDAY, 1:20 P.M. Paul turned off the highway and drove down a long, golden driveway of crushed leaves from the poplars that lined the road, a windbreak planted fifty years before by a visionary farmer. The blanket of clouds had lifted near its western edge so that the Cascade mountains rose jaggedly behind the barn and other out-buildings. At the sound of the Mercedes' diesel clatter, a black appaloosa, its hindquarters speckled with white spots, came charging across the rolling pasture. The sight of Yakima running free always gladdened his heart.

After his trip to the morgue with Father Janowsky, he needed cheering up. Even after checking out all the John Does, they hadn't found Nicholas Tambakis. What they had uncovered, however, was plenty disturbing.

Within seconds of his turning off the engine in front of the modest, Victorian-era farmhouse, Bernice Horn was out the door running to him, her jet-black hair pulled back in a braid that trailed behind her. She nearly beat the dog, a big, sand-colored animal that was all tongue and feet. Paul rested easy in Bern's embrace. Then she pecked him on the lips while the dog's tail beat time against his leg.

"Whose woman are you anyway?" came a gruff male voice from the porch.

Paul turned to see his best friend, Charley, wearing a cowboy hat and boots, jeans, and a white shirt, a toothpick hanging from the corner of his mouth.

"If I was his woman, would I be hanging around this hole with someone as ugly as you?"

"There you go," Paul said, petting the dog.

"C'mon," Bernice said and began to haul him by the arm up the steps. "Have you had lunch yet? I'll make you a sandwich."

"First, I need to talk to Charley."

She gave him a look, more curious than disappointed, then said, "Go. I'll get you some coffee."

"We'll be over by the stable," Charley said.

The two men exchanged pleasantries during the short walk through the wet grass. As they approached the split-rail fence that enclosed the stable and pasture, the appaloosa, which had been eagerly waiting, pranced a little ways off, stepping high, tossing his head and snorting.

"He wants you to ride him," Charley said.

"No he doesn't. He's pissed. It's been over three weeks."

"He's pissed, but he still wants you to ride him."

"Wish I could."

"It's a good day for a ride."

"In the rain?"

"The horse doesn't mind. It makes the ground softer. Everything smells nicer. Less dust. No flies. So quiet you can barely hear the traffic on I-90."

"Well, I can't ride today," Paul said.

"What's the matter, Poco? You look like your dick fell off."

Paul frowned. Both men rested their arms on the top rail, one foot up on the lower rail. "You're the only one that can understand what I'm going to tell you," Paul said.

"Oh, hell. I always knew you were gay," Charley said. "You wanna kiss me, is that it?"

"Get!" Paul shoved his friend away. He smiled and waited for the older man to stop laughing, his breath escaping in small clouds. They were so close to the mountains that the air raked your lungs with its claws. As if aware that they were no longer talking about him, the horse began to edge closer to the two men. Paul reached out a hand which the horse pretended to ignore. The dog, on the other hand, was considerably less fussy.

"I've run into something that I need your counsel on." Paul turned to face Charley. "You know all this weather-related stuff that's been going on in Seattle? Panels from buildings falling on people, a police helicopter crashing?"

"They didn't say what caused the copter crash, but we heard about it on the news."

"Let me ask you, have you had any stuff like that up here?"

"Nah."

"Strange, don't you think?"

"Nothing that happens in the flat lands really surprises me," Charley said.

Tired of being ignored, the horse stuck his nose over the fence and nuzzled Paul's shoulder. Paul winced in pain.

"What's the matter? Yakima bite you?"

"No. I lost a bit of skin last night."

Charley's eyebrows rose. "Does your sore shoulder have something to do with all of this?"

"It has a lot to do with it." Paul stroked the horse's nose. "I was there when the chopper went down." He pulled an object from his jacket pocket.

"What happened?" Charley asked, examining the chunk of melted plastic.

"The wind grabbed it."

The other man was silent for a minute. "If you say it is so, then I accept it. What I really want to know, Poco, is what grabbed you."

"Same thing. I was looking for this missing deaf kid—tracked him to the Seattle Center. When I found him, he was holding on to a tree in the center of a miniature cyclone. Then, when I tried to grab the kid, the wind nearly killed me. It came this close, Charley." He held a thumb and finger nearly together.

"How'd you get away?"

"I didn't. The deaf kid blew this thing that looked like a dog whistle and the wind stopped."

They heard a door slam and the dog went racing back to the house.

"That's Bern with the coffee," Charley said. "Is there more to this story?"

Paul nodded. "This morning, I visited the morgue with a priest and this Chinese doctor asks me to help identify an Indian that was murdered last Friday. First, she shows me a necklace that's like something out of a time machine. Then, she takes me into this huge meat locker and pulls out a drawer with this spooky-looking old guy, all stitched up." He indicated a circle around his head.

Bernice appeared, wearing a cowboy hat and wool coat, and presented them with steaming mugs of coffee that had been laced with bourbon. She held Paul's arm against her body while he sipped his coffee. Between his wagging tail and grinning face, the dog looked happy as hell.

"You look good, kid," Bernice said to Paul.

192

"Thanks. So do you."

"Not bad for an old lady, if I do say so myself." She kicked at her husband.

"Poco just told me he's queer," Charley said.

"You wish, you old fart." She kicked at him again. "Now what was that about somebody all stitched up?"

"A dead Indian," Charley said.

"What dead Indian?"

"It's a long story, Bern," Paul said.

"I wanna hear about who died."

Paul shrugged and sipped his coffee. "I don't know who he was, but from the look of him, he was mighty important."

"Poco thinks the winds that have been raising hell in Seattle might be connected to this guy's death," Charley explained.

Bern gave Paul a hard look. "How old was this guy?"

"A great-grandfather."

"And what was he wearing?"

"Hide body wrap, the doctor said. Plus this ancient necklace of claws, medicine bag and stuff."

"Sounds like a shaman to me," Bern said.

"And it sounds to me like you're getting into something that maybe you shouldn't," Charley said.

"What do you mean?"

"Sounds like a 'white' problem. When it hits the res, then I want to be the first to know."

"But it also tried to kill me."

" 'Cause you got in its way."

"I have to help."

"Why?" Charley asked.

"There's this kid. And his mother."

"His mother? Poco, you got a white woman?"

"No. She's just someone I met."

"I don't think so," Bernice said with a smile. "I'm happy for you, Paul."

"Wait a minute. I just met the woman."

"Charley," Bern said, "if we ever want to see any papooses from this one before we die, you better help him figure out a way to stop this wind and help this woman and her kid."

"What can be done," Paul asked, "if anything?"

Charley stared at the torn peak of one of the nearby Cascades. "I remember a story my father told me one time, about a spirit wind.

This was in Oklahoma where my people are from. It blew like hell for a month, until they finally pacified it."

"How'd they stop it?" Paul asked.

"I don't remember."

"Oh, great," Bern said. "Sometimes I think you got less brains than Big Duck here." She patted the dog.

"You ever been fishing at Neah Bay?" Charley asked.

"Charley!" Bern said.

"Once," Paul answered. "Why?"

"I think maybe it's time you go fishing there again."

Paul sighed. "I don't have time, Charley. People could die."

"I didn't say you should go fishing for fish." He looked back at Paul. "You're gonna drive right on through Neah Bay and the whole Makah reservation until you come to The Edge of the World."

17

Stalking Wind

SEATTLE, TUESDAY, 3:25 P.M. Evan stood ninja-still, resting most of his weight on the ball of one foot. Slowly, he swiveled his head, trying to move as little of his body as possible as he searched the sidewalk, trees, and modest homes behind him for anything unusual among the carved pumpkins and windows spider-webbed with black crepe paper. From Fiftieth and First where the school bus had dropped him was a distance of only six blocks through a well-populated, working-class neighborhood, a route he had traveled hundreds of times. Yet today, for some unknown reason, it felt deserted and a little scary. He turned up the collar of his raincoat. It had stopped raining and the sky was clearing rapidly, but it felt cooler.

Yesterday's encounter with the wind-thing still haunted him. Although there wasn't the slightest sign of actual danger, the sight of leaves drifting down the street or a political poster fluttering in a yard sent his heartbeat racing. And the longer he looked at the Halloween pumpkin perched on a nearby porch railing, the more it seemed to be looking back at him, its evil-looking eyes and gap-toothed grin reminding him of Rawhide.

He resumed walking, faster now. He had promised his mother on his word of honor that he would go straight home from school and he was eager, for maybe the first time in his life, to obey. Fortuno was waiting for him. There was also the strange feeling that he was being stalked.

As he crossed the street and approached Meridian Playground, he caught a glimpse of something white as it darted between the tall hedgerows that surrounded the former convent. Probably just some kid. He hesitated at the gate set in the hedgerow. He could easily walk around the playground, but it was much faster to cut through it. Trying to notice everything at once, he hurried along the well-worn path. The grounds smelled of decaying wood, wet earth, and leaves. The winter sun was cold and distant.

With increasing alarm, Evan noted the absence of people. Usu-

195

ally there were two or three mothers talking while their toddlers swung on the rusting swing set or rode the teeter-totter and once he'd come upon an older boy and girl making out under a tree. But that was summertime when the ground was dry. Today, there was just the old, three-story brick convent surrounded by its garden of bare rosebushes and the orchard of ancient, twisted trees. The gnarled limbs of one especially barren tree contained row after row of sleek, black starlings whose tiny eyes seemed to follow him.

There went the flash of white again. Evan peeked around a Japanese maple whose leaves had turned blood red. He didn't know the names of many trees, just the really outstanding ones and the ones with fruit or nuts. On the grass beneath a large chestnut tree lay a cloth. He stooped to examine the pillowcase into which two holes had been cut for eyes. The costume-wearer had disappeared. Funny thing, the birds were gone, too. That made the hairs stand up on the back of his neck.

About the time he had decided to run for it—who cared who saw him?—something hard bounced off his head and a horse chestnut rolled to a stop near his feet. Evan looked up into the tree from where it had fallen.

Touch the tree, whispered a voice in his head.

Evan suddenly needed to pee.

Touch the tree, the voice repeated, *and I will tell you a secret.*

What kind of secret? Evan thought without even meaning to.

I will tell you who I am.

You'll hurt me.

No I won't. I promise I won't hurt you if you touch the tree.

But why?

Then you can feel my thoughts as well as hear them, and I can feel yours.

Who are you? Evan thought, placing a trembling hand on the rough bark. It was cold, so cold that his hand stuck to it, as if frozen there.

I am called Williwaw by some. Taku by others. I have many names, but I am the wind. The wind's "voice" sounded hoarse in his head and its words were interrupted by many sighs.

You came to my room last night.

Yes.

You scared me.

I came only to find you, to speak as we are speaking now.

Why do you follow me?

The old one told me about you. You are chosen.

Chosen for what?

A great honor. You will see when the time is right.

Why should I believe you? Yesterday, you tried to hurt me and my friend, Paul. And you killed the men in the helicopter.

I did not mean to hurt you. I wanted only to tell you of my anger and sadness. Your friend is a meddler. He should stay out of what does not concern him. I hurt the others because they disturb the air and because they would stop me if they could. But they cannot. The wind's voice grew more forceful.

It's not right to hurt people.

What do you know? You are too young. Evan felt the wind's anger curling inside his head. *It was they who did the hurting first. Long before you were born, this was the land of my brothers and sisters. The land was taken from them by the whites. For many generations, it has been desecrated—the rivers stopped, the land scalped, the air made thick with stinking smoke. Now, it is fit for no one, not even the dead. The hare and the fish, the eagle and the maize—all die from the stench made by the whites. But this is only what makes me sick, not why I come. It is right to repay the new wrong many times over.*

What wrong? Evan asked, holding his free hand to the side of his head where his ear hurt.

They killed a holy one. There is no one left to avenge his death but me. But I am powerful. I will show them what they deal with.

Who's they? Who did this?

It does not matter.

Then a question came to his mind that Evan was afraid to ask.

You want to know if I killed the man with no eyes. The answer is yes. He and many others.

But why? He was my friend. He never hurt anyone. Evan wiped at a hot tear that sledded down his frozen cheek.

I kill because they are enemy: the young and the old, the strong and the weak, good and bad. They are all the same to me.

Then you're evil!

No. Evan felt the wind's anger exploding within his head and jerked his hand away from the tree. *It is they who are evil. Do you think I would visit this unholy place if I did not have to? I will make them pay for their ignorance and stupidity, like the people today on the great boat. They think they are safe in their machines.*

Boat? What boat? Evan didn't understand.

I rule all that stands upon the ground, floats upon the water or flies in

197

the air. Nothing can stop me. There, look into the sky. You don't believe me?

Evan looked up and saw a jet headed north.

Now, I will show you who I am and what I can do. Then you will know that what I say is true.

No, Evan screamed in his head. But the wind was gone.

Billy hung up the phone and looked away from the computer monitor long enough to rub his eyes. His was not a happy frame of mind. In addition to his tender rear, he had a headache that wouldn't quit. A migraine, actually. It started just behind his right eye, ran across his cheekbone and down to the corner of his jaw where it looped around to the back of his neck and his shoulders. The entire right side of his face felt twice its normal size.

"Are you sure you need to be here?" Olive, a senior copy editor, stuck her head in his office, a look of genuine concern behind her oversized plastic lenses. "You look like hell, Billy."

"Thanks," Billy said. "Same to you."

She withdrew hastily. He would probably regret his rudeness later, but right now, he felt too bad to feel bad.

He stood up, walked to his window and stared out at Puget Sound. The ferry story was coming together, much as he hated to admit it. There were eyewitnesses galore, from the people on the dock to several passengers who had managed to survive the crash. Even a couple of ferry attendants. The captain was undergoing breathalyzer and blood tests. All the survivors said the same thing—that the boat had missed the landing, but whether from a strong gust of wind, sloppy handling, or both, there was little agreement.

Being a phone call away from the story was frustrating. He couldn't tell someone else what questions to ask. You had to be there. A good story was in the eyes of the teller. Studying the eyes told Billy what questions to ask, where to go next and whether the person was lying. He hadn't felt this helpless since his daughter had been born.

But what was really wearing thin was all this crap about this being just another freak accident. Sure. Just like the Tower and the helicopter. A chain of freak accidents. "Pure coincidence," the weather service was saying. Well, bullshit. It was just too weird. And speaking of weird, where was Gretta? He'd called her apartment half a dozen times. Nothing.

Remembrance of the missing intern brought his mind and his eyes into clearer focus. Billy saw the city outside his window for the first time since driving in. It had stopped raining, the clouds had lifted, and he could see the Olympics. Below, a ferry approached the terminal. He watched as it slowed to a virtual standstill before docking gently.

"Where the hell did you go, Gretta?"

The phone rang. Billy picked it up on the second ring. "Mossman." The voice that spoke was so faint he had to ask the person to speak up.

"Mr. Mossman, this is Ann Bessani."

In the short silence that followed, Billy tried to place where he had heard the name. "Oh, yes. The sailboat lady."

"Am I that well known?"

"I'm sorry about your family. How are you and your daughter doing?"

"Better. Thank you for asking. Megan has been staying with her grandparents. I just returned home from the hospital. When I listened to my messages, I heard something that has me very concerned. It's the reason I'm calling. Mr. Mossman, do you recognize the name Helen Anderson?"

Billy felt his heart leap uncomfortably in his chest. "From San Juan Island?"

"Two for two, Mr. Mossman. She left word that she was on her way to Seattle to tell you what she had learned about the wind. Did you know she was coming?"

"Not at all." Another coincidence. "Oddly enough, however, I've been trying to reach her."

"That could be difficult based on what I just heard on the radio."

"Why's that?" He moved his foam donut into the center of his chair and sat down with a small grunt.

"I think she may have been on the Hiyu."

Billy was speechless.

"I don't suppose there's a passenger list?" Ann said.

"None," he said, still in shock.

"I've tried calling her, but there's no answer."

"Wait a minute. Does she have family? Or maybe friends we could check with?"

"I don't know about friends. With regards to family, I don't think so." She coughed and it sounded to Billy as if her voice was growing weaker.

"Did she tell you anything?"

"Yes. She thought she had discovered what was causing all the wind-related accidents. She called it a 'Williwaw,'' said it was an Eskimo spirit wind."

"Spirit wind?" Billy wrote down the word "Williwaw" on the pad under where he had previously traced Gretta's "whirlwind." "Spirit wind" sounded like the name of a recording by some New Age group. "Do you think a *spirit wind* attacked your boat, Mrs. Bessani?" He was unable to keep the disbelief from showing in his voice.

"That tone of voice is very unflattering." Her voice grew icy. "In answer to your question, I couldn't say for sure, Mr. Mossman. But I've never seen a wind hit so hard and fast, switch directions and then leave, all within a matter of a few seconds. I can see that this is a complete waste of my time. Good-bye, Mr. Mossman."

"Wait," Billy said. "Look, Ms. Bessani, I'm sorry. 'Spirit winds' aren't my usual beat. Let me try another angle. What color are your eyes?"

"Brown," she said, her voice heavy with suspicion. "Why?"

Billy tried to imagine looking into her eyes. "Is there anything else—anything at all—that you can remember?"

"Not really."

"Did you see or hear anything strange—a cloud, airplane, another boat?"

"Oh."

"What?"

"I just remembered that it was very cold before the wind hit."

"Cold?"

"Very. Like Antarctica."

Billy hung up the phone, stood up and paced the floor, his headache and other pains temporarily forgotten.

"Everything okay?" Truitt walked into his office.

"Yeah, great," Billy answered. "Go ahead, be my guest." He motioned to his terminal.

Truitt sat down and scanned the story.

"Good lead," he nodded his head and continued to read. "Let's downplay the Tower and police helicopter angle, Billy. If there's a connection, which I seriously doubt, tomorrow's edition can cover it."

"So you think it's all random circumstance, too?" Billy asked.

"What else could it be? Actually, right this instant, I don't give a flying fig one way or the other," Truitt said. "We're selling out on the stands and subscriptions are up twenty percent for the month. Thanks for your help today, Billy. Now go home. We'll take it from here."

Billy waited until the editor was gone, then dialed the police.

"I'd like to report a missing person."

"Not another one?" The voice sounded tired.

"Getting a lot of calls?" Billy asked, the needle on his curiosity meter had suddenly shot up into the red zone.

"Lots."

Billy told the officer about Gretta's mysterious disappearance.

"Is her car there?"

Billy was momentarily speechless. "That's a damn good question," he said finally. After hanging up, he racked his brain trying to remember what kind of car Gretta had driven. Buick? Oldsmobile? Billy had ridden in it once when his own car had been in the shop. What the hell was it? A big thing, he remembered.

Billy tried Personnel. They kept records on damn near everything and everybody. All kinds of arcane stuff, from where your nearest relative lived to how often you were late getting back from lunch. Five minutes later, after a good deal of badgering, he not only knew what kind of car Gretta drove but its license number. On sudden inspiration, he flipped through his directory of city and county offices until he found the number for the Police Department's vehicle impound lot.

"You got a Buick, royal blue, license IGA473?" he asked.

"Just a sec," a older woman's voice answered. Five minutes later, he was still waiting. One of the news desk's other copy interns handed him a fax. He scanned the victims names from the ferry accident. So far, less than a dozen names had been released. Helen Anderson wasn't among them. It would be a coincidence of the first magnitude, like winning the Lotto and the Pulitzer in the same week, if she were one of the victims. He didn't believe in coincidences and he sure as hell didn't believe in spirit winds, but somehow, he had the strangest feeling that Helen was going to turn up on the list, sooner or later.

"C'mon, for God's sake," Billy said into the receiver. "Somebody say something or do something. Cough, fart, anything."

"Running out of patience, are we?" The woman's voice suddenly came back on the line.

"Sorry. I thought maybe you'd died."

"I'm not *that* old, sweetheart. The reason it took so long was that I couldn't find your car listed on the computer printout, so I had to check the latest hand-written lists."

"Don't tell me you found it?"

"Lot two. Bring cash or check and two pieces of I.D., including a valid driver's license."

"Wait a minute. Mind telling me where it was when it was picked up?"

"Not at all. Just a sec."

"Oh, sweet Jesus, no," Billy pleaded.

"Here it is," the voice resumed after a blessedly brief pause. "We picked up a blue Buick, license number IGA473, at ten this morning in front of Pier 65 on Alaskan Way."

"Thank you," Billy said. "You've been a big help."

Ten minutes later, after turning over the ferry story to Truitt and promising to drive straight home, Billy was hurrying toward the parking garage, foam rubber donut tucked under one arm.

"You better watch out, Mr. Mossman."

Billy looked up in time to see Andy, the bandy-legged janitor coming the other way. "Why's that?"

"You startin' to walk like me."

SEATTLE, TUESDAY, 4:55 P.M., Billy found a parking spot on Alaskan Way near Pier 65, climbed stiffly out of the car and walked the short distance to the pier. The air reeked of decomposing fish and oysters. It was enough to make you swear off seafood for the rest of your life. His butt ached and the booming traffic noise from the viaduct rubbed against his already frayed nerves like sandpaper, intensifying his migraine. He paused to inspect a temporary barrier. The parking meter had been sheared off level with the sidewalk. Probably a drunk; there weren't even skid marks.

Gulls screeched and wheeled in an aerial battle above a young Asian couple who tossed them french fries. The man wore a black leather jacket with a map of California on the back.

Billy leaned against a concrete railing and searched the oily water that lapped at the pilings below, revealing a pale starfish like a hand clinging among the shiny blue-black mussels. He tried the door of the cannery building that commanded the pier and found it locked. The sign said they closed at four. Across the street, a handful of people walked quickly to the few cars remaining in the parking lot before joining the other commuters headed out of the city.

While waiting for the light to change, Billy noticed the long flight of stairs leading up to the Pike Street Market. As he made his way slowly toward it, he searched the ground carefully for car keys, a shoe, or any other clues to Gretta's disappearance.

At the base of the stairs, he discovered a large cardboard box. When he looked inside, he was startled to find a body partially buried beneath a pile of newspapers and tattered belongings.

"Gretta?" A muscle began to twitch in his face and he fought the urge to gag from the stench of mildewed clothing, sodden cardboard, sweat, urine, and vomit. He bent down on one knee to examine the corpse when it suddenly rolled over and stared at him.

"What chu looking at?" a bearded face snarled.

"Sorry for intruding," Billy said, rising. "You live here?"

"What's it look like? Go away."

"An associate of mine left her car parked across the street all last night. I wonder if you might have seen her?"

"I ain't seen nothin'."

"She was a kid, tall, early 20s."

"I told you, I ain't seen nothing. 'Sides, I just moved in today."

"Is that so?" Billy studied the man's haggard features; it could have been the face of a fifty-year-old man, and he might have been only thirty. "Someone live here before you?"

"What if they did? Finders keepers. Now get. Leave me be."

"Thanks," Billy said.

As he walked back to his car, Billy tried to decipher the graffiti scrawled on pilings, buildings and damn near everywhere you looked. You couldn't go anywhere without being assaulted by it. Someone had thrown a can of paint against one of the viaduct support posts, making a long smear that started ten feet up and ran down the dirty gray concrete nearly to the ground. In the rapidly fading light, it almost looked like blood. But how the hell would blood get there, so high up? He stared up into the nightmare black recesses of the viaduct where the cooing of pigeons was so loud as to be nearly deafening. He wished he had thought to bring a flashlight. At last, he gave up and walked back to his car. He was stiff and sore and tired, and he needed a drink.

Billy started the car and turned on the radio. He was pulling out into traffic when he heard the news about the downed Micronesia flight. Suddenly, he wasn't tired anymore.

SEATTLE, TUESDAY, 5:25 P.M. Denise parked in the dark driveway and opened the tailgate of the station wagon. She grabbed one of the plastic sacks full of groceries with her free hand; the other held her briefcase. Evan held the door open for her when she got to the porch.

More? he signed and pointed to her bag.

Denise nodded in the direction of the car and he was out the door and down the porch almost before she was in the house, the dog streaking right behind him.

Evan first checked out the bags' contents and was glad to see that she had remembered dog food. Anxious to make as few trips as possible, he looped the handles of four, heavy bags over his hands before starting for the house. Halfway up the stairs, Fortuno bolted in front of him, grazing his legs. He managed to keep from falling by putting one hand down, but the two bags in his hand hit the step hard. He hurried through the house to the kitchen where he set the bags down on the countertop, and then rushed back outside for the last load. When he returned, his mother was scowling as she pulled dripping items from one of the bags which had held a dozen eggs. A loaf of bread looked like it had been sat on by the circus fat lady. Out of the other bag, she gingerly lifted the broken half of a jar of mayonnaise. He watched her drop the eggs and jar into the trash, then empty the mostly liquid contents of the bag into the sink. She brushed by him without a word or sign on the way to the stairs.

He emptied the rest of the bags, washed the egg off the bag of broken potato chips and was putting away the rest of the groceries when he sensed her behind him. She had changed out of her business suit and into jeans and a shirt, but her frown was still there.

Bad day? he signed.

She nodded.

He studied her lips, waiting for her to say something, anything. *Car cost a lot?* he signed.

Denise shrugged. "Too much, but we'll manage," she signed and spoke simultaneously.

Work? he tried again.

She turned away to get a glass from the cupboard, but before she did, he saw hurt reflected in her eyes. Like she had a rock in her shoe, or maybe something worse.

"What about you?" she signed a moment later. "How was school?"

Fine. Much as he wanted to—needed to—it wouldn't help to tell her about his latest meeting with the wind. Especially not now.

"*I don't feel up to cooking,*" his mother signed, "*and there's not much left to eat.*"

Not even scrambled eggs? That got her. She looked away, tried not to let it show, but he could see the corner of her mouth pulling up. When she smiled, she was incredibly, awesomely beautiful.

"You turkey," she said at last and pulled him to her. He hugged her back. Hard.

"*Go get your homework for me to see and turn on the TV, okay? I'll call for pizza and be in to join you in a couple of minutes.*"

Evan retrieved his papers from his desk upstairs, then found the remote control hidden under yesterday's newspaper. The television flickered on to reveal a local news program. In the corner of the screen, a woman made rapid signing motions. One of his favorite games was to practice lip reading by studying the mouth of the news anchor and then checking against the signing. He rarely did this for long periods of time, however. The spoken words seemed dull in comparison to sign.

Fortuno jumped into his lap and licked his face. The dog wasn't supposed to be on the furniture, but it would be okay if it was for just a minute, Evan thought, as he stroked the dog's head and scratched behind his ears. When he glanced back at the television, the screen had filled with a jittery aerial view of something that looked like a junkyard surrounded by flashing blue, red, and yellow lights. A beam from a search light picked out scattered heaps of smoldering debris. The words "Special Report," were superimposed over the picture. Evan concentrated on the signing woman's flying hands.

"We're hovering over the scene of what officials are calling the worst aviation accident in Seattle history. A fully-loaded 747-400, returning from Tahiti, went down in the past hour just four and a half miles south of SeaTac Airport. At this time, there is no official estimate of injuries or fatalities."

"Do we know what caused the crash?" a woman news anchor asked.

Evan watched intently.

"Nothing at this time. The FAA will be combing the wreckage for clues as to whether the crash was the result of human error, mechanical failure, or some external factor, such as wind shear."

Evan stopped petting the dog. His heart began to walk like an elephant and the smell of burning plastic and aircraft fuel filled his nose as his mind replayed the helicopter spinning out of control, falling into the fountain, exploding into a yellow ball. In his head, he heard again the wind's warning, "Now, I will show you who I am and what I can do."

"There has been no official word from either the airline or the FAA yet," the signing continued, "other than to acknowledge that flight M-169 is missing and presumed down."

"Can you tell if there were survivors?" the anchor asked.

"No. We can see the lights of more and more emergency vehicles arriving every minute. I have yet to see any vehicles leave, however."

"About how many people would a plane like that hold?"

"Without knowing the seating configuration, probably three fifty to four hundred with crew."

Denise was hanging up the phone when she heard a strange sound. At first, she thought it was the dog whining. Then she heard a crash. She rushed into the living room to find the table overturned and Evan rolling on the floor as Fortuno cowered in the corner.

"What is it?"

Evan continued to thrash about and moan. A juice glass toppled off the corner table, spilling its contents on the hardwood floor.

"Stop it!" Denise tried grabbing his arms. Evan lashed out at her, striking her on the arms and shoulders. She sat on his stomach, straddling him with her legs in order to pin his arms with her own. She couldn't believe how strong he was.

"What is it? What's wrong?" she screamed, even though he couldn't hear, didn't even seem to see her. One of his arms came loose and his elbow struck her on the nose. Pain imploded in her brain. Dots of bright red blood appeared on her son's shirt and pants.

"Evan!" She struggled to regain control of his arms and fight back her panic. Now he was hammering the back of his head against the floor. "Oh, my God! Please, not again!" Unable to sign him, she pressed herself against his twitching body and breathed into his face, "It's okay, Evan, it's okay." Her breath came in ragged gulps. Beneath her, she could feel his heart running like a wild horse, the muscles in his arms and legs continuing to spasm.

At last, his struggling stopped. Soon thereafter, his respiration and heart beat settled into a regular—if still too fast—rhythm. When she was certain he wouldn't hurt himself or her, Denise pulled him up by the arms and half carried, half dragged him out onto the porch. She held him on her lap in the cool, night air. Fortuno licked his face.

"Get out of here!" Denise yelled and was immediately sorry. The dog ran down a few steps, looking stricken, his tail tucked between his rear legs. Evan put out a hand for the dog. Fortuno belly-crawled back, put his head on the boy's knee and licked his blue jeans.

"What was that all about?" Denise signed.

TV. Crash. I caused.

Denise listened to the television still blaring inside, her thoughts still racing out of control. Nothing added up. "The TV? You broke the TV? What are you talking about?"

He kicked the porch column a solid thunk in frustration.

"Evan Baker, that's it," she yelled, momentarily forgetting to sign. "I'm calling the paramedics."

He grabbed her arm so that she couldn't rise, then signed her. *Don't. I'll be fine. Promise.*

"Tell me now then. What was it that set you off? You owe me an explanation. You almost broke my nose."

He told her about wanting to come straight home, of being scared that someone or thing might be following him, how he'd seen the white sheet and thought it was only a kid playing games, didn't realize the wind was doing it, setting a trap. Then he told her about the voice in his head, the whispery, dry voice that said he was chosen and that nothing could stop it. And he started to cry, his lower lip quivering and two big tears rolling, one down each of his cheeks. She had wanted to hold him so much, but couldn't while he signed. And finally, he told her about the airplane and the wind's threat.

Now Denise understood. She didn't really believe in the "stalking wind" business, but if her son believed it was real—and he obviously did—she could see how news of the plane crash could have triggered his self-destructive fit. Her coming home stressed from her meeting with Bud and then her anger at his dropping the groceries were obviously to blame for his overloaded imagination. It was her fault.

Five minutes later, they were able to move back into the house. Together, they sat and watched the frequent updates from the scene of the airplane crash. The pizza was delivered and sat unopened on the table before them. The smell of garlic and pepperoni quickly filled the downstairs area. Denise was unable to eat—not because she believed Evan was responsible for the crash, but because he so obviously did. Equally alarming was his loss of control. It had happened once two years before. The doctor had said that the deaf sometimes exhibited violent behavior toward themselves and others, a result of being unable to express emotions verbally. The rest of us took the ability to swear or shout when stressed out for granted, never realizing the therapeutic value. Denise touched her swollen nose and wondered what she was going to do when Evan got a little bigger and stronger. His fits might actually get worse, the doctor had warned, as he got older. That was nothing she looked forward to.

At 6:30, the news was replaced by a game show. Denise patted Evan's leg. *"Sure you don't want me to call the doctor—just in case?"*

No, he signed. *I feel okay now.*

Denise didn't like what she saw, however. There were blue depressions under his eyes and his cheeks wore bright red blotches against his otherwise pale skin. *"Let's go to bed early tonight,"* she signed. *"Put on your jams and I'll play you a game of computer chess."*

Can I sleep with Fortuno? Just this once? I promise I'll never ask again.

The dog sat down, lifted one paw and looked at her with an expression that seemed to promise, "I'll be good."

"Maybe next time, okay?" Denise signed. *"And no fair teaching the dog sign."*

18

Truth Seekers

OLYMPIC PENINSULA, TUESDAY, 6:38 P.M. His people were Crow and, when he was a young boy, Paul had begged his grandmother to tell him all that she knew about the Crow Indians. Perhaps because he had no immediate family, it was all the more important to him to belong to a tribe and all the traditions that implied. The reservation became his extended family: his aunts, uncles, and cousins. Whenever he needed a playmate, a ride home, or just someone to talk to, one of them was always there.

From his grandmother, he learned that the Crow were among the fiercest and most proud of the Plains Indians. Their lodges, clothing and horse trappings were considered among the finest of all Indian peoples. Crow women had their own societies, just like the men, and enjoyed considerable status which, no doubt, contributed to his grandmother's position of respect within the tribe. Although related to the Sioux, they were nevertheless bitter enemies and quite willing to befriend the whites. Crow Indians had been among the scouts who fought and died with Custer at the Little Big Horn. Shattered by wars, devastated by smallpox, and betrayed by whites, they had finally dwindled to a few hundred people living on a reservation in southern Montana, including the enclave at Lodge Grass where Paul had been raised.

It was a long way from Lodge Grass to his present location in more ways than one. Yet, the farther west Paul drove, the more familiar the land became. Billboards, political signs, and the claustrophobic clutter of civilization had given way little by little to a more primitive landscape. Older and fewer were the houses, or more often trailers, separated by miles of field and forest. And the last shopping mall had disappeared in his rearview mirror over an hour ago.

Speed was one of his few indulgences whether mounted on a horse, riding a motorcycle, or driving a car, and he had driven as fast as the thin traffic would allow. Reluctantly, he had made the decision to take the four-lane freeway to the coast. It was by far the longer and slower of the two routes to the Makah reservation. The shorter route was north through Port Angeles. Soon after taking leave of his friends, however, the radio had reported that the Anacortes ferry was down. That meant everyone trying to get to the islands would be forced to leave from Port Angeles, creating even more traffic when he would be passing through the area.

As the dying sun deepened from yellow to gold and then maroon, he turned north at Hoqium onto Highway 101, two lanes of twisting blacktop that curled between thousands of acres of clear-cut land on either side. Rolling hills that had once been sheathed in moss-covered cedar and fir were now reduced to stumps that rose like tombstones from the surrounding scrub. In the fading light, the scattered branches appeared like bleached bones against the dark and torn earth.

The western side of the Olympic peninsula was still largely wilderness, populated by a handful of loggers and Indians who were equally anxious that it stay that way. State Highway 101 would take him north through Quinault and Hoh lands. Proceeding north and west from Sappho on county roads, he would eventually reach the rugged, coastal lands of the Makah, Ozette, and Quillayute. Given the reclusive nature of these peoples, he would probably not see anyone but whites—and damn few of those—until he left the highway.

Though he still had half a tank, he stopped for refueling and coffee at the south end of Lake Quinault. He needed the caffeine and finding diesel fuel would not be easy from this point on. While he paid for the items, he spotted a pay telephone.

Denise's voice sounded anxious when she answered. "Paul? I'm so glad you called. Where are you?"

"Olympic peninsula—west end of Lake Quinault. Everything okay?"

"Not really. You heard about the jet that crashed?"

"Can't pick up much over here. I've had the radio turned off. What happened?"

Denise proceeded to tell him about the air disaster followed by Evan's reaction to the television news story. "He thinks he caused the crash! Evan said the wind warned him, that it talked in his head again. What's happening to him? Is my son crazy?"

"No, Denise. I don't think Evan's crazy." Paul glanced at the store clerk who was engrossed in watching a small, black and white television. "I don't know exactly what we're dealing with—or why it's targeting Evan—but I'm going to do my best to find out."

"What's on the Olympic peninsula?"

"I discovered something at the morgue today. Something that may provide some answers."

"Couldn't you have called?"

"These aren't exactly the kind of questions you can discuss on the phone. Besides, I'm not even sure they have phones where I'm going."

"No phones? Is all this really necessary? Couldn't we just wait a few days? Let things settle back to normal?"

"I don't think so. Besides, there are other lives at stake—especially if the wind was really responsible for the plane crash."

"Wait a minute—you don't really think Evan caused an airplane crash?" Denise sounded incredulous, but fearful, too.

"No." Paul spun a rack of risqué greeting cards in frustration, causing the bored store clerk to look up. He wanted to be there to comfort Denise and protect her and the boy. Instead, here he was standing in a minimarket two hundred miles away.

"I don't think he caused it. But after what happened to that helicopter last night, it wouldn't surprise me if the wind could cause a plane to crash. I believe the wind is capable of almost anything—and I've got the bruises to prove it. As to talking in his head, I found out something interesting earlier today. Remember the dog whistle—the one that Evan used to call off the wind? Some researchers have had success using high frequency sound to communicate to the profoundly deaf."

"I've read about it," Denise said. "Unlike sounds in the normal range of hearing, they think ultrasonic sound causes vibrations that the deaf are unusually sensitive to. But what's that got to do with the dog whistle?"

"Probably nothing. But maybe—just maybe—ultrasound is how the wind communicates to Evan. If that's so, he may in fact be communicating back, by blowing the whistle."

"I'm not sure I'm ready to buy into any of this," Denise said. "But just supposing there is a wind of some kind chasing Evan, what if it decides to pay us another visit, like it did last night? What do we do—break out the kites?"

"Get below ground if you can. Stay away from windows—just as you would if your home was in the path of a tornado. And if you need a place to hide out, you're more than welcome to stay at my place. It's not much, but it's close and there's food in the fridge. I even cleaned it once."

"I appreciate your offer, but I'm not sure I'd feel safer there than here."

"A rabbit always has two escape routes—a front door and a back. Consider my place a backdoor."

"Thanks. Right now, I need all the options I can get. I wish you could be here, Paul." Her voice softened. "You've been great. You saved my son—twice. Thanks to you, the car's even fixed."

"I'm sorry I had to leave," Paul said. "Driving out here was the only way I could think of to get to the bottom of this. I hoped that the wind wouldn't come back so soon."

"I didn't mean to make you upset," Denise said. "Besides, as much as I probably sound like it, I'm not helpless. I must confess, however, you're becoming awfully indispensable."

After hanging up, Paul savored Denise's words. He had been called a lot of things, but indispensable wasn't one of them. It sounded nice.

A minute later, he was again driving north in search of The Edge of the World. According to Charley, the Edge people were a small tribe of perhaps a hundred Indians who claimed descendance from the distant Haida of the Queen Charlotte Islands in Canada. Raiding other tribes in their swift longboats, the Haida had once been lords of the Northwest coast from the Gulf of Alaska to Puget Sound. Unlike the Haida, however, the Edge people had never been defeated by whites. They lived today in virtual isolation in a single, tiny village located on lands technically belonging to the Makah. Charley said they had a reputation among the tribes as being violent even today, treating non-tribal members, white and Indian alike, with great hostility. So remote was their village, reachable only by an unpaved forest service road, that they lived virtually unknown to all but a few Indians and anthropologists. An incident back in the seventies had resulted in unwanted publicity when a Volkswagen van-load of foolish hippies had tried to establish a commune nearby. Evidently, a reservation—with its absence of police—had seemed like just the place to kick back and grow a little weed. Unfortunately, no one thought to ask the Indians their opinion. The FBI and the Bureau of Indian Affairs had spent several weeks looking around and asking questions, but neither the commune members nor the van had ever been found.

212

The Edge people were led by a paraplegic, seer-shaman whose Indian name meant The Light That Illuminates The Truth and who Charley believed might provide the answers that Paul sought if, indeed, he were still alive. Charley had met him once, more than twenty years before, at a fish-in when the statewide war over tribal fishing rights was just in its infancy. The Light was then already in his fifties, his limbs wasted from lack of use, yet, according to Charley, his personality and determination were more vital than most men half his age. From a wheelchair in the stern of a rolling fishing boat and with a voice that thundered even without a megaphone, he had marshaled hundreds of Indian men, women, and children who had stood up to the state troopers and gun-toting, angry fishermen, forever changing the fishing industry in the State of Washington. Charley's role that day, which in typical fashion he had refused to discuss, had earned him a rare invitation to visit The Light's village.

A surge of adrenaline shot through Paul as he crossed the Hoh River and saw in the fading light the nets strung by Indians. It gladdened his heart to see his people holding onto their traditional way of life. Even the car seemed to come alive; all four wheels momentarily left the ground as he exited the bridge. He swung out in the oncoming traffic lane to pass a logging truck. Ahead, he saw a sharp turn. Charley had pressed him to take his four-wheel drive pickup truck, but he had stuck with the Mercedes with whose idiosyncrasies he was well familiar. Now, as he pressed the accelerator to the floor, Paul was grateful that the heavy, turbo-diesel engine wasn't designed for city roads, but for the Autobahn. At the last possible moment, he darted in front of the Kenworth just in time to take the corner, tires complaining bitterly every inch of the way. Pebbles clattered against the undercarriage as he drifted wide before regaining control. Still traveling at a high rate of speed, Paul found himself fingering the beads in his shirt pocket, a parting gift from Father Janowsky.

"Please, do me just one more favor," the priest had said after their visit to the morgue when Paul was driving them both back to the shelter. With those few words, he had removed from the pocket of his coat a string of rosary beads from which hung a small silver crucifix and pressed them into Paul's hand. "They were given to me by my mother when I was confirmed."

Paul protested, but the priest had insisted.

"Keep them," he ordered. "When this is all over, if you still want to give them back, please do." And then he had turned away from

Paul's questioning look. "I regret very much to say that I have a strong feeling you're going to need them more than me."

Paul thought again of the mysterious dead Indian, the icy-feeling necklace and his earlier vision of the boy and something chasing him. He had learned what was stalking Evan. But why? In addition to his deafness, did the boy have special powers that made him a target? Somehow these clues were all linked. Could he unlink them? Or was the death he had felt while wearing the necklace waiting for him and the boy?

Tendrils of fog began to creep from the shadows and onto the road. As he drove northward, Paul strained to pick out where the blacktop began and ended, keeping a wary eye out for any unlucky whitetail deer or Roosevelt elk that might have chosen tonight to cross the highway. The odds of a successful mission were daunting at best. In addition to ingratiating himself among a people not known for their hospitality, he would first have to find their village. Even with Charley's map and careful instructions, it would be next to impossible, driving at night, to find the correct road, a knife-like scar bulldozed through the dense forest. Unless he could spot the Forest Service marker, he would likely have to spend the night in his car.

For the third time in as many hours, he wondered if he was on a wild goose chase. He might well be wasting precious time when the very people he was trying to protect were in danger. The acid in his stomach urged him to hurry back, but he was traveling as fast as he dared to the only place where he thought he might find an answer that would help Denise and Evan.

"One way or another, grandmother," he said aloud over the engine's steady growl, "I think it will all be over soon."

SEATTLE, TUESDAY, 7:02 P.M. How promiscuous death is, Billy pondered for the hundredth time. And capricious. She could come barreling along with the next drunk driver and greet us head-on, stand behind us in the 7–Eleven spewing anger from a machine pistol over a lost job or bitter divorce, silently infiltrate our veins and lymph nodes, or she could simply drop from the sky one afternoon. Death didn't scare Billy. It infuriated him. Whenever he suspected it of some new advantage, he felt compelled to warn his readers.

He smoked a fat cigar, one of many tricks he'd learned in 'Nam, and stood near the edge of the crash site where the all-too-arbitrary and asymmetrical line between life and death had recently been broached. The cigar helped mask the burnt plastic, aircraft fuel, and other, more repellent odors. Even with a flashlight, he could see that the twisted pipe, chain, and plastic had once been a swing set. What had once been a peaceful, suburban backyard was now cooked earth gouged by a ten-foot deep trench. Where a house had stood a few hours earlier was now reduced to a burned-out basement. The broken tail of the plane, what was left of it, was lying in the driveway. The rest of the plane, consisting of ragged sections of sheet metal and melted lumps of plastic, was distributed among an entire city block of formerly modest homes. Perhaps a hundred King County sheriffs' deputies and volunteers combed the scorched earth and rubble for body parts. A flock of helicopters traced a figure eight in the sky, using spotlights to illuminate the disaster for cameras so the scene could be photographed, video taped, printed, and distributed around the world. On the ground, an army of reporters descended on neighbors, officials, a pizza delivery boy—anyone who could say, "I saw it." Soon, they would be joined by the lawyers.

Billy kicked at a small pile of dirt and debris. Something caught his eye. His light illuminated a Barbie doll, missing one arm. He held it for a long moment before gently setting it back on the ground. Of such small details were his stories often made. Tonight, however, another issue occupied his mind, something more than just the human tragedy, albeit enormous, of an air crash. He thought back to Ann Bessani's phone call. He wasn't ready to subscribe to her "spirit wind" explanation. Might as well blame the tooth fairy or Santa Clause for what was happening. Nevertheless, *something* odd was going on, that was for damn sure.

On the street nearby, lit up like a star at a movie premiere, stood a thin woman wearing a dark raincoat, speaking calmly and circumspectly to the horde of press gathered in front of her. The tag that twisted in the breeze identified her as NTSB, National Transportation Safety Board. From here, he thought she looked too elegant for the Northwest. Probably from the east, he guessed. D.C., perhaps. People from Washington State never called Washington, D.C. "Washington." It was always "D.C."

Billy was in his "mood," as his wife called it. He was as tired as he had ever been and his ass was way past sore. Even so, he waited patiently until the woman had finished speaking. He didn't much like press conferences. "Cattle calls," he liked to refer to them. The good questions either never got asked or were never answered and everybody ended up with the same story. While the other reporters and broadcast crews hurried to car phones, packed up lights and cameras, or shot last minute takes, he watched the woman and her young male companion as they threaded their way along the debris-strewn street toward the command post that had been set up in a large tent. They walked fast. His injuries and the uneven terrain—even the asphalt was broken and furrowed—made it difficult to overtake them. Every step was agony. When he was within hailing distance, he called out.

"Lady?"

They ignored him.

"Lady," he tried again. "Can I just ask a couple of questions?" He was wheezing now, seriously out of breath. He tossed the cigar aside. "Ma'am, if you don't stop soon, I may have a heart attack and die."

At last, she stopped and stood waiting, arms crossed over her chest. Her assistant tried to head him off, but Billy walked right past him.

"Mossman, *Times*," Billy panted.

She took his hand reluctantly. "Marilyn Davis, Deputy Director, and this is David Redstone, my assistant."

The young man opened his leather briefcase and offered a typed page to Billy who refused to acknowledge it. "This is a summary of all we know, Mr. Mossman. I believe the *Times* was well represented at the press conference just concluded, by the way. Now, if you don't mind, we have work to do." They started to turn away.

"I figured maybe some questions you'd rather answer privately. Of course, if you'd just as soon have everyone think the skies are unsafe . . ."

The two exchanged looks. "So, what penetrating questions have you been holding back until now, Mr. Mossman? Have we a pet theory?" Ms. Davis looked like she'd just as soon eat slugs as answer his questions. Of course, some people liked that kind of thing: they sprinkled garlic on 'em and called it escargot.

"For one, how come there's so little damage? Why isn't the accident site a lot bigger? After all, this was a 747, not a Cessna. That crash site in Ohio covered half a mile."

Davis nodded. "Very perceptive. As you can see, it looks like the pilot firewalled the throttles and flew it right straight into the ground. Why, I have no idea. We'll know more when we hear what's on the black boxes. Unfortunately, it may take a while. They tell me the tapes are so badly damaged, they don't know what—if anything—we'll be able to retrieve."

"You think this was caused by wind shear?"

"It's much too early to speculate," she said. "Everything was normal up until the crash. Controllers received no communication from the plane that indicated they were in trouble. Wind shear is certainly one area of our investigation, along with major mechanical failure or something unusual happening in the cockpit. There were no reports of heavy precipitation or gusting winds before the accident, however. Now, we really must go."

That was no big help, Billy thought as they turned to leave. C'mon ace reporter, what else you got? Might as well haul out the spirit wind theory. "You ever hear of a 'Williwaw'?" he called out to their retreating backs.

His question must have touched a nerve; Ms. Davis stopped in her tracks. "Mr. Mossman," she wagged a finger at him, "you're getting in way over your head. A Williwaw is a mariner's term for a particularly violent wind like they experience in the Strait of Magellan or the Gulf of Alaska. Seattle is a long, long way from either of those latitudes."

"So, you *do* know about it."

"This isn't the first time I've heard of the Williwaw hypothesis," she said, "and I doubt very much it will be the last."

"Given the local geography, we're much more apt to have experienced a rotor wind," the assistant jumped in. "The plane was on final approach and the pilot couldn't recover in time."

"Yeah," Billy answered. "Rotor wind. Of course." He slapped his forehead. "Why didn't I think of that?"

"Rotor winds are not unusual where large mountain barriers exist, such as the Cascades."

"Mountains, huh? So why didn't this 'rotor wind' show up on radar? You got gear on the ground not to mention gear on the plane to watch out for that stuff, right?"

"No precipitation," the assistant said. "Plus, microbursts are highly unstable and unpredictable."

"Microburst? Isn't that a tiny, intense fart? What happened to 'rotor wind'?"

"Ignore him," Ms. Davis said. "He's just fishing for a quote."

"Sounds to me like you got a lot of fancy, techno-babble words for obscuring the fact that you don't have a clue what killed all these innocent people."

"You're right, Mr. Mossman." She was angry now; her answers short and clipped. "I don't have an answer for you. I wish I did. We'll have an update tomorrow. Until then,"—she began walking—"goodnight."

Billy watched them as they disappeared into the tent. He sure didn't have a story. Not even close. Yet. He looked at his watch. It was almost 7:30. Then he remembered. It was their anniversary. "Shit." He'd better call Julie.

He called home from the pay phone in front of Safeway. He had just paid too much for a good bottle of champagne and a wilted bunch of cut flowers, but his guilt was riding him high and tight like a Derby jockey and he would have spent damn near anything. He'd learned the hard way with his first marriage. Sweat the small details like birthdays and anniversaries, and the larger, more incendiary things would pass.

"Happy anniversary, babe."

"Where on earth have you been?" Julie answered, exasperation clearly evident in her husky voice. "You had me frightened another building had fallen on you! And why aren't you resting?"

"I had to check out the plane crash."

"The doctor said you were supposed to take it easy for a few days."

"Yeah, well, he didn't know we were gonna have two separate disasters on the same day."

"How's your tush doing?"

"Fine." There was no need to mention the blood he'd found on his foam rubber donut. "I've got to swing by the *Times*. Won't take five minutes. Want me to pick something up at the Chinese place?"

"Just come home, Billy. I've had dinner waiting here for the past two hours and there are people here to see you."

Billy immediately thought of his daughter, but she was in college in Oregon. Gretta? It would greatly unburden his mind if the kid had turned up. "Who?" he asked.

"Ann Bessani, for one. She said you'd know who she was."

"Oh, great. That's just terrific. How the hell did she find where we live?" Their phone number was unlisted.

"How should I know? I figured you told her. She seems nice enough, Billy. Now, hurry home."

Billy shook his head and hung up. Whatever happened to nice, quiet days at the office followed by peaceful evenings at home in front of the TV, the lights of the city reflected in the water outside their houseboat? Billy slammed the car door. Who was he kidding? He hated being bored.

He parked in the area marked "deliveries only." On his desk was the latest fax of those people confirmed dead or missing from the ferry accident. Helen Anderson was listed as missing and presumed drowned at the top of page two. Evidently, they'd found her car. He kicked at his wastebasket, sending it spinning into his office wall. Heads looked up in the newsroom. Okay, so the broad was dead and the coincidences were thick as a bus full of Republicans on their way to the Nixon Library. He still didn't have one tiny fact to go on.

On the way back downstairs, he stopped the elevator at the third floor and entered the office marked "Supplies."

"Evening, Mr. Mossman." The woman looked up from her word processor. "What can I do for you?"

"I need to check out one of those," Billy said, pointing. He hated even to say the word.

"Last one," she said a moment later. "All our pagers are checked out, too. How long you need it?"

Billy looked at her. "Now there's a question I'd give anything to know the answer to."

"Just sign your name and put seventy-two hours," the woman advised. "You can always check it out again."

"Thanks." He stuck the scuffed Motorola in one pocket of his raincoat. He was firmly convinced that portable phones were another nail in the coffin of individual privacy, not to mention sanity. What the hell. He might be a trifle archaic, but he wasn't a fool. The way stuff was happening around here lately, he could use a few tricks.

Julie met him at the front door, having no doubt heard his tired footsteps approaching on the dock. She held out a drink and two aspirin. "I'm sorry for losing my temper on the phone. It's good to have you home. Take your medicine."

"Thanks. I'll trade you." He handed her the flowers and wine.

219

"By the way, happy anniversary." He popped the aspirin in his mouth, sipped the drink, then set it on the dock railing. "I admit I should have called earlier, but I still don't understand how you could do this to me." He nodded toward the houseboat.

"She said it was important." She slipped her arms around him. "A matter of life and death."

"That's what crazy people always say." He kissed her, the whiskey and her soft lips tasting fine together.

"Now be nice, Billy."

"Sorry. Nice wasn't in the genes I was born with."

"Pretend." She pecked his lips.

"Can I get cleaned up first?"

"Yeah, but be quiet. There's a girl watching TV in our bedroom."

Billy had to walk through the living room to get to their bedroom which was located in the back of the houseboat. The two women sat at the dining table. There was something oddly familiar about the older woman. The younger one stood and held out a hand for him to shake. She was slim and pretty, probably in her early thirties, with dark hair and a wounded look in her intelligent eyes.

"Ann Bessani," she said. "I'm sorry for disturbing your evening, especially on your anniversary, Mr. Mossman, but I wanted you to meet someone. This is Helen Anderson."

Billy set his drink on the table, trying hard not to spill, and turned to face her. Now he saw that she was wearing some of Julie's clothes. He took her hand; it was very cool. "You get around pretty good," he said. "For a dead lady."

Julie had laid fresh clothes in the bathroom. After showering, Billy studied his rear end in the mirror and applied a couple of fresh bandages before getting dressed. He knocked on the bedroom door.

"Yes?" a small female voice answered.

"May I come in?"

"Okay."

She was sitting on the bed. Laughter came from the color TV. She watched him with her mother's large, dark, wounded eyes.

He sat on the bed beside her. "I'm sorry about your dad and grandpa," he said. She nodded and turned back to the television. "Do you remember the wind?"

"Yes." She blinked several times, never looking away from the TV.

"What was it like?"

"Mean," she said. "It even stole my Paddington Bear." She turned toward him. "Daddy and Grandpa are in heaven now."

"Yes," he said. "I'm sure they are." The girl went back to watching her program. He walked to the built-in bookcase that took up an entire wall of their bedroom. "Do you like to read?"

"Uh huh."

"Ever read *The Lion, The Witch & The Wardrobe?*"

"What's that?"

"Only a great book. Here, you can keep it."

"Thanks. What's your name?"

"Mossman."

"Like Superman?"

"Kinda."

She smiled.

Kid's gonna be okay, he thought. "So, who's dealer?" he asked as he approached the table where all three women were talking and sipping the champagne. Helen Anderson threw back her head and laughed.

"Helen was just saying how much she enjoys playing Twenty-one on the Indian reservation," Julie said.

"I wouldn't want to bet against her," Billy said. He poured himself another shot of Wild Turkey before sitting down. The thought entered his mind that he could like both of these women, even develop friendships, but they had invaded his house.

"Just after I spoke with you," Ann said, "I got a call. The voice on the other end was so incoherent, I almost hung up. Then I heard the word 'Williwaw,' and I knew it was Helen. She was calling from the pay phone at a restaurant. Can you imagine? I yelled for Megan and we jumped in the car and drove to Anacortes as fast as we could go. We found her, still wearing her soaked clothing, drinking a cup of hot tea like nothing had happened."

"You wouldn't be related to Houdini, by any chance?" Billy asked. "You seem to have his knack for escape."

"Just too stubborn to die, Mr. Mossman." Helen's eyes locked onto his. "A man—I think it was the guy from the car behind mine, God rest his soul—helped me to the surface. I managed to grab onto a section of wooden hand railing from the pier. He tried kicking us in to shore, but the tide was headed out and the current was too strong. Twenty minutes or so went by—it felt like hours. It was all I could do to just hang on. I kept expecting to be dead. When I

221

finally bumped up against the beach, I looked around and discovered that it was just me there. He—whoever he was—must have given up."

"I've been seeking the proverbial scoop for over twenty years now," Billy said, "but this is the first time one's come to my home. We better call the *Times*, by the way. They have you listed as missing and presumed dead, along with seventeen other people from the ferry accident and another three hundred fifty-seven from the plane crash." In the silence that followed, he could hear water lapping at their houseboat from a passing boat.

"What are they blaming the accidents on?" Julie asked. "The news reports were pretty vague."

"I don't think anybody has a clue at this point," Billy said. "They're throwing out the usual weather-related crap, but at this point, they're not ruling out mechanical or human failure. Or anything else, for that matter."

"Are you ready yet," Ann asked, "to listen to another possible explanation?"

"Look, Ms. Bessani—Ann. I warned you that I don't believe in ghosts or witch doctors."

"Billy . . ." Julie started to interrupt.

"But I also said that I wouldn't bet against this lady." He nodded at Helen. "So, deal the cards."

"Show Mr. Mossman the message you showed me about Taku, Helen."

"This came by way of an electronic bulletin board I subscribe to. It's from a Inuit woman by the name of Sally Light Feather who lives in Anchorage." She handed him a fragile sheet of crumpled and sodden computer paper, torn along one fold, but still readable.

"White people don't believe there is such a thing as a wind spirit," the letter began. "But this is only their ignorance of nature talking. Long ago, when I am a little girl, my mother tell me the legend of Taku. Back in the time of the first people, the wind was just like the other creatures: bear, owl, deer, beaver. All these creatures were very competitive—they like to bet, just like Indian people today. They race one another to see who is fastest, shoot arrows at the sun to see which one can shoot farthest, fight each other to see who is strongest. But the wind—Taku—always win. This made the other creatures very angry, so one day they complain to Great Spirit.

"Great Spirit say to Taku, 'It is true what the other creatures say.

222

You are too swift and strong for the others. Because I cannot take these things away from you, I will make you invisible.'

"This pleased the wind very much. Now, he thinks, I will not only be faster and stronger than the others, but I can sneak up on them, too.

"Taku was right, but he was loser. Now, no one wanted to play with him because he was invisible. Wind became very lonely. In time, he move to mountain top to be with other wind spirits. Now, when he visit, you can hear him crying in the trees."

"Excuse me, Helen. This is a very pretty story," Billy said, "but what's the point?"

"Billy!" Julie said.

The old woman smiled gently and patted his hand. "I gave you the story to help you find Taku."

Billy looked around the table from one face to another. "I'm sorry, but I'm not receiving. My batteries must be low."

"Helen heard about this wind called a 'Williwaw' from a pilot in Alaska," Ann said. "Sally's people call it a 'Taku.'" Ann leaned across the table toward Helen. "Did Sally say whether this Taku creature still lives on the mountains?"

"At home, yes," Helen answered. "But here, in the city, she said he would seek out the highest place to make camp."

"You mean like Queen Anne Hill? The Space Needle?" Ann asked.

"Cancel my dinner reservations," Julie said.

"Holy hog shit," Billy said.

They all looked at him.

"Excuse my language, ladies, but you just described the Olympic Life Tower."

19

Sentinels

MAKAH TRIBAL LANDS, TUESDAY, 8:33 P.M. Beneath a dense evergreen canopy, the Mercedes' high beams sought passage from among the millions of silent sentinels that guarded the way to The Edge of the World. Each tree revealed in the car's headlights appeared identical to the previous one. Paul yawned and stretched cramped fingers, grooved from the steering wheel. He felt as if he had been driving forever, as if he had somehow driven past The Edge of the World and entered into another time zone where clocks ran in reverse. Here was mile after mile, thousands upon thousands of acres of primitive forest, uninhabited except for a solitary cougar whose eyes glowed with red-amber fire before muscular legs launched him from view.

Seeing the big cat had definitely been the highlight of his journey so far. For the past hour, the car's springs had produced an unceasing riot of indignation as he lurched and bounced over a knobby bed of tree roots and rocks, carved decades earlier by a bulldozer—and from the looks of it, seldom used since. More than once he had been forced to stop the car and drag downed tree limbs from his path. At such moments, he would stand in the blinding headlights, facing out into the limitless black void, not knowing whether he was now heading east or west, north or south, up or down, and he would listen for frogs, crickets, or any living thing that might reassure him that he had not passed through an invisible barrier and entered the spirit world.

Just when he was certain he had indeed chosen the wrong route, the trail suddenly veered left between two cedar trees, wide as horse trailers, and without warning, the forest stopped. Stars littered the night sky like shattered glass and a hissing, jet-like roar followed by a thunderous slap told him he had reached the Pacific Ocean. In the center of the clearing, a large, windowless lodge perched near the edge of a cliff. Monstrous totem poles towered over forty feet high at each of the building's four corners. Another pole, shorter but much thicker, stood guard at the center, facing the sea. Paul parked near an enormous war canoe to have a look around. A stream had cut a trench down to the ocean, providing a natural boat launching ramp. Dwarf firs, victimized by decades of wind and salt, clung to the bluffs on either side of the channel. He peered down from one of the precipices into a roiling white cauldron. A wave exploded with a booming crash, blasting spray three-quarters of the way up the cliff and wetting his face with cold mist. Two hundred yards out, bathed by moonlight and phosphorescence from the surf, a craggy hunchback of an island squatted, protecting the small, rocky beach from the full fury of the sea.

Back by the lodge, he ran one hand over the satin-smooth rail of the dugout canoe. He estimated that it was capable of carrying at least twenty warriors. A scowling bird-man jutted from its tall prow, wooden wings swept back at his sides. The incredible size of the few man-made objects and the total absence of familiar landmarks gave him pause. There were no trucks or cars, no stores or post office. Nor were there any lights or other signs of life. Beyond the rhythmic pounding of the surf, there wasn't a sound. He felt like an archaeologist happening upon a lost city in the jungle. He stared in wonder at the visages of bears, eagles, wolves, killer whales, and ravens carved into the lofty totem poles. Whoever had labored over those fierce images had been in a highly antisocial frame of mind. Charley's story about the missing hippies seemed highly possible, if not probable. Paul shivered in the damp night air and touched the priest's rosary beads in his pocket, as if they might somehow bring him warmth. "Hello?" he called out, and listened for an answer over the crash of the surf. In reply, he heard the whistle of a club just before it struck.

The blow landed behind his left ear and knocked him to the ground. Nausea enveloped him. He retched, then managed to roll over. As he fought to remain conscious, he heard a war cry. Paul blinked and rubbed a hand over his eyes trying to clear them. The last thing he saw was an eagle towering over him. And then he blacked out.

When he came to, he heard voices discussing him.

"Looks Indian," said one.

"A dead Indian," said another voice nearer his face.

"Nah, he's coming around," said the first. A war club hung from his hand.

"Too bad. Who are you and why are you here?" asked the second.

Paul struggled to focus on his questioners. Unlike the tall, lean Plains Indians with whom he was familiar, these were two short, stocky men in their mid-twenties, dressed identically in buckskins and wearing mustaches—rare for Indians—and carved wooden helmets: one helmet was in the shape of an eagle, the other, displaying a longer beak, a raven. But there was something else about them that made him blink his eyes and shake his head to clear it. He had just figured out that the Indians were indeed twins and not a result of double vision when a foot landed in his side, driving the wind out of his lungs.

"See that cliff?" the second man pointed. "People who have come uninvited to The Edge of the World have been known to have accidents."

"No one ever finds their bodies," his brother added.

"I'll ask you one last time: who are you and why have you come?" A long, narrow blade, the type used for filleting fish, whickered out of its leather sheath. "Answer now or begin your journey to the Great Spirit. It's all the same to us."

"My name is Paul Judge," he wheezed. "I'm looking for The Light That Illuminates The Truth."

That got them talking between themselves.

"Why do you seek The Light?" the first one asked a minute later.

Paul tried to rise up onto his elbows. A moccasined foot on his chest pushed him back. "It's a long story."

The knife flashed above his face. "We got no time for stories."

"The people of Seattle need his help," Paul tried again.

The twins snickered.

Paul realized how foolish his answer sounded. These men could care less whether he—or anyone else—lived or died. He'd better be plenty resourceful, he decided, if he didn't want to become the next unexplained disappearance. On the other hand, you didn't reach manhood living on a reservation without knowing life was fleeting as a shadow fleeing before the sun. "Hoka hey!" was the Sioux war cry—a good day to die. It was also the favorite fighting slogan of the Indian boys he grew up with.

"You're trespassing on our land," said the one with his foot on Paul's chest.

"Sign says trespassers will be shot," the brother said.

"It was dark. I didn't see the sign."

The foot tried to kick him again. This time, he caught it in both hands, twisted, and dropped his attacker who landed with a loud grunt.

"Watch it!" the first one attempted to warn his brother, but Paul had already rolled away and up. The fallen Indian was on his feet an instant later. Both men began circling him. The knife glinted in the moonlight. The other Indian gripped his war club.

"Before I kill you," the one who had fallen asked, "tell me what kind of Indian you are, so I will know when I tell the story on potlatch day."

"I am Crow," Paul answered, backing toward the lodge.

"Crow, hah!" The first one laughed. "Look at his 'Eye-talian' shoes, fancy leather coat, and Mercedes. Looks more like a peacock to me."

"You're a long way from the city, peacock." The other Indian feinted left with the knife. "Take a wrong turn at the drive-in?"

"Careful," the one with the club warned. "He's quick." But his twin was eager. He rushed in, faked right, and slashed left. Paul whirled to his right. The knife grazed his stomach. He grabbed the knife arm with his left hand and yanked the now off-balance man forward. He continued to spin so that his back was to his attacker, throwing his right elbow in a savage arc. His elbow connected with the man's nose with a sound like crunching snow, followed by a howl. Paul found himself in front of the center totem and saw that it was also a doorway. As the two men closed in again, he dove into the snarling mouth of a bear.

He rolled to a stop in a short passage lined by fishing nets, canoe paddles, and harpoons. A dozen faces looked up in amazement from the main room. A naked toddler cried for his mother. Paul's attackers immediately followed him through the opening. Blood painted the lips of the twin Paul had struck. Each man grabbed one of his arms and began to drag him back outside.

"I come in peace to speak to The Light," Paul called out. There was stunned silence in reply.

"You've said too much already." The one with the knife pressed it against his throat. Paul felt a trickle of warm blood roll down his neck. "Now you die."

"Stop!" a deep voice commanded. Everyone turned toward the sound. An older man wearing only a breechcloth approached the entryway. Crest tattoos covered his thin arms and legs and gaunt face. A thin bone pierced his nose. He wore a heavy mustache and, amazingly, a pair of black-plastic-framed glasses.

"Bring him to my fire," he said.

The men holding him protested with angry shouts.

"He is a thief," said the one with the knife.

"A spy," yelled the other.

"We shall soon see," said the older man. "Bring him."

"His feet dishonor the lodge of our people," said the knife-wielder.

"Then you shall carry him," the older man said. Half-hidden behind thick lenses, his dark eyes fell upon Paul's. "And if, as you say, his feet bring dishonor to our people, then, before the sun rises, you shall cut them off."

With a grunt of disgust, the Indian handed his knife to his brother.

"No way," Paul said, backing up. But before he had taken two steps, the Indian tackled him around the legs, then hefted all six-feet-two of him over his shoulder. A large number of Indians, young and old, had gathered to watch. Paul was forced to endure their stares and laughter as he was carried like a sack of feed to the back of the building. Flickering light from a large fire in the center of the room and strategically placed oil lamps illuminated the lodge's cavernous interior. Raised platforms constructed of heavy planks provided sleeping and sitting areas.

He was thrown to the dirt floor near a second fire pit.

"Sit here," the older man said and pointed to a spot near the blazing fire. "Closer," he said, when Paul tried to sit a more reasonable distance from the fire. Smoke curled up to an opening in the roof past massive ridge poles made of cedar trees. At a nod from the older man, the brother with the war club laid another log on the fire. Flames leapt higher, throwing dancing shadows high upon a house post in the shape of a frog that held up one of the ridge poles. Still wearing his leather jacket, Paul felt the heat rising rapidly. In less than a minute, his cheeks were flushed and sweat had broken out around his scalp, yet he knew that it would be a sign of weakness to let his discomfort show.

The older man sat down in front of him, the fire reflecting on his tattooed skin. "I am Strong Hands, leader of my people."

Paul couldn't avoid studying the man's hands which were dark with calluses, probably from handling fishing nets, he guessed.

"I think you have already met Eagle Brother and Raven Brother."

228

The twins glared at Paul. "How is it that you know about The Light?" the chief asked.

He explained about Charley's visit.

"This happened over twenty years ago and still you travel so far?" the chief said. "Your vision quest must be very strong."

"Bullshit!" Eagle Brother yelled. "He's got Bureau of Indian Affairs written all over him."

"Let me have a minute with him," his brother said, drawing the knife blade across his palm, "and he will tell us everything he knows."

Paul glanced uneasily at the twins who stood slightly behind and on either side of the chief. "What's their problem?"

The chief raised his hand. The brothers sulked.

"They believe there is still honor in fighting and bloodshed, as all Indians once did. But that was another time. Answer with the truth," the chief said as he stirred the embers with a long stick, "and they will not harm you."

"First, tell me why you try to cook me," Paul said, removing his jacket. Sweat trickled down the back of his legs and soaked his shirt.

"You don't get to ask questions," the chief said. "And besides," he added less sternly, "when you get to be as old as me, there are few things better than a good fire."

Paul spent the next five minutes describing the events in Seattle leading up to his rescuing Evan from the wind and the wind's later tracking the boy to his home. He ended with a description of the Indian in the morgue. While he spoke, the brothers paced and the chief stared into the fire. When he finished, an argument broke out among them.

"Peacock brings good news after all!"

"Let us hold a potlatch to celebrate the deaths of our enemies."

"Where is the victory in innocent deaths?"

"The whites deserve to die."

"The wind is our avenger."

"Since when did you learn so much about the spirits, Raven Brother?" the chief asked. "Perhaps you will teach me from your great storehouse of wisdom?"

The verbal sparring ended with the older man directing the brothers to make some sort of preparations. After they had departed, he continued to stare into the fire for another few minutes.

"You have come at a very bad time," he said at last. "What are you called and who are your people?"

Paul told him his name and tribal heritage.

"I never met a Crow before. Are all your people as tall as you?"

Paul shrugged. "Some."

The chief nodded and resumed stirring the embers of the fire. Several more minutes passed without any further talk until the brothers reappeared with two young women, one of them obviously pregnant, bearing wooden platters of food which they set before Paul. He recognized salmon. There was also a small, stone bowl in the shape of an otter filled with what smelled strongly of fish oil.

"In the days of my forefathers," the chief began when the women had left, "ours was a strong people, known far and wide for the number of our slaves and the size of our potlatches. The sea was very generous to us. She gave us whale, halibut, seal, salmon, and sent the eulachon to our shores for our feasts and lights." He gestured toward the food and to one of the oil lamps that burned nearby. "The sea carried us on her back to make war on our enemies. With her help, we won many victories and brought back many slaves. When we became too many for one place, she showed us where to set our lodge poles. By canoe, we spread out far to the north and south. And we were content."

He stood up slowly and walked to a nearby platform where he climbed through an oval hole in a tall partition. When he returned, he was carrying a box. He set it down between them. It was made of wood carved in the design of a killer whale and inlaid with shark teeth. "Then the white man came and our day turned to night." He reached into the box, drew out an old Colt army revolver and held it with two hands on his thighs, turning it as he inspected it. "The whites brought guns, disease, and drink. They killed many hundreds, many thousands of us. Whole villages were wiped out. Still, we did not give up like other tribes. We retreated, instead, to the furthest, most distant place we could go, and we said to our mother, the sea, if you will take care of us, we will stay and fight here. Even to the death, if necessary."

Unable to quiet the rumbling in his stomach, Paul tried a bite of the salmon. It was rich in smoky flavor and delicious.

"Try it with the oil." The old man pantomimed dipping his fingers in the bowl. Not wishing to insult the chief, Paul followed his instructions and did his best not to gag. His jeans had to serve as napkin.

"For many generations, we lived in peace," the chief continued. "The whites left us alone. We kept to ourselves. Then we became lazy. My people saw the Makah and the Quillayute fishing with store-bought nets from boats with motors. Their women watched color TVs and stored their food in refrigerators. The men drove pickup trucks. Our people wanted these things, too. The Light was wise, wiser than all the rest of us put together. He warned us, but we closed our ears and would not listen. My people began to send their children to school where they learned to speak English. Some built houses and even our own school. In a short time, we forgot our own language, who we were; we forgot the spirit world and who provided for us. And the Ocean Spirits were very angry.

"First, the whale quit coming. Next, the seal and the otter went away. A few years ago, the salmon and the eulachon began to disappear along our coast. We were forced to send our boats farther and farther to find them. And even then we did not learn. We didn't know that the worst was still to come."

One of the brothers hissed loudly.

"Why do you waste your breath?" asked the other.

"Because he is Indian, because he has come a long way, and because we cannot help him."

"What happened?" Paul asked quietly.

"About two years ago, a strange thing began to take place," the chief said, a note of wonder in his voice. "One of the young women gave birth, her first time, but the baby was dead. At first, we blamed the mother. When it happened again to another, we began to suspect. Then, it happened a third time. This was a hard thing. As you can see," the chief spread his arms to include the entire lodge, "we are no longer a people of large numbers. We could not afford to lose one child, let alone three."

"The Light had said all along how we must go back to living as before or suffer the spirits' anger. He said we must give up the motor boats and color TVs. This was very painful to us, but what choice did we have? We sold the boats and built the canoe in the old way. We took back the trucks, TVs, and refrigerators. We closed the school and moved everyone into the lodge. As much as possible, we went back to the old ways. This was very hard to do; much harder than you might think. Without these," he removed his glasses, "I am as blind as a starfish and twice as useless. The Light even had us throw his wheelchair into the sea. After all this, we fasted. But it was not enough. Two more babies died within a month of each other.

"I'm sorry you had to come all this way, Paul Judge of the Crow tribe. You see before you a dying people. The spirits have turned their backs on us. This is why we cannot help you."

Paul stared into the fire. A thought had fastened itself onto a place in his mind and would not let go. In his mind's eye, he could see a small woman dressed in white; a woman who knew the secrets of death better than anyone. If he solved the riddle of the ancient Indian in the morgue, she would owe him a favor.

"Would you help me if I promised to help you find the answer to the babies dying?"

"Hah!" Eagle Brother spat.

"Are you a shaman?" Raven Brother asked.

The chief raised his hand for silence. "How could you help us?"

"Well, not me actually," Paul explained. "It's a woman I know."

"A white woman?" Eagle Brother was incredulous.

"We would rather die!" his brother said.

"Actually, I think she is Chinese. But what does it matter whether she is black or white, red or yellow, if she can help you find what is killing your babies?" He recalled the young, pregnant woman who had served him and guessed that she was the wife of one of the twins. "Are you so stubborn that you would throw away the life of your child because of the doctor's name or color?"

Eagle Brother looked as if he had been clubbed between the eyes.

The chief nodded. "My heart tells me you are right. But still I cannot help you. Of all our people, only The Light could find the answers to your question."

"Can I meet him?"

"It would be too dangerous."

"I don't understand."

"The Light is old now and very near the end. Even when he was young, he was difficult to approach. I do not know how it is with the Crow people, but our shaman is not like other men. His medicine is so strong that he must live apart. Only at potlatch do we eat and sing together without fear. As The Light grew older, he became more and more remote. Since the tribe's trouble started, he spends much of the time visiting the spirit world. To intrude upon him even in the best of times is to risk his anger and that of the spirits.

"Ga-git come," said Eagle Brother. His brother nodded.

"What is Ga-git?" Paul asked.

"Ga-git is half man, half spirit creature," the chief said. "They say his body is covered with hair, that he has claws longer than the fingers on my hands and can fly. Since he has come to The Edge of the World, we no longer go into the forest at night. To seek The Light now, when only bad spirits visit the Edge people, could be fatal."

"For who?" Paul stared at the older man. "The Light or me?"

"For all of us."

Paul clasped his hands over his knees and hung his head. It had been a stupid idea to come here. What did he expect to find? He could have done a better job of protecting Evan and Denise if he had stayed in Seattle, not driven halfway across the state in search of a ghost. Then, a strange peace settled over him. Defeat at least could be honorable. He looked up into the faces of the three men who were watching him.

"Perhaps you can't help me," he said. "But I would still like to try to help you, if I can."

"You?" Eagle Brother scoffed.

"Who's going to help you get out of here alive?" the other asked.

The chief raised his hand. "What is it you do, Paul Judge?"

"I'm a lawyer."

"Ah. You see?" He turned to the twins. "He has many powerful friends."

The brothers threw him suspicious looks.

"No," Paul admitted. "I'm afraid I don't have many friends. And none of them are what you would call powerful."

"Then you are worthless as sea foam," Raven Brother said.

"I will cut him up into little pieces for the fish," Eagle Brother added.

"You sound like a couple of jealous squaws. Go back to your wives," ordered the chief. "And leave us in peace."

"Did you happen to bring any tobacco?" he asked when they had left.

Paul was embarrassed. "I'm sorry. I left in such a hurry, I didn't think."

"Never mind." The chief smiled. "I have enough to share a pipe." He rose and limped back to the partition. When he returned, he carried a long pipe and another, smaller box. The bowl was elaborately carved in the shape of a bear's head with a smaller bear's head in its mouth. The eyes were polished abalone shells. Sea otter

233

teeth and small copper images of various birds and animals hung from braided human hair. The box held a leather pouch containing tobacco. After lighting it with a brand from the fire, the older man took several long pulls before handing the pipe to Paul. Paul sucked the smoke into his lungs before exhaling it in a blue cloud. For several minutes, they smoked in silence. After quickly becoming light-headed, Paul took very small drags.

"You are a good man," the chief spoke at last. "You told the truth before. Tell me now. Can you help us? Truly?"

"I don't know. I promise I will try."

The chief gazed thoughtfully at the fire before answering. "It is enough."

"Come," he said when they had finished the pipe. "I have something to show you." He led Paul past his partitioned sleeping area and out a back entrance. The air was cool and clean, washed by seventy million square miles of salt water.

They crossed the clearing to the north of the lodge. Soon, they were swallowed by the forest, wading down a narrow path through waist-high sword ferns. Without the moon and stars, Paul could see almost nothing and stayed close on the heels of the chief. The boom of the surf on his left told him they were headed north.

After several minutes, they came to a small clearing dominated by yet another totem pole, this one so old that the features had been nearly weathered away and whose raked pitch foretold an ignominious end one day in the not so distant future. An invisible owl hooted upon their arrival. The chief turned to him. "Ga-git may be near," he whispered. "You must be very quiet. Do not speak unless you are spoken to. And, whatever you do, do not run or show fear."

Paul nodded. They crossed the clearing slowly, stepping carefully over bones that gleamed white in the moonlight. A yellow banana slug, larger than any Paul had ever seen, left a silvery wake in the wet grass. Skulls, large and small, including that of a human and another that looked like a huge sea monster, hung from tall posts. On the opposite side of the clearing, they came to the stump of a large spruce tree whose jagged and blackened crown testified to having been struck by lightning. The skull of an elk with a full rack of antlers guarded a narrow opening in the tree. They were about to enter, when the chief stopped him again.

"Take off your clothes," he said.

"What?"

"Take off your clothes."

"Why?"

"The spirits are easily offended."

Paul took off his jacket and pulled his sweatshirt over his head. "It's cold." he said.

"Better cold than dead." The older man crossed his arms and waited patiently while Paul stripped off his shoes, pants, and shorts and laid them at the base of the tree.

"Have you no medicine bag to protect you?" Strong Hands asked when he was done.

Paul started to reply, "No," and then he remembered. "What about this?" He found the rosary beads and held them for the chief to inspect.

The chief fingered the tiny crucifix with interest. "This contains very strong medicine, does it not?"

"Yes."

The chief nodded. "Then you should wear it."

They entered the opening in the tree and descended several steps into the ground beneath. The air was thick with the pungent smells of smoke and earth. The stairway opened up into a small cave-like room whose walls were formed by the twisted roots of the tree. A small fire burned in one corner. A noise from the wall to his right drew Paul's attention to a sleeping platform. A weak cough was followed by a voice like the rustle of dry leaves.

"I have been expecting you."

20

Howl of the Wolf

THE EDGE OF THE WORLD, TUESDAY, 11:40 P.M.
Propped up on animal hides was a small man whose dirty hair hung
in thin braids around a gaunt face so heavily tattooed that no skin
remained that was not part of a crest design. Like the chief, a bone
pierced his nose. From his elongated ears hung fetishes of carved
ivory. The twisting tentacles of an octopus were painted on his skin
shirt. Over it, he wore a necklace of small bits of bone, sea urchin
spines, shells, and sea lion teeth. It reminded Paul of the necklace he
had tried on at the morgue.

"You knew I was coming?" he asked The Light. He turned to
Chief Strong Hands. "Did you tell him?"

The chief shook his head.

"Many things are hidden from me," the shaman said, "but you
and the boy with no ears I have seen."

Startled, Paul strained to hear The Light's dry whisper. "You
know about Evan?"

"I know of him, though I did not know what he—or you—are
called."

"But how?" Paul pressed.

The chief waved him silent. "He is Paul Judge, a great warrior
among the Crow people. He has come far to see you."

"Judge," said the shaman. "This is a most interesting name." He
nodded. "Yes. I see now another thing that was hidden." He
coughed several times, struggling after each exhalation to find
the air necessary to cough again. He called out an Indian word Paul
didn't understand. A heavyset woman appeared out of the darkness
with a cup. She held The Light's head and helped him drink. As he
sipped, she looked up at Paul and smiled, displaying a couple of
missing teeth. Though she was at least sixty, Paul felt uncomfortable, crossing and uncrossing his hands in a vain effort to hide his
nakedness.

"Tell me what you know," The Light whispered.

Paul repeated the story he had told the chief.

"There is something else," he said when he had finished, "something I forgot to tell Chief Strong Hands. When I placed the Indian's necklace over my head, the room became dark. I had the feeling that I was in another place—a very strange place."

The shaman coughed again. "Describe."

Paul struggled to put into words what he had felt. "It was—I had the sensation that I was an animal. And that I was running through a tunnel. Into a mountain."

The Light's eyes blinked several times, as if some ancient memory had been awakened. When he finally spoke, it was so soft that the woman had to repeat what he said.

"He say this man, he must have been a great shaman with knowledge of the old ways. If so, he is protected by powerful spirits. Now, he say spirits angry. Must pacify before peace return."

Paul's hopes soared. Now we're getting somewhere, he thought. "What do I need to do?"

The shaman shook his head. "Not so easy."

"Can you help him?" Chief Strong Hands asked.

"Maybe," The Light said. "But it is he who must make the journey."

"How? It would kill him!" the chief said.

"Journey where?" Paul asked.

"He has no knowledge. There must be time to prepare him."

"It is only way," the shaman said. "Next time I go, I will not be coming back."

"What about me?" the chief asked.

"His name Judge. Ram's horn is horn of justice. The ram must go. This I have seen." The Light was interrupted by another coughing spell. Again he sipped from the cup. "It is true he has no training, but I think his medicine is strong."

"Where am I going?" Paul asked.

"To the spirit world," the chief said, a note of resignation in his voice.

"Me?" Paul stared at the chief in shock.

"You want an answer, you go."

Paul looked for his wrist watch and realized it was outside with his clothes. "How long will this journey take?" he asked.

"Before you visit spirits," Strong Hands said, "you must fast for four days and take baths so that you are clean inside and out."

"I can't stay that long," Paul protested. "The boy and woman I left in Seattle are in danger. If I'm going—wherever it is—I must go now."

"Are you willing to risk your life this way by angering the spirits?"

"I have to save the boy."

"Then, so be it."

The woman interrupted their discussion. "First, where is payment?" she asked.

"Payment?"

The chief pulled Paul to him with a steel-like grip. "You want to save the boy and woman?"

"Of course."

"Then get your jacket."

Paul climbed the stairway to the world outside the tree. His bare skin tingled from the cool air. The stars shone brightly as if they were but a mile instead of millions of light-years distant. He fingered the rosary beads that hung around his neck and thought of Evan and Denise. He wondered if they were asleep and if he would ever see them again. He was nervous, yet in an odd way, happy, too. His education and legal training seemed trifling compared to what he was experiencing now. It made him smile to imagine what his law professors would make of this. Then the owl hooted and he nearly jumped. He scanned the nearby forest until he discerned a spotted owl blinking at him from a branch in a Douglas fir. "Are you laughing at me, or trying to warn me?"

Again the owl hooted.

"Fine. Be that way."

When he returned, the chief motioned for him to give his jacket to The Light.

"Mind if I ask what this is buying?" Paul said.

"His services. Shaman always gets payment in advance. Besides, where you're going, you won't need it."

The woman took the jacket from him and laid it over The Light, placing his hand on the soft suede. Paul thought he saw the old man smile.

"What is the thing that he wears around his neck?" asked The Light.

"From his secret society," Strong Hands said, pointing to the rosary beads. "Very powerful medicine."

"Good." The shaman nodded. He spoke again in an Indian tongue.

The woman opened a finely carved trunk inlaid with crests. From it she brought out a ceremonial box drum and a bundle of leather which she handed to the chief. Then, she took out a wooden mask. The mask had a great mane of flowing black hair, slits for eyes and nostrils, and carved teeth. Its geometric crest shapes were painted in red and black. Finally, she withdrew a bear claw crown topped by tufts of eiderdown. She placed both the mask and crown upon the shaman's head. It made his withered body look even smaller. After these preparations had been made, she closed the covering over the smoke hole. The room began to fill with smoke.

Paul felt his skin grow taut as he inhaled. The veins in his arms and legs jumped as if, instead of blood, they were full of electricity. Something amazing was about to happen. Whatever it was, he felt as ready as he would ever be.

"Sit here," Strong Hands commanded.

Paul knelt at his side, watching carefully as the old man unwrapped the bundle of leather skins. It contained a rattle made from a gourd whose painted halves had been sewn together and bound to a handle.

The woman laid a rope of braided fiber in front of him.

"Tie one end around your waist," the chief said.

Paul knotted the cord around him. "What's this for?"

The chief tested the knot on the rope, then tied the other end around his own waist. "Just in case."

"In case what?"

"In case I need to pull you back from the spirit world."

The woman held a twisted piece of hemp in the fire until it was lit. Then she brought it to the chief who held it under Paul's nose.

"Breathe deep," he instructed. "I hope you realize this is a great honor. You are the only Indian in my lifetime to see this ceremony who is not of the Edge. It is death even to speak of it."

"I won't say a word."

"I'm not worried," Strong Hands said, and inhaled smoke from the glowing brand. "You probably won't live through it anyway."

The small underground chamber filled rapidly with a dense cloud of smoke. The woman beat a steady rhythm on the drum and The Light began to chant softly.

"Tell me what he is saying," Paul asked the chief.

"He says, 'O friends, turn your faces to me. I come to visit your world to beg your help, Spirit Ones, and this is what I ask you. The stranger is not one of us but he has come to learn why the Wind Spirit has such great anger with the white people. Show him, O Spirit Ones, to whom nothing is impossible and all mysteries are known, why the Wind Spirit seeks the boy with no ears. O Life Bringers, one more thing I ask. Take pity on the Edge People. Show me how we have offended you that our babies die before they are born. Show me how we can once more live in peace with your world.'"

Between the drumming and the buzzing that had started in his ears, Paul could barely hear the shaman's chanting. It sounded like the yapping of a dog. The chief stood and began to dance, shaking the rattle and moving his arms slowly as if he were a large bird. Paul felt his head becoming heavier and heavier. The smoke made his eyes burn. His vision blurred and he felt slightly nauseous. The yapping grew fainter.

And then, waking as from a light sleep, he found himself sitting in a gray and windless place where it was neither day nor night, nor was there any noise other than the barking. He stood and began following it. Soon, he came to the small clearing with the skulls. A very old woman, dressed in deerskin, stood among the bones, the fog swirling around her. She looked vaguely familiar. Then, she lifted her head and he knew why.

"Grandmother?"

"You are the ram," she said. "Remember ancestors. You are the ram." She began walking away.

"Grandmother! Wait!"

She paused. "Find the dog and you will find the boy. Remember ancestors. I can help you no more."

He sprinted after her retreating figure, but by the time he reached the last place he had seen her, she had disappeared into the fog. He spent several minutes searching for her trail but there was no trace of her among the thick, tangled salmonberry bushes. Again, he heard the barking, familiar-sounding now. He followed the sound up the steep side of a mountain, the barking growing louder, until finally he came upon the dog. It was Fortuno, the blind beggar's dog, tied to a tree. Evan must be up ahead. Then he heard the howl, a high, mournful falsetto that turned his blood into a river of ice. Although he had heard plenty of coyotes, he had never before that moment heard a wolf and yet, he knew without a doubt that was what it was.

Now, he was running up the hill, his breath coming in painful gasps, his legs stiff as wooden posts. At last, he reached the top and saw an old Indian wearing a fur coat and sitting with his back to him.

"Strong Hands?"

The Indian made no acknowledgment that he had heard him. Paul walked around to face the sitting figure and discovered that it was not an Indian. No. Not a human after all.

A large wolf glared back at him, a look of pure malevolence in its pale gray eyes. One large paw rested on a boy's chest. Recognition froze the blood in Paul's veins. Evan's silent mouth formed words that Paul couldn't understand. Didn't need to understand. The boy was bleeding from wounds on his arms, legs, and stomach.

"Stop!" Paul yelled and threw himself at the beast. The wolf shook him off as easily as if he were one of its cubs. It snarled at him, the muzzle drawn back in a savage grin that exposed all its fangs. Then, it stretched its neck toward the sky and unloosed a howl that soared up, higher and still higher into an unearthly register, piercing the fog and ramming a dagger of ice into Paul's heart. The message was brutally simple: "The boy is mine."

Before Paul could stop it, the wolf lowered its head and ripped out the boy's throat. Blood sprayed the air as the body spasmed and then lay still.

"No!" Paul screamed. Again the wolf snarled. Then, it leapt. The weight of its body knocked him down and pinned him to the ground. He grabbed it by the ruff around its neck, digging his thumbs into its throat, but the wolf was stronger. Its breath stank of death and Evan's blood dripped from its jaws as they reached for his throat. He heard his own flesh tearing.

He awoke with a scream, heart pounding, the air dense with smoke. The fire had nearly gone out and he was covered with cold sweat. His body hurt all over, especially his chest. He ran a hand over it. His hand felt sticky. He held it up close to his face to see. It was covered in blood.

"Jesus!" he sat up and looked at himself in the dim, flickering light. There was blood everywhere. On his chest, arms, and legs. He wiped his mouth with the back of his hand. More blood.

"Almost lost you."

Paul spun around and saw Chief Strong Hands lying behind him. He felt for the rope around his waist. It had been severed; the braided strands were frayed.

"How did you . . . ?"

"When the rope broke, I pulled you back with these." He opened his hand. There were three or four rosary beads and part of the string. "Help me sit up."

Paul had to use both hands. The chief was exhausted.

241

"Open the smoke hole and let any remaining bad spirits out." When Paul had done so, he saw the woman bending over the shaman, wetting his face with a rag. She looked at Paul.

"He wants you."

Paul stepped over the mask that grinned eyelessly from the floor beside the sleeping platform and bent over The Light. He looked gray, the color of meat gone bad. The Light motioned for him to come closer. He leaned down so that his ear was almost to the shaman's mouth.

"What did you see?" the shaman whispered.

"I saw a wolf, huge and black. The boy lay trapped beneath its paws." Paul hung his head, remembering the futility of his efforts to save the boy. "I couldn't stop it from tearing out Evan's throat. It was about to do the same thing to me when I woke up."

The shaman breathed so shallowly and for so long without responding that Paul thought he had gone to sleep.

"The wolf is a very powerful shaman. He wants the boy for a sacrifice. When the Wind Spirit has completed revenge, the boy's spirit will join the dead shaman's to serve him in the spirit world."

"How do I stop it?"

"Without big medicine, even with all your strength and wits, you cannot defeat one as powerful as this shaman."

"Then what can I do? I must help the boy, even if it kills me, too."

The ancient shaman stared past him for a time, as if calculating the answer to some indecipherable equation. "There is one thing that might help you." He turned to the woman. "Get Soul Catcher."

While Paul pondered how one went about catching a soul, the woman visited the trunk once more. This time she brought back a hollowed-out length of ivory with eyes and mouths carved at either end.

The Light clutched it to his chest as one might hold an infant, his eyes closed, fingers caressing it. "Use Soul Catcher to capture this shaman's angry spirit," he said. "Once you have done this, you must see that the body is properly taken care of. Leave in the top of a tall tree for at least ten days. After ten days, burn. Failure to do this is death."

Paul held the Soul Catcher reverently in his hands. Its smooth surface was etched nearly everywhere, but appeared to have been used so often or was so old that its markings were too worn to distinguish clearly.

"One more thing," came the whisper. "Must make sacrifice."

"Sacrifice?"

"To take boy's place. Blood for blood." He coughed.

"How does the wind track Evan?"

"Wind finds boy the same way I knew about your coming here. All thoughts, good and bad, live in spirit world. Go now." The voice was very faint. "Ga-git come." He breathed raggedly for several seconds. Paul started to pull away.

The old man clawed his shoulder with an effort that must have cost the frail paraplegic a great deal. "I heard raven croak," he rasped. "Two times." And then his hand fell from Paul's neck.

Paul squatted by the chief. "He gave me this," he held up the Soul Catcher, "but, I'm afraid I don't understand how it works."

Strong Hands's eyes were large, whether from surprise or fear, Paul wasn't sure. "Soul Catcher is very old. From way-back time when spirits ruled the earth and ancestors knew things, long time forgotten now, about how to deal with spirits. When the time comes to use it, perhaps you will know," the chief said. "Meanwhile, the sun comes soon. Let us both rest until then."

"I can't," Paul said. "Even if I could stay longer, The Light warned me to go now. He said Ga-git comes and something about hearing the raven two times."

The chief spat. "He means two will die."

"Who?" Paul's pulse quickened as he thought of Evan and Denise.

"Don't know. Maybe you, maybe him, maybe me. The raven is a trickster. You must go as fast as you can. Try to be out of the forest before dawn."

"But . . ."

"If you live, remember the Edge People and your promise."

"I'll remember." Paul squeezed the chief's arm.

The chief nodded. "Then go."

21

Nightmare

SEATTLE, WEDNESDAY, 12:01 A.M. It was so quiet, Denise could hear the furnace purring in the basement. Hours earlier, the door locks had been checked and double-checked and the lights turned off, all except the one in the bathroom, left on as much to soften the fearsome visage of night as to be a beacon in time of need. Denise lay in her bed, staring at the overhead lamp. In the shadows, it looked like the areola of a breast set in the center of the ceiling. Sleep was temporarily out of the question; her mind was far too busy attempting to sort out enormous heaps of conflicting information to let her have any rest.

During the previous night when Paul had stayed over, the wind-thing—whatever it was—had been all too terrifyingly real. Now, the more logical side of her was having a hard time accepting what Evan, Paul, and even her own senses said was true. For starters, how could a wind be anything more than a natural phenomenon? Winds were air currents caused by the earth's rotation and the differences in temperature between the poles and the equator—physics stuff. So how did one make sense of the events that had taken over her life for the past two days? What was it Evan had said? Something about everyone—good and bad, young and old—being the enemy for killing an "old one." Why everyone? And who was this "old one" who rated such fealty from one of Mother Nature's hitmen? It was as if sanity and science had suddenly been replaced with voodoo and fairy tales by the Brothers Grimm.

If Evan's explanation was bewildering, his recent behavior was downright disturbing. His disappearance yesterday and violent reaction to the television news tonight had rocked her to the soles of her Reeboks. What new psychological scar tissue would her son be trying to deal with years from now? Childhood was such an emotional minefield anyway. And that was without seeing people in helicopters die, or thinking that you were responsible for the deaths of hundreds of people in an airplane. To quiet him down and help him sleep, she had given him half of one of the sleeping pills she sometimes took for her insomnia.

Then there was the episode with Bud and the entire work issue. She had worked so hard to be the best P.R. professional she could be—as good as or better than the men she had to compete with— only to see it all threatening to unravel because she wouldn't fool around. The feeling that she had been wronged made her angry, but the knowledge that she was trapped made her crazy. If Bud became hostile over her rejection of his advances, he could make her life hell. She couldn't go around him; Bud and Grenitzer went way back. Going to her boss would do no better; the mayor was one of the agency's most profitable, as well as most visible, accounts. Besides, Phil had already insinuated that she shouldn't hesitate to use her "physical assets" to woo clients. Whenever the agency pitched an account, he made sure to parade Denise in front of any male prospects. And, when new accounts were assigned, more often than not she got the ones managed by lechers while the guys got the accounts run by sports freaks or women.

And, finally, there was Paul Judge. Who was this mystery man and what was he doing in her carefully—until now, at least—controlled mayhem of a life? Of all her dilemmas, this was possibly the most difficult one to understand. She was unsure where her fears ended and where her other feelings began. Initially, Paul had been just someone—albeit a damn good-looking someone—to fill the breech in an emergency. But something had changed since their conversations the previous night and again last night on the telephone. Now, there were these silly, long-forgotten feelings of wanting to share everything, no matter how trivial, and a word, a look, or a touch took on hyper-significance, staying in her mind to be replayed over and over.

Denise sighed and shook her head. There was altogether too much to consider for her over-stressed and over-tired mind. "Get real, Denise," she scolded herself. She would probably never see the man again. And even if she did, it would be foolish to add anything more to her life's stew, at least until she found out if she could eat what she already had on her plate.

Sometime later, she must have dropped off to sleep. When she awoke, the clock read a little after two A.M. She listened intently, trying to decipher what it was that might have awakened her. Methodically, she sorted through the sounds of creaking floors, a dripping faucet, a neighbor's barking dog, the distant backfire of a truck on the freeway. Denise's eyelids drooped as sleep returned. She pulled the comforter up to her neck. The air had turned frosty. Had the furnace quit? No, she could still hear its faint hum. Her eyes popped open. She remembered the eerie coldness she had experienced at the Tower just before the granite panel fell.

"Evan!" She jumped from bed, turned on the light and ran across the hall to wake him. Only Evan didn't want to wake up. He moaned in his sleep, his eyes roaming feverishly beneath their purple lids. She had to shake him for several anxious seconds before his eyes finally fluttered open. She helped him sit up.

What is it? What's wrong? His hands signed lazily, as if he were underwater.

"The wind!" she signed. "Can't you feel it?"

He yawned and shook his head.

Denise cocked her head and listened, but there wasn't a sound of wind or breath of air and the temperature was its usual, nighttime sixty degrees. On top of everything else, was she losing her mind, too?

"Sorry," she said. "I must have dreamed it." But, unused to the effects of the mild sleeping pill, Evan was already fast asleep. "Just a nightmare, I guess." She ran her fingers through his hair.

On the way back to her room, she visited the bathroom, found the prescription container in the medicine cabinet and shook one of the sleeping pills into her hand. She stared at it, tiny and white, in her palm. It would give her temporary rest from her worries, allow her to be fresh the next morning. She took a small paper cup from the dispenser, ran cold water into it. She put the pill to her lips, then stopped. What if, illogical as it sounded, there *were* a wind following her son, a wind capable of knocking airplanes from the sky? What then? She drank from the cup of water, then put the pill back in its bottle.

Denise was climbing into her own bed when she heard a strange noise. She paused, one foot still outside the comforter. It sounded like a train coming, fast and hard. Problem was, to her knowledge, there wasn't any track closer than Magnolia—surely too far to hear a train's passing. Then, Fortuno's howl, like an air-raid warning siren, joined with the noise which swelled louder and louder until it became a great, angry tsunami rushing toward them. The windows rattled in their frames and the milk glass shade on the nightstand lamp began vibrating, the dog's howl rising, rising, her own heart hammering in her ears, the wind noise so loud now that she couldn't hear herself think, couldn't move, until the shade vibrated right off the lamp and disintegrated on the floor. The explosion of glass brought her back to her senses.

"Oh, my God," she whispered. "Oh, my God!"

The wind struck with a resounding boom. The house shuddered and groaned, as if struck by a huge wave.

Instantly, Denise was out of bed for the second time, racing across the sharp glass that pebbled the floor and bit into the soles of her feet. Awake now, Evan met her in the hallway. In his baggy pajamas, he looked like a cruise passenger who knows the ship is about to go down.

She flipped on the lights in the hallway and Evan's room.

"Get dressed!" Denise signed. "We're getting out of here."

Where are we going?

"I don't know yet. Now hurry!"

Her first reaction was to flee to Paul's apartment, or anywhere for that matter—just away from this house. Back in her own room, the clamor made thinking difficult if not impossible. Tree limbs knocked and rattled against the side of the house. The wind whistled shrilly around the edges of the windows. The lace curtains fluttered and a magazine flapped its pages angrily. She found tennis shoes and a pair of jeans in her closet and was stuffing the tail of her nightshirt into the pants when the lights went out. She reached the doorway to Evan's room and couldn't see him in the blizzard of computer paper swirling about. Then the wind slammed into the house again. The double-hung windows popped like champagne corks and shot straight at her. She only had time to twist aside as the panes shattered against the door frame, showering her with fragments. A dagger-sized piece pierced her arm and she screamed. Denise fell to the floor, momentarily stunned by the force of the gust and the pain. Evan bent over her, so pale his skin seemed translucent. In his eyes, she read both concern and terror. Her confusion vanished. This was no nightmare, much as she wanted it to be. Something wanted her son.

She could feel the oak floorboards vibrating beneath her as the wind circled the house. With her right hand, she grasped the glass protruding from her arm, closed her eyes to the pain, and yanked it out. The darkened hallway swam before her eyes when she reopened them. Denise refused to faint; her son's life was at stake. The wind suddenly stopped. Fortuno's frantic howling continued unabated downstairs. Evan dabbed at the blood that was drenching her nightshirt. It was too dark and there was no time to sign. She grabbed his hand and struggled to her feet. Together, they made their way down the stairs. The living room was a disaster. Broken glass, torn curtains, and newspapers littered the floor. Her heavy brass Stieffel lamp, a Christmas present from her parents, protruded from the face of the television. The couch lay on its back, blocking the doorway to the guest bathroom. Denise released Evan's hand to find out whether the phone on the buffet still worked and he broke from her.

"Evan! Come back here!" she yelled at his back as he raced toward the porch where Fortuno whimpered.

She checked the phone, then dialed 911. After one ring, the line went dead. She slammed the receiver down.

In a drawer, she found a flashlight and was greatly relieved to discover that it worked. She used it to examine her arm. The cut was large, but the flow of blood was oozing, not spurting. Teeth gritted against the pain, she tied a doily, crocheted by her grandmother, around her arm. It would suffice until she had retrieved Evan. Then she hurried toward the back porch. She had just reached the kitchen and saw Evan entering from the opposite direction, his hands full of quivering dog, when another thunderous jolt shook the house. For a second, Denise thought a bomb had detonated. Walls cracked. Plaster fell in slabs from the ceiling. Thick dust roiled the air. Denise couldn't see Evan and, for one terrifying moment, thought the wind had managed to steal him. "No!" she yelled and began digging through the debris. She found Evan a few seconds later, still holding Fortuno beneath a pile of coats.

"Okay?" she signed with one hand while the other held the flashlight. She heard rafters tear and pop as the roof was ripped from the house. He nodded and Denise hauled him to his feet.

"C'mon!" she yelled and they ran, crouching, to the basement door which gave way grudgingly, only after she had used her good shoulder to batter against it. Fortuno raced downstairs as Denise kicked the door closed behind them. She and Evan scrambled down the narrow steps as the wind shrieked in fury. Denise stumbled and fell the last two steps, landing on her injured arm. Tears sprang to her eyes. Evan helped her crawl to shelter. The three of them huddled together under the utility sink. Above, there were the sounds of splintering wood and furniture being overturned.

Evan started back toward the stairs. Denise grabbed his ankle.

My whistle! He pantomimed blowing and signed into her hands. *Got to get it!*

Denise shook her head and pulled him back. She clutched him to her tightly. He was going nowhere without her. The wind would have to break her good arm to separate them.

The basement door began shuddering violently. Denise trained the flashlight on it.

"You can't have him!" she screamed. "He's mine!"

With a roar that shook the house, the door was torn off its hinges and flung down the stairs. It landed with a crash on the sink. Then the basement window blew in. They were in the center of a frigid, whirling nightmare. Glass and wood splinters stung them. Choking dust coated their tongues, nostrils, and eyes, making it impossible to see. A heavy support timber fell near their feet as the entire house began to shift off its foundation. Denise screamed, but couldn't hear herself above the raging wind.

22

Ga-git Comes

THE EDGE OF THE WORLD, WEDNESDAY, 4:02 A.M.
The owl was gone. Probably hunting, Paul thought as he dressed.
The woman had given him a wet buckskin to wipe away the blood.
Based on The Light's words and his own personal experience, the
body evidently became whole when it entered the spirit world;
whatever infirmities one had were left behind along with hunger
and disease. Traveling in the other direction, on the other hand, the
rules were reversed. One brought back any injuries received—if
one came back at all. Fortunately, his wounds were limited to several deep scratches on his throat and chest.

From the lightning-blasted spruce, he began working his way
south, keeping the surf on his right as he backtracked along his and
the chief's earlier footprints. The chilling encounter with the wolf
had increased his anxiety and sharpened his senses; around him, he
could hear the dew falling from the trees with frequent splats onto
the ferns below. It was cool, walking in his shirt-sleeves without a
jacket. Paul wondered if the shaman would live long enough to
enjoy his payment.

Back outside the lodge, there was no sign of the twins or anyone
else. Even the ocean seemed to be resting—the rhythmic rumble of
the waves sounded less violent, more subdued. There was no time
to enjoy the peaceful solitude of the moment, however. He was relieved to find the car still sitting where he had parked it. The Mercedes roared to life with a diesel clatter that was loud enough to
wake the dead, and within moments he was bouncing over the rutted road back to civilization.

The forest had the transitory quality of early morning. Mist
draped her ethereal fabric among the trees and shrubs. Nothing
stirred. And although the sun had not yet risen, the sky had light-
ened in preparation for its eventual appearance. The car groaned at
least as loudly as it had on the way in. But this time, it seemed to fit
the road more surely, anticipating the dips and turns, as if his mind
and the machine were one.

While it had been less than twenty-four hours since he had left Seattle, it felt like a week. He had not slept, other than the time spent in dream-trance—and that could hardly be called restful. Every bone and muscle ached, yet he felt clear-headed and energized. Connected. In a few hours, he had grown closer to Chief Strong Hands than anyone since his grandmother. It was as if he had sprouted instant roots, roots that had always been there, but too shallow to reach water. His grandmother's words, "Remember ancestors," came back to him now. He was not entirely sure what they meant, or how they might affect what he did from this point on in his life. There were many questions still to be answered. But he was convinced that he could never again let himself become so disconnected from his heritage. He had been living in a white world without benefit of family and with few friends, unaccepted by the whites who saw him as an alien aberration and equally disdained by the local Indians he often represented and who shared little of his education or ambition. If he was ever to enjoy the peace of mind that came with being comfortable with who he was, he knew that he must embrace his Indian-ness instead of running from it. How this change would affect his career and the rest of his life, he was unsure. One question was especially troubling: the boy and his mother had become more important to him than anyone else. If Denise was ever interested in the old Paul, would she still want the new model? He was nearly as anxious to hear the answer to that question as he was to learn if they were safe.

By now, he thought, the ferry that went down should have been replaced. He decided to gamble on the shorter return route through Port Angeles. With a little luck, he would be back in Seattle before nine A.M. One little detail, however, had to be handled first.

He stopped the car, letting the engine idle while he relieved his bladder by the side of the road. The silence of the primeval wilderness caused him to recall the chief's warning to be out of the forest before dawn. Then a distant sound made him pause mid-zip. He stood, frozen, straining to identify the strange sound as it grew louder by the second. In a flash of recognition, he ran to the car, slammed the door, jammed the gearshift into second, his foot already to the floorboards. The car bounced high and hard over the rutted road. Paul drove to the limits of his concentration and reflexes, glancing frequently into the rearview mirror. The forest rushed by in a blur of black and white as the car outpaced the ability of the headlights to distinguish the twisting road from trees and shrubs. His concern over what was behind him caused him to see one turn a moment too late. The back end drifted right and the rear quarter panel glanced off a tree trunk with a sickening thud.

He swore and kept the pedal pressed nearly to the floor. This time when he looked back in the mirror, there was something there—the eye of a drunken cyclops.

From the way the leaping and weaving light moved, Paul knew that it was a two-cycle dirt bike that followed him. He was also pretty certain that one or both of the twins was riding it. And he was willing to bet that they were not coming merely to say good-bye. If the brothers saw the wind spirit as their tribe's avenger, they would use any means necessary to stop him from interfering with its deadly purpose.

The gap was shrinking; the ever-growing light bobbing in his mirror as whoever was steering the bike navigated the trail. Then the rear window exploded. He ducked involuntarily as a glass shard stung his ear. In his rearview mirror, Paul saw that the window was one big jigsaw puzzle, each piece no larger than a pebble, except where the bullet had blown out a jagged hole the size of his fist. The roof liner contained a shallow trench to the right of the dome light. Over the throaty roar of the engine and the angry whine of the bike, he swore he could hear war cries.

Though he was already on the edge of losing control, he pressed the pedal as far into the carpeting as it would go. He flew through the forest, the car sometimes airborne, ricocheting off tree trunks with the sound of grinding metal. Tree boughs swept across the windshield, temporarily blinding him and raking the roof of the car. As he concentrated on seeing beyond the lighted perimeter provided by his headlights, he realized that it was only a matter of minutes—perhaps seconds—before they would catch up to him again and kill him. The Mercedes was built like a tank, but its oil pan, gas tank, and tires would only take so much abuse. He forced himself to breathe deeply and think rationally as he considered his options. He would not give up without a fight.

Despite his speed and the rough terrain, the bike closed rapidly. Paul anticipated another shot with every yard less distance. When they were within four car lengths, he slammed on the brakes. The car fishtailed wildly, seeking purchase on the wet grass and rocks. The bike slowed, swerving at the last moment to avoid the car, before rocketing past him. The Mercedes skidded to a halt. Paul turned off the car's lights and waited patiently, heart pounding, revving the engine, until the twins turned the bike around and came back for him. When they were within fifty feet, he flipped on his brights and charged straight for them. The driver was forced to send the bike hurtling into the forest to avoid a collision. Paul shot by them. "So much for that trick," he said and shook his head. Whichever brother was driving that dirt bike was damn good.

Within a minute, the motorcycle was again positioned right on Paul's bumper. Another gunshot punctuated the engine noise. This one missed. At a fork in the road, Paul threw the wheel to the left. The motorcycle moved off to his right and was now running parallel, separated by a narrow stand of slender saplings and intermittent foliage. Paul stole a glance to his right and saw the brothers, riding in tandem, their faces decorated in war paint. The one on the rear imitated drawing a bow and loosing arrows followed by shrill war cries. The car grazed a boulder that demolished a headlight and nearly tore the steering wheel from his hands.

Out of the corner of his eye, he saw a muzzle flash, simultaneously hearing the gunshot's report. This one punched through the passenger door. Paul was so certain he must be hit that he had to glance down to make sure his legs were still intact. Then his passenger window disappeared. The explosion seemed to come from within his head. He ducked as glass showered his face and arms. There were more war cries.

"Remember ancestors," Paul heard his grandmother's words.

Ahead, his remaining headlight illuminated little more than a massive cedar tree that seemed to fill the road. The turnout suddenly ended and the dirt bike shot back onto the road in front of the car. The twin on the bike's bouncing rear seat leveled a large handgun at Paul's head. The driver turned and grinned at something his brother said. In that instant, an enormous elk stepped squarely in front of the two vehicles.

Paul braked so hard that the Mercedes nearly flipped. The elk froze in his headlights as he skidded toward it, its large eyes staring directly into his own. A second later, the bike's driver saw the animal that blocked his path and he, too, hit his brakes. The bike skidded, swerved, hopped an exposed tree root, seemed to recover, then went down, striking something on the rutted road that flipped it through the air. It smacked into the cedar tree, sending a burst of flame boiling up into the night sky.

Paul jumped from the car and ran toward the wreck. The brother who had ridden on the back of the bike had fallen off before it crashed and now struggled to get up. Paul ran past him. Ignited by gasoline from the bike's ruptured fuel tank, the tree was engulfed in flames that crackled and soared high into the night, illuminating the surrounding forest. The driver remained pinned beneath the mangled bike. It was obvious he was dead. Behind him, over the sound of the inferno, Paul heard a noise. He turned to see the bloodied twin on his knees, holding the gun pointed at him.

"Bastard!" he screamed in a voice laced with pain and rage.

Paul heard the gun cock. "I promised Strong Hands to help your people and I will," he said. "Kill me and you kill more of your own people."

He walked slowly to the injured man. When he reached him, he saw that there were tears running down the other man's face. "I can take you back to your village," he offered.

But the brother shook his head. "No, you won't. Go," he said and lowered the gun. "I must protect my brother's body from Gagit."

"You could die of blood loss or shock before anyone finds you," Paul argued.

The man's anguished face darkened with rage. "Go, damn you, or I'll blow you to hell!"

Paul got back in the battered automobile. As he drove off, he saw the brother kneeling where he had left him, his shoulders shaking, head so low that his hair touched the ground. Paul planned to stop at the first place he saw to phone for aid, but he wondered if it would arrive in time, or, even if it did, whether the Indian's pride would permit anyone to help him.

The elk, he noticed, was nowhere to be seen. He wondered how it had managed to escape being hit by at least one of the two vehicles. And then he remembered the elk skull and antlers guarding the entrance to The Light's dwelling.

23

Black Clouds

SEATTLE, WEDNESDAY, 7:00 A.M. Denise woke with a start. It took a few seconds for her to understand where she was and why. Then she remembered.

"Evan," she said and jerked her head up, causing a mini-avalanche of plaster dust. She used her uninjured arm to raise the shower curtain under which they lay. A two-quart sauce pan, minus its handle, clattered onto the concrete floor. The air was cool and damp and the gray light of dawn filtered through the basement window.

Still under the effects of the sleeping pill, Evan slept beside her, his breathing normal. He looked like a war refugee, but, much to her relief, didn't appear to be injured. That they weren't both dead, buried under the rubble of their house, was a miracle. Denise remembered her father's words when she had bought the house: "It ain't gonna win no beauty contest, but it's been here for seventy years and it'll likely still be here in another seventy." In its fury, the wind had shaken the house to the point of collapse, and then, as suddenly as it had come, it was gone. Unable to see, too tired and frightened to move, they had spent the rest of the night huddled under the utility sink.

Pounding began somewhere near the front of the house. The walls trembled with the heavy blows. Evan and Fortuno's heads came up in tandem.

What's that? Evan signed.

"Someone hammering on our house, I think. How are you?" she signed back. She looked him over for any cuts or bruises.

Hungry!

Under other circumstances, Denise might have smiled, even laughed—the kid was obviously in no pain if his first consideration was food. But this time, tears began to well up in her eyes. She hugged Evan to her tightly. He mustn't see how scared she was.

She looked for her wristwatch and discovered that it was missing. Her grandmother's doily was a dull red and lifting her arm caused a

255

shooting pain. The beam from a flashlight suddenly appeared in the midst of the debris.

"Over here!" Denise called out. Evan waved his arms. A young man wearing a yellow slicker, fire helmet, and a full mustache crouched in the small, ground-level basement window. He spoke briefly into a walkie-talkie before returning his attention to them.

"Everyone okay?" he asked.

"Guess it depends on what you mean by okay." Denise crawled out from under the sink, stood up and brushed herself off.

The fireman wedged himself through the window, dropped down into the basement and shined his light around the room. Broken glass, chunks of plaster and pieces of lath were strewn among heaps of camping gear, paint cans, old clothes, and odds and ends left over from a previous garage sale. He examined a fallen support beam.

"Looks like you folks got the worst of it."

"Worst of what?" Denise asked, wondering what explanation he would give for the wind's attack. She brushed dust and grit from Evan's hair and clothes while he combed the dog's fur with his fingers.

"Weather service is calling it a tornado. Hey, you're injured. Why didn't you say so? I'll call for an EMT." He spoke into his radio again.

"A tornado, huh?" The tension and lack of sleep made her irritable. "So, where you guys been?"

"Pardon me?"

"We spent the night down here. Didn't anybody call?"

The fireman left off examining the damage to their house, a task he clearly relished, to face her. "Didn't get a call until about an hour ago. Phones are down, I guess."

"Nobody had a portable phone, or just got in their car to go for help?"

"Like I said, lady, most people just had their fences and garbage cans knocked down, maybe lost a few shingles off the roof. One guy had a tree fall on his car."

Oh, no. That would be the final straw. "Did you happen to notice the condition of our car?"

"The station wagon out front? It's seen better days. Couldn't say if it runs or not."

"Come on, Evan. Let's get out of here." Denise started up the stairs.

"Ah, sorry, lady, but no one's allowed in the house until repairs are made. You're going to have to jack up this floor and replace a couple of beams."

"That could take days or even weeks."

"Could." He nodded.

Here was the guy you'd probably want for your softball team, but his bedside manner left something to be desired.

"So arrest me." She began climbing again.

"Wait," he called out after apparently having second thoughts. "Anybody got hurt, I could lose my job. What do you need? I'll go."

"My purse, for one thing. Last I saw, it was on the kitchen table. A few clothes wouldn't hurt either." Denise had no doubt that the wind would be coming back. The sooner they were gone, the better.

"I'll see what I can do. You wait right here until the EMT arrives."

Denise managed to find Evan a clean shirt and socks in the dryer located next to the sink. A second fireman inserted a ladder through the basement window. After handing Fortuno up to him, Denise and Evan climbed to freedom. The fireman made her walk across her unmowed lawn and sit down on the open end of a bright yellow van so he could clean and bandage her wound.

He whistled when he cut away the doily. "Bet that hurt."

Denise nodded and tried not to look. Instead, she inspected the house. It looked abandoned. All the windows had been blown out. The front door sagged on its hinges. The rafters were exposed like ribs and a ten-foot section of roof now lay atop the car. Yet another fireman was cordoning off the house with yellow tape.

"This is going to hurt some more. Lie back if you feel like it. I'm gonna clean this out a little."

Evan watched him work while playing with the dog. Denise closed her eyes and laid back, her lower legs hanging down over the rear of the vehicle.

"What's your name?" the black man asked.

"Denise," she said.

"I was asking your boy here."

"His name is Evan. He's deaf."

"Mine's Rodney. I'm a little hard of hearing myself, but don't go telling the captain. You need to have this looked at and soon. Could be glass still in there. Probably need a couple of stitches to close it up right, keep the scarring down. When's the last time you had a tetanus shot?"

"I don't remember."

"It's a trick question." He smiled. "Nobody does. You best check with your doc whether you think you know the date or not. Otherwise, you'll be drinking your meals through a straw. What are you planning to do about the house?"

Denise looked at her house again. It had taken years of saving and a loan from her parents in order to buy it. She took in a lung-full of air, then blew it out. "I don't know. Fix it, I guess. Does insurance cover something like this?"

"Depends on your policy. Some policies don't cover acts of God—you know, earthquakes, stuff like that."

"I don't think this was an act of God," Denise said softly.

Rodney didn't hear the irony in her voice. "That's just what they call natural disasters as opposed to good, old, EPA-approved, man-made disasters. You married?" he asked.

"No, why?"

"Just wondering. You got family?" he asked. He applied something to her arm that made it burn as if he'd held a match to the skin.

"Yeah," she answered, a note of huskiness edging her voice.

"Good time to call on them. You read lips?" Rodney asked her son.

Evan nodded enthusiastically.

"I bet your mom's a good mom, huh?"

Evan smiled.

"You see that she gets to a doctor, okay?"

He patted Denise's shoulder. "Best I can do. Good luck."

Denise sat up and waited a moment before her head cleared so that she could stand. "One more thing," she said. "If we leave, what's to keep someone from helping themselves to all our stuff?"

"Don't you worry," Rodney said. "As soon as our inspection is done, we'll board up all your windows and doors. By the time we get finished, your house will be more secure than before."

"Thanks. For the first aid and the advice."

"My pleasure."

Denise stood in the ankle-high, dew-wet grass and glanced around. Though it was barely light out, clots of curious bystanders stood across the street gaping. A woman reporter and cameraman were interviewing one of them. From the other side of her driveway she could see her next-door neighbor approaching in his bathrobe and bedroom slippers and looking like he was about to have a stroke.

"Your tree has fallen across my fence, missy. Who's gonna pay for it, I'd like to know?"

"Your insurance company, more than likely." The contrast between the pale blue skin of her neighbor's feet and the deep red of his veined and unshaven face seemed pitiful. He was her father's age, working-class, and she was willing to cut him some slack, even if he was more than a little obnoxious. She began walking toward the car.

"But what about my deductible?" he shouted, following behind her. "Don't deny that it's your fault, missy. That tree should have been trimmed back years ago. Don't think I won't talk to my lawyer!"

Denise whirled to face him. "We just lost nearly everything we own, barely escaped with our lives, and you're threatening me with a lawsuit over a tree that's fallen on your stupid fence? Send me the bill! Now, let me offer one little piece of advice," she jabbed his chest, "if you want to live to see your next birthday, don't ever call me 'missy' again. Let's go, Evan," she signed.

Denise shook her head sadly as she walked away, leaving her neighbor standing there slack-jawed. She regretted losing it like that. One day, she'd have to apologize. Right now, she just hoped there would be a day when this was all over. She spotted the fireman with the mustache carrying her purse like it was a douche bag in one hand and their ski parkas in the other.

"Couldn't find any clothes except these," he said.

"Thanks. Can I get a hand with my car?"

When he saw what she wanted to do, he used the chain saw to cut the section of roof that had landed on the station wagon into two sections, then helped her remove them. The top and hood were badly dented and scraped, but the car's appearance was the least of her worries.

Evan tugged on her bandaged arm and she jerked it away before she realized who it was.

"What?"

He pointed to the second floor. The siding had been ripped away so that you could see into his room. The computer desk, bed, and dresser were smashed to bits, more tangible proof of the wind's aggression. And its purpose.

"Get into the car," Denise signed. "Right now."

She tried the key and was greatly relieved when the car started. She looked in the rearview mirror and saw the news reporter and cameraman coming up the driveway.

"Excuse me," the reporter called out. "I'm Dixie Delmont with KOMO TV. Can we have just a minute?" She shoved a microphone through the window and into Denise's face. Denise noted the woman's carefully coiffed hair and expensive suit as the cameraman focused in on her. She glanced down at herself, saw that her nipples were showing through the thin and dirty nightshirt and realized that her disheveled appearance was probably going to be the highlight of the evening news. She'd be lucky if she didn't end up on network television. She could just hear Tom Brokaw: "And from Seattle, woman and son lose home and belongings to vengeance-seeking wind."

"Sorry," Denise said. "I just used up my last available minute. Watch your toes."

She roared down the driveway in reverse, shifted into drive and gunned it. Two stoplights later, they were headed south on Interstate 5 into the city.

Where are we going? Evan signed. He leaned forward so he could better read her lips. Fortuno rode in his lap, his head hanging out the open passenger window. For once, Denise didn't mind. The cool air helped her think.

"Spokane," she answered. "We can stay with Grandma and Grandpa." As long as they stayed away from their house, Denise hoped they'd be safe from the wind, but she wasn't taking any chances.

No school?

"No school."

Evan bounced on the seat. Fortuno licked his face, as if he, too, thought this was a great idea.

What about Paul? He'll be worried about us.

Denise considered this. Evan had been a fan of Paul's from the beginning. For her own selfish reasons, she hoped he was right about Paul's concern.

"I've got to go by the office. We'll call and leave a message on his answering machine."

She took the Columbia Street exit and drove west through downtown Seattle to First Avenue where she turned south. The early morning sky was uniformly gray except for some black clouds clustered near the waterfront. Although it was a workday, there wasn't much traffic yet in Pioneer Square. She'd prefer to be headed out of town as fast as the old wagon would go, but she'd been raised to believe you didn't just run out on people who were depending on you without an explanation. The mayoral election was a week away, the memorial ceremony in just two days. Of course, even with an explanation, leaving now would probably doom her career, but she had a deeper responsibility to her son and herself.

At First and James, they passed a man covered in newspapers sleeping on a bus bench beneath the glass and iron pergola, and a policeman buying coffee from a sidewalk vendor. Fortuno began a low, mournful whine deep in his throat. Evan noticed the dog's agitation and tugged Denise's arm urgently to show her.

"Maybe he just remembers this neighborhood," she said, wary now. The back of her neck had begun to cramp and she had to grip the steering wheel hard to keep her hands from trembling.

Fortuno's whine changed to a guttural growl as they proceeded south on First Avenue and his jaws snapped at the window, as if he saw something. Denise searched for any sign of the wind, but the air was still as death. The trees that lined the center divider might as well have been petrified. Then a newspaper flew onto the car's windshield, startling her and blocking her view. She stopped quickly—too quickly. Behind her, she heard the squeal of brakes followed by a hard jolt and the anguished convergence of metal and glass. Cold air flooded into the car from the vent and her partially opened window. She rolled it shut. The wind began to whistle around windows and doors.

The smell, Evan signed.

It was true. Close your eyes and you would have thought you were in a snow-bound forest, not downtown Seattle.

She looked at Evan. His breath made steam and his freckles stood out against his pale face.

"Stay here," she said.

Heart pounding, she opened the door and started to get out in order to remove the newspaper and make sure the other driver wasn't hurt. With a snarl, the wind slammed the door shut, just missing her foot. Fortuno's paws scrabbled against the window and the car began to rock as if they were parked beside a freeway with large trucks rolling past.

It wants me, Evan signed. *It won't leave us alone until it wins.*

Denise grabbed Evan by the shoulders. "Read my lips carefully:

It's not going to win, Evan! Whatever it is, it's like a spoiled child. We can outwit it, but I need your help!"

The car springs groaned as they continued to rock and the newspaper remained plastered to their windshield. She searched behind them for an escape route. The driver of the car that had hit them was clinging to his car door while his raincoat flapped in the wind. She heard him swear over the wind's howl, then he lost his grip and was sucked into the air. He landed with a crash on top of the pergola where he hung, spread-eagled. The cop was next. He was leaning into the wind, crossing the street with his head down, trying to get to the man on the pergola, or perhaps Denise and Evan, when the park bench, still carrying the reclining man, flew straight at him and caught him up like a cow catcher on an old train engine. Bench, bum, and cop disappeared through a large storefront window with a crack like gunfire.

Denise held Evan's face between her hands. "I want you to put the dog down. If he's smart, he'll follow. You see that doorway, the one with the panther on the sign over the door?"

Evan nodded.

"When I push you, we're going to run in there."

What if the door's locked?

"If it is, it won't be much longer. Scrunch down and cover your head."

Still unable to see through the windshield, Denise steered the car in the general direction of the doorway. The car hit the curb harder than she expected; the steering wheel tore from her hands. She recovered quickly, stepped again on the gas and they lurched into the brick and glass storefront. She missed the door, but the building was so old that the wall caved in, creating an opening large enough for them to get through. Bricks and glass thundered onto the car. Denise quickly shifted into reverse, pulling back just enough to clear the rubble.

"Now go! Go!"

Evan had the door open and she pushed him out. Before she could escape from her own door, the wind seized the car and dragged it backward into the street. She tried stepping on the gas. Though the tires squealed, louder and louder, the stench of burning rubber filling the passenger compartment, the car continued in reverse. There was another wrenching collision as the car snapped off a fire hydrant. A torrent of water shot high into the air. Denise jammed her foot on the brake pedal. In slow motion, she felt the front end lift. The newspaper fluttered from her window and she could see buildings falling away, then gray sky. Water from the hydrant cascaded heavily onto the car, drumming on the hood, drowning the windshield. The car continued over and landed with a crash on its top. The windshield popped out. Denise hung upside down, her safety belt sawing her in half and her head resting against the headliner. A trickle of something warm ran down the outside of her nose and onto her forehead. She couldn't tell if it was blood. At this point, she didn't care. She hadn't had the time to see if Evan had made it safely into the building. Adding to her panic, smoke began to escape from under the hood.

Denise forced herself to examine her surroundings. There was asphalt just beyond the hole left by the windshield. The top of the car had been pancaked, but she might be able to escape through the remaining narrow opening if she held her breath—and if the wind let her.

In the dim light of the store, a face stared up at him from the pile of rubble. Evan inhaled sharply, stumbled, and fell to his knees. In addition to collapsing the storefront, the force of the collision had destroyed a number of display cases. Antique jewelry, windup cars, old dolls, and a brass telescope were strewn among the broken glass and bricks. He knelt to clear the dust and debris from the face and heaved a sigh of relief with the discovery that it belonged to a store mannequin. Fortuno sniffed at it suspiciously. Evan grabbed the dog and hurried to the back of the store, as far from the wind as possible. There was no exit, however. The dead bolt on the back door had been locked with a key. He huddled with Fortuno under a roll top desk to wait for his mother. When she didn't appear immediately, he began to worry. The vibration from another crash told him something had gone wrong with her plan.

He made the letter Y with both hands and gestured firmly at Fortuno, *Stay!* Although the dog didn't understand sign language, it seemed to sense his intent.

Back at the street, Evan's fears charged into full-scale terror. Less than three minutes had passed since they had arrived in Pioneer Square, but the scene that greeted him was altered almost beyond recognition. Water from a broken fire hydrant shot high into the air. The station wagon was in the center median, upside down, and his mother was nowhere to be seen. She might still be trapped inside the car. Traffic was stopped in both directions. One of the towering maple trees was uprooted and a light standard sprawled across the road. A handful of people crouched behind cars or hid in doorways. A cyclist chased his bicycle until he stumbled, landed on his back and was blown down the street like a tumbleweed. The first police car was just pulling up, lights flashing. Evan waved his arms and began running to warn the officer, but the wind was faster. A bronze bust of Chief Sealth sped down the street, striking the cruiser with such force that it demolished the top and sent the car spinning into the other cars.

Evan stopped, unsure where to turn or what to do. He couldn't see or hear the wind, but could sense it as it soared and twisted among the trees and buildings. It was enormous—the size of a building itself—and incredibly fast and powerful. One moment it was shoving you around so hard you had to grab on to something to keep from blowing away, and the next it was gone. He could also sense the wind's anger and he knew that his mother and all these people would die unless he could stop it.

The shooting water from the hydrant gave Evan an idea.

Here I am! He sent the thought hurtling toward the wind. *Bet you can't do the trick with the water again.*

Without a tree to put his hand on, Evan was afraid that the wind wouldn't "hear" him, but he felt it change direction instantly and come rushing toward him. The wind blasted him off his feet and threw him against a large blue mailbox. For a moment, he was afraid that he had pushed it too far. His elbow was numb, and he couldn't lift his arm.

Do you still dare to doubt me, boy? The wind whirled about him so that it was hard to see or breathe. *Nothing is impossible for me.*

Show me! Evan thought. *Show me the water trick if you think you can!*

He thought he felt the wind laugh. Then it swatted the column of water so that it shot out hundreds of feet, raining down on cars, buildings, people and all that was below.

Higher! Evan thought.

And again the wind sent the water flying, this time carrying it high into the sky before letting it fall back to earth. But Evan had turned his attention to the upside-down station wagon where first an arm and then a head now protruded as his mother tried to wriggle out of the car. Fear instantly replaced his hope. What if the wind read his mind? He forced his thoughts back to the water.

Is that the best you can do? Evan asked.

Enough games! the wind shrieked, batting the water violently. *Do you remember what I said I would do to the air machine? I threw it to the ground as easily as you would a stick. Now, it is time. You must come with me!*

But why? he asked it. *I hurt no one.*

Your innocence and strong medicine are fitting for sacrifice. Besides, it is honor to die.

I don't think it's honorable to kill or hurt people.

This just proves how little you know. Your words tire me. The water became a funnel, rushing up in the center and overflowing at the top.

If I must be the sacrifice, why hurt all these other people?

They could have provided the Old One sanctuary, allowed him to die in his own time. Instead, he was murdered. Now revenge is at hand for their treachery. Today is the day you and I have been destined for. All is in readiness so that the Old One may pass peacefully from this world to the next. Only then can I return to my home.

Evan sagged against the mailbox. Tears filled his eyes. The finality of the wind's thoughts overwhelmed him, making all of his arguments sound futile. Then a blur of white charged by him. The dog leapt and snapped at the column of water.

Fortuno!

Evan started after the dog when a hand seized him by the wrist. He looked up in surprise at his mother, fresh blood smears on her forehead and previously injured arm. She pointed to the collapsed storefront and they ran, Denise limping, her grip painfully strong. At the entrance to the store, Evan turned in time to see a sign whirling through the air toward the leaping dog. The force of the blow sent the dog crashing into a wall. The sign pinned him to the ground where he lay in a lifeless heap.

"No!" Evan screamed.

His mother was so surprised that she lost her grip.

I hate you! You're evil and I hate you!

His angry thoughts only made the wind laugh. Then his mother was swinging him into the building, hoisting him over the tumbled bricks. They collapsed in a heaving pile on the floor. Evan was unable to stop crying. He grabbed a broken brick and pounded it against the other bricks.

"Stop it!" Denise shook him. When that didn't work, she slapped him. "We've got to get out of here!" she signed.

Why? Evan rubbed at his eyes, then signed. *Why did it have to kill Fortuno?*

265

"I don't know. But I do know that the dog gave his life so that you could escape. Now, let's go." She pointed to the back of the store.

Evan shook his head. *That way won't work. I checked already. The door's locked.*

"Then we'll just have to find another way out."

Denise had no sooner finished signing than the station wagon came smashing back into the store. Bricks and glass flew all around them. The odor of fuel filled the air. A spark from a broken neon sign ignited gasoline from the car's ruptured gas tank. There was a *whoosh* as flames shot up from the demolished car.

Denise grabbed Evan's arm and helped him to his feet. The light of the fire illuminated a maze of corridors leading to small rooms. As they passed one, Evan jerked out of her grasp.

I'll try down there, he signed and pointed to steps leading downstairs. Before Denise could object, he was gone.

Eieeyha!

Williwaw was furious with himself for letting the boy with no ears escape. He spotted the blue coats and the yellow hats setting up barricades at opposite ends of the street and he swept them away, people, barricades, and machines. He had counted plenty coup; now it was time for the real battle to begin. The enemy would see. There was nothing they could do to stop him. Those who had died before were the lucky ones.

He hurled the upside-down car at the building where he had seen the boy run. When the tongues of flame leaped up a moment later, he rejoiced. Here was something better than water to play with. Much better.

"Spirit wind!" Billy slammed the door shut on the elevator cage. "I must be out of my fucking mind!" Teenage mutant Easter bunnies was more likely. The Bessani woman was either very gutsy or a blue-ribboned, pedigreed lunatic for barging into their houseboat last night with her daughter and Helen Anderson in tow. The older woman was a hoot and a half; would probably be a popular guest on TV talk shows. As full of hot air as she appeared to be, however, Helen *had* offered the first potentially verifiable lead. She claimed there would be some sign of the Williwaw, or "Taku" as Sallie Light Feather called it.

After they had all agreed that Helen's description of a Williwaw's preference for penthouse lodging fit the Olympic Tower to a T, she had indicated that it should be a relatively easy thing to determine its presence. In the old days, she said, Indian warriors would often collect scalps to memorialize acts of bravery, stringing them on a coup stick decorated with feathers and paint. According to Helen, Indian spirits were closely related to Indians and therefore similar in their behavior. All Billy had to do was check out the top of the Tower. Find sign, find Williwaw. Simple. And there was a pot of gold waiting at the end of the rainbow, too.

Billy thought Helen's tales were precious. Also baloney. But, faced with three determined women—one of whom also happened to be his wife—there was no way he could not agree to check it out. Besides, Billy reflected as he sipped the last of his Starbucks coffee from the stand across the street, there was still a tiny germ remaining of the curiosity that had made him become a journalist in the first place. Back when he was fresh out of Ohio State University's School of Journalism, he would have chased down the slightest rumor. But that was long ago. Back when he still believed in God and the innate goodness of people. Before his gung-ho illusions met bloody, shit-smelling reality in the rice paddies of Vietnam and he'd come back to find an entire country turned against itself. Now, he believed in only one thing. Facts. A couple of facts and some reasoned commentary thrown in for good measure and you had a column.

After Ann Bessani and company had departed and while Julie slept, he had used the modem on his computer to tap into the *Times'* databank of information. What he'd found was startling to say the least. Over a period of just four days, three police officers and nearly five hundred civilians had died from weather-related causes. Reports of missing persons were up over one thousand percent. A follow-up call to the U.S. Weather Service, however, had turned up less than nothing. The man on duty claimed the reports of intense tornado-like winds were merely the result of a high-level storm front, too weak to turn up on satellite weather photos. A second late-night phone call had been more intriguing, however. The Director of North American Indian Studies at Seattle's Coastline Community College was a bright woman whom Billy had once heard speak at one of those boring lectures Julie was always dragging him to. Roberta Satiacum was also no slouch when it came to being politically astute.

"You're asking me if I think an Indian spirit is responsible for the destruction of property and loss of life?" she asked, sounding both tired and incredulous. "Are you kidding? If I said yes or even maybe, I'd be lucky to keep my job twenty-four hours. Make that twelve. My own children would disown me. Indians have taken a bad rap for too long as bloodthirsty savages without you quoting me saying something as stupid as that."

"What about off the record then?" Billy persisted. "I promise I'll never mention that this conversation took place. Just answer for my own personal knowledge, could such a think happen?"

"You must believe me to be a complete fool, Mr. Mossman, to trust a white newspaperman. What I will tell you is this: this town was stolen from Native Americans. Seattle is literally built on top of an Indian burial ground. So in answer to your question, maybe what we're seeing is long overdue."

"You're saying it's possible that a spirit wind is causing this?"

"Like I told you before, I'm not saying anything. Now, if you'll excuse me, I'd like to return to the much-needed sleep you interrupted."

"Just one last question: if there was a spirit wind, how would you stop it?"

"Stop it?" She laughed mirthlessly. "No way you could stop it."

Still unconvinced, Billy had tapped out the column on death that he had composed in his head at the plane crash. He had even managed to use the one-armed Barbie doll. It had not been the story he wanted to write: it dealt only with effect, not cause. That subject, if he was lucky, would come later. Perhaps as early as today, depending upon what he found waiting for him at the top of the Tower.

If it panned out, Billy admitted to himself, this would be one hell of a story. But, after his misfire with his earlier column on the Tower, he wasn't about to further sully his already marred reputation. Especially with another "theory" advanced by so-called experts. In that first column he had gone off half-cocked at best, blaming the deaths and injuries from falling panels on political improprieties and faulty construction. Even if his accusations were true—and the jury was still out—it was hardly a major news item. Such things were happening more and more all the time. A government official disappeared after embezzling millions of dollars in public funds. A bridge collapsed from faulty construction work, killing innocent people. It was getting so commonplace that people almost didn't care. But if a mythological spirit wind had knocked a 747 out of the sky and capsized a ferry, causing hundreds of fatalities, now *that* would be front page news all over the country, if not the entire world! Which was why he was riding this slow, creaky, construction elevator up the side of a half-finished building while most people were still home eating their stale bran muffins. It had been easy enough to bribe the security guard to let him take the elevator to the Tower's ninety-eighth floor where he could climb the stairs to the roof. Then he would find out if Helen Anderson and Ann Bessani were the crackpots he thought they were. Or—as ridiculous as it sounded—whether a Williwaw had taken up residence in Seattle and was kicking the bejesus out of it without so much as a cry of alarm.

Billy watched another of the large floor numbers that someone had spray-painted on plywood panels pass slowly by the opening of the cage, and shivered in his nylon windbreaker. He'd never been particularly fond of heights, nor had he found the time to replace the heavy, fleece-lined trench coat ruined in the Tower accident. This was probably just another dead end, like last night's search of the waterfront for clues to Gretta's disappearance. Oh well, Billy thought as the elevator rose higher and higher, at least this dead end came with a hell of a view.

At first, Paul thought he had turned down the wrong street. When he realized that it was indeed Denise and Evan's house boarded up and taped off, he felt panic. Yellow tape was what the police used to seal off an area when someone had died. While the motor continued to clatter in the driveway, he hurried up to a neighbor's house. The red-faced older man who answered the doorbell wore baggy pants, a threadbare flannel shirt, and slippers. His breath reeked of booze though it was barely 9:00 A.M.

"If you're looking for handouts," he said after checking out Paul's appearance, "you come to the wrong place."

"What happened next door?" Paul said, ignoring the man's comment.

The older man scratched an unshaven cheek then turned and shouted at someone in the house. "What'd they call that thing? She's a bit hard of hearing," he explained. "The wind!" he yelled again. "What'd they say it was?"

Though Paul listened intently he couldn't hear the response.

"Tornado. That was it!" the man said at last. "Hammered the place pretty good, didn't it? Blew a tree down on my fence, too!" He gestured toward the backyard. "Say, you with the insurance company?"

"No. Anybody hurt?"

"Nah. We're okay."

"I meant next door."

"She had a bandaged arm, but that's all I seen. Kid looked okay." He looked over Paul's shoulder at the ruined Mercedes and back at Paul. "What's it to you, anyway?"

"I'm a friend," Paul said. "Know where they went?"

"No and I don't care. Bitch was rude to me. I said she was fucking rude!" he shouted for the benefit of the person inside.

Paul turned and strode back to his car.

"I wouldn't go in there if I was you!" the man shouted after him. "Police are watching the place."

Paul raised a hand in acknowledgment. Before getting in the car, he stood for a moment, inspecting the damage to Denise's house and imagining her and Evan's terror. He hoped they had holed up at his apartment, because he needed to find them fast. Based on what he'd learned from The Light, he didn't think the wind was through with them yet.

Against all her maternal instincts, Denise had forced herself to search the other rooms in the antique mall. Her first and nearly overpowering urge had been to rush after Evan when he'd run off to explore downstairs. Letting him out of her sight was the most difficult thing she'd ever done. If anything happened to Evan, she would rather go over Snoqualmie Falls in a Hefty bag than face life without him. But they didn't have much time. Already the fire had spread from the entrance to engulf the larger front room, generating a fearsome rushing noise like a blast furnace and interspersed by sudden and unexplained explosions. Her cheeks felt hot and the smoke made her eyes burn so that she had to squint. To control her panic, she made herself keep moving, keep searching for a way out.

The mall was the worst sort of firetrap. The turn-of-the-century building was a maze of tiny cubicles in which small-time entrepreneurs had crammed every available square inch of wall, floor, and even airspace with old furniture and collectibles—merchandise that, whatever its value as heirlooms, made excellent fuel, bursting all too readily into flames. As the fire feasted, smoke, dense as cat fur, swelled and spread into the mall like a cancer.

Denise found another stairway that led down to still more shops. It would be so easy to get lost. There was a knot in her throat as she ran from room to room in the flickering light of the fire. She feared that Evan might already have become disoriented, unable to find her, and was even now choking to death in the smoke. After all, kids had smaller lungs than adults. A single breath of smoke was all it took.

When she had completed her hurried inspection without success, she retraced her steps to where she had begun. In less than a minute, the fire had engulfed the entire upstairs area. Nothing remained untouched by its fury. The heat was overwhelming. She saw a beam fall and the entire ceiling looked like it might cave in at any moment. "Evan!" she screamed vainly. Even if he weren't deaf, she knew he couldn't have heard her over the roar of the fire. Then, remembering how well he picked up vibrations, she stamped her feet and pounded her fists on the wall. Coughs tore at the back of her throat. The air was becoming too thick with acrid fumes to breathe. She felt light-headed and her sinuses throbbed with pain. Still, she wouldn't leave. She knew she couldn't remain where she was any longer and hope to live, but without Evan, there was nothing to live for. Then, just when she knew she'd never see her son again, a fantastic apparition materialized through the smoke: a bipedal insect with long proboscis and dressed in blue jeans waved for her to follow. Evan wore a World War I–era gas mask.

Denise wanted to sweep him into her arms, kiss him, tell him that she loved him. Instead, she followed him down the stairway he had taken earlier. They ran through one room, around a corner, down a hallway past a sepia portrait of some turn-of-the-century family and through yet another room and then . . .

"What?"

At first, Denise couldn't understand. What was a large picture window doing below ground? A window to see what? She pressed her face against the glass and saw a tunnel lined with old bricks, earth and wooden beams. And then she understood. It was not the escape route she would have preferred, but right now it looked like the only chance they had.

She pointed at Evan's gas mask. "That thing work?" she signed.

He shrugged and removed it. He nodded at the window. *What is it?*

"You know that Underground Seattle tour you've been pestering me to take you on? You're about to get your wish. Help me find something heavy to break the glass."

The first chair she threw at the window merely bounced off. Evan tried a bowling ball still in the bag with some success. A three-foot crack appeared in the room-sized window. Now, however, there was a wall of flames at the top of the stairs. Frantically, she searched the room for something heavy enough to break through into the tunnel.

"Shove," she signed.

Together, they pushed a desk from the other side of the room. The heavy desk began to slide ever so slowly on the wooden floor, gaining momentum as they covered the short distance. Denise grunted as they let go. The window shattered and collapsed and the desk toppled into the tunnel. Denise leaned inside. There was no light with which to see in the dark corridor.

"I don't know, Evan," she signed. "This could be a dead end." Instantly, she regretted her choice of words.

He jerked a thumb at the fire behind them. It was nearly at the bottom of the stairs.

"No choice," Denise nodded and signed. "Wish we had a light."

Evan ran back to where she'd found the desk. He held up a wooden flagpole, a little taller than he, from which hung an old American flag. Denise furled the flag tightly around the pole and tied it with the fringe from a Victorian lamp shade. A crazy thought flitted through her mind: flag-burning was against the Constitution. I wonder if they'll arrest me.

While she held the flagpole into the flames near the stairwell, the ceiling gave way over her. Flaming plasterboard fell on her head. Evan pulled her back and brushed cinders from her hair. The thin cotton flag had ignited and Denise picked up the makeshift torch. How much light it would provide or how long it would last, they would just have to find out.

Evan ran into the tunnel and Denise followed him. Which way? Their dilemma was solved when the tunnel section where they had entered collapsed with a crash and shower of sparks. They fled through the serpentine labyrinth in the only direction not blocked by the fire.

Billy opened the door at the top of the stairs and stepped out onto the roof of the world. All he could see was sky—miles and miles of it in every direction. In the backs of his legs, the muscles quivered like cheap guitar strings.

Except for the dark, tumultuous clouds hanging over the waterfront, it was a typical Seattle morning: indistinct, gray, vaporous shapes tumbled against each other, blotting the Cascade and Olympic mountains from view.

As he approached the building's eastern periphery, the city began to come into view and his breathing quickened. First rose the tips of its somewhat shorter but still imposing skyscrapers: the dark, slightly sinister-looking spire of Columbia Center, the AT&T Gateway Tower, the pie-shaped Two Union Square and the Sheraton Hotel. Next, the city's surrounding hills and shorter landmarks appeared: To the north, the Space Needle, Queen Anne Hill, and the University of Washington. To the east, Capitol Hill, St. Mark's Cathedral, and the twin spires of St. James. To the south, First Hill and the Kingdome. High overhead, a jet headed east. As his eyes followed the jet, Billy stumbled over a man's badly worn shoe. The sole had long since separated from the leather upper. He slowed as he neared the eight-inch-wide and thirty-inch-high wall that marked the building's outer edge.

Billy tried to whistle and failed. He stood a good two feet behind the wall, sweating in the damp morning air. He wanted to get on his hands and knees and crawl back to the safety of the stairwell. What kept him from doing so was a sensation so awesome it temporarily overwhelmed his powers of description.

Even at this early hour, 1,212 feet high, the noise from traffic was impressive. Much of the city had still to wake; windows in office buildings remained dark. The freeway canyon, however, was a river flowing with cars of every color, trucks—one with JESUS SAVES stenciled in bold black letters on top of its forty-foot trailer—and articulated buses, some with trolley antennae folded back along their tops like giant insects. Billy watched the vehicles streaming along gray ribbons of concrete that disappeared beneath the green expanse of Freeway Park and the sprawling Convention Center and couldn't help feeling superior to all those drivers. For a few moments, he let himself share a sense of the egotism a man like Earl Massey must have felt when he built such a monument. He could see how it corrupted men like Massey and Grenitzer into thinking the sky wasn't the limit. It was hard to perceive limits when you stood like this, on top of the world. Perhaps it was this arrogant lack of human scale that prompted the taggers to scrawl their spraypainted calling cards on bridges and buildings—a single digit salute to all those who would try to rise above the less fortunate. Up here, ironically, there was not hint of graffiti, poverty, or crime.

Even flying over it, Billy had never experienced the city as such a living, breathing entity. Seattle was a city of neighborhoods: West Seattle, First Hill, the International District, Capitol Hill, University, Roosevelt, Windemere, Wallingford, Madrona, Ballard. Here was the city's heart, its hub and intelligence center, where all the appendages came together. It made perfect sense, he thought as he gazed down on the tiny cars and even smaller people: what better location for a lookout post? You could see the entire city from here. Choose your target from the hundreds, thousands that presented themselves.

As his eyes swept toward the west, he saw the wheeling blue-black mass beyond the green dome of the Second and Seneca Building and he realized with a chill that what he had thought were storm clouds were in fact birds. Now he could hear the grisly squeaking of their wings, a sound that he had earlier confused with the traffic noise.

"What in the hell are they up to?" The birds were such an unusual event that Billy nearly missed seeing the smoke.

At first, it was just a wispy plume coming from the area of Pioneer Square. As he watched, fascinated, it grew quickly into a tall, mushroom-like cloud. He remembered the cellular phone in his pocket. By the time someone answered at the city desk, the smoke had risen higher than the top of the Tower.

Paul drove south on Highway 99 at only fifteen miles over the fifty-mile-per-hour posted speed limit. He fought the urge to drive faster. He could ill afford the delay if he was pulled over now for a speeding ticket, but the reason for his caution was mechanical and not legal. The Mercedes' oil pressure gauge was again reading alarmingly low, though he had added two quarts of oil in Port Angeles. He passed a billboard that displayed a handsome white couple and child sailing on Puget Sound with a sparkling Seattle cityscape in the background. The headline proclaimed Seattle America's most livable city. Beyond the billboard, he could see what looked to be dark, squall clouds preparing to enter the city.

At the end of the Battery Street Tunnel, the highway opened onto the Alaskan Way Viaduct. Cars began to slow, as if there had been an accident somewhere ahead. What was strange, however, was the ominous-looking clouds building over the roadway. It took a few seconds and another eighth of a mile for Paul to determine that what appeared to be storm clouds were in fact pigeons—thousands and thousands of them. It looked like every pigeon in the city had congregated over the viaduct. The noise from their wings was deafening. Paul ducked instinctively as, adding insult to previous injury, the car was peppered with their droppings. He was forced to slow while the wipers labored to clear the windshield.

He had no sooner cleared the cloud of pigeons than he passed a line of cars, nearly a quarter of a mile long, trying to get off at the King Street exit. Traffic often backed up when there was a game at the Kingdome, but this could hardly be the problem on a Wednesday morning. Then he saw the bloated cloud of black smoke billowing from among the historic, brick and granite buildings of Pioneer Square. Paul clenched his jaw. The deserted house, the pigeons, and now the fire—it was too peculiar to be just coincidence.

His apartment was located on one of the upper floors of a recycled pharmaceutical warehouse that bordered the International District. To reach it, he had to drive two miles out of his way, past a forest of orange ship-loading cranes and acres of blue and orange containers, to the next exit at Spokane Street, and double back. Rerouted traffic caused several additional delays so that, by the time he arrived at his apartment and determined that the station wagon was nowhere to be seen, he was as tense as a bull rider the moment before the chute opens.

The car door wouldn't close all the way and Paul kicked it. The long drive, the vision in the shaman's cave followed by his flight from the Edge were all starting to tell. At the very least, he needed coffee, a shower, and a change of clothes. At worse, he needed a good eight hours sleep and a visit to Doctor Diesel's Autowerks.

A helicopter swooped by, strobe light flashing, as Paul used the last of his energy to take the stairs two at a time rather than wait for the elevator. The spare key was still taped beneath the window frame when he checked. Adding to his unease, the sounds of sirens seemed to come from every direction. He unlocked the door to his apartment and was further dismayed. The newspaper and unopened mail on the floor beneath the mail slot, the half-empty coffee mug on the table, the tidy rows of books and recorded tapes—it was obvious that Denise and Evan hadn't been here.

He fed Sitting Bull, his goldfish, while he listened to the messages on his answering machine. He slammed the fish food down in frustration when the tape reached the end with no message from Denise. He tried calling her office, but the phone didn't work. He walked out on the balcony and faced the city, trying to think where they might have gone. Dense smoke boiled up a half-mile away.

Flames flickered among them. You could almost feel the heat. While he watched, a police cruiser screeched to a halt on the street below and a cop jumped out.

"What's going on?" Paul called out.

"We're sealing off downtown," the cop answered. He took a portable barricade out of the back of his car. "Power's been knocked out and the traffic lights aren't working. Ambulances are having trouble getting to the injured. Wind's spreading the fire."

Wind? What wind? Paul glanced at the scarlet leaves that drooped from his neighbor's Japanese maple. While the officer positioned the barricade in the intersection, Paul ran back into his apartment. When he had what he needed, he ran downstairs and unlocked the garage. A few moments later, a four-stroke engine coughed, then boomed into life. Paul coasted out of the garage on his lovingly-restored '65 Harley-Davidson, the heavy exhaust pounding loud as artillery. He wore an old black motorcycle jacket and cowboy boots, his long hair held by a faded bandanna. Slung over his shoulder by a leather thong was the ivory Soul Catcher entrusted to him by The Light.

"Hey!" the cop shouted as Paul blasted down the sidewalk past his carefully placed barricade. "Where do you think you're going?"

In response, Paul gunned the bike toward Pioneer Square. His tiredness was gone. In its place was rage. He had no doubt that Evan and Denise's disappearance was the result of the wind. At the next intersection, he heard before he actually saw the yellow fire chief's car bearing down on him from the right. Smoke poured from the rear tires as its driver stood on the brakes to avoid hitting him. With his heart in his ears, Paul skidded around the car's bumper, dragging one boot for balance, and never looked back.

His anger made him strong, but it also made him reckless. He knew there was little chance of his finding Denise and Evan, let alone defeating the wind, if he made any stupid mistakes. "Remember ancestors," he cautioned himself. Something else his grandmother told him long ago came back to him now: "To defeat your enemies, you must be cunning as the fox, swift as the hawk."

As he neared the scene of the fire, he drove on the sidewalk to avoid more police barricades and the dozens of police cars and fire and aid trucks that jammed the streets and alleys. Weaving around the lengths of fat fire hoses and ignoring the shouts of police and firefighters, Paul arrived at the hissing inferno. The only thing not yet engulfed by the fire was the Tlingit totem pole which towered

276

above the shattered remains of the glass pergola at Pioneer Place.

Flames soared a hundred feet high above an entire block of buildings. An army of firefighters shot streams of water at the fire from every direction, but the wind swatted their spray awry, blew men from ladders and carried embers from one crackling building to others hundreds of feet away. The air reeked of burning plastic and wood. Windows on upper floors popped and came crashing down. Water ran gurgling down storm drains from the flooded streets. The stifling heat blistered paint on cars and trucks and singed his hair and eyelashes. Ash and soot rained from the Stygian sky and were whipped into a hailstorm of miniature missiles that stung his eyes and cheeks. Far more dangerous were the glass shards and other projectiles that came whizzing from whatever direction you happened not to be looking. While he watched, a flying brick struck a firefighter in the face and he dropped his hose. The hose, like a living thing, whipped about furiously, toppling men, dousing people and machines with water until another firefighter caught and controlled it. Riding slowly by the wreckage of one totally demolished building, he spotted a car too mangled to identify. It was obvious that whoever had been inside it had perished. A rumble came from the midst of the fire, as if it hungered for more, and the sickening feeling he'd had while trying to find Evan returned. Then he saw the dog.

Fortuno lay on his side, pinned beneath a street sign, his white fur blood-soaked and sooty. Paul parked the bike. He was certain the dog was dead, but as he knelt over it, he thought he heard it whimper. He lifted the heavy metal sign. Fortuno yelped and jerked a front leg back.

"That's a good dog." Paul stroked the dog's head and inspected the bloody shoulder. "Where's the boy?"

The dog lifted its head weakly.

"Can you find the boy for me?"

Fortuno struggled and stood. Testing the injured leg, he stumbled, but didn't fall, and hobbled determinedly across the street on three legs. The dog sniffed for several seconds in front of the gutted building where Paul had seen the skeleton of the wrecked car. Then he barked and snapped at the charred and smoldering ruins.

"Lord God, no," Paul whispered as the dog confirmed his worst fears.

Overwhelmed, he sank to his knees in the center of the street. A river of ash and debris from the flooded buildings swirled around him. It was all his fault. He never should have left Denise and Evan. Instead of delivering them, his journey to The Edge of the World had cost them their lives. He had lost his mother and father, then his grandmother, and now Denise and Evan. Would he never have a family? Was he meant to live his life alone, like an outcast?

As if listening to something within the roar of the fire, Fortuno cocked his ears and faced down the street. Paul watched, silent, as the dog sniffed the air. When he suddenly set off again with his awkward but determined three-legged gait, Paul was up and running to the motorcycle. The bad feeling had been replaced by a new, even stronger one. Whatever price he must pay for challenging the wind, he was ready to pay it.

A war cry rose in his throat as he leapt upon the bike and gunned the engine. "I am Paul Judge of the Crow. I come to find the boy and the woman and to send you back from where you came! You will have to kill me to stop me!"

He followed the dog up Yessler Way, throwing up a rooster tail of water behind the rear wheel. Then, Fortuno turned behind a long hook and ladder truck and Paul lost him. He grew more and more frantic while he searched for a route among the hoses and vehicles. He spotted two fire captains wearing slickers and helmets as they squatted behind a Mercer Island fire truck. One was talking into a portable radio.

Both men stared as Paul rode up.

"See a dog just now?" Paul had to shout.

The men looked at each other. The one with the radio turned his haggard gaze on Paul.

"Look, mister," he yelled. "We're fighting a war and you're looking for a runaway dog. Do us a favor and go home."

Ignoring the instructions, Paul turned down Occidental Avenue and took a quick survey. The last he'd seen the dog, he was heading south. A helicopter buzzed by overhead. Painted on its side in large type were the call letters of a local television station. Paul could see a cameraman leaning out, no doubt shooting video tape for the evening news. The pilot was already flying low, but the cameraman motioned for him to fly still lower.

Paul eased the rear wheel of the motorcycle over a hose that blocked his way and glanced again at the chopper. It was jerking about like a puppet on a string. Suddenly, the wind swatted it to one side. If not for his harness, the cameraman would have fallen out. The pilot seemed to regain control; the copter scooted forward as he made a run for it, but the wind was only toying with it. Like the police helicopter the night before last, it flipped, and down it came.

It narrowly missed a ladder from a fire truck, then struck the side of a building. The metal rotor blades disintegrated, their pieces whirling off in all directions. The chopper struck a hook and ladder truck broadside. With a scream of twisting metal, truck and ladder started to go over. One firefighter high up on the ladder fell to the street. Another managed to hang on, waited until the ladder was near the ground and jumped. Then the chopper's fuel tank exploded and it and the truck were bathed in flames. Chest flattened against the motorcycle's gas tank, Paul sped away from the flying shrapnel through Occidental Park.

Douglas Truitt wasn't in yet. After describing the fire's location and leaving his cellular phone number with the assistant editor at the city desk, Billy walked back to where he'd seen the shoe and stopped to examine it. Nobody earning what these construction guys were making would wear a shoe that looked as bad as this worn-out excuse for cowhide. He left it lying there and continued his inspection of the roof. Other than the small cubicle that housed the stairway, the roof contained only a few bulky crates, roughly the size of automobiles, containing equipment wrapped in heavy plastic. Billy guessed they held air-conditioning and heating equipment. Thirty feet away from the shoe, he found a purse. He was just starting to dump out its contents when the phone in his pocket chirtled.

"Mossman."

"Where the hell are you?" It was Truitt. The keening of sirens came from every direction and Billy had to hold the phone close to his ear.

"Top of the Olympic Life Tower. Twelve hundred feet up if you believe their flak."

"What on earth . . . ? Don't answer. What can you see from up there?"

"I see a woman's purse." Billy reached for the leather wallet that lay among the pile of lipstick, change, half a stale but not yet moldy bagel wrapped in a napkin, and other items from the purse that now lay spread before him. "It would seem to belong to an Edna Shumski, sixty-eight years old, a resident of Kent."

Truitt was incredulous. "What the hell are you doing, Billy? The city's burning down and you're going through a woman's purse?"

"There's something weird going on up here, Doug."

"Sounds to me like it's you that's weird, Billy. What's going on with the fire? Can you see enough to help me direct our limited resources?"

"Sure. Hold on a sec."

Billy's view was blocked by the Century Square building next door and he had to walk to the Tower's southwest corner to get a clear view of Pioneer Square. He was shocked by the fire's rapid progress. It had been ten minutes at most since he'd seen the first sign of smoke, but already the fire had totally engulfed the block bordered by First and Second and Cherry and James. Even as he watched, the flames leapt across First Avenue and began attacking neighboring buildings. The smoke was spreading out in a foul smelling black pall over the southern part of the city. At the rate it was going, he wouldn't be able to see the fire much longer from this height.

"What's going on? Are you there?" Truitt was obviously running out of patience.

"Oh, yeah, I'm here all right."

"Fine. Will you please tell me what you see?"

"I can see Tacoma being the new home of the Seahawks if the fire department doesn't get a handle on this thing."

"That bad, huh?"

"You know that tree planting crusade the parks department has been on? Bad idea. Fire's going right down the median."

"Well, damn," Truitt said. "There goes the tourism industry."

"They've got about ten minutes to pull the plug on this," Billy said, "before it's into the financial district. Then it's good-bye tourism and good-bye business, too."

"I don't know, Billy. Ferguson's at ground zero and he says every time the fire department looks like they might get a handle on it, the wind blows it somewhere else."

"The wind?" Billy looked around. Puget Sound was an unruffled sheet of gray steel.

"What? Isn't it blowing up there? Listen, how's your butt? I need you on the ground. Get me some good interviews: fire crews, bystanders, injured—the usual."

"You got it. Do me a favor, Doug. Check on this Edna Shumski woman for me."

"For Christ's sake, Billy! It's not like I don't have anything to do!"

"Just have someone call her home. I'll give you her address and driver's license number."

"Anything else?"

"No." Again, Billy noticed the host of birds that continued to wheel and whirl to the west. If anything, it had grown even larger.

"Say, Doug, any idea why the pigeons got a mass orgy going on down by the waterfront?"

"Pigeons?"

"Yeah. Must be a million of them."

"Remember the fire, Billy. The fire!" Truitt said, and then he hung up.

Billy turned from the perimeter and began walking toward the stairway that would take him down to the ninety-eighth floor and the elevator. If he didn't want to give Doug anymore reasons to fire him, he'd better get his sore ass over to the fire. First, however, he'd just take a small detour. When he reached the shoe, he followed a hunch and headed in the opposite direction from the purse. He couldn't just leave without taking one last look around. Besides, he rationalized, it would only take a minute.

Thirty feet from the shoe, there was yet another pallet of equipment. This one, however, looked damaged. The plastic was torn and one of the boards from the crate had been broken. He was nearly past it when he spotted the small patch of blue and yellow hidden within a cavity of the machinery. A hint of recognition sent a surge of something like electricity rushing through him: his hair felt as if it were standing on end and his fingertips tingled. He heard himself swallow as he reached a hand into the crate. His fingers closed on something soft and furry and still a bit damp. Billy wished he had brought some aspirin to ease the steel bands now tightening around his forehead. He sat down and focused on taking deep breaths. Large, meaty hands clutched Paddington Bear to his chest.

24

Black Wolf's Revenge

SEATTLE, WEDNESDAY, 8:24 A.M. Denise tried to recall anything that might help them find a way out. When the city had been destroyed by fire in 1889, its leaders had decided it would be cheaper and better to build the new city on top of the old. The unrestored remains of what was early Seattle's thriving if somewhat seedy business district lay damp and crumbling beneath the sidewalks of Pioneer Square. Some years back, a businessman had the brilliant idea to reopen the passageways and charge admission. No matter that the tunnels were dirty and smelled slightly of sewage, they had become a popular attraction for tourists.

Even if she could have remembered how the tunnels linked, after they had made a couple of turns, she quickly lost track of which direction they were headed. Once, they had crossed under a street. Sirens wailed and trucks rumbled above them. There are probably people right over our heads, Denise thought, but there was far too much noise for them to hear her shouts.

Their spirits soared when, after trudging through unlit passageways for what seemed like miles, they reached a doorway. Through a small window in the door, Denise saw daylight. Freedom was inches away, but iron gates prevented their escape. Meanwhile, smoke and fire pursued them, herding them ever onward. After failing to attract attention by beating on the door with their fists and Denise shouting, they had to retreat back into the tunnels to avoid becoming trapped. Grimly, Denise realized that the fire was spreading rapidly, leapfrogging from one street to the next. There was no way to know when their escape route might be cut off. As if that weren't enough, there was also another problem. Even as the roof of the tunnel threatened to collapse in places from the fire, water from the large-scale firefighting efforts poured in from all directions. In a few short minutes, it had risen over their ankles. They were sloshing through it when something clutched Denise's leg. Before she realized what was happening, it had climbed her leg, raced up her back and leaped onto her head. She screamed and dropped the flag. Their torch light sizzled out in the water as Denise knocked the wet rat off. Another started up her leg and again she screamed, stamped her feet, and brushed madly until it fell off and was swept away in the rising waters.

Without the torch, Denise was blind and terrified. She heard Evan cry out behind her in his awkward, unused voice, and she hurried back to find him battling a large rat. The huge rodent sank its fangs into the base of her thumb as she wrestled it from her son's hair. She dashed it against the wall of the tunnel and heard it plop into the water. Evan moaned. She clutched him to her tightly. It was too dark for reading lips, but they could sign into one another's hands.

They continued on more slowly now, holding hands and feeling their way along the rough, cobweb-covered walls. Gradually, her eyes grew accustomed to the lack of light. A faint red glow could be seen behind them. Occasional hints of daylight came from above, filtered through thick prism glass imbedded in the sidewalk. They came at last to a Y in the tunnel. Denise could feel cool air against her sweaty cheeks. She licked a finger and held it up as she remembered doing as a girl, but there wasn't enough breeze to tell her which way the air came from. Afraid that too much indecision might frighten Evan, she decided to try the left branch first. After less than a minute, during which time the water had risen to her thighs, Denise decided to turn back and try the other route. It, too, began to look like a poor choice. Water rose past her hips and then waist as the floor descended gradually. The water was cold and Denise began to shake as her body temperature dropped. She knew it was worse for Evan. The water level was already to his chest. Behind them, the shadows danced and glowed brighter as the fire neared. If they were going to change direction again, it had to be now. They had reached the point of no return. It was the worst nightmare imaginable: They were trapped underground with the water rising, fire threatening from above, and smoke pursuing them from behind.

"Please, God," Denise whispered.

She wet a numbed finger again and held it up. This time, she felt a gentle draft coming from the direction they were headed. She squeezed Evan's hand and he squeezed back. A minute later, they made another turn and saw a fissure of light. Evan slipped from her grasp and waded past her. When she caught up to him again, he was flattened against a large door. Excited, he pointed to the narrow gap between door and sill. Cheek pressed against the door, Denise could see concrete steps leading up to daylight. She sought and found a door handle in the water, but it wouldn't turn. She tried inserting her fingers in the crack between door and frame, but it didn't begin to budge. She was desperate enough to try picking at the wood with her fingernails. All she succeeded in doing was getting a sliver lodged under one. For the next several minutes, they searched walls, ceiling, and even underwater with their toes for loose bricks, scraps of wood, anything they could use to smash, cut or pry their way out. In the end, they had nothing but numbed and bloody fingers to show for their efforts and the water had risen nearly up to Evan's chin. The angry red glow behind them was bright enough to light the tunnel and the first wisps of smoke were catching up to them again. Evan had his eye to the crack, beating on the door with his fists. Denise felt tears roll down her cheeks. Nobody said life was fair, but come on. Even rats deserved better.

When Evan suddenly leapt up, making a great splash, Denise thought another rat had attacked him. He made hasty signs and pointed at the narrow wedge of light. Denise peered out. At first she could see nothing through her tears. She wiped her eyes and looked again. This time, she saw a dog sniffing the air at the top of the stairway. It took her several seconds to realize that it wasn't just any dog.

"I don't believe it! Good dog! Go, boy. Go get help!"

Fortuno cocked an ear toward her as if listening. He hobbled down three or four steps, then back up to street level, all the while barking his head off. Denise was never so glad to see a flea-breeding, hair-shedding animal in her life.

Evan crowded against her and the door to see. Denise hugged him and, for the first time in what seemed like a very long while, she felt hope.

The phone in the pocket of his windbreaker continued to ring every couple of minutes. Billy turned it off to conserve battery power. The last time he'd bothered to look, the fire that had started in Pioneer Square was threatening to repeat the results of the one that had destroyed the city in 1889. He was supposed to be there on the ground covering the once-in-a-lifetime story, but right now, he had other, more urgent priorities.

His continuing explorations had turned up a number of scavenged odds and ends arranged in a ragged circle on the rooftop. In addition to the shoe, purse, and stuffed animal, he had found some two dozen "trophies," including a man's fringed leather coat, a life jacket stenciled with "Hiyu," a wool cap with "Huskies" printed on it, an empty plastic spool of twenty-pound monofilament line, a seat cushion of the type used on commercial airplanes, a scorched piece of black cloth uniform with a barely recognizable SPD Helicopter Patrol patch, a studded black leather arm band, and a boy's jacket.

Like a child hunting Easter eggs in the park, Billy crisscrossed the football-field-sized roof, even lay on his stomach to peek under crates, until he had combed every inch of it except the top of the stairway shed. He found an empty wooden pallet and leaned it against the small cubicle that stood at the center of the Tower's roof. Standing on its top rung, he could see that there was indeed something there—something wrapped in dirty cloth or leather. He removed his belt. The pallet shifted an inch, and for a moment Billy thought he was going to fall. When his improvised ladder remained standing, he made a small loop in one end of the belt and cast it in an effort to snag the knapsack or whatever it was and pull it within reach. His first two efforts failed. On the third try, the buckle dragged across the heap, peeling back a flap of leather. A breeze lifted the remaining layers for a moment and a cloud of yellowish powder rose and immediately dissipated into the air.

Something told Billy he'd better hurry.

The wind watched the figure on the motorcycle approach. Here was the meddlesome Indian who had taken the boy with no ears two days before.

The restaurant awning was far enough away that it had so far escaped damage. Then a large ember landed on its canopy. Fanned by the wind, the stretched canvas flared into greedy flames. The clamor of sirens, engines, and fire drowned out the pop of lag bolts as the awning's steel supports tore away from the brick entryway.

Frustrated by his lack of success and the number of obstacles in his path, Paul was beginning to think that riding the bike had been a mistake. He continued his search for Fortuno, searching up South Main for any sign of the dog when, out of the corner of his eye, he saw the flaming awning descending upon him. It was too late to react beyond braking and throwing up an arm to shield his face. Then the burning cloth and steel framework were on him and the bike like a shroud. The bike went down, skidding on its primary. Heat seared his throat and lungs. The shafts beat him like clubs. Paul fought to keep his head above the ground and prayed desperately for the skid to stop. The bike slewed up enough water from the street to knock down most of the fire, but the metal stanchions and cobblestones were not as forgiving. When the bike finally came to rest, Paul crawled out from the wreckage, splashed ditch water on his smoking hair and collapsed against the curb.

He did not lie there long. His pain and his fears for the boy and his mother would not let him rest. He rolled over on his right side where he could inspect the damage. His left boot was destroyed and the jeans were ripped away from the calf to his thigh, the skin marbled with blood. Although his left hand and forearm were encased in leather, they had suffered serious road rash. He removed the shredded leather glove from his trembling left hand. What remained of his little finger was folded back on top of itself. The nail on his ring finger was peeled back, hanging by a piece of skin. He tore it off. He needed both hands to open the small, silver knife from his pants pocket. He used it to slit the denim the rest of the way down his leg. Where his leg entered the mangled leather cowboy boot, he could see a white sliver of bone sticking out. His foot was still there. Beyond that, he couldn't tell how bad it was. The pain was so great, he had to fight to keep from passing out. "Remember . . . ancestors," he choked between gritted teeth. He rolled onto his stomach and crawled on his hands and knees. Someone had piled office furniture and computers on the sidewalk in a mostly futile effort to save them from damage. He swept a computer off a chair, then sat down on the curb and smashed the chair against the concrete sidewalk until a leg broke off. With the bandanna that held his hair and the broken chair leg, he fashioned a makeshift splint for his leg. He managed to stand on one leg, using the rest of the chair as a crutch.

He began to shuffle on one leg back to the bike. He was halfway there when he saw a manhole cover pop up from the street some distance away. It rolled several feet, then hurtled toward him like a giant discus. He started to back up, then, realizing that he couldn't walk—much less run—with his broken leg, forced himself to wait. He guessed that the wind would change the spinning disk's course to intercept whatever evasive tactics he might make if he moved too soon, so he watched the cast bronze cover lock in on him at sixty miles per hour. When it was less than twenty feet away—so close he could hear its whirring drone above the other noise—he dove right at it. He landed on his face and chest in the water. The cover sailed over his head, sliced a lamppost in half, skipped once on the street with a mighty splash, and buried itself in the marble wall of a building. The decapitated lamppost toppled forward. Paul rolled away and it landed where he had been a split second earlier, drenching him in its wash.

He gasped in pain and looked around for whatever new trick the wind had in store for him, but it had apparently tired of him. He saw a Dumpster rumbling down the street, smoke and flames pouring from the opened top. The wind rammed the Dumpster into a building, fueling yet another fire. Then, on the opposite side of the street, at the entrance to an underground stairwell, Paul saw something white. He raised up so that he could better see.

Fortuno appeared to be barking in an effort to attract attention. Whatever the dog thought might be down that stairwell, Paul could understand the reason for its concern—smoke was pouring from the windows on the second floor. If there was anybody in there, they were within minutes, perhaps seconds, of being cooked. Paul glanced at the bike and then once more at Fortuno who dodged a falling cornice and continued to bark. He checked to see that the Soul Catcher was still tied to his back and crawled to the wrecked bike. Once again, he had to use the smashed chair to stand. He pulled the bent and tangled awning framework from the bike. The grip was missing from the left side and the shifter was bent, a few dents, otherwise the bike looked okay. He used strength born of adrenaline and desperate hope to lift and then push the 500-pound Harley up. When it was standing, he nearly lost it. He stood panting, temporarily exhausted. To climb on the bike, he had to maneuver around it and get on from the right side. He lifted his broken left leg. The end of his makeshift splint caught on the saddle and he nearly blacked out with the pain. He tried the electric starter, but the engine only coughed.

"Come on, baby. Don't quit on me now."

He tried again. This time, the engine caught and he nursed the throttle carefully. When it was running smoothly, he eased the clutch lever out. Still in gear, the bike began to roll forward. Paul lifted his left leg until his numb foot rested on what remained of the left pedal and turned the bike slowly around toward where he'd seen the dog.

*

The underground had become a death trap. Less than fifty feet away, the tunnel roof had collapsed with a great *sploosh* of steam and water. Denise could plainly observe the fire gorging itself on the inside of the building immediately above them. Smoke snaked around them, trying to steal the oxygen from their lungs. Even stood on tiptoes and they traded turns breathing through the crack in the door. Thinking was reduced to the most basic, sub-human level: there was only this breath and the next.

The fire was so loud she couldn't hear herself cough. Nevertheless, she heard the guns blasting outside the door. Evan turned so quickly, she was afraid he'd been shot. Cheeks puffed out from holding his breath, he pointed at the fissure of light.

Again, Denise pressed against the door to see. The stairway was filling up with water and Fortuno was still barking, but now there was a crazed-looking man wearing a leather jacket and sitting astride a motorcycle which made loud noises like gunfire.

"Denise?" the motorcycle rider yelled.

"Paul!" she shouted into the crack. "Hurry. We're trapped."

"Get away from the door."

"Can't," she sputtered, swallowing water. "No more air."

"The building is going to collapse," he shouted. "Only chance is to break the door down. Get back as far as you can and count to ten." The motorcycle roared away before she could argue.

She turned Evan's face to hers and pantomimed taking a deep breath, then held up ten fingers. They sucked in as much air as they could, then started swimming back toward the blazing inferno. The heat weighed down upon them, scalding backs and singeing hair. Caught halfway between incineration and drowning, death hovering so near that she could touch his ragged garment, Denise's mind drifted away from her body. This must be how Icarus felt before he plunged to his death, she thought as she watched herself. The peaceful calm of resignation settled over her. Then the roof of the tunnel caved in just in front of Evan.

Instantly, she was back in her body. Denise grabbed Evan's hand and they dove into the water beneath the fire. In awe, Denise looked up into the hungry maw of the inferno. She tried to shield her son from the horror, knowing it was futile. Then, as if from some great distance, she heard the bike coming back fast followed by a thunderous crash. The door burst open and they and the water surged out of the tunnel.

Denise wrestled one side of the broken door open and they half-swam, half-climbed over the motorcycle at the bottom of the stairway. She groped her way to the stairs, gulping air into her lungs. Evan had reached the top first and now held Fortuno's head to his own, getting his face cleaned by the dog's tongue.

She wanted to just sit there for a day, a week—perhaps forever—and watch them, but the fire still threatened and somewhere out there was a demon wind determined to destroy her son. On the street, a fire truck was moving into position, men shouting directions over the engines. Two other men were connecting a hose to a hydrant across the street. One waved at her urgently and pointed above her. Denise looked up and saw that the wall immediately above them was bulging outward, smoke escaping from its mortar joints, and she realized Paul was missing.

Denise stumbled back down the stairwell. Beneath the water, she saw a sweeping motion of something dark and colorless. Paul was trapped beneath the bike, drowning.

"Oh, Jesus. Oh, God. Help!"

She grabbed a handlebar and yanked but the bike wouldn't budge. The front wheel was still lodged in the broken door. Evan splashed into the water beside her. She saw Paul point to the back of the bike. Denise climbed the stairway quickly to the rear of the bike and found a chrome bar near the back of the seat. While Paul pushed from below, Denise lifted. The bike raised only a few inches. Evan tried to pull Paul out from under it, but was having difficulty. Denise knew she couldn't hold the bike up much longer by herself.

"Help!" she yelled again.

Then two firemen jumped in beside them. One helped lift the bike and the other grabbed Paul under the armpits and dragged him up the stairway. Face contorted with pain, Paul lay on his back and coughed up water.

"Can't work on him here," one man shouted. "Building's gonna bury us all."

The two men linked arms beneath Paul and picked him up. Paul groaned, then his eyes fluttered open and found Denise's.

"The dog. Around his neck."

Denise knelt where Evan was petting Fortuno. The dog held his injured leg back against his side like a broken wing, but she didn't see anything around his neck.

"Did Fortuno have something of Paul's?" she signed.

Evan reached behind one shoulder where something was strung

on a leather thong and brought around a carved ivory tube.

What is it? Can I keep it for him?

Denise shook her head. Something about the artifact sent chills racing through her body.

"Better let me have it. Let's go ride in the ambulance with Paul."

But Evan refused to give it up and there wasn't time to argue.

"No dog," a paramedic ordered when they were climbing into the vehicle.

"This dog saved our lives. Not only that, he's injured," Denise argued.

But the man was adamant. "No dog, I said."

"C'mon, Scott. Where's your heart?" the other paramedic, a freckled, redheaded young woman, asked.

"Up yours, Jesse. I don't give a damn. Just don't run off and leave my ass hanging in the wind if the captain wants to know whose idiotic idea this was."

"No problem," Jesse said. She winked at Evan.

Denise stroked Paul's head while Jesse took his pulse and Scott started an IV. She pulled the long, wet hair from Paul's face. Half the eyebrow was gone over his right eye and an angry red burn angled across his forehead. His jeans were shredded and bloody and the remains of a chair leg hung from where he had tied it with a bandanna to his left leg. She tried not to look at the hand that lay across his stomach.

"Paul," was all she could say.

Billy wiped a hand across his brow. He had coaxed and worried the curious-looking bundle with his belt until it was nearly within his grasp. He was sweating hard in the nylon jacket and didn't immediately register the sudden drop in temperature until a cold draft blew open the skins and nearly toppled him from his perch. For an instant, a moldy heap of bones, ocher, several black stones, and a small skull lashed to a handle lay exposed to the morning air. And then they vanished, as the wind snatched them up, skins and all. Billy stared at the place where the bundle had been and knew he'd been caught with his hand in the cookie jar.

The realization that he had overstayed his welcome was followed by remembrance that the stairway was just inside the cubicle upon which he now leaned. One foot was reaching for the next board down from the top of the pallet when, without warning, the wind returned. He was hurled backward, arms flailing. He landed on his side with a painful crash. Before he could right himself, the wind tumbled him to the very edge of the building. Only the retaining wall saved him from falling off the roof. He heard the wind snarl and saw one of the large crates nearby beginning to rock. Then it came barreling toward him.

Billy rolled to his right and the pallet of equipment smashed through the wall and sailed into space. He didn't wait to hear it land. Wheezing like an asthmatic rhino, he sprinted to the stairway door, jerked it open and leaped inside. The wind shrieked and the door slammed behind him. Billy leaned against it, gasping for breath, his heart trying to escape his chest. His respite was brief.

The shed exploded. Billy somersaulted down the corrugated metal stairway and landed on his back, the breath knocked out of him and one ankle twisted beneath him. Pain stabbed in the back of his head and his hand came away smeared with blood. It hurt just to open his eyes, but he forced himself to look for a way to escape. The wind rumbled overhead among the exposed sprinkler system, forced air shafts, and shiny electrical conduit. Billy did a quick survey of the unfinished ninety-eighth floor. He was trapped in a gigantic skeleton with no place to hide. There were no walls, partitions or ceiling. Just a poured concrete floor and steel girders that had been sprayed with grayish insulation. Large vertical pipes flanked the empty elevator shafts.

"So I've finally met a Williwaw," Billy said when at last he could breathe. He rolled over and clutched the stairway with two hands. "And I thought I'd seen everything."

The wind whistled through the girders. It seemed to be stalking him, so fast that he could barely follow it. Dust and dirt, metal scraps and bolts, a T-shirt and anything else that wasn't tied down hurtled around him. The reporter half of him marveled, while the other half—the scared-shitless part—wanted to be as far away as possible.

"It was you!" Billy had to shout to hear himself. "You killed all those people on the ferry and the airplane. And the people on the street below. I didn't believe in such things, but Helen Anderson, bless her heart, was right. What about Gretta? Did you kill her, too?" He shook his head. "I get out of this—and the odds aren't looking great—I'll see that you're remembered, girl."

Again the wind shrieked. The stairway was torn from Billy's grasp and he hurtled across the concrete floor. A single girder stood between him and almost a quarter mile of nothing but air. He had less than a second to stretch his body to the right. He struck the girder with his ribs and armpit. An insulation-wrapped section of aluminum ducting struck his head a glancing blow and disappeared into the void. Pain and numbness devastated his right side so that he couldn't hold onto the steel I beam, could only lie there, curled around it, waiting for the wind's next move.

"Why'd you pick Seattle? You could've trashed Tacoma and hardly anyone would have noticed." Billy started to chuckle, but coughed instead. "Ooh, that hurt."

The wind wasn't through. Billy heard it rushing toward him and snatched at a coil of conduit hanging from the open ceiling with his left hand. Then he was flung underneath the metal safety rail.

Out, out and down he fell, the conduit streaming out behind him like an aluminum umbilical cord. Was there no fastened end? Billy wrapped his legs around the metal tubing the way he had learned to climb ropes in high school and looked down on the plaza with its tiny fountain, tiny trees, and tiny figures rushing up to greet him.

The conduit stopped paying out with a jerk that stripped the flesh from his legs and hand, and Billy found himself swinging toward the face of the Tower like a deranged Tarzan.

"Oh, Julie," he said.

Nearly all the injured victims of the Pioneer Square fire, Denise learned, were being taken to Harborview. It bore the twin distinction of being the county hospital where most emergency victims ended up. and it was close. During the short ambulance ride there, the paramedics had secured Paul's IV, taken his pulse, and taped the fingers together on his left hand. Now, as if saving the best for last, they were immobilizing his ankle. The young woman named Jesse held a large cardboard splint in place while the dark-haired man she called Scott, her senior by a few years at best, wound Ace bandages around it.

"This is only temporary," Jesse said to Denise. "With luck, it should get him into ER without further complications."

While they worked on his leg, Denise wiped away the sweat that had broken out on Paul's forehead. His eyes were closed, the pupils roaming behind their lids as if he were dreaming. His silence scared her. Evan held Fortuno and watched the paramedics work. He pointed at the bone splinter sticking out of Paul's ankle and made a face as if gagging. Denise nodded. She'd been thinking the same thing.

292

"Shouldn't you do something about that compound fracture first, before you wrap up his leg?" she asked.

"Can't. Not without endangering his life," the man said without looking up.

"Bone infections are killers," the woman added. "Bad as it looks, it's better to leave it alone."

"What about the pain? The least you could do is give him some aspirin."

"Sorry," the man said. "Can't do that either. They're gonna knock him out to set the ankle. If he's had anything, he'll just puke it right up."

"Can't knock me out," Paul said, his voice edged with pain. "No drugs. We're leaving Seattle soon as I can find a way."

"Hey, buddy." The man looked at Paul with some interest. "Sorry, but you ain't going nowhere until the doc sets this. Never mind the fact that if you get a bone infection, they may have to cut off your leg. One bad move with a break like this, a splinter pops the artery and you're history."

"Scott!" The redheaded EMT scowled. "Pardon my partner's poor bedside manner."

"Just settin' the guy straight," her partner said. "Thinks he's gonna play tennis this afternoon, he's got a surprise comin'."

"Thanks for the advice," Paul said, "but this match won't wait."

Billy lay face down in a small pool of blood. It was not reassuring, but there was nothing he could do about it. He felt like he'd been run over by stampeding elephants. He had struck the window feet first, destroying the heavy plate glass. Near as he could tell, the impact had broken both his legs and he was bleeding from somewhere he could neither see or feel. His earlier collision with the girder had left him with ribs that made it painful to breathe and with only one arm that still functioned reasonably well. With it, he retrieved the cellular phone. Useful damn things, Billy decided as he laid the Motorola in front of his face. He pushed the buttons carefully— now was not a good time for a wrong number—and fought off another round of lightheadedness.

The decision about who to call first—Julie, 911, or the *Times*— wasn't difficult. If he died now, he'd only regret one thing: if he didn't get to file this story, perhaps no one would ever know about there being a Williwaw in Seattle. Julie would understand.

"News," the young voice answered.

"It's Mossman," he panted. "Get Truitt. Tell him to hurry."

A moment later, the exasperated city editor was on the phone. "Where the hell are you? I've tried to call you at least ten times."

"Ran into a slight complication."

"I don't even want to hear about it."

"Yes, you do."

"No, I don't, Billy. Get your ass down here. I've had it up to here with you and your freelance bullshit. All I asked you to do was . . ."

"Damn it, Doug!" The pain in his ribs stabbed, forcing him to pause. "I'm hurt and don't have a lot of time to chitchat. So skip the whining, okay?"

"You're hurt? Why didn't you say so? Have you called an ambulance yet?"

"No, I haven't. Now, will you shut up?" For perhaps the first time in Billy's memory, Doug was quiet. "Did you check out the woman's name I gave you earlier?"

"Yeah. Wait a sec—it's right here. Edna turns out to be one of the people killed last Saturday by falling granite. I hope you can appreciate her family wasn't in the best frame of mind when we called. I told them a workman must have found her purse and forgotten to turn it in."

"A workman didn't find her purse."

"Yeah? So how did it get to the top of that building—a bald eagle?"

"Listen good, Doug, because this could be my last story. But first, I want a conference call with the mayor."

"The mayor? Shit, Billy! What do I look like—the genie from Aladdin? Grenitzer's dealing with a major league disaster. You, of all people, are hardly the person he'd want to take a call from."

"Aren't you the one always saying 'never second guess yourself, just do it'?"

Doug sighed. "Actually, that's a shoe company's slogan. Let me call an ambulance first."

"No time. I'm not even sure what floor I'm on—probably somewhere in the lower nineties. Call Grenitzer. He might be able to save some lives if he acts fast."

"Okay, but it's gonna take a few minutes—that's if we can find the little son of a bitch."

*

Paul was back in Montana, remembering the time his horse had stepped in a prairie dog hole and fallen, snapping a cannon bone and breaking one of his own legs when it had landed on him. When his grandmother and a neighbor found him, she had dispatched his horse with an old Winchester, then built a travois and hauled him home behind the neighbor's horse. On their slow and painful journey, she had walked beside him and told him the story of his great-great-grandfather. One especially long and cold winter, Spotted Horse had been hunting for meat when he'd been surrounded by a Sioux war party. Before they overcame him and cut out his heart, he had killed ten of the enemy. "You have his blood," his grandmother said. "Whenever you must call on all your strength and know-how, remember ancestors. Then you, too, can be a great warrior like Spotted Horse."

He used the story now, as his grandmother had used it then, to block the searing messages from his finger and ankle. Later, if there was a later, there would be time for the pain.

The ambulance halted and Paul brought himself back to the present. "Where are we?" he asked.

"Harborview," the woman answered.

"Good." Paul reached up and clenched the Denise's still soggy parka in his good right hand as they were opening the rear of the van, preparing to unload him. "Find the Medical Examiner's Office. When you get there, ask for Dr. Chan. Tell her it's extremely urgent that I see her."

"What about you?"

"I'll be all right. I'm more worried about you and the boy if the wind returns. It's apt to destroy this hospital just like it's done to Pioneer Square."

"Doesn't this thing ever quit?" Denise's anger flared. "What do we need to do to get it to stop? Shoot it with silver bullets and throw holy water on it?"

"Not a bad idea," Paul said, his voice growing weaker.

"Okay. Evan," she signed and spoke, "you're coming with me."

"Hurry, Denise," Paul said as they unloaded him from the paramedic van. "There isn't much time."

The emergency ward was overflowing with patients. Gurneys were set up in the hallway and the lobby. They parked Paul next to an obese woman who moaned loudly and continuously. Fortunately, he did not have to wait long before a middle-aged nurse appeared with a clipboard.

"Name?"

"Paul Judge." Paul raised up on his elbows. "Look, I know you're just trying to do your job, but I don't have time for an operation right now."

"Judge, Paul." She ignored him. "What's the nature of your problem, Mr. Judge?" She looked over his ankle with the indifference of a service station attendant studying a flat tire and jotted some notes on her clipboard.

"My problem is there's something stalking the woman and her son who just arrived with me. I have to get them out of here before it finds them again."

The nurse looked at him over her thick glasses. "I see." She continued to write. "Are you on any medication, Mr. Judge? Drugs or alcohol?"

"No." Paul sighed in frustration. It was difficult to argue and fight the pain at the same time and it was obvious that his story wasn't being taken seriously. But then, why should it? The wind could destroy the entire city, kill half the people in it, and still no one would believe him.

"As you can see, Mr. Judge, we're very busy this morning. Open." She thrust a thermometer under his tongue. "You're in line for X-rays, but you're going to have to be patient."

He closed his eyes and opened the door in his mind that his grandmother had taught him how to find and use. Within seconds, he was back in Montana.

When Dr. Chan found him ten minutes later, he was listening to the swish of his feet in the tall, sunburnt grass and the buzzing of grasshoppers as they scattered before him.

Dr. Chan touched his arm. "Mr. Judge?"

Regretfully, he opened his eyes to the bright sterile lights and controlled mayhem of the hospital.

"Dr. Chan. Where's Denise and the boy?"

"In my office. One of my staff is attending to his dog," Dr. Chan said while she timed his pulse. "You must be very tired. I am amazed that anyone could sleep in this place." She examined his ankle. "This needs immediate attention. Let me try to get you some help." She started to leave.

Paul grabbed her wrist. She winced at his grip. "That's not why I had Denise find you. The Indian you showed me—we've got to get his body out of here before the spirit that's taking revenge for his death does any more damage."

The obese woman's moaning stopped.

"Perhaps we had better find a more private location to talk," Dr. Chan said.

After she had wheeled him to a space that had recently opened up in the hallway, Paul quickly recounted his journey to The Edge of the World and the shaman's advice. "There's a wind following the boy—not an ordinary wind, but a Native American spirit wind. It's bent on revenging the Indian's death and nothing can stop it. Nothing!"

Dr. Chan stared at him, her nose wrinkled in disgust. "I'm sorry, Mr. Judge, but you don't seriously expect me to believe this?"

"Look," he pleaded, "I know how incredible this must sound to you, but I swear, not only this woman and her son, but many others' lives could be in jeopardy if we don't follow The Light's instructions."

Dr. Chan shook her head. "Even if I could do as you ask and release the body to you—a very big if, I might add—where would you take him?"

"My friends in Issaquah. I'm certain they'd be willing to permit the ceremony to take place on their property. Once the body is cremated, the ashes can be taken to an Indian burial ground or another holy place and dispersed."

"What you are asking is highly unusual, not to mention illegal. Without the consent of next of kin, we must go through proper procedures to remove a body, or obtain a special release from higher authorities. Forgive me, but I cannot very well go to the County Commissioner with a crazy story like this."

"What if the mayor were on our side?" Paul asked.

"Mayor Grenitzer?"

"Denise works with him."

"That would help, but, excuse me for asking, if I do not believe your story, why do you think he would believe it?"

"I may be dreaming, but considering the lives at stake, it's worth a try."

Arms folded over her chest, Dr. Chan chewed her lip as she considered his request. "I will tell Ms. Baker of your plan," she said at last. She can use the phone in my office."

"As soon as Denise is through, I'll call my friends in Issaquah," Paul said.

"You, Mr. Judge, are another matter. You really must not be moved. The risk of infection or further complications is too great."

"I understand, and I'm not anxious to die—especially now. But I also know that none of us are safe if the Williwaw comes for the boy while he is here. And I'm certain that is just what it will do. Tell me, how would one go about stealing an ambulance, Dr. Chan?"

"Hah! You are delirious, Mr. Judge. Just finding one that is not being used would be a miracle. Right now, they are using buses, pickup trucks—anything that moves."

Once again, Paul held her arm to prevent her from leaving. "One more thing, Dr. Chan. I promised that when this is all over, I'd try to help an Indian tribe whose children are being stillborn. I was hoping you might lend your expertise."

"First, let us fix your foot, Mr. Judge. Then we can look at other problems."

Billy was so tired. Why wouldn't the strange, insistent noise stop so he could sleep? Then he remembered the phone.

"Mossman," he mumbled.

It chirped again. He jabbed fingers at buttons until at last he heard a voice.

"Billy? You there?"

"Yeah."

"You don't sound so good."

"Right now, I'd give a week's pay for a shot of Jack Daniels and some pain pills. Did you find Grenitzer?"

"Sorry. Bud Phillips says he's taking a helicopter tour of the damage."

"Helicopter? This thing eats helicopters for breakfast!"

"What thing?"

"Tell Grenitzer to get his butt down on the ground where it belongs—fast."

"Sure, Billy, whatever you say. Want to speak to Phillips?"

"That weasel wouldn't know the truth if it made its nest in his shorts." Billy coughed, sending pain spiking into his right side.

"There's a paramedic team on its way. Should arrive any minute. Meanwhile, are you gonna tell me what's going on, or do I have to beg?"

"Promise me one thing: give me the benefit of the doubt."

"Hey, I'm an editor. Doubt is what I do best."

*

Bud Phillips had just hung up from talking with Doug Truitt for the second time in the past fifteen minutes when the phone rang again.

"Mayor's office," he answered. He put his feet up on Grenitzer's desk and leaned back in his leather chair.

"Where is he?"

"Denise. I didn't expect to hear from you."

"This has nothing to do with us. I need to talk to him."

"Why?"

"Number one, it's a long story. Number two, it concerns the welfare of people other than just yourself. I don't think you'd be interested on both counts."

"Oh, you'd be surprised what I'm interested in, Denise." He fingered the cards in Grenitzer's Rolodex file, removed Denise's business card and put it in his pocket. "I really don't think His Honor is going to be available anytime in the foreseeable future, if you get my meaning."

"Why are you doing this, Bud?"

"For the same reasons I spank the dog with a rolled up newspaper: it teaches him a lesson and it also feels good."

"I refused to play your little game, so now you're gonna take your ball and go home, is that it?"

"To use your analogy, I offered you a spot on the team, but you missed the bus. Now, why don't you just fly away, like a good witch." Bud hung up the phone.

"Who was that?"

He looked up at a slump-shouldered Grenitzer standing in the doorway. His deeply lined face conveyed the results of his tour better than any words.

"Nobody important. How was the flight?" Bud brought his feet down from the desk.

"Too much turbulence. We never left the fucking ground." Grenitzer took off his coat and threw it on a chair. "I got a pretty good look from the observation deck of the old Smith Tower though. Pioneer Square's a total loss. Looks like pictures from the war, Dresden, or Nagasaki. Did the governor return my call yet?"

"Not yet."

"Any other important messages?"

"Right here." Bud stood up and handed him a sheaf of pink message forms.

While Grenitzer went through them, he poured himself a shot of bourbon from a leaded crystal decanter.

"Oh, Truitt from the *Times* called twice," Bud said.

"Probably trying to set up an interview. Have we scheduled a press conference yet?"

"Actually, he claimed to have some information about what caused the accident at the Tower."

Grenitzer looked up and frowned. "Talk about old news."

"He said it could tie up a lot of loose ends."

The mayor sat down in his vacated chair. "I've got no time for loose ends. You should have seen it, Bud. A goddamn nightmare. Most of six blocks is gutted. Power's out. People stuck in elevators. Every fire company in the world is down there and they can't get it under control because of the fucking wind!"

The phone rang again. Bud hurried over and snatched it up. "Mayor's office."

"Dammit, Bud," Denise said. "I want to speak to the mayor and I'm not giving up, not when my son's life is at stake."

"For the last time, I told you he's unavailable!" He slammed down the receiver. Grenitzer's bushy eyebrows shot up a couple of notches.

"Just another crank call," Bud explained.

"I appreciate your trying to keep all my political affairs in order, Bud, but this is my office, my phone."

The phone rang again. This time, Grenitzer pushed the speaker button.

"Bud! Are you there? Don't hang up on me again, for God's sake."

"Denise?"

"Oh, Mayor Grenitzer. Thank God. I desperately need your help."

"This is hardly the time for handling your personal business," Bud said, reaching for the speaker button.

Grenitzer waved him off. "What's wrong, Denise?"

While Bud paced the room, she told him about the wind's following Evan, the attack on her house, how it had started the fire that morning and how Paul Judge thought it was all connected to the death last week of an Indian shaman.

"I've heard some amazing yarns in my time," Grenitzer said when Denise had finished explaining why she needed to remove a dead body from the morgue, "but that is absolutely the most far-fetched, ridiculous story I have heard in my eight years in office—hell, in my life." He chuckled.

"I'm sorry you're not taking this seriously, Mayor. A lot of lives are at stake—not to mention the costs to repair the damage the wind has caused."

"Now, don't go jumping to conclusions, Denise. I didn't say I don't believe you, I just said it was an awful lot to swallow in one bite. I'll admit the weather conditions have seemed diabolical lately, but an Indian spirit wind—that's a hell of a leap! You mentioned the Tower; I want to check something out. Let me have a number where I can call you back."

Grenitzer hung up. "Where's that number for Truitt?"

"Don't tell me you believe that horseshit?"

"Right now, I couldn't tell you what I believe, Bud. What I do know is this: in the past week, we have either suffered the greatest run of municipal catastrophes in history, or Denise's story—crazy as it sounds—at least deserves a phone call to check out. Wouldn't you agree?"

"Yeah, right."

"Get some coffee. And Bud? One more thing—don't let me catch you putting your damned feet on my desk again."

Over Paul's heated arguments, Dr. Chan had steadfastly refused to permit him to leave the emergency ward until he had the ankle wound cleaned, X-rays taken, and the bones set. When Denise rejoined him, Paul was arguing with two orderlies and a nurse who were attempting to give him an injection.

"You've got two choices," a burly man in hospital greens said. "Either cooperate and let us do our job, or you can lie there until you croak, for all I care. You decide, Mr. Judge. We'll be back in five minutes."

Paul fell back onto the gurney. Denise put one hand on his sweaty cheek and squeezed his other hand.

"I don't want you dead," she said.

"Nor do I," he said in a voice that was considerably weaker than before she'd left to phone Grenitzer. "My priorities are just different than theirs. How's Evan?"

"Fine. He's holed up in Dr. Chan's office." Of all the places he could be in Seattle, Denise figured a hospital was the safest. "I'll head back downstairs in a minute. I just thought you'd like to hear about my conversation with the mayor."

"Did he laugh?"

"No."

"Don't tell me he believed you?"

"Not exactly. Said he'd check it out."

Paul shook his head, eyes closed. "No time for that. We've got to get out of here now."

"You're one tough hombre, you know? How do you feel?"

"Not so good. The pain is wearing me down. Don't know how much longer I can stand it."

"You could let them fix it, get it over with."

"Can't do it, Denise. Not now."

"Maybe it's through with us."

"You know that's not true."

She closed her eyes, drew in a deep breath and let it out slowly. "You're right."

"What about you?" he asked, studying her. "You look tired."

"Me?" Her face temporarily brightened. "I feel like I could do anything. It's amazing. I'm probably brain dead—or at least I know I should be—but I don't feel tired. Since escaping from the fire, I have the strangest urge to go line dancing."

He frowned. "Sorry, can't help you there. Maybe when this is all over."

Denise felt a solitary hot tear burn her cheek. "And just when is that, I'd like to know? This wind-spirit, spirit-wind, or whatever it is nearly killed you, me, and Evan. It's destroyed my house, my car, and my career—not to mention your motorcycle."

"You should see the Mercedes."

"Why us?" Denise used the sleeve of her jacket to dry her cheek. "Some people seem to have all the luck. And some—like you, me, and Evan—have none."

An orderly walking past raised his eyebrows and gave her a look that communicated she'd been speaking too loudly.

Paul squeezed her hand back. "Wish I knew what to say."

"What I really want is to be held."

"That I could maybe help you with, if you don't mind an IV wrapped around you."

Denise laid her head against his chest. With his good arm—the one with the IV attached—he held her to him, gently at first, then more firmly. Her hands tightened their grip on his shirt where it covered his ribs and he could feel her breasts pressed against his stomach and the beating of her heart. With his ruined hand, he stroked Denise's short blond hair. Once, on the reservation, he had caught a baby jack rabbit so small that he could hold it in one closed hand and he had felt its tiny heart racing so fast that he was afraid it might burst from fear and so he had released it. The pain from his injuries was intense and he started to move his arms away and let Denise go, but then her head lifted. Her blue eyes were soft, cloudy and barely half-open as her lips sought his, and, for a few blissful seconds, he forgot his pain.

While Fortuno, his shoulder bandaged, slept under Dr. Chan's desk, Evan sat in her chair and studied the ivory tube. Carved on either end were monsters with closed eyes and gaping mouths filled with teeth. It offered no clue as to its use, if it had one. He was dying to ask Paul what it was for. It felt strangely alive in his hands, as if it carried an electrical charge. He tried swinging it over his head like a badminton racket until he noticed two lab workers watching him. He quit out of fear that it would be taken away. He had already disobeyed his mother in keeping it, but he was worried about Paul and his mother. Paul's leg was so badly hurt that it totally grossed out Evan to look at it, and his mother's normally brilliant blue eyes were dull and sunk in shadows. If the wind came again, he was afraid they wouldn't be able to save him.

When Dr. Chan finished using the telephone, she took a manila envelope from her file cabinet. Then she hunted through her desk until she found a small card that she studied briefly. When she laid it on the desktop, Evan saw that it contained illustrations of basic American Sign Language.

"Don't let me forget to give this to Mr. Judge," Dr. Chan said, wiping her hand across her forehead and speaking slowly to aid him in reading her lips. Then she left.

He waited until Dr. Chan was out of sight before sneaking a peek inside the envelope. Whatever it was looked very interesting. Gingerly, he poured it out on the desk. It made a curious rattling noise as it slid from the envelope and, for a moment, he thought it was a snake and jumped back. Then, as he spread it out in a circle, he saw that it was an Indian necklace. He touched the long fangs, so cold that they stuck to his fingers. With a quick glance around to make sure no one was watching, he picked up the necklace in both hands and slipped it over his head. Instantly, the room became dark and began to spin. He grabbed the desk to steady himself. He was surrounded by huge beasts running side by side, deeper and deeper into a mountain. At the far end of the tunnel, he saw a light that grew brighter as he neared it.

25

Sacrifice

SEATTLE, WEDNESDAY, 10:30 A.M. Paul noticed it first.

As Dr. Chan was describing the fruitless results of her search for an ambulance, a hemostat vibrated off the stainless steel countertop nearby and dropped to the floor. Then the overhead lights began to flicker and the metal blinds shuddered against the windows.

"What's that?" Denise said.

"Earthquake. About a five-point-o on the Richter scale, I would estimate," Dr. Chan said.

A specimen bottle jumped off a rack and fell to the tiled floor, miraculously avoided breaking, rolled past an orderly who tried to grab it but missed, and smashed against a metal cabinet. Then the gurneys began to shuffle and hop along the floor and cries of fear from both patients and staff merged in a cresting wave.

"That's no earthquake," Paul said.

"Evan!" Denise screamed.

A thunderous explosion rocked the building. The power went out and the room plunged into darkness. An ambulance, emergency lights still rotating, slammed through the emergency room doors, scattering bodies and furniture before it and showering the room with glass. The wind whirled into the emergency room. Screams were drowned out by a deafening roar and a blizzard of ceiling tiles cartwheeled through the air. A computer monitor exploded against the wall. An unoccupied gurney crashed into Paul's, toppling him to the floor. Drawers full of bandages, medicines, syringes, surgical instruments, and linens shot out from every direction; their contents caught up in a vortex. And then the wind was gone. Enough supplies to support the emergency room of the county's largest hospital clattered to the floor with a sound like a volley of rifle shots.

"Denise!" Paul called.

"Here! Dr. Chan's been hurt."

Paul's IV had been ripped away and the gurney had fallen on him.

He crawled out from beneath it and over to where Denise bent over Dr. Chan.

"I'm okay," the doctor said. Denise helped her sit up.

Over screams and further sounds of destruction, they could hear the wind rumbling through the hospital's upper floors.

"It's trying to find Evan," Paul said. "You two go. I'll follow."

When Denise and Dr. Chan were gone, Paul searched the wreckage for a crutch. He found a small cabinet on wheels and used it to lean on, pushing it before him and dragging his broken leg behind, his pain momentarily forgotten.

The ambulance driver was slumped against the steering wheel, unconscious.

"You came to the right place," Paul said as he opened the door. He unfastened the man's safety belt and dragged him from the vehicle. A noise from the rear caused him to check the back where he found an elderly man who appeared to be none the worse for wear.

"Damn, that was fun! Do her again?"

"Maybe next time," Paul said.

He offered the man a hand to climb down before returning to the front of the ambulance. He crawled into the vacated driver's seat and noted with relief that the transmission was automatic. The engine started on the first try. He shifted into reverse and started backing up.

"Out of the way," he shouted.

Those who could move scrambled out of the way or helped others less fortunate. On the other side of the emergency room doors, the admittance desk lay on its side. Paul used the ambulance like a bulldozer to clear a path through the debris.

Outside the hospital, the signs of the wind's destruction were everywhere. Falling trees had downed power lines which snapped and spat blue sparks like giant, electric cobras. Cars were piled against each other. A motel sign announced NO VACANCY from atop a Cadillac. The hospital's entrance overhang was torn off and a large portion blocked the exit. Paul rammed it with enough force to push it out of the way, then drove around to the side of the building where the medical examiner's office was located. The garage door was crumpled and hanging at an angle like the top of a TV dinner that had been peeled away. Paul climbed through the opening.

"Denise?"

Ominously, there was no sign or sound of life. The condition of the coroner's offices was perhaps even worse than the emergency room. He found an office chair with wheels and used it as a walker to make his way to Dr. Chan's office. Sitting on the floor among reams of scattered paper, the base of a telephone and an overturned potted plant, was a salt water aquarium whose colorful occupants appeared to have been the only ones to escape harm. Nearby, a desk had been hurled through one wall. In the dim, spooky interior, Paul stepped in something slippery. Grimly, he followed a pool of blood to a young woman who lay pinned beneath a fallen file cabinet. Paul lifted the woman's head; vacant eyes stared back at him. He swallowed with some difficulty, grateful that it wasn't Denise.

The few remaining lights flickered on as emergency generators kicked in. A pair of fluorescent tubes hissed, then exploded in a brilliant blast of white light.

He found Denise sitting on the floor of Dr. Chan's darkened office, cradling Fortuno, and rocking silently back and forth. Dr. Chan sat slumped in her chair and stared at the top of her desk as if the answer to what had just happened might be lying there among the scattered papers, dust and debris. Adding to the room's physical destruction was the oppressive gloom of defeat. Exhausted from his short but difficult journey, he sat down in his walker-chair, used his hands to stretch his splintered leg out in front of him and then put his arm around her.

"He's gone, Paul," she whispered. "The wind took him."

"Don't," he said, holding her tightly against him. "Don't give up now."

"What's the use? He's gone." She blinked tears away.

"I know you've already been through a lot," he said quietly, his cheek pressed against the top of her head, "but you've got to have faith."

"Faith? Faith in what? I want my son back!"

"Look at me." He waited until she did. "There's nothing I won't do to get Evan back. I can feel in my gut it's not over yet. But sitting here won't help. Grandmother taught me, 'Defeat is a heavy rider. Never let him climb on your back or he will ride you into the dust.'"

"Your damn grandmother." She shook her head. "How did she find the time to tell you all this shit?"

"No TV." His eyes searched the room. "Where's the Soul Catcher?"

"The what?"

"The ivory tube."

"Gone."

"And the necklace?"

Dr. Chan nodded. She looked dazed, her skin pale and blotchy.

"What about the body?"

"As far as I know, still here." Her hands lay on her lap, palms up, as if she no longer believed the veracity of her own answers.

"I've got an ambulance in back. I'm going to need help getting it loaded."

"But why?" Denise asked. "What's the point?"

"We can't quit yet. Not while we've still got one card left to play."

"What card?"

"The shaman. He started all this. Maybe we can make a trade." He paused, not sure if he believed it himself, but knowing Denise needed a grain of hope to hang onto. "His body for Evan."

Fifteen minutes later, a yellow plastic body bag containing the shaman's remains was strapped to a portable gurney in the back of the ambulance. Denise helped Paul to the driver's compartment; he dragged his broken left leg behind him.

"Why not let me drive?" she asked as he panted from the exertion of heaving himself into the seat.

"Can't."

She threw him a skeptical look. "Is this a macho thing?"

His mouth formed a tight smile in spite of the pain. "I bet you've never been carsick when you've been the driver. This is the same. My ankle's only unbearable when I have time to think about it."

"Okay," she said, "but give me a minute. I forgot something." When she reappeared, she was holding Fortuno. "Maybe he can find Evan one more time," she said as she climbed into the passenger seat.

Paul started the engine and began to pull away.

"Wait." Denise pointed.

Dr. Chan approached, holding a pair of aluminum crutches. "I found these," she said. Her lab coat, pristine less than half an hour earlier, was torn and smudged with bloodstains. She used a sleeve to wipe her red-rimmed eyes. "Maybe you were right about the spirit wind coming, Mr. Judge. My training says this isn't possible. Now, half my staff is either dead or injured. The offices and equipment are destroyed. If I had believed you, perhaps I could have prevented this."

"Don't take it out on yourself, doctor. You didn't cause the destruction. You were just a victim, same as everyone else. If we're going to have even a small chance of stopping it, we've got to go now."

"Good luck."

"Thanks. We'll need it."

Denise waited until Paul drove away before commenting. "For someone who's used to seeing death every day, she didn't look like she's handling this very well. I guess it's different when the bodies are people you know and work with."

"There's that," he agreed. "And she just discovered something they didn't teach her in medical school, something that's going to affect the way she looks at corpses for the rest of her life."

Tires squealed as he turned down a narrow street. A previously tall Douglas fir blocked traffic. Paul drove through a hedge to avoid the slowdown, wincing as the van bounded across several front lawns.

"Where to?" Denise said.

"East," he answered.

"Mind if I ask what the plan is? It's my son, after all." Fortuno sat in her lap, his bandaged foreleg held against his side and head resting on the open window.

"Of course." He had to swerve to avoid a black limousine coming the other way.

Denise spun in her seat. "I wonder if that was the mayor?"

"Too late to help us," Paul said. "The plan is still to head to Issaquah with the body, build a coffin, haul it up in a tree for ten days, and then cremate it in a ceremonial fire to release the shaman's spirit."

Denise stared at him as if she couldn't believe a word he'd just said. "Are you serious?"

"Don't worry," he said. "I'm almost certain the wind will never let us carry it out. Not without a fight, anyway."

"Then why? What are we doing this for?" A look of comprehension suddenly swept over her face. "Are we the bait?"

"That's pretty accurate. Actually, he's the bait." Paul nodded his head toward the back. "We're more like the red cape."

"So we're trying to make it angry? Like a bullfighter?"

"Make it angry and—if we're incredibly lucky—make it miss. That's my hope."

Denise stared ahead for a few moments. "It won't hurt Evan? I mean, us making it angry won't cause it to take it out on him?"

"I don't think so. I expect it'll come for us."

"Good."

She removed the parka, still heavy with dampness. Paul noticed her shivering beneath the nightshirt that clung to her body.

"Cold?"

"Not really," she said. "Just scared."

"Me, too."

They were entering Interstate 90 freeway and traffic was stalled. Paul found the switch for the siren and flipped it on. "Hang on."

Billy was beginning to worry that he'd been forgotten. He clutched the Motorola cellular phone in his left hand, afraid he might somehow lose his link to the rest of the world. He still hadn't heard from Grenitzer and Truitt hadn't called back in nearly half an hour. Adding to his frustration, he had tried calling Julie several times, but the line was busy. Who could she be talking to at a time like this? Didn't she realize he was hurt, might be dying? "Of course not, you jerk," he said.

He coughed, wincing with the effort. The pain in his legs and ribs prevented him from rolling over or sitting up. He had lost a fair amount of blood and either the temperature was dropping, or his shivering meant he was beginning to go into shock. There was also the possibility that the wind would return at any moment to finish the job it had started.

He was saved from further such deliberations by the phone's chirp. His other hand was so numb that he had trouble pushing the right button. "Hello?"

"I heard you were looking for me."

"Well, well, if it isn't his lordship. I never thought I'd be saying this, but it's good to hear your voice."

"Cut the crap, Mossman. I've got you on the speaker phone in my car. I'm here with Dr. Chan, Deputy Medical Examiner, and Les Martin, Chief of Police. Dr. Chan has provided professional if reluctant confirmation of your theory of a Williwaw. I want to make it perfectly clear that I'm personally reserving judgment until this is all over."

"Would that be before or after the election?" Billy said.

"We're parked in front of Harborview," Grenitzer continued as if he hadn't heard him. "Evidently, it struck here earlier. Either that or there was a Pearl Jam concert. The hospital is totally trashed. I doubt there's an unbroken window or a fresh bed sheet in the place.

Your Williwaw also apparently kidnapped the son of Denise Baker, my P.R. agency's account manager."

"Kidnapped?" Billy was astonished.

"For once, we agree," Grenitzer said. "Dr. Chan? Perhaps you could enlighten Mr. Mossman."

"I'll try," Dr. Chan said without conviction. "Mr. Judge warned that the wind would come to take boy, but I didn't believe him. Then it happened, just as he said it would. The wind caused much destruction and hurt many people." Her voice had begun to quiver and she paused.

"Dr. Chan, you were saying?" Billy said.

"I'm not sure that I understand who or what is responsible. Ms. Baker left with Mr. Judge in an ambulance to find her son. They took the body of a John Doe that was discovered last week. Mr. Judge believes this Native American's murder may have been responsible for the wind's attack."

"Where are they headed?" Billy asked. "Can we contact them?"

"East," Dr. Chan said. "Mr. Judge said they are going to try to reach Issaquah."

"We can call them on the shortwave," the fire captain said, "if he hasn't turned it off."

"Let's get on with it," Grenitzer said. "Now what do we do about this Williwaw or tornado or whatever the hell it is?"

"Nothing much we can do," Martin said, "except warn people to hole up in their basements."

"You might also save some lives if you could track it," Billy said.

"Track it?" Grenitzer said. "How would you suggest we go about tracking the wind? Or did this Williwaw kidnap your brains, too?"

"Radar," Billy offered.

The short silence that followed was interrupted by Martin. "I thought you had to have precipitation for radar to be effective."

"Me, too," Billy said. "But I was researching wind shear last night and I found something about a new radar capable of tracking Clear Air Turbulence, or CAT as it's called. The reason that Micronesia plane didn't have time to react was because—unluckily for them—for once it wasn't raining in Seattle. This new gear is supposed to prevent that."

"So who's got this new radar?" Grenitzer asked.

"The FAA, NOAA, National Weather Service—I don't know."

"If anybody's got it," Martin said, "I'd bet that Whidbey Naval Air Station does."

"All right," Grenitzer said. "We'll check it out. Oh, and Moss-man, hang in there. A paramedic team is on the way."

"Thanks," Billy said, and meant it.

Billy ended the call and tried Julie again. This time he got through. "Julie? It's me."

"Julie isn't here," a voice said. "This is Ann Bessani. Megan's with her grandmother. Just Helen and I are here. Are you okay? Your editor called and told Julie what happened."

"I've been better. Where the hell's Julie?"

"She's on her way to the Tower to be with you."

"What? Has she lost her mind? What if the wind comes back?"

"We tried to stop her, but she wouldn't listen. Where is the Wil-liwaw now?"

"I don't know. I just spoke to Mayor Grenitzer. He claims it de-stroyed Harborview and stole the son of a PR consultant by the name of Denise Baker. She and a guy named Judge are headed after it."

"Why would it take the boy?"

"Wish I knew. The coroner said something about an Indian that was murdered possibly being responsible."

"Did they say which way they were headed?"

"No. Wait. Yes, they did. East. East toward Issaquah."

"Helen wants to know if you found the sign you were looking for."

"Tell Helen I found enough sign up here to write a pretty damn good story about this Williwaw—that's if I live long enough. I even met the bastard personally and it's just like you described it—one mean son-of-a-bitch."

Helen spread the map that Ann had retrieved from her car out on the Mossmans' kitchen table. Outside the sliding glass doors, a pair of mallards slept on the houseboat's boardwalk, heads tucked into their wings, oblivious of the human lives that were at stake.

"There's Harborview." Ann pointed. "Why did you want to know where it was?"

"Just a crazy idea," Helen said as she traced a line heading east toward Issaquah with her finger.

Paul turned off the siren. "That's it. We're stuck." The radio con-tinued to chatter in the background.

Even with siren and flashing emergency lights, their progress had been slowed by heavy traffic. For the first few miles of travel on Interstate 90, he had driven down the narrow median to the left of the express lanes. Having reached the tunnel approach to the Mercer Island Floating Bridge, they had run out of median. They were trapped until at least one of the two stalled lanes began moving.

"What now?" Denise said.

"Just have to wait it out."

"I can't sit. I'm going to check it out." She settled Fortuno on the floor, opened the door and jumped out.

"Denise?"

"Yeah?"

"Be careful." He watched her thread her way through the lines of vehicles leading into the tunnel. When she was out of sight, he tried moving his leg. Since getting in the van, he had lost all feeling below the knee. Now, it felt as if a railroad spike had been driven through it. Though the muscles in his body quivered with the strain, he couldn't budge his leg. He opened his door, grabbed his leg in both hands and lifted. The leg shifted an inch causing a flash of lightning behind his eyes. He rested his head on the steering wheel, panting.

Denise returned and climbed back into the van. "A driver ran out of gas in the right lane. Another driver slowed in the left lane to see what was happening and her car died. A third driver wasn't paying attention and ran into the back of the second car which spun into yet another car."

Paul made no acknowledgment that he had heard her.

"Paul?"

She touched his arm. When he still didn't respond, she became alarmed. She lifted his head from the steering wheel. It was bathed in sweat again, but this time, his closed eyes weren't moving. She felt for his pulse and couldn't feel one. The thought that he was dying and that she might have to find and fight the wind alone panicked her.

"Jesus, Paul! Wake up, please!"

His eyes remained closed. "You're back."

"What happened?"

"Nothing." His voice was so faint that she could barely hear him and he still hadn't lifted his head from the steering wheel. "Just resting."

She jumped out of the van, hurried around to his side and opened the door. "Let me see your leg." The bandages were soaked with blood. "It's bleeding again. I'm going to get clean bandages."

"Leave it."

"Listen up," she instructed. "I don't want to lose you, too. Besides," she added, "we serve no martyrs before their time."

He tried to smile.

"Be right back."

Denise opened one of the rear doors and crawled in. The body bag lay where Paul and Dr. Chan had strapped it in. The urge to see the man that had caused a powerful wind to stalk and then kidnap her son was strong. She searched for and found a first aid kit and a bottle of drinking water. Glancing down at the body, she started to move past it, then halted. Slowly, she bent down. Unaware that she had stopped breathing, she unzipped the bag from around the face.

Except when her grandparents had died, Denise hadn't seen death. Here it was in spades: the unnaturally gray skin, sutured hairline, faded tattoos, eyes closed and sunken. She turned her face away. Still, she couldn't leave. As repugnant as the corpse was, there was something strangely familiar about the face. She forced herself to study the features again. Then she remembered the incident at the McDonald's a week before. It seemed like another lifetime.

She closed the doors and hurried back to Paul. In her haste, she forgot to zip the body bag closed. Now, in the darkened van, Black Wolf's eyes were open.

"I've seen that guy before." She nodded toward the back as she rebandaged Paul's ankle.

Paul's head lifted from the steering wheel. "Where?"

"Last week. In the Pike Place Market. Evan and I were waiting in line at McDonald's when this man came up to Evan."

"What did he say?"

"Not a word. He just tried to touch Evan's ears. Scared me and I freaked out. I don't think he meant to harm him, so I apologized. Then he left."

"What day was this?"

"Friday, after work."

"Was he with anyone?"

"Not that I saw. There were some tough-looking punks in the restaurant, so we didn't stick around, just got our food and left."

"According to Dr. Chan, he died Friday. You and Evan may have been the last ones to see him alive—other than whoever killed him.

See which way he went, or if anyone followed him?"

"Sorry. I wasn't thinking of anything except eating and getting home."

"Incredible," Paul said.

Denise finished bandaging Paul's leg. "How's that feel?" she asked. "Better?"

But Paul was somewhere else. "So that's why the wind's been tracking Evan. It's all starting to come together."

Denise was about to ask for an explanation when she was startled to hear the radio calling them.

"Hey, that's us!"

She ran around to her side of the van, climbed in, and grabbed the telephone-like handset. Fortuno sat up.

"This is Denise Baker. Who's this?"

"Chief Martin, Seattle Police Department. Where are you now, over?"

"We're trapped in traffic just before the west side of the I 90 tunnel. Paul's broken leg is bleeding again. He needs medical attention. We also need help in clearing a path through the traffic."

"There's a wrecker on its way from Mercer Island, but, from what they tell me, it's going to take awhile. I'd send you a back-up aid vehicle, but we don't have any to spare, over."

"Ask them about the wind," Paul said.

"Any sign of the wind?"

"Nothing for the last thirty minutes, Ms. Baker. There are high wind advisories posted for the entire Puget Sound region. We've shut down the airports and all Seattle-area ferries as a precaution. You'll also be interested to know that five minutes ago, a P-3 Orion took off from Whidbey Island Naval Air Station. The P-3 is equipped with all the latest radar tracking devices. We're hoping to get a picture of this thing. We'll let you know if we spot something, over."

"Thanks," Denise said.

"This is Grenitzer," said another voice. "Sorry about your boy, Denise. Someone whose opinion I must now give unexpected credence to is calling this thing a 'Williwaw.' Whatever it's called, just wanted you to know that you're not alone."

Denise hung up and didn't say anything. After a minute had gone by, Paul looked over in time to see her wipe away a tear.

"What is it?"

"I can't believe it," she said to Paul. "They're actually trying to help us. But, I don't really see how they can. I mean, what can they do?"

"Nothing," he admitted.

"How does the Williwaw, or whatever he called it, even know how to find us?"

"Don't worry. It'll find us. It's tuned in on the ultimate frequency. Like ESP only better." He handed her a box of tissues from behind her seatback. "I know it's hard to accept. It's hard for me and I was raised in a world of spirits: earth, sky, animals—you name it."

Denise shook her head. "I wish I knew what I believed in. The God I knew in my childhood disappeared along with Santa Claus and the Tooth Fairy. Now, He—She—suddenly seems essential, but, after so much neglect, I'm embarrassed to ask for help. Besides, even if He heard me, I'm afraid my prayers would be too little, too late. Look at the trees." She pointed to the tall Douglas firs that lined the road. "There's no wind. Why should there be? It got what it wanted."

"It's coming."

"Yeah?" She stared at him. "How can you be so damned sure?"

He nodded at Fortuno, still sitting on the seat, nose out the window, sniffing. "He knows. It's out there somewhere."

"I hope you're right. Lord, do I hope you're right!" She reached over, stroked the back of his neck beneath his long hair. "Here. Rest your head on my shoulder. I'll wake you when the traffic starts moving."

Sleep had overtaken them both when Chief Martin's agitated voice erupted from the radio. "Baker and Judge, the P-3 just spotted something mean looking headed your way and moving very fast, over."

As if in confirmation, the dog's mouth had formed an O shape, as if he were trying to imitate a coyote howl.

"Got it," Paul replied.

"Take care." The well-wisher sounded less than hopeful.

"Now what?" Denise turned to Paul.

"A good time for prayers, even tardy ones. Other than that, I'm not really sure. Keep an eye out for trouble. You're in charge of recovering Evan. I'm going to be tied up with the Old One."

"Paul?"

"Yeah?"

"There's something I want to tell you. I have the awful feeling I may not get a chance to say it later."

"Don't say it, Denise. Don't even think that there won't be a time and a place for whatever it is."

"Okay." She sighed. Then, "Look!"

Two lines of traffic had begun moving. Paul started the van, took off the emergency brake, turned on the siren and emergency lights.

"Ready?" he asked.

The stubborn set of her jaw was his answer.

Halfway through the brightly lit tunnel, the lights went out and the wind slipped in among them, moaning, rattling windows and jostling vehicles. Several drivers slowed or stopped as they fumbled for the controls to turn on headlights and tried to cope with the unexpected succussion and darkness. A few changed lanes without signaling, creating near misses in their haste to escape the narrow confines of the tunnel. Fortuno climbed onto Denise's lap and let out a terrified yowl.

"My thoughts exactly," Denise said and she held the dog tightly.

"Come on, faster," Paul urged the other drivers. He watched for an opening, spotted a space of a few feet, and pulled out from behind a lumbering RV that swayed from side to side. At the far end of the tunnel, they passed a wrecker and a number of mangled cars from the previous accident lined up on the far right. A handful of people huddled among them, seeking refuge. Then the ambulance shot into daylight and the full fury of the wind. A gust batted the van across another lane and onto the shoulder. Fortunately, the traffic emerging from the tunnel was light enough that Paul was able to avoid a collision.

Denise threw one hand up on the dashboard and clung with the other to the suicide strap overhead.

"I don't think I'm going to like this," she said.

Paul couldn't hear her over the raging wind, but he shared her concern. The normally tranquil waters of Lake Washington had been transformed into a frenzied cauldron of gray and white seas into whose midst stretched the Mercer Island Floating Bridge, two fragile threads of concrete nearly a mile long. Two-story-tall waves smashed into the bridge, cascading over cars and trucks and causing the spans to flex and roll. Most drivers hesitated or pulled over to avoid crossing, but Paul knew that for them, there was nowhere to hide. If they were to find Evan, they needed also to be found.

Grimly, he steered them into the maelstrom.

Navigating the pitching bridge was like driving on a concrete trampoline in a wind tunnel. The muscles and tendons stood out on his arms as Paul fought to maintain the van's forward direction. Visibility was hit or miss, mostly miss. He was forced to slow down when a wave drenched the van's windshield, but when the wipers finally cleared it, he floored the accelerator. Their only chance was to get across before the floating bridge came apart. Then he saw the truck.

Its tanker trailer yawing in the heavy wind, a fuel truck was headed in the other direction. With the roar of a jet, a towering wall of water slammed into the bridge and pushed the tail end of the trailer out into the left lane. Paul saw the driver turn the steering wheel with little effect as the tractor was pulled into the center lane by its heavy load. The truck wobbled unsteadily as its driver locked up the brakes; then it toppled, the trailer going over first, landing on the concrete divider and sliding along it with a shower of sparks. The weight of the huge trailer yanked the cab over on its side and dragged it like a toy. The trailer climbed over the divider and rushed toward them, sliding sideways, blocking all three eastbound lanes and leaving them no room to get by.

Fighting wind and waves, steering with minimal traction, Paul sought an escape route in the far right lane. He pumped the brakes, but the van was hydroplaning, tires barely skimming the surface of the water-covered bridge as they slid toward the approaching tanker. He saw that there was neither room enough to pass nor time to stop. Denise cried out and threw an arm over her face. Then a Metro bus skidded past them and slammed into the trailer. Flames jetted from the ruptured tank, igniting the bus whose momentum pushed the trailer back toward the middle of the bridge and created a small opening on the far right side. It was too small, but their options were down to none.

They were less than a second from impact when Paul stepped on the gas pedal and aimed the ambulance at the gap. They caromed off the end of the tanker and into the guard rail. The impact temporarily dazed him, but he felt no pain. Now they were pointed at the sky as the van climbed the railing. The scream of twisting and tearing metal competed with the thunderous whoosh of the tanker fire as they passed through a wall of flame. For a moment, he thought they were going into the lake. Then they tipped over. They landed on Paul's side, sliding with enough momentum to swing clear of the tanker and leave several car lengths between them and the inferno.

Still strapped in their seats, too stunned to move, Paul and Denise watched as waves attacked the bridge in phalanxes, hammering the concrete and steel span and rapidly drowning out the fire. The southern side of the bridge reared up and water began to pour over its opposite side. A sepulchral thrumming rose from the watery depths as the bridge began to vibrate from the relentless pounding. A small Japanese car floated down toward the northern edge of the bridge where it came to rest against the retaining wall. A young man managed to climb out. Denise and Paul watched helplessly as waves carried first him and then the car away.

Unable to withstand the combined forces of wind and waves, steel bolts the size of a man's arm snapped and the bridge began to separate at its joints. Below the water line, an anchoring cable was stretched beyond its maximum load. It gave way and ripped out a pontoon seal. The pontoon quickly began to fill with water which increased the force still more on the remaining cables and pontoons. As the wind continued to roar, the center bridge section began to settle into the churning water.

"It's going down!" Denise yelled.

Paul pulled her to him, shouted in her ear. "Go!" He pointed at her door, above them now. "Head for the far side. Forget me, forget the dog, forget everything but Evan!" She had barely managed to open the door a crack when the wind tore it off. He pushed her from behind as she scrambled up through the opening.

Denise turned for just an instant.

"Love you," she said and crossed her hands across her chest. Then she dropped past the windshield.

Without hearing her or knowing sign language, Paul understood. Anxiously, he watched as she tried to duck-walk on the heaving concrete bridge. Then a huge wave threw her to the pavement and carried her away. Witnessing Denise vanish was agony, but there was no time for feelings. The Light had warned that the price for getting Evan back would not come cheaply. For an instant, he remembered the shaman's words about a sacrifice, then he was forced to turn his full attention to his own predicament. The same wave that had taken Denise had also twisted the bridge still higher on its south side. Caught in the wave's backwash, the van slid toward the tanker. Signaling that the end was near, the bridge groaned and listed further. Fortuno stood on his hind legs and whimpered.

318

"You next. Time to abandon ship."

Paul lifted the dog up and out the door. While the dog cowered above, Paul climbed over the driver's seat, now on its side, and crawled into the back of the ambulance. Wind and waves rocked the van like an empty beer can. Compartments sprang open, spilling their contents. He was thrown against the stretcher that held the shaman, banging his ankle in the process. He swore out of equal parts pain and frustration. Then he saw something that made him forget his pain. Eyes old and hard as glacier-scarred rocks watched him from the partially unzipped body bag.

"Give back the boy," Paul ordered, "or we go down together."

As if in answer to his request, a wave exploded over the van. Water flooded through the open passenger door. The inside of the van was a violent confusion of first aid supplies and equipment bobbing in foot-deep water. Water sloshed over the body bag. Paul found a rope and lashed one end around his waist. He was tying the other end around the body bag when there was a deafening crack. The bridge section pitched forward, then plunged abruptly to the bottom of the lake. Paul's head struck the corner of a metal cabinet as the van wallowed helplessly in the hungry water and began to sink, nose first. Pain short-circuited his mind and everything went blank.

Seconds later, the rising water drenched and revived him. He grabbed the body bag and discovered with a start that it was empty. His eyes searched the van's partially-submerged interior with increasing panic. Frantically, he rummaged beneath a water-logged blanket. Then he saw that the rear door was slightly ajar. Half-crawling, half-swimming, he struggled to reach it, but before he could escape, a torrent of water rushed in and swept him back into the van as it, too, dived to the bottom.

So this was death.

The first thing he noticed was the absence of pain. Relief flooded through him as he checked his leg and hand. His wounds were gone. There weren't even scars. Next, he examined his surroundings. Like his vision at The Edge of the World, he stood in a cold, gray, and windless place where there was neither day nor night. His tattered shirt and jeans were gone. In their place, he wore only a loincloth of soft buckskin. Then, through the dense, swirling mists, he saw again a familiar shape.

"Grandmother." He hurried toward her.

She held up a hand in warning. "Come no closer, son of my daughter, or the bond between our two hearts may become too strong for you to leave."

"I don't know if I can go back, grandmother. There, the pain from my wounds is very great and my strength is all but gone."

"Even death can be a blessing," she nodded. "I regret that you have had to learn this truth so early. But there can be no life without pain. Besides, there are many who depend upon you."

Her words reverberated within him. His hand and leg no longer hurt—his body was whole—but his heart ached with loss and the bitter knowledge that he had failed to rescue the boy.

"What must I do?" he asked.

"The spider's web of your life is not yet complete. You may yet go back to finish its weaving. But first, you must overcome the spirit of the one who has called on the wind for vengeance. His medicine is very strong, too strong for you alone. To defeat him, you will need help from the boy with no ears."

A primitive howl pierced the mists, cutting off her words of advice and freezing the blood in his veins.

"Go now," his grandmother said. "There is not much time. And remember ancestors," she called after him.

Paul raced toward the receding howl. As before in his vision, he came to the steep mountain. Ice formed a thin crust on the loose shale, making it treacherous to climb. He scrambled up the shifting incline, the muscles in his thighs screaming and his lungs threatening to burst. When at last he reached the fog-shrouded summit, he found the huge, black wolf waiting for him as if it knew he was coming. Like before, Evan was trapped beneath its paws. The necklace and the Soul Catcher lay nearby on a flat rock.

"Tell me, Old One, why do you want the boy?" Paul asked, still panting from his climb. "Take me if you must have a sacrifice, but let the boy go."

The wolf's eyes glowed a malignant red and it grinned, exposing its long and deadly fangs. A cry of warning came from the boy's lips. Paul whirled. The long, slender blade of a fish filleting knife missed his heart and plunged instead into his shoulder. He gasped and fell to the ground. Eagle Brother did not give him time to recover. He let out a war whoop and leapt again. Still on his back, Paul got his feet up just in time to catch the diving man in the stomach and pitch him over his head. Paul rolled to his feet and clutched his shoulder.

"How's that feel, peacock?" Eagle Brother asked, circling him. He *wore only the wooden helmet and leather breeches, his stocky, muscular body showing none of the effects of the fire and crash that had killed him. "There is no one to protect you here. I'll carve you into little pieces before I'm done."*

Paul backed up warily, keeping the other man in front of him. He was bleeding only a little from the deep puncture wound, but his left arm hung numb and nearly useless. Out of the corner of his eye, he could see the wolf watching intently. Before he could think of a strategy, Eagle Brother darted in again. The knife slashed. Paul twisted to avoid it, but wasn't fast enough to escape unharmed as the finely-honed blade sliced open his right forearm. Bright red blood coursed down his arm, dripping from his hand.

Now fear dragged at his heart as he backed away from the other man. Any more wounds and he would be unable to defend himself, let alone try to free the boy. Evan was still alive, but for how much longer? There was simply no margin for error.

"Remember ancestors," he whispered.

"What's that, peacock?" Eagle Brother asked, circling again. "Do you cry 'Uncle' so soon?"

"Uncle? I defeated you easily enough before, why not again?" Paul taunted.

Eagle Brother's face darkened in rage. "You bastard!" Impetuous in death as he had been in life, he charged forward, lunging at Paul's left leg. But Paul had anticipated that he meant to cripple him before taking his time with the actual kill. He pulled his left leg back, pivoted on his right, and threw a right cross that connected solidly with the other man's cheek.

Caught off-guard, Eagle Brother stumbled and swore. "I'll teach you to—" He didn't get to finish. Paul was already on the offensive, loosing a ferocious kick. His right foot caught the other man on his Adam's apple. Eagle Brother landed on his back, rolled to his knees and gagged. Before he could recover, Paul leapt on him from behind, hooked his right arm around the man's neck and locked his hand through his own left elbow while, with his left hand, he pushed down upon the back of Eagle Brother's head. He had to lean back to keep the other man's flailing hands from reaching his face, but he would not relax his headlock. It was only a matter of time before Eagle Brother's frantic efforts failed and he pitched forward onto his face.

The wolf snarled in fury, then stretched his neck toward the sky and howled. Instead of pausing as he had in their earlier meeting, Paul threw himself on the animal, tackling it around the throat. Together, they fell to the rocky ground. *The wolf shook him off, but not before he had gouged a finger into one of its eyes. He rejoiced when it yelped in pain.*

Paul turned quickly to Evan who had scrambled a short distance away. "Get the Soul Catcher," he said and pointed.

What do I do with it? *Evan signed, turning his palms up to indicate his lack of understanding.*

In the split second that Paul hesitated, the wolf charged. Its momentum carried them down the steep hill and onto sharp rocks. Even before they had stopped rolling, the wolf's paws were ripping at his stomach and thighs, the fangs tearing at his already injured shoulder. Paul heard the sound of teeth crunching on bone and gristle. He was down to his last resources, until they failed he would give no quarter. His hands closed on the wolf's neck, thumbs searching out the animal's carotid arteries.

Evan slid the necklace over his head. When he picked up the Soul Catcher, he saw for the first time hidden in its intricately carved details, a boy much like himself, except for his missing ears, who held the Soul Catcher high in the air. As Evan raised it over his head, the ivory tube began to vibrate and make the tingling feeling in his head like the whistle given to him by the blind beggar. Now the ground vibrated, too, as if a herd of large animals approached.

Paul felt the mountain tremble beneath him, but had no time to wonder at the cause. His thumbs and fingers were buried in the wolf's muscular neck as he used the last of his strength to kill it. His final hope was that they would die together and that his death might be as worthy as that of his great-great-grandfather, Spotted Horse.

It took him a moment to understand what had happened when the wolf's fangs released his shoulder. A moan escaped its bloody snout and the red fire in its eyes flickered. Then, it jumped as if it had been shot and fell onto its hindquarters. It tried to rise, but its forelegs buckled and gave way and it tumbled several feet on the loose shale. Mist drifted over the ice-covered rocks, hiding the body from view.

Too weak to follow it, Paul examined his shoulder. While the flesh was badly torn and drenched in blood, the telltale spurt of a punctured artery was missing. He scooped up a handful of ice granules and packed it over the wound to staunch the bleeding.

When he could stand, he worked his way down to where the wolf's body had come to rest. The wolf, however, was gone. In its place, an ancient Indian, gaunt and frail, now lay among the rocks. Black war paint decorated his abundantly-tattooed face and body. At first, Paul thought he was dead. Then the lids opened and his dark eyes flashed.

"It is I who should be gloating over you," the Old One said. He coughed and a thin line of black drool ran from his lips.

Paul knelt and lifted the man's head. "I don't gloat," he said. "Besides, you are old."

"You speak true." Black Wolf nodded. "I am old and tired and my heart is sick." His eyes closed. "You are strong and the boy's medicine is even more powerful than I thought. Tell me, what kind of Indian are you who helps his enemies?"

"They aren't my enemy," Paul said. "You have murdered and injured hundreds of innocent people."

"Now you lie!" He winced and clutched one gnarled hand to the skin over his heart. When he spoke again, he sounded out of breath. "Is it wrong to desire to die with one's own family? I came only to rest, not to fight. The whites murdered me, took my money, and trampled my dignity. They stole from me not only the beauty of life, but even the terrible beauty of death." His voice was choked with emotion. "Now, my daughter will never know that I came to be with her at the end. My anger and sadness at this injustice will not let my spirit rest."

"You speak of injustice; why then does the Williwaw hurt the innocent? Doesn't this perpetuate the injustice?"

The Old One hissed between his teeth. "You are same as all the rest. Because you think only one way, you try to make the world the same as you. Does the osprey fish for only this or that salmon, or the fox hunt only one hare? I called upon the wind for vengeance against my white enemy and also to teach him respect for his red brother. At the end of time, when the Creator calls on all men for a final accounting, this shall be the judgment upon the whites: that they held nothing sacred—earth or sky, river or sea, not even life."

Paul was silent for a moment. Memories of a hundred racial insults and indignities threatened to come spilling out if he let them. But there were other memories, too. Of schoolmates whose eyes knew no color. And of his grandmother who taught him that the Creator made all hearts the same no matter what color the skin.

"What is your daughter's name?"

"She is called Quiet As The Deer, daughter of Black Wolf and Talks With Moon."

"Then hear my oath, Black Wolf. Let the boy go and I will find your daughter. I swear also to see that your body is put to the fire and your ashes scattered in the proper way, according to your custom, so that your spirit can be free of this place of death."

323

"No!" Black Wolf's mouth twisted with anger. "The boy is mine! He shall bring me comfort in the spirit world. So it has always been among the Caribou People. My own sister was sacrificed that she might serve my uncle. Only an innocent—one whose hands have not yet spilled blood— and whose medicine is strong is worthy to serve."

Paul hung his head. "Then, I can't help you. I won't go back without him."

Now, Black Wolf was silent for a very long time. At last, he spoke, "I do not understand this riddle. You have defeated me, yet you do not wish to leave. And the boy with no ears is not your son, yet you care for him like a father?"

Paul stared into the Old One's dark eyes. "Is your heart so hard that you can't understand? Have you no love for your family?"

Black Wolf turned away.

"If this is so," Paul continued, "I pity you. Your medicine may be strong, but without a heart to rule it, of what use is it except to create mischief and evil? Look around you. You can stay in this ugly place, The Land of Forever Dead, or you can join your ancestors, the moon and the stars. But choose well, Old One. The honor of the Caribou People is at stake."

Black Wolf grimaced as if he had been struck and Paul feared he'd pushed him too hard. A muscle twitched in the smooth skin beneath his left eye and his lips drew back in a thin line. Reluctantly, he surveyed his bleak surroundings. When at last he turned back to Paul, his dark eyes had softened. "Perhaps you are right," he said, his voice reflecting his weariness. "My season was finished long ago. The boy's tree has only begun to bear fruit and yours is just now reaching fullness. But heed my words." He pointed a bony finger at Paul. "For those without the proper knowledge and medicine, the price of travel between the two worlds is death. He who would try to cheat death must be prepared to lose."

"I understand," Paul said.

"Then go. Quickly, before I regret my decision." The Old One turned his eyes to the sky and began to chant. Almost immediately, the air turned colder and smelled of spruce. A sharp breeze began to blow. As it swept across the hill, it whined and picked up ice crystals that cut like tiny razors. The mists boiled up, forming a dark cloud that hung like a wolf's head high in the sky. Lightning flashed and thunder clapped from within its seething midst and the swelling sound of hoofbeats surrounded them.

Standing on the wave-lashed, eastern edge of the bridge near its abrupt end, stood a small boy. He wore only the necklace and a leather breechcloth. His ribs shown plainly against his thin body. He shivered, but not from the cold, as he surveyed where the center section had been torn away. His fear was less for himself, however, and more for his mother and Paul. Above his head, he held the ivory Soul Catcher firmly in two hands. It made the eerie, tingling sensation inside his head as the wind traveled through it.

Fortuno's ears perked up and he paddled toward the sound.

Denise clung to the pontoon of a small fragment of bridge that had broken free and remained floating. Around her, the water eddied and whirled. Soon her strength would be gone and her hands too numb to hang on and it would suck her down to a watery grave.

Above the wind's shrill keening, she heard another sound, a sound that caused her to raise her head as she strained to identify it. When she heard it again, she recognized the unmistakable howl. Determinedly, she began swimming toward it. Wind and waves quickly battered her to the point of exhaustion. Then she saw Evan standing, alone and vulnerable, among the tempest.

"Evan!" She waved her arms, knowing he couldn't hear her cry.

He had just seemed to see her when a large, foaming white wave, hissing with power, swept over the end of the bridge and he was gone. When she was still more than a hundred feet away, she saw his head bob to the surface. Instead of filling her with relief, however, she was horrified to see a large dismasted schooner bearing down upon him.

The necklace had become so cold that it burned Evan's skin and the Soul Catcher glowed as if a fire burned within it, yet it, too, felt as if it were made of ice. Though the wind bullied him, he would not let go. Then he saw Fortuno. Not far behind, a determined swimmer battled the waves and current. The tiny figure waved. Recognition brought a cry, instinctual and unheard, that the wind tore from his lips. Even before he saw the wave coming, rising up, towering over him, he felt its raw, brutal power like a heavy fist crashing down. Then the cold water swallowed him, pulled him down, and tumbled him like a tennis shoe in an enormous washing machine. The Soul Catcher was torn from his hands. The glow from within it flickered out and it sank, silent now, to its final resting place, two hundred feet beneath the surface of Lake Washington.

*

Denise stroked unconsciously, her arms and legs dead of all feeling, as if the rubber bands that controlled them had been stretched too far and broken. The schooner was now almost upon them. Everything she had left she spent in an effort to make it to the last place where she had seen Evan. A hand, small and pale, rose from a wave. Denise dove for it. Her arms found his body and wrapped around him, but she had no strength left to swim. She could only kiss his face one last time, a face she had feared she might never see again. Then she heard the hoarse rumble of engines approaching followed by a violent crash and the sound of splintering wood. She looked up in time to see the bow of the oncoming schooner veer sharply to the left, shoved aside by the bow of another boat. A rope stung her face as it landed across her. Her hand somehow grabbed it and hung on. Too tired to close her mouth, she swallowed water and felt them towed toward the side of the large fishing boat. A man jumped into the water beside them. Another reached down and lifted first Evan and then herself from the water. Gently, they were laid side by side on the boat deck. Waves no longer caused the boat to roll and the wind was now silent, as if it had given up. For a moment, Denise thought they had died and gone to heaven. She lay looking up into the face bending over her thinking, God really is a woman, an old woman with gray hair.

"You the Baker woman?" God asked.

She nodded and coughed. "How's my son?"

"Gonna be just fine—both of you."

The man who had pulled them from the lake now wrapped them in blankets. "Just rest easy," he said.

Another man, lean and silver-haired, appeared from the cabin. "That was close, Helen," he said. "Everybody okay?"

"Just need a hand grabbing this poor old dog, Ted," Helen answered.

"Please," Denise sputtered, "you've got to find Paul."

"Any idea where we should look?" Ted asked.

She shook her head, her teeth chattering. "Last I saw him, he was still in the ambulance."

"Take care of these two, Arturo," Ted said to the other man. "And grab the dog before the kid or Helen dives in after him." He hurried aft to where a woman Denise's age was helping to towel dry the young man who had jumped into the water to rescue them. "Let's launch the Zodiac, Brian," the older man ordered. "You search over there," he pointed, "and we'll comb the waters around here."

The young man threw down the towels and raced to where a rubber boat was lashed to the deck. Within seconds, the two men had the boat in the water. Before they could stop her, the other woman jumped down into the boat with Brian. "Don't argue," she shouted over the inflatable boat's outboard engine. "I know CPR and can probably swim better than either of you."

The young man stared at his father with raised eyebrows. Ted shrugged. "Get going then!"

The motor's whine increased and they pulled away, headed toward the middle of the channel.

The paramedics were outfitted like Sherpas. Nylon climbing ropes hung from their shoulders. There was just room enough in the construction elevator for the two men and Billy's stretcher. One of the men, Kanaloa—called Kana by his partner—was huge and brown-skinned, built like a native Hawaiian. Billy actually felt small next to him. Kana held the plasma bag daintily between two oversized fingers. A tube ran from the lower end of the bag into Billy's good arm. The younger man, Shultz, according to his name tag, carried portable oxygen equipment. The power had been knocked out when they arrived, but the mechanically-inclined Shultz had been able to hot-wire the elevator with a portable on-site generator.

As the elevator descended, Billy clutched the Motorola phone to his chest with his bandaged left hand. He still hadn't managed to reach Julie to tell her he was all right. When at last they reached the ground and the elevator door opened, Billy was surprised to see Bud Phillips standing there, hands shoved in the pockets of his Burberry, and looking like he might have had a few too many shots of something stronger than coffee.

"What happened to you, Mossman? Trip over your purple prose?"

"Phillips? What in God's name are you doing here?"

"Grenitzer sent me to check out this treasure trove of trash you supposedly discovered on the roof. I swear, you'd make a damn good science fiction writer, if you knew how to write."

"You're not going up there?" Billy was dumbfounded.

"Why? The boogeyman going to get me?" He pulled a silver flask from an inside pocket of the Burberry, unscrewed the top, and took a deep draught.

"Trust me." Billy coughed. "You don't want to be up there if the Williwaw returns."

"Williwaw!" Bud snorted. "Save your breath, Mossman." Phillips closed the gate behind him and turned the lever to go up. "I don't need a fat-ass incompetent like you to tell me how to do my job."

"Suit yourself," Billy had to shout over the elevator motor's noise. Pain shot through his right side. "Where's Grenitzer now?"

"Hell if I know. He can go fly a kite, for all I care."

"Is that any way to talk about your meal ticket?"

"He needs me a hell of a lot more than I need him," Bud said. He disappeared slowly from view as the elevator ascended.

"Nice guy," Kana said as they rolled his stretcher toward the waiting van.

"A prince."

They had slid his stretcher into the van and were locking it in place when he heard a familiar voice.

"Billy?" Julie peered in the open doors.

"It ain't the Pope."

"You belong to this sack of trouble?" Kana asked.

"He's mine all right," Julie answered.

"Then let me offer both my condolences and a ride to the hospital."

Kana unfolded a small jump seat and Julie climbed in to sit beside Billy. She held his hand while Kana monitored his pulse, and they listened to a continuous travelogue punctuated by energetic epithets as Shultz was forced to navigate city streets where traffic lights didn't operate and it was every driver and pedestrian for himself.

"See if you can learn anything about the wind." Billy held out the Motorola to Julie. It was covered in bloody fingerprints.

"If he's as nasty as he talks, you might be needing a pair of these," Kana said, tossing her a package of latex gloves.

As they skipped toward the small clusters of floating debris in the middle of the channel, Ann scanned the water for bodies. Her search was made easier due to the wind dying down and by the unfortunate lack of survivors. Of those who had been crossing the bridge when the wind struck, most had either gone down with their vehicles or drowned quickly afterwards in the violent seas. A lucky handful had been pulled to safety by the heroic efforts of a few by-standers.

Ann searched the choppy waters anxiously. Unless they found the one called Paul very shortly, their efforts would be futile—if they weren't already.

A minute later, their rescue mission had turned up a Styrofoam ice chest, a bright orange parka, and a child's plastic lunch box, but no bodies. Brian had all but decided to give up and turn back when she spotted the floating body bag. "There!" She pointed. The engine roared as Brian maneuvered the Zodiac closer. Ann tore off her coat and pants and, before he could stop her, dove into the water.

Using a crawl to cut quickly through the chilly water, Ann soon reached the yellow plastic bag. Inside, she found nothing but water and stale-smelling air. Nor were there any bodies nearby. Then she discovered the rope tied to one end. The sight of the line trailing off into the murky depths reminded her of her own recent ordeal. "I can't do this," she whispered.

"Hey lady, you okay?" Brian called out.

No, she wasn't okay. She wanted to flee, go back to Megan as fast as she could, never leave her daughter's side. If she never saw water again, it would be too soon. Then she remembered the boy and his mother. They were counting on her. She sucked in a lungful of air and dove beneath the gloomy water, following the line down until her lungs threatened to burst, following it down until she saw the bodies tied to it.

In the dim, watery light, it was difficult to tell which body was which. Ann lifted the head of the first. The corpse of Black Wolf stared back at her and she jerked her hand away in horror. She untied the line from around Paul's waist, wrapped an arm under his chin and kicked toward the surface. The other body remained below, still tethered to the body bag. Though Paul's body was much larger than her own, his buoyancy combined with her adrenaline made his weight manageable for her. A moment after she had brought Paul to the surface, Brian was there in the Zodiac, reaching for him. Still in the water, Ann blew four quick breaths into his lungs. When he didn't respond she checked his throat for a pulse. "Nothing," she said. "Get him into the boat." She climbed in after him and immediately started cardiopulmonary resuscitation. Several chest thrusts later, she tried two more quick breaths. Still nothing. "C'mon, Paul," she coaxed. "You can do it!" She pressed her hands down on his lower sternum and repeated the entire process.

"Now breathe!" she commanded and blew two more blasts into his mouth. This time, he coughed and inhaled sharply.

"That's what we like to hear," Brian said.

Paul's eyelids fluttered and he began to breathe on his own. Brian handed Ann her jacket, then wrapped his own around Paul. "You did good, lady," he said. "He ain't out of the woods yet, but he's alive. Gonna need some medical attention in a hurry though. Got to get his body temp back up, or he'll die from hypothermia. His leg needs to be resplinted and his hand looks like it must have been bandaged once before. No idea how he got these deep puncture wounds in his shoulder and some shallower cuts on his stomach and thighs, but at least the cold has stopped the bleeding."

Ann sat in the bow, cradling Paul's unconscious head in her lap as Brian restarted the engine and they raced back to meet the other boat. She turned so that he wouldn't see the tears that ran down her frozen cheeks. Just four days before, death had claimed her husband and father-in-law. She could never bring them back, but it would help knowing that she had spared someone else the pain she and Megan still felt, would continue to feel for a very, very long time.

Billy was on his way to the prep room at Group Health Hospital before going into surgery. Julie held his hand as the orderly steered the gurney down a crowded hallway. The cellular phone worked poorly in the hospital and its battery was nearly dead, but she had managed to raise Truitt and carry on a fuzzy conversation that faded in and out.

"Doug says the I 90 bridge is history. They lost contact with the couple in the ambulance just before it went down."

"Those poor bastards," Billy said. "Where's the wind now?"

"Any more information on the wind?" she asked Truitt.

"He says the P-3 crew reported it heading back downtown. The mayor's ordered everyone except emergency personnel to stay inside."

Billy's eyes widened. The swinging metal doors that would separate him from all that was happening were just ahead.

"Wait!" He raised his hand. "Tell Doug that, last time I saw him, Bud Phillips was on his way to the top of the Tower."

Except for one last task, Williwaw's mission was complete. He had avenged the shaman's death. Now, he could return to the serenity of his mountainous northern home and leave the stench and ugliness of the white man's city far behind. The boy with no ears had managed to escape the blood sacrifice, but he and his friends had fought bravely and this, too, brought honor to the shaman.

The flag on top of the Kingdome hung limply. The metal pole snapped easily and he carried it like a lance toward the cage that crawled down the face of his temporary home. Those who trespass on a holy place and show no respect must suffer the consequences.

Epilogue

ISSAQUAH, SEVERAL DAYS LATER, 11:00 A.M.
They held the ceremony at Bernice and Charley Horn's ranch.
Nearly three hundred Indians, many dressed in traditional ceremonial finery, attended from numerous Northwest tribes, some from as far away as Alaska. Ann and Helen had made up flyers with an artist's rendering of Black Wolf and distributed them in downtown Seattle and at all the nearby reservations.

Two days before the ceremony was to take place, Ann received a call on her answering machine from a Mary "Quiet As the Deer" Pangborn. A friend had seen the flyer, recognized the style of facial tattoos which Mary also wore, and called her. Mary lived with her husband, Joe, in a trailer by the Snohomish River. The oldest of her two grown boys was in the navy, currently touring the Mediterranean, and the youngest had just begun pre-med studies. All the Pangborns except the oldest boy were able to attend the ceremony.

The breeze soughed softly in the trees and shadows danced among the fallen leaves. Wearing black cowboy hat and boots, a red-checked Pendleton shirt tucked in his blue jeans, Virgil Twelve Ponies of the Nez Pierce read the long-forgotten words of Chief Sealth, "Seattle" as he was called by the whites.

"There was a time when our people covered the whole land, as the waves of a wind-ruffled sea cover its shell-paved floor. But that time has long since passed away with the greatness of tribes almost forgotten.

"When the last red man shall have perished from the earth and the memory of my tribe shall have become a myth among the white men, these shores shall swarm with the invisible dead of my tribe . . . .

"At night, when the streets of your cities and villages shall be silent, and you think them deserted, they will throng with the returning hosts that once filled and still love this beautiful land.

"The white man will never be alone. Let him be just and deal

kindly with my people, for the dead are not altogether powerless.
Dead, I say? There is no death, only a change of worlds."

When he finished speaking, several men lowered the pine coffin
from the branches high in the cedar tree where it had rested the
previous ten days. Their grunts and the creaking of the rope rang
clearly in the crisp mountain air. The coffin was placed on a
wooden platform constructed of two-by-fours under which a
goodly amount of kindling had been strategically placed. The Pangborns' Congregationalist minister said a prayer, then Mary stepped
forward. Though she was in her early fifties and her hair had long
since turned gray, her face remained wrinkle-free except for the tiny
laugh lines around her eyes. By far the most remarkable facial features, however, were her lower lip and chin which were tattooed
with a finely-drawn geometric pattern that never failed to elicit the
stares and pointing of children.

A jet passed overhead and a frown momentarily creased the placid forehead of the heavyset woman as she strained to raise her soft
voice over the intrusion. "My father, Black Wolf, shaman of the
Caribou People, is dead. We release him from this world into the
next. But his spirit lives on in the breeze that stirs our hearts."

Then, the chanting and beating of the drums began. Wiping away
tears on the sleeve of her dress, Mary lit the pyre. The alder wood
fire soon crackled and popped with intensity. Smoke rose in a twisting column that soared above the treetops and obscured the mountain peaks, already dusted with the first snow.

"Such a beautiful, healing sort of day, wouldn't you say, Mr.
Mossman?"

Billy turned to see Ann and Megan Bessani bundled in woolen
scarves and coats. "Yes, I couldn't agree more. Glad to see you
could make it. And how's my favorite little girl?"

Megan beamed. "I finished the book you loaned me. It was
great."

"Where's Julie?" Ann asked.

"Last I saw, she had her Nikon loaded and was headed in the direction of the tom toms. Thinks she's going to be the next Edward
S. Curtis. I was just going to motor on over to those people," he
pointed. "Why don't you come along?"

Using his good arm to steer and his other to operate the throttle,
Billy drove toward one side of the large gathering.

"You must have some pretty good pull to rate an electric wheelchair," Ann said as she walked beside him. "Aren't they difficult to come by?"

"Very. It's a gift from a very well-to-do and grateful benefactor who wishes to remain anonymous."

"Would it happen to be the same well-to-do person who owns a certain downtown highrise?" Ann asked.

"You know, you have a very suspicious mind. Have you thought about becoming a reporter? By the way, how's Helen? I had hoped to run into her here."

"Me, too. In fact, I asked her to come with us, but she refused. Said she wasn't much for funerals. I think she's still a little depressed."

"Her dog?"

Ann nodded. "Her anger held her up for the days immediately following his death. Now she's faced with mourning his loss."

"She'll get over it. She's a tough old broad."

"Strong, yes. Tough—I don't think so. In some ways, Megan and I are more fortunate, as strange as that may sound." Ann put her arm around her daughter. "At least we have each other."

A minute later, they arrived at a small cluster of people who were sitting on folding chairs and talking among themselves.

"Hello." He stuck out a hand to the pretty blond-haired woman. "I'm Billy Mossman."

"I know," Denise said, rising. "This is Paul Judge and his friends, Bernice and Charley Horn. And this is Dr. Chan."

"Dr. Chan," Billy said, seizing the small woman's hand. "I'm glad to finally meet you. And this must be Evan."

Evan smiled, his large green eyes darting from face to face, tracking the conversation. A white dog sat next to his chair, its head resting in Evan's lap. Another larger dog pressed his wet nose into Megan's hand.

"That's Big Duck," Bernice said. "He's real picky about who he chooses for friends. You must be a very special girl."

"Ann and her daughter, Megan, were responsible for my learning the truth about the Williwaw," Billy said. "Being a trifle hardheaded, it took a while to convince me. But since my story was picked up by the Associated Press, I'd be willing to bet that half the meteorological world is out hunting for one."

"What do you think, Evan?" he asked. "Are there any more Williwaws out there?"

334

Evan's smile disappeared and his eyes dropped, but not before Billy read the fear hidden within. For one so young, Billy thought the boy's eyes guarded many secrets. There were other questions he would have liked to ask, but now was not the time.

Denise spoke for her son, "He thinks the wind has returned home and is gone for good. Now he can concentrate on school and soccer."

"I believe I have something of yours." Billy reached behind him. "I found this on top of the Olympic Life Tower. It has your name sewn into the collar."

Following his momentary surprise, the first thing Evan did was to check the pockets of his jacket. He removed a small glass item—it looked like a horse—and a folded piece of paper.

"Important?" Billy asked.

Evan blushed and nodded shyly. He touched the tips of his fingers to his lips, then extended his hands out, palms up.

"He said, 'Thank you.'" Denise turned to her son, signing and speaking simultaneously, "Why don't you take Megan to meet your other new friend, the one I could hear whinnying all during the ceremony?"

Evan and Megan headed for the paddock area. Fortuno hopped on three legs beside them. Big Duck ran circles around the three.

"Paul's teaching Evan to ride," she explained. "Mom's hoping to get a few lessons herself."

"My sources tell me you quit your job," Billy said.

"I've decided to start my own business, as long as Evan promises not to complain too much about missed meals and the long hours."

"Public relations?"

"Yes."

Billy nodded. "I'm sure you'll be successful. I hear you're very good at it. How's your house?"

"Demolished, I'm afraid," Denise said. "But the insurance company is paying for an apartment while it's rebuilt. Six months, they say, and we should be able to move back in."

"What about you?" Billy studied the Indian. Paul stood off to one side of the group with the aide of crutches, his leg in a cast. "We seem to owe the return of our city's normalcy to your heroism."

"Your words are very kind," Paul said, "but quite mistaken. If not for Ann and several others, I wouldn't be here today. Besides, I was only trying to help save one boy, not a city."

"Maybe that's all any of us are capable of," Ann said.

" 'Save a child, save a nation,' I heard somebody say once," Bernice said.

"Wasn't that on *Wheel of Fortune?*" Charley asked.

Bernice kicked at him.

"My grandmother used to say, 'Even the seed of the mighty oak tree can fit easily within the hand of a child.' "

"Thank you, Ms. Baker," Billy said. "You've just given me the hook for my next column. And now, if you'll excuse me, I'm going to find my date."

"Your grandmother?" Paul said to Denise after Billy had departed.

"It might have been my aunt."

Bernice turned to her husband and Ann. "Something tells me these two are going to make a good pair."

A loud roar turned everyone's attention back to the fire where the wooden structure and coffin were now totally engulfed in flames.

"Isn't that the mayor coming this way?" Paul asked Denise.

"Oh, geez. Wonder what he wants."

"I didn't expect to see you here," she said a moment later. "Congratulations."

"Thank you." Grenitzer shook her hand. "I was probably as surprised as anyone by the final margin. Thought I better come. I may owe my job to this Black Wolf. Besides, the news media are here. How about taking a walk with me for just a minute?"

He waited until they were out of hearing range from the others. "I thought you might be interested to know that I fired my P.R. firm yesterday."

"Really?"

"Not worth a damn since their account exec left." He continued to walk slowly. "Did you know they got many of their clients based on my recommendation?"

"You mean all those presentations I had to prepare and then do my best Vanna White imitation weren't necessary?"

"It's not an easy account to handle," he continued. "Someone's going to have to work very hard. We've got a lot of hurdles to overcome and the city needs a whole new campaign."

"Mayor Grenitzer, are you offering me your account?"

"If you don't mind working with an old fogey who swears and smokes cigars."

336

"Don't city contracts have to be put out to bid?"

"Technically, that's correct." Grenitzer waved his hand as if shooing away a fly. "But you're in a highly favored position, what with being a woman, and let's not overlook your experience. Now that Bud's gone, no one else knows the city so well. I'm not guaranteeing anything you understand, but with the weight my vote still carries among the council, I think you might safely assume victory."

"I want you to know that I'm flattered, but I'll have to think about it."

"Guess I could learn to cut down on my swearing some, but there's no way I could give up cigars. Of course," he added, "we'll make it worth your while."

"You're very kind. How about if I call you tomorrow?"

Denise watched as he headed back toward the long line of parked cars.

"What was that all about?" Paul met her halfway, walking with the aid of his crutches.

"Possibly my first client. You can't accuse God of not having a sense of humor. The mayor promised to clean up his language *and* to make it worth my while."

"As your attorney, let me advise you to get it in writing."

"My attorney? And what about as my friend?"

"As your friend, I advise you to kiss your attorney." He pulled her to him.

Each kiss was still a tiny miracle of lips and tongues, the heat of this one contrasting with their cold noses and cheeks.

"Mmm." Denise pressed against him and breathed in his ear. "Isn't this a conflict of interest?"

"Yeah." He kissed her neck. "Sue me."

"Whatever you say; you're the lawyer."

"Promise me just one thing," Paul said. "If you decide to take on Seattle as your client, retire that 'America's Most Livable City' stuff."

"Done. Anything else?"

"Yeah, kiss me again."

They had nearly reached the paddock when Fortuno stopped to sniff the air. He smells the smoke from the funeral fire, Evan thought. Then, abruptly, the dog began trotting back toward the ceremony, nose lifted high.

"Where's he going?" Megan asked.

Evan shrugged. He was excited about showing Megan the horse, but was troubled by the way the dog's ears had been cocked, as if he heard something. He turned to watch the dog disappear into the alder and fir trees that surrounded the farm. Rising behind the trees, the jagged, snow-covered Cascade mountains gleamed like sharp white teeth. *Wait here*, he signed, pointing to where Yakima stood, tossing his head impatiently.

Fortuno had picked up a leaf-and-horse-dung-strewn trail that cut through the woods and Evan followed him. It was cool in the deep shadows. The limbs of the tall fir trees were black and skeletal and frost lay in glistening, scab-like patches where the sun didn't reach. He began to worry when he had walked for what seemed like far too long a time to cover the short distance back to the ceremony. He stopped and scanned the surrounding forest, trying to orient himself. Where were all the people? And Fortuno? Was it his imagination, or was the temperature dropping? He began to shiver. He felt the back of his neck prickle as the boughs of the surrounding trees swayed and the few remaining leaves shook or took flight in the freshening breeze. He rested a hand against the furrowed bark of an ancient Douglas fir and then jerked it away, afraid that it might tell him what he already suspected. A pair of pheasants erupted suddenly from the bushes to his right and disappeared rapidly from sight. They knew. It was here! He'd been tricked. Now, when his mother wasn't paying attention and Paul was too injured to fight, the wind had come for him.

Panic seized him and he started to run, his chest tight, his breathing shallow. Reaching the clearing and the people there was his only hope. A branch tore at his shoulder; he stumbled and nearly lost his balance. Just ahead, the trees thinned and he could see sunlight. The clearing! He was running flat out now, the Williwaw's words repeating endlessly in his head, *You are chosen. You are chosen. You are chosen . . .*

Like a river delta, the trail opened up into tiny tributaries where horses or livestock had trampled the ground. Evan raced through what looked to be the straightest, shortest course. He threw a look over his shoulder for signs of the wind and missed seeing until it was too late that the route he'd selected was a dead end. He tripped over a creeping blackberry vine and fell. He managed to stand, but couldn't escape the canes that clutched at his sleeves and pant legs. He worked feverishly to free himself, ripping thorns from clothing and skin, all the while darting anxious glances behind him. Beyond the tree line, the main gathering stood around the funeral pyre which was blazing now, the flames soaring up into the chilly November sky. A half-dozen Indian men wearing buckskin shirts and pants danced around the fire, their breath rising from them in ghost-like mists. Heavy war paint decorated their faces and eagle feathers hung from their long black hair. There was no sign of the dog, or his mother and Paul.

As he gaped, open-mouthed, the supports upon which Black Wolf's coffin rested suddenly gave way, dropping the wooden box with an explosion of sparks onto the remaining bed of kindling. The sides of the coffin burst open, revealing a dark, sinister-looking shape among the flames. Due to the extreme heat of the fire or some unknown cause, the corpse sat up, arms crossed over its chest. To his horror, he saw that Black Wolf appeared to be looking right at him. The arms loosened from the chest and fell forward as if readying to gather him in.

A hand grasped his arm and he must have screamed.

"Evan?" It was the girl, Megan. A grinning Big Duck was right behind her. Fortuno appeared a moment later and the two dogs went through their sniffing routine.

"Are you hurt?" Gingerly, Megan lifted a vine away from his jacket. A row of holes remained in the nylon where the thorns had pierced it. Tracks of blood crisscrossed the pale skin on the backs of his hands.

No, he signed.

Evan cast a wary look over his shoulder toward the bonfire while Megan helped him pull away the last of the vines. In just a few short minutes, bones, flesh, and wood had been reduced to a fiery stew of coals and ashes. The dancers and the rest of the assembled mourners were already packing up or walking to their cars.

Megan looked uneasy. "Is anything wrong?"

He paused. He wanted to find his mother and Paul as quickly as possible. Megan needed reassurance, too, however, and wouldn't understand if he signed her. So he shook his head, then took her hand and, together, they began the walk back to the paddock.

A leaf fluttered on a tree branch as they passed. The fragile link between it and tree broke and it wafted upwards, spinning lazily. As it climbed toward the treetops, it flew faster, joined now by other leaves, small twigs, fir needles, a feather, until all were swept into a funnel spout. The whirlwind made a mournful, sighing sound not unlike a small waterfall. The snow-covered mountains looked on impassively, silent, serene.